Unseen Warriors

Gavin Parmar

PublishAmerica
Baltimore

© 2005 by Gavin Parmar.
All rights reserved. No part of this book may be reproduced, stored in a retrieval system or transmitted in any form or by any means without the prior written permission of the publishers, except by a reviewer who may quote brief passages in a review to be printed in a newspaper, magazine or journal.

First printing

This is a work of fiction. Names, characters, places and incidents are either the product of the author's imagination, or are used fictitiously. Any resemblance to actual persons, living or dead, business establishments, events, or locales is entirely coincidental.

ISBN: 1-4137-9305-3
PUBLISHED BY PUBLISHAMERICA, LLLP
www.publishamerica.com
Baltimore

Printed in the United States of America

I dedicate this to all those men and women in uniform. Every day you put your lives on the line so we may live in a free and just society. Your sacrifice takes special courage and dedication that shall never be forgotten. Because of your sacrifice, we live in a free and just society. We all owe you a debt of gratitude that can never be fully repaid.

Acknowledgment

I would like to give thanks to the many people who made this book possible. First of all I would like to thank my wife who has given me so much patience through my adventure of writing this book. Secondly, thank you Jim Eisele for providing me with a wealth of technical information. Without such assistance, this book would not be possible. Thank you Jan Eisele for helping me with numerous storyline edits and ideas. Michael Witt, former Staff Sergeant 82nd ABN US Army, you were totally instrumental in providing me with your real life experiences. These events eventually became the character of Staff Sergeant Walters. Also, I thoroughly enjoyed spending the many days doing photo shoots with you for the front cover. Thank you Dave Taylor for helping me proofread the final draft. I know the long hours and heavy workload was a large drain and a major disruption on your personal time. With your assistance, the final draft came out as a piece of literature that I can be proud of. Finally, thank you Doug Vernier and Mike Peace for your insightful recollections of combat in Vietnam. Your recollections of the war eventually became one of the driving forces for my novel.

Prologue

Chinese/Russian Border
18-April-2010
1800 Hours Local Time

    Sergeant Stevens stood in the open field. His transport, a twin-engine turboprop, rose into the sky and out of view. Stevens knew this was going to be an unorthodox mission. His only real Intel was a planned meeting with a Russian soldier named Sergeant Kotov. The goal was some high level terrorist named Sadr. Other than Kotov, no other man had seen Sadr face to face. Stevens hoped this wasn't another one of colonel Griswalt's wild goose chases.
    Corporal Ortega walked up to Stevens with Private Wong and Garcia. "No sign of our contact, do you think Kotov's squad got ambushed?"
    Stevens rubbed his chin. "I don't know. We are a little early. Corporal Schneider, take Private Wong, and Bouchard. Set up a lookout point on the north side of the field." The soldiers quickly ran off to their assigned duty.
    Ortega gave a glum look to Stevens. "What is it?" Stevens barked to Ortega.

Ortega rolled his eyes. "I can't pinpoint it but I just have a real weird feeling about all of this."

Stevens sighed. "I feel it too. I had a tuna fish for lunch just like you."

Ortega gave an angry look. "Not funny!"

Stevens dismissed Ortega with a wave of his hand. Stevens looked at the muddy field and rain soaked hills and around him. His mind was immediately lost in thoughts of spending two weeks stateside. The warmth and sun of his California home immediately made his wet socks and muddy pants that much more unbearable.

Stevens pulled out a bundle of papers from his pocket. He reread the top-secret orders several times, trying to see what he missed. Steven rechecked his watch several times. His frustration growing, Stevens wondered, *Why isn't the contact at the LZ?*

"Sergeant Stevens, come here! We have a big problem!" cried out Schneider. Stevens ran across the field. Huffing and puffing, Stevens ran through the deep mud and stagnant water. Stevens stopped short of Schneider's position looked down to a small valley. His eyes grew huge at the terrifying sight.

Part 1

Jungle Fever

Chapter 1

World Airways freedom flight
14-May-2010
2300 Hours Local Time

The soldiers were flying over the East China Sea on their way to Seoul from Seattle. The engines whined on the World Airways MD-11 as the shimmering blue water passed underneath while wispy clouds passed by the fuselage. They sat in uncomfortable seats packed like Sardines. It just made that long ride that much longer staring into strange faces. Everyone wanted to say, "Hello," but none were daring enough to say anything.

Accompanying an Army platoon was a band of unruly Marines who made "Dog face" jokes while the Army grunts made "Jar Head" jokes. Deep inside, they all felt uneasy about their posting in the hotbed of the Korean peninsula. It was a place where the possibility of war was a daily remainder for both the civilian and soldier

Settling the boys down was Richard Townsend. The platoon commander and a stern voiced, salty veteran of the Iraq invasion. He had plenty of experience under his belt, as well as an equal amount of bitterness for such young men. His crew knew not to challenge him; he was hardheaded and always right. He believed that his platoon was an elite strike force. A force that should only include the best the Army could provide. He had his aces that he always depended on. They gave him his due respect in return. The rest of the platoon he called idiots even though he had never seen them in action

Sitting directly to the right of Townsend was Sergeant Martin, Townsend's right-hand man. The two had spent two years together at Ft. Lewis, making them able to almost read each other's minds while under the stress of combat. Martin was the son of a four star Navy Admiral. He had all the connections and privilege that came with his birthright. He was six feet tall with jet-black hair and a deep tan. He could walk into a room and women would flock to him. For all his perfect features on the outside, his mind was tormented by the vices of womanizing and alcoholism.

A graying Marine, Staff Sergeant Buckmaster called out to Martin in his thick southern accent, "How long are you guys going to be in country?"

"They say about a year. Of course the brass always says that to keep us from asking questions," Martin answered.

"I've been here for a couple of years now. This is the place to be. Seoul is just the happening place. Maybe later I can show you where to get some good beer."

"Sounds good," Martin said. He soon drifted off to thoughts of home and his children. Dreams always crashed into reality after he thought of his ex-wife. Martin felt anger and rage at her. He felt she bore all the responsibility for his divorce. He conveniently chose to forget about his unfaithfulness and alcohol abuse during his five rocky years of marriage.

Several rows down sat Private Sarah Matthews. She was the only female in the squad. It may have been 2010, but to her it was still 1970. She felt she had to work twice as hard as any of the male Soldiers to be accepted as a competent soldier. She knew

Townsend didn't consider her part of his elite team and resented it. Unknown to her the feeling of resentment was shared by many in the platoon.

Across from Matthews sat Private Nishan. He was the oxymoron in every way possible. An Indian born Canadian who joined the US Army to escape what he thought was the oppression of his Indian culture. Coming from a devout Hindu family, he still worshiped the Hindu God Krishna in his quiet hours. But, he couldn't keep from sneaking looks at Matthews' blue eyes and sandy blonde hair peeking from underneath her helmet. He was lost in her eyes. He wondered if she felt the attraction he felt.

Sitting beside Nishan was Private Jonathan Jacobs or JJ, as he was known by most. He was the newest member to the Platoon. He was just twenty, barely out of infantry school. His father had been a Vietnam vet and avid gun enthusiast. He learned at an early young age on how to handle a rifle, and become a steady shot even before boot camp. He was of small stature, shy and timid. He lacked the courage to confront his superiors in a forceful way.

A Marine Private finally broke the ice with Nishan, "I like your gun. It looks like a real rifle, instead of this toy that we get. What is that thing?"

"It's called an HK-91, man this is some serious firepower" Nishan hastily replied, caught off guard by the Marine's question. The standard issue 5.56x45 mm M4 continued to have poor reliability, and questionable stopping power in Iraq and Afghanistan. Coupled with the huge troop deployments and shortages of small arms, the Army decided it wanted something different fast. A few target shooters in the Pentagon came with a novel idea. They took DC Industries aluminum receiver version of Heckler and Koch's venerable .308 rifles, the HK 91. They shortened the barrel to 14.5 inches, added the wide forearm grip with the bipod clip, 1X45mm compact red dot sight on the integral rail on the top of the receiver coupled with twenty round aluminum magazines and a side-folding buttstock. The HK-91 was born. Using off the shelf parts, DC Industries was manufacturing HK-91s in record numbers. All the upgrades significantly lowered the weight of the rifle to only about a pound greater than the standard issue M-16A2. The red dot sight was an ease to shoot while still allowing the shooter to use the standard iron sights for backup. Coupled with millions of 7.62X51mm rounds still sitting in Pentagons stockpiles, ammunition shortages were not an issue. Neither was the stopping power of the venerable .30 caliber, 147 grain round.

The MD-11 rolled its wing over to the left, as the pilot started on his ILS approach to Osan Air Force Base. The plane was buffeted by winds as gear came down and the flaps lowered. The soldiers were happy they were near the end of their flight. Still, they felt uneasiness about living a top of the powder keg of the world.

The platoon members quickly got off the flight and were whisked away to their barracks. Many of them were happy to finally be done with the lumbering Military flights across the Pacific. To them Ft Lewis, Washington was as much a memory as was basic training.

Private Steven Patrick lay on his bunk strumming his guitar. For him it was the only way to deal with the boredom of Army life. To others his guitar was the annoyance of Army life.

"Put that ridiculous thing away, all you're doing is scaring the dogs outside," Nishan called to Patrick in an irritated voice.

"No, he's trying to scare the cats away and entice the rats here with that torture device," Private Watson called lying on the top bunk from across the aisle.

Patrick replied, "This torture device you refer to has made some of the best music known to man."

"I wasn't talking about the guitar. The torture is listening to you play it," Watson joked. The barracks broke out in laughter.

Suddenly, Martin walked into the hallway. The laughter in the room immediately hushed. "Folks, now that we're here safe and sound Lieutenant Townsend has allowed you guys out for the night. Remember, curfew is at ten o'clock, anybody coming back drunk will be cleaning the latrine and scuff marks from the floor for a week." He walked away casually thinking about Sergeant Buckmaster's offer from the flight.

Watson looked at Nishan. The two men nodded and in about ten minutes they were ready to go. On their way out they grabbed JJ to see the excitement of town. Watson and Nishan had a special friendship. They had both come from the Seventh Battalion, Delta squad. They were close, but they seemed so much a part. Watson knew almost nothing about Nishan's personal life, he didn't even know Nishan's hometown. To him, Nishan was a mysterious friend who seemed to always be hiding something. On the outside he seemed to be just another American small town boy.

Nishan and Watson decided they wanted to see the nightlife of Seoul. To boot they wanted to take JJ along to get out of his shell. "So, what do you want to see JJ? How about checking out some hard drinks and soft women?" Watson shouted exuberantly.

"Easy, Watsy! Do you want to corrupt the boy on his first night out in Korea?" Nishan calmly interrupted. JJ felt out of place, but comfortable with the two six footers. They reminded him of his father and uncle. The distance from home seemed that much easier to take with their presence.

The trio rode a small cramped taxi into downtown Seoul. The roads were filled with bars, nightclubs and many ethnic restaurants. The city lights lit up the streets like daytime. JJ was filled with awe as he tried to enjoy his first night out in a foreign city. The trio picked an American looking restaurant just off the main stretch. They sat down inside at a cramped table and checked the scenery in the window.

"Now remember, Martin said no drunkenness tonight. After all you're too heavy for me and JJ to drag back down to base," Nishan lectured Watson.

"I don't care what that Peacock has to say, heck he'll be the first dipstick to get drunk tonight. If I'm not in his clique, what's the point of following his orders?"

"He could throw you into the brig, Watsy"

"The brig? When did we become gay sailors?" Watson loudly blurted out.

"Careful, that kind of talk's gonna have us thrown out. You do remember that bar in Virginia, don't you?"

All of the sudden with wide-open eyes, JJ announced, "Those guys are staring at us!"

Ten tall men wearing blue dungarees approached the trio. "What do you mean gay sailors?" A tall muscular built sailor shouted to the men.

*****

Martin sat in the airport bar drinking his beer. He couldn't help but look at the pictures of his children Kyle and Christie. It had been almost one year since he had seen them. His heart ached and his eyes watered at the sight of the photographs.

"Hollywood, fancy meeting you in a place like this," Boxman shouted at Martin with glee. Boxman-who's real name was Earl Johnson-was one of Martin's old high-school friends. Boxman entered Army flight Ops and quickly became a respected Blackhawk pilot. Boxman shared Martin's penchant for alcohol and loose women. In so doing never failed to give Martin a memorable encounter.

Martin discreetly hid away his photographs, "Always a pleasure dude, always. Tell me, how true are the rumors about hit and run attacks around the DMZ?"

Boxman paused, and whispered, "I lost a supply chopper to a SAM last week. Luckily it landed on its feet. But it took heavy damage. It was the second hull I lost in a week. The kicker's that the SAM originated from this side of the DMZ. Recon looked all day, they couldn't find any trace of the launcher."

Martin gasped. "So, are the stories about the raiders crossing the DMZ true?"

"I don't know. It doesn't seem too likely with all the security forces in the area. It could be a bunch of locals ticked off at us. Word has it that HQ is really concerned about the whole situation. They want to send a Black Ops team across the wall."

"That is a high risked mission and defiantly a night time stunt. Nothing I would want to do," Martin said as he winked to Boxman.

The Flight attendants from Delta Airlines filed into the bar. Giggling and chatting, they showed no signs of fatigue from their long flight. The women elegantly sat down beside a nearby table and ordered a round of beers.

Boxman looked lustily into their direction and gulped his beer. "Time to get some Hollywood."

* * * * *

The sailor took a long swing. Watson immediately dove for the floor. The sailor's fist hit JJ square into the jaw. JJ immediately went down to floor unconscious. Nishan picked up a chair and threw it at the sailor missing him by inches. The chair crashed into the counter breaking all the bottles. The bartender dove to the floor, glass shards flew all around him.

The sailors picked up Nishan and held him still while their leader punched Nishan in the face, stomach and chest several times. Several sailors grabbed Watson and tried to hold him still. Watson desperately struggled to free himself. Looking over in Watson's direction, the leader stopped beating Nishan. He proceeded to violently beat Watson. He hit Watson several times in the chest and gave him a sharp blow to the face.

Suddenly a chair crashed into the back of the sailor's head and knocking him unconscious. His mates stood in stunned silence. Hearing the alarms of distant Military Police vehicles, they scattered.

Matthews casually walked into the destroyed bar. Broken pieces of furniture, glass and spilt alcohol covered the floor. Matthews looked at her injured teammates and shook her head with displeasure. "Why do you two always get yourselves into so much trouble every time you leave the base? Worst of all, you got JJ involved."

Watson grinned, barely able to open his swollen eyes. "Well, if we didn't get into fights we would never be able to have any fun. After all we are guys."

Nishan smiled, captivated by her blue eyes, "I could never have a nicer rescue party."

Matthews picked up JJ, still groggy and his face swollen. "If you guys are going to get into trouble all the time, at least leave JJ out of it"

Nishan could kick himself, the harder he tried to get close Matthews, the further away she seemed to drift. JJ took one shot to the face and she was all over him. Nishan felt as distant from Matthews as Watson was from JJ. He needed to figure out a way, but what? Well, he was going to have lots of time to think about it in custody.

* * * * *

"Holy cow!" shouted Townsend in an infuriated tone. "You idiots weren't even gone an hour and you already got in a brawl? What the hell is wrong with you? Is there not enough action for you in the infantry?" Eyeing Matthews, he stepped up to her face. "What the hell's with throwing chairs? I've seen you in action. You can't even throw a grenade. I'm surprised you were even able to lift that chair. I have a mind to lock you guys up in Leavenworth and throw away the key into the Sea of Japan!

"Luckily for me there is another option. Black Ops are short heads. The casualty rate in Iraq and Afghanistan is consuming troops faster than they can train them. I'm sending you four to their Pacific HQ. If you ever make it back alive, I'm making sure you never come back to this Battalion, understood?"

Matthews, Nishan, Watson and JJ gave Townsend a collective "Yes, sir!" Townsend stormed out in anger.

Nishan looked over to Watson, "Nice going, buddy."

"Any place in Black Ops is got to be better than this outfit," Watson muttered.

The next morning the four were put on an unmarked turboprop transport at Osan. They knew the Army adage. The fewer the markings on the plane the riskier the mission was.

Chapter 2

Black Ops Camp Zulu
15-May-2010
1300 Hours Local Time

"Welcome to Black Ops, Camp Zulu," called out Colonel Griswalt. Black Ops' real name was 731 SOG. It was an elite counter terrorism team set up after 2001 to fight terrorism on foreign soil. Its organization was totally separate from regular Army Ops. Even the Green berets and Special Ops remained unable to penetrate Black Ops' super secret organization. Many outsiders referred to Black Ops as the CIA. Even more in Black Ops felt the same.

Terrorist attacks aimed at Russia increased greatly in the twenty-first century. Russian forces short on equipment and cash desperately tried to cope without foreign intervention. All that changed when Pakistani terrorist Ahmed Hassan blew up an Aeroflot jet over New York City. The calamity of the incident caused the Russian government to invite Black Ops to set up a base in Eastern Russia.

The simple camp soon became a sprawling city of aircraft, armor and infantry. The base directed operations along the

Pacific theatre. Russia, China, Korea, Canada and Japan all funneled Intel to the base. The Pentagon eventually made the base the Pacific HQ. Camp Zulu was now born. Located 100 miles west of Vladivostok close to the Chinese border, access was by air only. It was totally isolated from the outside world. The base was used for clandestine missions into China and Siberia among other things.

"Your former Platoon commander gave you high marks for marksmanship and basic skills in you last fitness report. You will do well in Black Ops. I run an informal camp. We don't spend all day saluting each other and critiquing uniforms. But we are a tight-knit operation. You will perform all required duties at Camp Zulu. There are no specialists in my camp. Your weapons are being modified to our specs. You'll get them back at the firing range tomorrow. Your new uniforms will be available tomorrow. Remember, unlike the regular Army. We do not carry any names on our uniforms or ID cards. Everything we do here is off the record. Report there at 0600 to begin your counter terrorism training. Dismissed." Griswalt leaned back into his chair and waved the team off.

The four walked down the hall to the barracks while quietly mumbling to themselves. "High marks for marksmanship, the old goat must have really hated us to falsify our fitness reports," muttered Nishan.

"I don't like the looks around here. Look, every plane, Jeep, truck, and building. They're all unmarked, what's going on here," whispered Matthews.

"You'd think we joined the CIA," grimaced Watson.

Main Conference room, Camp Zulu
16-May-2010
0600 Local time

Every morning Colonel Griswalt had an action meeting with his senior staff. This morning it would be like almost every other with a real twist.

"Spetsnaz recon teams report Hassan was sighted at the Chinese border 500 miles from our location. Seems he's talking to some of his foreign contacts about locating some nuclear material from them. Documents indicate that North Koreans are getting in on the act, possibly providing transport," Major Fleming noted.

"Captain York, when will our new soldiers will be able to be ready for combat?" Griswalt asked while thumbing through a stack of documents.

"I say about two to three weeks. We've been having some ammunition shortages lately. Say Colonel, do you really believe Townsend's fitness reports? After all with fitness reports like those, that four should have been picked up by Delta Force."

Griswalt chuckled for a second. "Of course not, but after losing the entire squad on the recon mission near the Chinese border last week, I don't have a choice. Major Fleming, has Spetsnaz provided any more Intel about our missing squad?"

"Negative! Spetsnaz never made contact with them. The LZ was totally abandoned when they arrived. Sir, can I be frank with you?"

"Shoot," Griswalt answered while stirring his coffee.

"Shouldn't we tell the families of the missing soldiers now?"

"No, right now that would bring too much attention. We could be on the verge of uncovering a large terrorist plot, and I don't want to blow the chance. Dismissed"

* * * * *

"Greetings soldiers," announced Staff Sergeant Walters. "Today you will start training in counter terrorism. First off, we do not have 6X6 trucks delivering us ammo, what you can carry on a mission is what you have. You have to make every bullet count.

"Second, stealth is the key. We do not jump into rooms guns blazing. Leave that to Hollywood. Let's begin."

Walters had the team run up and down concrete walls and under barbed wire and brush, around obstacles while shooting at popup targets. Then he had them collapse their stocks and clear houses one after the other all at a brisk pace. Over and over, he worked them until they achieved perfection. After completing one stage of their training, the team was elevated to another, far more difficult level. Over and over, Walter's made sure they performed every task with random surprised until they achieved perfection.

Main Conference room, Camp Zulu
01-June-2010
0600 Hours Local Time

Griswalt looked around, even though he knew Captain York and Major Fleming were already seated. "Good morning Gentlemen, what new intelligence do you have Fleming?"

Fleming cleared his throat. "Spetsnaz reports Hassan's top Lieutenants will have a high level meeting at an old castle on the Chinese border at 1300 hrs tomorrow."

"Captain York, I want a team in the air by 0600 tomorrow headed for that castle. Are those newbies ready yet?"

York madly shuffled through some papers while he spoke to Griswalt. "Yes, sir, in many ways they live up to old man Townsend's report"

"Put them on with the team, if they don't work out, I want them on the first plane stateside. Also, I want another Recon mission to the Chinese border set up, this time don't tell Spetsnaz."

"Colonel, do you think Spetsnaz is selling us out?"

"I don't know, but I do like to have my bases covered." Fleming and York looked at each other with a stunned look as Griswalt curled his lip.

Gavin Parmar

02-June-2010
0700 Local time

The twin engine Dash 8 – 400 troop transport shone in the morning sunlight. It was 107 feet nose to tail but its cabin was a mere eight feet wide. It was able to achieve 355 Knots top speed with a range of 1800 nautical miles. The seats were uncomfortable and crammed. This meant the soldiers were jammed against each other, with no room to move while the plane raced down the runway on its journey to a distant rain soaked land.

Nishan sat between Watson and Matthews while he looked across to JJ. JJ's eyes were full of fear and anguish. None of the four had ever been in combat. This would be their first mission, a baptism of fire. Nishan couldn't help but wonder what combat was going to be like, what would be the feeling when you took another man's life. Yes, they were terrorists and they had killed thousands of people around the world. But Nishan couldn't help but wonder what difference this one raid could make. Nishan's drifted off to thoughts of September 11th. The sights and sounds were still fresh in his mind. The men he hunted were no different. How men could kill women and children in cold blood like this. Nishan continued to ponder about the rights and wrongs of the war on terrorism. He knew he'd spent years training for this moment, but he was still confused and scared. It was just…

Matthews was nudging Nishan. Nishan shuddered for a second and looked over. She was passing him a bottle of water. He took it and blurted out, "Thank you, Sarah." *I called her by her first name, what an idiot I am*, he thought. Matthews smiled, and started blushing.

* * * * *

Unseen Warriors

The airplane shook and rocked as it was buffeted by ground winds while it flew at treetop level. Major "Rooster" Jones commanded the plane. He threaded it between mountains and down through the valleys with ease. His years of experience of nap of the earth flying made their dangerous trek seem simple.

Rooster straddled the Chinese border as he headed north, following the Shikhote-Alin mountain range. Flying over Nakhodka, he turned right flying over rivers pouring east to the Sea of Oshkosh. He continued to fly north eventually turning into China, west of Kabarovsk following the Amur River inland.

As he approached the LZ he pulled up high and began circling. He quickly scanned around for snipers and hidden artillery. He checked his wind gage, banked the left wing hard and swung the nose into the wind. He threw the throttles into idle, the airplane plunged earthward falling out of the sky. Rooster punched the throttles forward. The engines raced forward while the props screamed under the strain of being forced to spin up to 850 RPM. Rooster leveled the wings, lowered the flap to 35 degrees and lowered the gear. The wheels hit the grass hard, throwing dirt and grass everywhere as they spun up. The ground spoilers popped, Rooster threw the props into reverse pitch and sat on the brakes. The plane stopped in a muddy patch of grass just 1500 ft past where the wheel first hit. The aft door flew open as Rooster feathered the props. The squad ran out as fast as they could. Walters prided himself on fast turns and this would be no different.

"Saddle up!" Walters shouted to his team. It was time to start the long hike up the mountain to the castle. As the team started moving, the rain started falling. The soft soil quickly turned into huge rivers of mud. The squad trudged through the mud, slipping and sliding while going up the hill. They lost their footing several times. Sometimes their boots got stuck in the mud. Their heavy packs and weapons only increased their difficulty on their trek up the mountain.

After a long three-hour hike they arrived at the plateau where the castle was located. A shot rang out through the still mountain air. The squad went down into the mud while a quick burst erupted again. Walters looked up with his binoculars. They were about a mile from the castle entrance. Three guards carrying AKS-74U's stood in front of entrance to a towering wall. The wall circled the castle ruins while guards were seen walking the walkway on the top of the wall.

The squad members crawled through the muddy grass. They finally positioned themselves 1000 yards from the entrance behind an old farmhouse. The entrance was slightly west, about 100 yards from the road. Walters looked through his binoculars again. The two guards were shooting a handgun at the grass toward the east. Their target, Walters could not see.

Walters ordered the team into attack positions. Corporal Timothy and Jones covered the left flank. They wadded through the grass, stopping 230 yards of the entrance. Lying in the muddy vegetation, they had a clear view of the castle wall. Matthews and Watson went on the right flank. They stopped about the same distance ahead of the old farmhouse while out of sight of the entrance. Walters led Nishan and JJ forward until they found a large rock to hide behind.

"Guns up!" Walters proclaimed to his team. Jones fired the first bullet. The shot rang out. The bullet struck a guard standing on top of the wall. It tore through his neck, causing him to fall back over hitting the pavement below. Timothy hit the other guard in the chest causing him to fall down in a similar manner.

The entrance guard opened full auto fire toward the left flank. The bullets slammed into the dirt around Jones and Timothy spraying them with gravel and mud. JJ opened with a short burst at the leader. Bullets slammed into his leg and blew out his knee. He started to fall down. Another round tore into his heart ripping at his aorta, blood spraying everywhere.

The remaining guards fired toward their unseen foes with wild spurts of automatic fire. Walters and company replied with several short bursts of gunfire. Rounds slammed into the three guards burying in their chests. They fell lifelessly to the ground as their blood soaked the earth.

The team ran up to the entrance. Jones and Timothy hid beside the left wall, Matthews and Watson on the right side. Walters, JJ and Nishan hid behind a nearby boulder. AK gunfire erupted from the heart of the castle. Bullets struck all around the team peppering them with sand and gravel. Nishan raised his rifle and pulled the trigger, a bullet screamed into a shooter hitting him in the shoulder blowing out muscle and bone on the backside. Before he could feel any pain, another bullet slammed into his neck cutting through his carotid artery causing blood to spray out his neck as he fell over. Another bullet tore into his windpipe sheering it into two pieces and burying it into his spine. He fell over and hit the ground. He made a gurgling sound that was heard by his friends as he drowned in his own blood.

Two men scurried around, finally hiding behind a Jeep. Walters fired more automatic gunfire. Bullets buried themselves into the tires. The Jeep immediately lurched over throwing a man off balance. He raised his head and grabbed his rifle. A bullet struck him in the forehead causing brain matter to be torn up and sprayed out as a bullet exited at the base of his skull.

JJ threw a grenade at the Jeep as two more men rushed in to use the Jeep as cover. The grenade passed behind the Jeep and exploded several feet in the air. Dirt and rocks were thrown up on the men. The men stopped shooting, immediately becoming dazed and confused from the explosion.

Matthews rushed in with Watson. She jammed her rifle into the first shooter and opened with a short burst into his stomach. As Watson beat the other shooter with his buttstock, the terrorist put his hands up and started sobbing.

Walters regrouped in front of the remaining terrorist. JJ and Timmons guarded the entrance.

"Nishan, do you speak Punjabi?" Walters demanded to know.

"Yes, I do!" Nishan answered in a confused voice.

"Interrogate him!" Walters shot back. Nishan questioned the man for several minutes, he answered back appearing agitated and nervous.

"Wow," Nishan gasped.

"Well, what did he say?" Walters impatiently remarked.

"He says the Sheik was here early in the morning, possibly 0600. He came with a 6x6 truck carrying a large bomb looking device in the back. It had Pakistani markings on it. The Sheik said it was for his next big US attack." The prisoner started jabbering something, he handed Nishan something shiny.

"What is it?" Walters asked

"It's a dog tag, Sergeant Richard Stevens," Nishan answered in a nervous tone.

Walters' eyes grew big, his face turned white as a sheet. "Stevens is MIA from a recon mission about a month ago, what does he say about him?"

"They claim the Sheik executed him this morning. He took the body with him for him for display purposes."

"Jones, radio a progress report to HQ, looks like we made it here a little late." Walters looked around at the crumbling ruins all around him. "I want you guys find any reliable forms of transportation."

The team scattered around. The castle's main walls were solid, unadulterated by hundreds of years of weather. The inside buildings were different. Piles of old wood and rock were scattered everywhere. Rusting Jeeps and motorcycles littered the compound. Each team member tried starting anything that had wheels. Too often the vehicles were neglected too badly to even crank.

Matthews finally found an old 6x6, "Looks like this is all we have got. I'll try to start it," she said to Watson. Watson looked on, fascinated by her skills. Matthews turned the ignition key.

Unseen Warriors

The truck loudly rumpled and shook but failed to fire. Matthews ran around and opened the hood. She smelled the carburetor, shook and rattled the mechanical linkage. She carefully pulled off several leads of the spark plugs and inspected the wiring in the boot. Satisfied, she removed wires of the distributor cap and straightened the wires. Matthews pulled off the distributor cap and wiped all the water and debris from the inside. She quickly reassembled everything and slammed the hood shut. She patiently tried starting the truck a second time. The truck coughed and shook before starting up. The truck idled at low smooth speed. Gently purring like a new car.

Walters smiled at Matthew for a second. "Tie the prisoner up and put him in the back of the truck. Collect all the weapons you can find and put them in the back too." The team searched through the old castle. In every nook and cranny small quantities of ammunition, magazines and grenades were stored. The team gathered up what they could rummage from the old ruins and dead soldiers.

Walters intently watched the goings on around him. Out of the corner of his eye, Jones approached, "What do we have for enemy weapons?" Walters impatiently questioned Jones.

"About 12 AKS-74U rifles, about 2000 rounds of 5.45x39.5 mm ammunition and 12 Russian grenades," Jones meekly answered

"Good, we'll take the truck to the LZ. If we don't use the weapons, we'll destroy them and the truck." Walters then tightened the strap on his helmet as he looked up at the sky. Rain was falling heavier and heavier.

* * * * *

JJ gestured to Timothy, "I hear something, like branches breaking."

Timothy turned his head, "I don't hear anything." He pulled out his binoculars and scanned the area around the ridge. "I don't see anything, wait, something's..." A bullet buried itself into his chest tearing up his heart and left lung. Timothy crashed down still clutching his binoculars.

JJ started shouting and screaming in horror. Walters ran up to JJ and started scanning the distance with his binoculars. About thirty fighters approached from the road followed by Jeeps. "Everybody into the truck," ordered Walters.

Watson jumped into the driver's seat and threw the truck into gear. The rest of the team quickly jumped in the back. He circled inside the ruins for several minutes, madly searching for an alternate exit. Driving around, he found a small exit deep in the back. He revved the engine and raced out the exit. The truck sailed through the air and crashed into the muddy road at top speed.

Walters shouted over the loud noise of the engine, "Everyone arm with the AK, use full auto. Use up the enemy ammo before using our own. If the gun jams, throw it overboard."

The truck danced along the bumpy road. Mud, dirt and gravel ejected from its wheels. Several Jeeps pulled in behind hot pursuit, troops firing automatic weapons. Rounds flew by the truck, some burying themselves into the wood side rails of the box.

Walters' squad returned fire, spraying the Jeeps with automatic fire. A round hit the one of the troops in the Jeep. The terrorist fell over out of the Jeep rolling into a ravine. Another bullet tore into the front tire, the tire burst throwing rubber over the front fender. The driver lost control and the Jeep flipped over several times. Bodies flew out every direction like rag dolls.

Two 6x6 trucks joined in behind the Jeeps several hundred yards away. The backs were full of troops firing automatic guns. A bandanna clad figure armed with an RPG aimed and then fired from the lead truck. Watson noticed a sharp curve through the mist. He yanked the steering wheel to the left. The rear end swung out on the muddy road throwing up dirt rocks and mud into the distance. The rear wheels barely missing going off the edge of the cliff. The lead Jeep spun its tires trying to gain traction while maneuvering the tight corner. An RPG slammed into Jeep. It burst into flames and rolled into the canyon.

Watson plunged down the hill on the muddy trail, feverishly trying to keep the truck on the road. He saw a checkpoint coming up. The guards immediately opened fire on the fast approaching truck. Bullets smashed all around and into the headlights causing them to explode into a cloud of glass shards. Another bullet tore through the windshield narrowly missing Watson and burying itself into the back of the cab.

Matthews opened fire on the guards, missing them wildly. The truck blew by the guards spraying them with mud. The guards staggered into the road firing their weapons at the disappearing truck while flying gravel continued to pepper them. A Jeep crashed into the guards. The driver immediately lost control and spun out into the middle of the roadway. The occupants were launched into the brush. The trucks slammed into on their brakes trying to avoid a collision with the Jeep.

Jones called into the radio, "This is Fox. We need a pick up at the LZ, Charlie in hot pursuit. Can you accommodate Devil one?"

"This is Devil one, I'm a half hour out from pick up point," Rooster called into Jones' radio.

"Fox is ready, expect a real hairy LZ"

Watson swung over the wooden bridge crossing the stream. "Boom," the left rear tire blew causing the truck to shudder. Watson hung on the steering wheel for dear life as the tires slid around the wet wood.

Walters' crew threw their Russian weapons overboard. They quickly changed over to their HK-91 rifles. Relief filled the crew as they saw the grassy field come into view. High above in the rain clouds, Rooster circled overhead in preparation for landing.

Rooster looked saw the truck approach. Confused at first, he realized danger of the situation and began his plunge earthward. He jammed the throttles into the flight idle gates and aimed just short of the speeding truck. The tires slammed into the grass spinning up in the mud, he put #1 engine into feather and slowed down while the truck raced to his position.

Suddenly the two 6x6s firing automatic weapons appeared crossing the bridge. They raced through the mud, madly trying to meet the taxing plane. The trucks slid around and slowed, barely able to keep traction in the soupy mess of mud and grass.

Watson skidded to a stop behind the idling plane. He rapidly jumped out of the cab and provided covering fire. Walters dragged Timothy into the back of the plane. JJ and Mathews aided in providing suppressive fire. Explosions popped all around the plane, Nishan grabbed the prisoner from the truck and threw him into the open doorway.

"Get in!" Walters shouted.

Watson ran in as the aircraft started to roll. JJ soon followed behind, Walters helped pull him in. Matthews took several steps toward the plane. A bullet hit Matthews in the leg and she went down, the feeling of intense pain burning in her leg. She watched the plane roll forward at a brisker pace. Horrifying thoughts that she would be left behind filled her mind. Nishan rushed out into the mud and picked her up. He ran as fast as could to the door. He passed her to Watson and jumped into the back of the plane.

Rooster slammed the throttles full forward. The airplane shuddered while the props strained to transfer the torque to the blades from the engine. The 6x6s flanked the Dash on either side and quickly closed while spraying the airplane with gunfire.

"Keep your heads down!" Walters shouted to his team. Bullets tore through the aft door narrowly missing Matthews who was lying in Nishan's arms. Matthews looked up at Nishan's face and smiled. Bullets continued pass overhead.

Rooster yanked back on the yoke. The airplane strained to lift off out of the mud. The nose rose up and dragged the fuselage up into the air. The right flank 6x6 pulled up and poured gunfire into the right engine nacelle. Bullets tore into the aft gear doors, shattering them into fiberglass splinters. Rooster slapped the gear handle up. The gear legs retracted while bullets smashed into the flaps.

The plane shuddered as Rooster turned it into a sharp right-hand bank. The retracting flaps immediately ground to a halt. "Boom," an RPG exploded after it contacted the right nacelle, sparks and flames raced around the nacelle. The oil cooler door blew off and fell to earth. Rooster trimmed the right wing down and continued full speed toward camp Zulu. He called to his first officer, Captain "Speedster" Swisher, "What warning lights are illuminated?"

"Looks like we have Flap power, Hot SPU, right gear door unsafe and low system 2 hydraulic fluid level caution lights. Flaps are frozen around 15 degrees."

"They hit the right engine nacelle hard. Keep an eye on Engine 2 oil pressure," Rooster commanded

"Hyd 2 light is illuminated. We've lost all pressure and quantity. We aren't going to have nose wheel steering on touchdown," Swisher warned.

The airplane continued on its trek back to Camp Zulu. The team members remained quiet. An eerie silence quickly befell the cabin. The gunfire had left dozens of holes through the cabin. In the cockpit, Rooster and Swisher watched their warning lights with boredom. They knew the emergency procedures by heart. But for them, this emergency had all the smells, sights and feelings that they never had seen in training.

Rooster looked at the fuel gage. Only 1300 pounds were left in each tank. The low altitude and the extra drag of the flaps hanging out were making an immense increase in fuel consumption. Rooster knew there was only thirty minutes of flying time left. The fuel supply would last until Campy Zulu. But there would nothing to spare.

Rooster approached the camp and lined his aircraft up for the unseen runway, "Gear down" he shouted. Swisher reached above, opened the landing gear bypass door and pulled the cord. The doors flew opened. The gear fell out of the wheel wells and hung limply in the air. He the opened the alternate release door and pulled the cord, the nose fell out and locked from its own weight. Swisher installed the emergency handle and started pumping the main gear until they locked forward.

Rooster throttled up the engines, consuming precious fuel as the plane fought the gear's drag. He looked to the right. Three green lights were illuminated. The gear was down and locked. The winds violently rocked the plane. Rooster struggled to keep the plane lined up.

Slowly, the runway appeared through the haze. Rooster was a quarter mile out and in the groove. The master caution flashed, he looked over the low fuel lights. Both were on. He only had 325lbs of fuel left. At his current fuel consumption rate, the plane would barely have enough fuel at landing.

"Number two engine's out of oil," Swisher announced as the master warning light flashed in Rooster's eyes.

"We're going in both engines turning," shot back Rooster

The left main tires were the first to hit the runway. The right tires hit the runway seconds later. The right engine flamed out, causing the airplane to swerve violently to the right. The right wing clipped a line of barracks as the plane crashed into a ditch at the end of the runway. Its tail stood high in the air. Smoke poured out from the number 2 engine nacelle.

Watson looked over to Walters, "Great mission. Do all Black Ops missions go as smooth as this one?"

Walters Grinned, "No, this one went just as we planned." Watson scowled.

Chapter 3

Black Ops Camp Zulu
04-June-2010
1300 Hours Local Time

Griswalt walked into the conference room, coffee in one hand and a stack of file folders in the other. Sitting down he glanced around, as was his usual routine before starting every morning meeting. "Gentlemen, I can see you read the report from last night's mission. Captain York, how is Private Matthews doing?"

"She is doing fine; it was only a flesh wound," he hastily replied while shuffling through his documents.

Griswalt stared at list of names while he spoke "Give my condolences to Corporal Timothy's family." York nodded in agreement.

"Major Scott, how is our aircraft availability?"

"Well, Colonel I can have another Dash 8 ready to fly in a couple of days, Aircraft 507 was badly damaged, and I don't think it will be ready for at least four weeks."

"Major Fleming, why was our Intel that inaccurate yesterday?"

"I don't know, Colonel. I am investigating our intelligence failure with Spetsnaz right now. Apparently the CIA said their Intel wasn't any different."

Griswalt took a long sip of his coffee and spoke again, "Has the prisoner provided any info?"

"No, it appears he was a low level thug. He had nothing about Sergeant Stevens either. But I can say confidently that the dog tag was legit"

"Interrogate him for a couple more days. If you don't get any details; ship him off to Camp X-ray."

The door flung open, Colonel Griswalt's aid came rushing in. "Sir, sir, I've..."

"Lieutenant Dempsey, you are interrupting a high level meeting. I don't want to be disturbed during any of my meetings again. Speak, this better be good!" Griswalt angrily barked.

"A General Chui from the People's Republic of China is on our secure line. He called for you specifically and says he has an important security matter to discuss."

"Looks like yesterday's raid riled up the Chinese," muttered Fleming.

"Put him on the speaker phone!" Griswalt ordered. The room fell silent. Griswalt leaned into his phone's microphone and spoke. "Good morning General Chui, I am Colonel Griswalt. It is my pleasure to speak to you?"

"Cut the crap." The harsh tone disturbed Griswalt. "We know you were on our soil yesterday. We also know where your base is located. Stop the intrusions into our soil and airspace. If you violate our airspace again, we will attack, understood?"

"General, I know that you have concerns about terrorist factions operating around the old castle. We suspect they are trying to steal nuclear weapons. They could be a threat to China as well..."

"We can take care of our own problems ourselves. Just keep out of our airspace, understood?" The general abruptly hung up the telephone.

"He doesn't seem too happy does he," commented Fleming.

"Sir, may I interject?" queried Dempsey.

"If you must," gasped Griswalt.

"The Chinese aren't the most forgiving people in the world. We've violated their border countless times. This is the first time they've ever said anything."

"I don't have all day. Get to your point," Griswalt angrily lectured Dempsey

"Do you think we've stumbled upon something that could be embarrassing to them?"

"What would that be?" Griswalt asked. His eyes focused on Dempsey with rapt attention.

"Maybe they are unable to control terrorist activities on their soil. Yesterday's raid was on a major terrorist operation located on their soil. They probably didn't even know that base was there. Their fear is that we'll let it be known that they're unable to control terrorism on their own soil. The Chinese are a proud people; a revelation like this would severely tarnish their image abroad."

"Possible." Griswalt rubbed his graying hair. The events of the preceding night were now rapidly spinning into a confusing mess.

04-June-2010
2200 Hours Local Time

Nishan hated guard duty. Here he was at the most secretive base in the US Army and all he was doing was standing watch. He wanted some excitement. This was going to be a long night for him.

"Want some coffee?" Watson asked waking Nishan out of his daydream.

"Yeah, give me half a cup of that diesel fuel."

"Diesel fuel? This is my famous Watson family coffee recipe."

"Like I said Diesel fuel. That stuff would wake the dead."

"This just like old times, isn't it Nishan?"

Nishan rolled his eyes then quibbled, "Every time you say that we get in trouble somehow. Don't you remember the brawl in Korea?"

"You worry too much. Townsend had it in for us."

"He may have had it in for us Watsy. But you got JJ and Matthews thrown out too." *How was Sarah doing?* Nishan wondered. He hadn't seen since coming back from the Castle mission. Word was she would be back to active duty soon. He couldn't wait to see her blue eyes and sandy blonde hair again.

"You're dreaming about her again aren't you?"

"What?"

"Your girlfriend, Matthews."

"Well, we're not really…"

"Look, we've all been watching 'Sarah' as you called her from the moment she joined Townsend's platoon. She's smart, well disciplined and best of all, she's hot. When are you going to take her over to see mom and dad Gandhi?"

"Watsy"

"Let's face it, buddy, you got the hots and she got a thing or two for you"

Nishan raised his eyes and excitedly asked, "You really think so?"

"Yeah, you keep talking about her in your sleep, ever since you laid you're…"

"Not me, the girl!" Nishan rolled his eyes.

"Look, you're the only guy who can call her by her first name. You don't think she just happened to be at the bar that we had a fight at, do you?"

"Well, I don't know." Nishan pondered his thoughts for a second.

"She wanted to be alone with you hoping that she could start something. I saw her coming toward us in the window. That's why I started things up with the sailors. I was going to get in a nice discussion with them and take JJ away so you two could be alone. But, things didn't go quite as planned."

"You're a real friend, Watsy. Sometimes in lot more ways than I give you credit."

JJ came rushing toward the two, "I heard something back in the woods, sounds like branches crashing."

Watson sighed. "JJ, this is guard duty. We aren't supposed to be rushing around like a lost boy panicking at every sound he hears."

"Hold it, Watsy. If JJ says he heard something, there's something out there. Give me the night vision binoculars, I'll have a look." Nishan scanned the forest, "I see something, it's, there's a bunch of men with AK's approaching! Sound the alarm!"

Watson grabbed a flare gun and fired a flare above the enemy forces. The area ahead lit up like daybreak. Gunfire erupted into Watson's position, "There are hundreds of them out there. We don't even have a belt fed machine gun to fight them off," Watson shouted over the popping sounds of gunfire.

"Grenade," JJ threw a grenade into the trees at the bottom of the hill. A fireball erupted. Dirt and rocks flew everywhere. The enemy gunfire continued unabated. Nishan opened with automatic fire with his HK-91. Spent cases flew out the ejection port, narrowly missing Watson.

Gunfire tore into the bunker; Nishan, JJ and Watson dove for cover. A rocket-propelled grenade flew above them hitting the barbed wires. Dirt and sand rained on them, temporarily blinding them with a cloud of dust. Nishan crawled forward and looked through his red dot scope. A fighter hid behind several small trees, a grenade in his hand. Nishan opened with a short burst. The rounds tore through the tree and then buried into the fighter's chest. A fighter fell back, another round slammed into his forehead. His turban blossomed red with blood.

JJ fired a short burst into the tall grass. Three fighters came out of the grass and ran toward the bunker. JJ immediately cut them down in a flash. Two more fighters came running, firing wildly. JJ fired several single shots at the approaching men. The first fighter took a bullet to his leg. Falling over, another bullet slammed into the base of his skull blowing out his brain. The next fighter stopped dead in his tracks and retreated to the tall grass. A burst of semiautomatic gunfire hit his back. The rounds exited out of his stomach and sprayed blood and internal organs over the grass.

Nishan threw a grenade behind some small trees. Clothing, dirt, and foliage erupted into the air. Gunfire returned from the trees in response, slamming into the bunker's sand bags in front of them.

The pair of Cobra Gunships took off flying in a wedge formation. They hovered ahead of the trio scouring the area for enemy combatants. A flash lit up from the ground and an RPG flew straight into the engine of the lead gunship. The intake cowling exploded, flames and smoke blew out of the engine compartment and killing the pilot. The Cobra's nose began to fall as the copilot struggled to maintain control of the wounded Gunship. Another RPG rose from the ground and slammed into the Cobra's tail rotor. The tail rotor exploded into pieces causing the gunship to spin out of control. The stricken helicopter crashed into the trees exploding into a ball of flames. Enemy combatants madly scurried to be clear of the burning wreckage.

The other gunship pointed its nose toward the tree line and fired a long salvo of 2.75 inch folding fin rockets. The rockets exploded into the brush, massive trees fell down on fighters trapping then underneath. Fires burned them alive as they struggled to free themselves.

Fighters hiding in the forest fired their AKs at the gunship. The rounds clanged and cut through the thin aluminum hull. The gunship let another salvo of rockets into the ridge. Fires exploded around the ridge. Men screamed in pain, their limbs amputated by the rockets. Their team members ran out of the brush to offer any assistance. The Gunship quickly covered the forest with 20mm cannon gunfire. The dying men's screaming drowned out the noise of the helicopter's engines.

Fighters continued rushing out of the brush to escape burning trees and gunfire. Flanking the gunship, they swarmed up the hill with confidence. The gunship swung its nose over, taking aim at the fleeing men. A pair of RPGs slammed into the nose. The nose exploded, killing the both pilots instantly. The stricken hull crashed to the forest floor. The ammunition in the fuselage exploded with the burning fuselage setting the hillside ablaze.

"All units, retreat to the inner perimeter," commanded Staff Sergeant Walters over the radio. The trio jumped out of the bunker and ran to the inner perimeter. Bullets slammed all around the men, narrowly missing Watson by inches. JJ fell to the ground screaming in pain. Nishan stopped and ran back to give aid.

"Are you crazy, we're going to be overrun any second now!" screamed Watson.

"I am not going without JJ! Give me a hand!" Nishan shouted above the noise of gunfire.

"We don't have time!" Gunfire ripped into the rocks beside Watson spraying him with rocks and dirt.

"He'd do the same for you!" Nishan replied.

Watson cringed for a moment, thoughts raced through his mind. He then ran over and helped Nishan carry JJ. The two took JJ back within the inner perimeter. The barbed wire was in sight. Suddenly a grenade exploded behind them. JJ flew up into the air and crashed down into a gravel bank just short of the wire. Nishan rolled to his left bouncing on crates and ammo boxes before landing into a patch of grass. Watson flew to the right, crashed into rocks and rolled down the hillside out of view.

Corporal Jones and Corporal Ward crawled under the wire. Bullets grazed by as they tried hard to keep their heads down. They grabbed JJ and pulled him out of the brush and dragged him back to the wall.

Medics rushed to JJ feverishly treating his leg wound. JJ screamed to the medics, "They're still out there! My friends are still out there! You got to go get them! You got to go get them!" JJ cried. His heart hurt almost as much as his leg.

"Staff Sergeant Waters, have all our guard units returned yet?" Captain York asked.

"All but two members, sir," Walters replied

"We can't wait. We lost two gunships already. Open up with the machine guns and set off the perimeter explosives!"

A dozen M-60s opened with automatic fire followed by dozens of Mk-19 grenade launchers. Insurgents surging over the wire were immediately cut down by the M-60s. Automatic grenade fire blew through the second wave. Fighters screamed in pain, but still charged forward toward the heavy weapons.

At the north side of the camp, fighters ran over a field beyond the end of the runway. Their guns blazed with automatic fire. Crossing the field, mines exploded. Arms, legs and bodies were hurled into the air. When the bodies hit the ground, mines exploded blowing more body parts off. The field became soaked with the blood of so many men.

* * * * *

A group of insurgents ran over the bodies of their dead comrades and stormed into the cavernous hanger. They fired wildly at the Dash 8 400 sitting on jacks. Corporal Jones slid in through the hanger doors and fired a 40mm grenade from his M-203. The grenade hit the lead shooter in the chest and exploded. His head and torso disappeared in the explosion. Shrapnel and body parts impaled the second shooter, killing him instantly also.

Unseen Warriors

An insurgent ran by his dead teammates and pulled the pin from his grenade. He threw the grenade in the direction of Corporal Jones. The grenade bounced off the plane's fuselage and onto the open fwd cabin door. An explosion rocked the plane, destroying the cockpit floor and nose gear. The plane shook and rattled on its jacks. Jones fired another grenade. The grenade missed wildly and hit the left main jack. The airplane shuddered and fell off the jacks. The falling fuselage crashed earthward, trapping several screaming insurgents underneath its belly.

Private Zale ran to Jones' side and opened up with the HK-91. The rounds cut down an RPG armed shooter. Another terrorist threw a grenade at the two men. It exploded high above, knocking them to the ground. Several other shooters joined in, firing their automatic weapons in Jones' direction. Bullets crashed around the injured Black Ops soldiers.

Private Flag came to the rescue of his stricken comrades. He fired his HK-91 in short bursts of automatic fire. Thirty cal bullets slammed into the fighters' legs blowing out their knees and flesh. A bleeding insurgent loaded up an RPG and fired it at Flag. The RPG slammed into a nearby beam killing Flag.

Jones and Zale regained their senses. They sprayed the wounded terrorists with automatic fire mercilessly. Blood sprayed the fuselage of the plane. The two men walked over to look at the dead. An RPG armed fighter moved his head to look at the two, blood dripped from his mouth. Zale pointed his gun at the fighters' head. He fired a quick shot, killing the terrorist. He proceeded to kick the bloody corps repeatedly. Jones pushed aside Zale. Zale gave Jones an angry look. Jones looked back, "Private Zale, I order you to stop." Zale gave Jones a dirty look and followed him out of the hanger.

* * * * *

A dozen fighters ran up the hill. Burned and wounded, they tried to close in on the hanger. Zale and Jones gunned them down before they had a chance. Their fellow combatants changed direction and tried to sneak behind the machine guns. When they approached the inner perimeter barbed wire, Walters set off the perimeter explosives. The fence was pelted with blood and body parts.

The morning sun slowly rose in the sky and cast light on the charred battlefield. Colonel Griswalt looked through his binoculars. He shook his head with disgust and horror. *What waste, what total disregard for personal safety. Why did they attack, what did they want?* Griswalt wondered.

"Well, how are you doing?" Major Fleming asked.

"This is unbelievable, utter suicide! Who was behind this?"

Fleming shrugged his shoulder. "From the looks of it, all of the attackers were Arab men in their twenties. They were poorly trained, but highly motivated."

"Do you think the Chinese backed this incursion?" Griswalt asked

"I don't think so. They were using Russian-made weapons. If the Chinese were to attack, they would use something more sophisticated than RPGs and small arms."

"Colonel, we have a live one here," shouted someone from the battlefield.

Griswalt walked over and looked at the bleeding fighter. His turban was soaked with blood, his arm burned and his leg torn was open exposing bone.

"Why did you attack us?" Griswalt asked in a calm, nonchalant voice.

"The Sheik ordered us!" The man whispered in a heavily accented voice.

"Who is the Sheik? Is he Hassan?"

"The Sheik, Mansoor, Ali Mansoor." The fighter closed his eyes and life left his body. Ali Mansoor was a warlord from the Northeast region of Pakistan. Mansoor helped Bin Laden hide from the US for several years after 9/11. He had extensive connections to terrorists across the world. He was suspected of everything from car bombings in Baghdad to shooting down airliners in Europe. In 2008 President Musharaff was assassinated in his palace. Pakistan was immediately plunged into civil war. Chaos reigned everywhere. Mansoor quickly dispatched his private militia. Very quickly he became the only person in charge Pakistan. Terrorist activities across the world quickly grew as his area of control expanded.

Griswalt shook his head in utter disbelief, "Why would Mansoor be around here? After all he's got his haven in Pakistan?"

Fleming shrugged his shoulders as he spoke. "He's got terrorist cells all around the world. This just may be one of those we didn't know about."

"That is possible. But why would he order an attack on such a heavily defended base? There are plenty of soft targets all around Southwest Russia."

Unable to answer, Fleming blurted out the first thought in his mind. "They're crazy. They'll do anything to see Allah."

"No, they want something. They came here in force for it, what is it?"

"I know," Dempsey interrupted.

"Lieutenant Dempsey, you are supposed to be helping me in my office. I don't want you following me around like a lost puppy dog!"

"Sir, if you would listen, I can explain."

"Go ahead, if you must."

"Like you said, they came for a high value target. We must have Hassan."

"What?" Griswalt's facial expression turned to confusion. Fleming rolled his eyes and looked up into the sky.

"Preposterous!" Fleming shouted.

"Hassan is a Pakistani. He speaks the same language as Nishan! Nishan spoke to the prisoner in his native tongue at the castle. Hassan hasn't been seen or heard from ever since our raid at the castle. Multiple, independent sources of Intel from various countries said that Hassan would at the castle last night. How could they all be wrong?"

Griswalt shook his head for a second. "Staff Sergeant Walters, get me Private Nishan. I want him to help with an interrogation."

"There's a problem, sir," Walters answered. "Private Nishan and Watson are missing since last night's raid. They never made it into the inner perimeter."

Chapter 4

Army Intelligence HQ
Puchon, Korea
06-June-2010
0600 Hours Local Time

Lieutenant Townsend walked down the empty halls of the Army Intelligence building. He had been called by his commanding officer to personally to appear before a Top Secret panel. He knew that either he was being relieved of his command or a new, extremely dangerous mission was being planned for him. Either way he was very uneasy about this invitation to appear.

Townsend entered a large room. In the center there was a large oval table. Seated at the head of it was General Lewis Mackenzie, a three star general who was in command of the entire Asian-Pacific theatre. To the left of him sat Townsend's Commanding officer, Colonel Stevens. To the right were several Colonels that Townsend had never seen before.

"You can be seated," Commanded the general. "First of all, anything said or seen in this room is Top Secret. Nothing shall be leaked out of this room, understood?"

"Yes, sir," Townsend emphatically responded.

"Okay let's begin. Yesterday another Apache was shot down near Chorwan. The Apache's wingman watched several figures wearing black pajamas rush north toward DMZ after the attack. This leads to a total of six helicopters down in the last three weeks. All the attacks seem to be the same. A SAM, possibly an SA-7, is launched from the South Korean side at night at helicopters flying at low level. Intel suggests the aggressors are not necessarily North Korean military forces but possibly a band of insurgents seeking to wreck havoc along the DMZ. Lieutenant Townsend, your team has been doing quite well patrolling along the DMZ. From fitness reports, you have quite an elite team of soldiers. Your mission is simple. You are to lead your platoon across the wall on a Top-secret mission. Colonel Jones, please give the Lieutenant the full details."

Jones lifted a sheet of paper and spoke. "You will be transported from Chorwan across the DMZ to a point east of Ichon. From there you will meet up with one of our intelligence moles. Use him as a guide, seek out and destroy the raiders at will. Use whatever intelligence you can pick up in your travels. When you have completed your mission, send us a cowboy six message over the radio. We'll pick you up at an undetermined LZ at exactly 0300 hours the following day. Other than your pickup call there are to be no other radio contacts with us. Remember your mission does not officially exist. If you get caught, we will deny knowledge. Do you have any questions?"

"Isn't this one of those stealth missions that Black Ops would normally do?" Townsend hesitantly asked.

"Yes, normally a Black Ops outfit would do it. But Camp Zulu was attacked yesterday. They'll be out of action for a while. Lieutenant, we have the confidence your platoon has the skill to complete the mission successfully."

"One further note, Lieutenant Townsend. Be very careful. Do not trust anyone. That includes our mole," Colonel Spielman said.

"Your platoon ships out from Kimpo at 0800 hours. You are dismissed," Mackenzie commanded in a stern tone.

Townsend walked away stunned yet relieved. He would lead a high-risk mission across the DMZ. He would finally get a chance to show the top brass what his men were made of. But if they got caught, the North Koreans would consider this an act of war. Townsend knew in such a case he would never see his family ever again.

Upon arrival back to his base, Townsend stormed into the barracks. Standing his troops to attention he took roll call. "Where's that clown Martin?" he shouted, his eyes burning with anger.

"Sir, Ahh, he's incapacitated in his bunk right now," Patrick meekly replied.

Townsend stormed into Martin's quarters. Finding Martin asleep in his bunk, Townsend anger exploded. He tossed Martin and his mattress out of the bunk and onto the cold hard floor.

Martin awoke, groggy, barely ably to keep his eyes open.

"I want this platoon ready with its gear for a flight at Kimpo by 0800. Understood?"

"Yes, sir." Martin saluted Townsend. Townsend stormed out leaving Martin dazed and confused. A massive hangover reminded Martin of his previous night of partying.

The platoon loaded their gear into Hummers and drove off to Kimpo. Many wondered what this mission was all about. The way Townsend burst into their barracks made them fear the worst.

Patrick leaned over to Martin, "How was your big night with Boxman?"

Clutching his head, Martin meekly answered, "I don't remember too much, boy my head is booming."

"Well, I caught you two in action for about an hour before I headed back to base. You two were dancing up a storm with those Northwest Airlines flight attendants. Boy, those women had to be at least fifty. You guys were making them dance like they were twenty. One of them even wanted to marry you. She chased you around the bar all night all night long. You and Boxman know how to have a good time!"

Martin couldn't believe it. He had too much to drink and he got himself into trouble again. He knew he had to stop, but drinking was the only way to dull the pain of loneliness. *I spent the night chasing around senior citizens*, he thought. *Man I'm slipping.* Martin knew his head wasn't clear. He didn't think he was prepared for this mission. This was the combat mission he had been longing for since he joined Townsend's platoon. But, deep inside, he wished he could have stayed behind. He knew Townsend's hard head was going to make sure that the platoon put out 100% effort during this mission. But Martin wasn't sure he was up to the task.

Arriving at Kimpo, a Blackhawk waited. Its rotors cutting through the air making that distinctive beating sound that all grunts knew. The platoon charged in carrying their heavy gear. They scampered inside, trying to find a comfortable place in the cramped cabin. Martin took a seat by the open door.

The Blackhawk headed northeast. Winds buffeted it, causing it vibrate and shake on its travels above the Jmjia-gang River. The platoon felt uneasy looking over to the DMZ. The mountains broke through the haze. Martin's stomach felt queasy. He shifted his attention out the door to the vegetation rushing below him. Martin couldn't it hold anymore. He vomited and sprayed the contents of his stomach out the door, hitting the tail boom.

The Blackhawk approached Chorwan. It turned south to a hill overlooking the town. The helicopter landed in a makeshift LZ beside a couple of rundown wooden buildings. The troops immediately rushed to one of the dilapidated buildings. Townsend continued to shout orders at every point of their journey.

Inside the old building, Townsend gave his briefing to the platoon. Many of the soldiers couldn't believe their eyes and

Unseen Warriors

ears. A vague goal, sketchy details, rigid pick up times and no re-supply helicopters. They wondered if HQ was serious. Many didn't believe this was an actual mission. Martin' hangover worsened through the briefing. He was unable to concentrate on mission details. His thoughts quickly drifted to his children, whom he had not seen for almost two years. He wished he could just talk to them for five minutes. He figured that's all it would take for him to say how he felt he felt about them.

After the briefing the troops went to the ammunition table and picked up all the ammunition they could carry. For their HK-91 rifles they collected twenty-five twenty round magazines, six grenades a 9mm HK USP pistol, a gallon of water and food for a week. Each team member carried a combined load of about fifty pounds of gear. Many still wondered if they carried enough ammunition for their mission.

At 2100 hours the platoon loaded into another Blackhawk and took off into the clear night. At the helm, Captain William "Cobra" Johnson made a smooth transition from vertical to forward flight. He didn't fly the helicopter in as much as he wore it. He smoothly banked around the hills, flying low under the cloak of darkness. He plunged down valleys using the terrain to mask his presence. Crossing the DMZ, his heart began to pound as he looked down. The Blackhawk crossed mere feet above the invisible border at top speed. Johnson constantly monitored to his threat indicator for radar sweeps. There was nothing but silence. His copilot looked into blackness of the night for SAMs and their trademark fireballs after launch.

The Blackhawk turned a corner and headed northeast, delicately balancing the distance between Chorwan, Ichon and Pyongyang to avoid detection by the rings of radar control stations that circled the cities.

Johnson knew the mission was high risk. Any second he could be detected. Detection would be a major international incident, an act of war that would send shockwaves across the globe. But Johnson knew his duty and flew on with apprehension. This was a real mission and he knew it. Johnson had spent countless years practicing for what ifs and maybes with fake weapons staged enemies and staged outcomes. The training missions had become dull routine. Sweeps along the DMZ contributed to his boredom making him ponder his future in the Army. But this mission was with real bullets and enemies excited him. The danger somehow aroused him and made him feel his training finally could be put to real use.

The Blackhawk rose slightly and crossed the Ichon/Kimhwa highway. Johnson's stomach tightened as he scanned around for vehicles. Outside there was nothing but blackness. The lack of life made the 80-degree night feel that much hotter.

Thirty miles east of Ichon, Johnson approached the LZ. He could see railroad tracks shimmering in the distance. Closing in on the LZ, a grass field appeared out of the darkness. An old man wearing a traditional Korean hat, carrying a staff in one hand and a dim lantern in the other appeared out of nowhere. Johnson flashed his taxi light with two quick bursts. The lantern flickered four times and went out. Contact with the mole had been made.

The Blackhawk touched down a hundred feet short of the old man. The platoon ran out the helicopter while lugging their battle gear. Townsend was the last to step out of the throbbing machine. Taking a quick headcount, he casually made his was to the old man. The Blackhawk lifted up and banked sharply to the left. The team looked on at their transport as it disappeared into the stillness of the night.

"Hello, Lieutenant Townsend, I am Colonel Pak of the North Korean army," the old man said in a timid voice.

Townsend's eyes grew big. He held his hand out. "Nice to meet you, err, you speak very good English, sir."

"Thank you. Even here in North Korea we know that the international community will never accept us if we don't learn the ways of modern commerce and diplomacy. Speaking English is a basic skill that we are all required to master."

"If you don't mind me asking, why you are helping us? You are, what we would call, the enemy. Your soldiers have been regularly shooting down our aircraft."

"Lieutenant Townsend, we want North Korea to be a prosperous country again. Years of famine, economic sanctions and diplomatic isolationism have left our country poor and economically ravaged. These raiders who shoot at your aircraft only increase our suffering. They have short term political goals, but they risk the long term health of North Korea in the process."

"Why doesn't your central government do something about the raiders? They have the firepower and the troops. After all, if you want to improve your image you need…"

"You don't understand. The central government has become weak from years of corruption and mismanagement. It is a mere shell of its former self. The Army has broken down into several factions. The generals have carved the country up into several fiefdoms. The generals act like rival warlords. They savagely raid each other for food and supplies. The law or rule is that the men with the weapons are the ones in control now. Come, we need to hike toward Hoe yang. It's about twenty miles from here. General Luck controls the area. He is very anti-American and extremely savage. Often he will kill any villager who he thinks is consorting with a rival militia. Several villagers have reported General Luck's militia travel to Hoe yang for supplies."

The team turned on their night vision monocles and hiked over the steep terrain. Colonel. Pak, despite his old age and frail condition, lead the team. Several platoon members, barely half his age, had trouble keeping up with the brisk pace. They crossed over the railroad tracks, the heat and the humidity radiated from the ground. Sweat-soaked the soldiers' uniforms. The heat of the night became as unbearable as the heat from the day.

"Over the crest there is a deep canyon with steep walls. The raiders often set up positions there in order to send raiding parties across the DMZ," Col Pak announced to the team.

Approaching the crest, Townsend shouted, "Guns up!" Each one of the members crouched down behind the ravine. They set their HK-91s to auto and waited for the command to fire.

Ahead, inside a gully, a dirt road ran parallel to a shallow stream. A convoy of run down trucks and assorted tracked vehicles slowly drove by. Troops sat on the roofs, turrets and any other flat space they could find. Armed with AK-47s, they looked nervously around for threats. The equipment continued to limber along to a dead end in the canyon. Steep cliffs surrounded the convoy, hiding its presence from the outside world.

"These are the raiders. They are poorly trained and armed. They don't have any night vision devices, or any body amour. They must be going out on another mission, stay very quiet," Park whispered.

An officer walked out a T-55 tank. He looked around toward the team's direction. He smelled the air. Walking forward a few feet toward the stream, he looked up to the sky with anger.

* * * * *

High above, Major Chiang of the Chinese Air Force flew overhead with his Mig-29A. His wingman, Major Ziang, followed closely behind. Ziang scanned the ground as they made lazy circles in the sky. "Sounds like General Luck has very busy. He shot down another one of the American's electric helicopters again. He must be very pleased with himself," Chiang announced to his wingman.

"Yes, you are right Comrade Chiang. The American's have the largest, most technologically advanced military. But they cannot protect themselves from on rouge, General with barely enough food to feed his troops. Comrade, why does our government want us to do these missions, wouldn't it be better if we allowed the general to provoke a war with South Koreans?"

"Patience Comrade Ziang, if the general provoked war, we would have a new strong man in charge of North Korea. The nuclear weapons North Korea has would be not only a threat to the South, but also to the People's Republic of China. Our war against the Muslim insurgents is not going well. The insurgents have attacked many of the American manufacturing plants. The American companies are threatening to leave if we do not stop the attacks. We need the help of America against the insurgents. Don't forget Beijing is just as corrupt and mismanaged as Pyongyang. If it weren't for the American dollars that the manufacturing exports to America bring in, we could just as well suffer the same fate as North Korea. Our fate is linked with the success of the American war on Terrorism."

"What are we supposed to be looking for? This is a futile effort. We cannot see anything from up here. We are just playing around. What we can do stop this general anyway," Ziang complained.

"All we have to do is make noise. The general is a weak man. He will be scared when he sees our Air Force in the sky. He will go back to fighting with his fellow generals. North Korea will stay weak."

Ziang looked at the black ground below. A flash erupted from the ground, his aircraft's threat indicator display chirped then beeped constantly. "SAM, SAM twelve o'clock!" Chiang screamed over the radio. Both planes jammed into tight 8g turns in opposite directions while dumping chaff into the air. Looking over his shoulder, Chiang could see a missile approaching on his right wing. When the missile leveled off, Chiang performed a right turn. At first he started a wide turn, as the missile approached closer he tightened up his turn while dumping chaff at the same time. Crossing paths with the missile, he pulled up hard while dumping chaff. The missile flew by the plane and exploded harmlessly out of range. Chiang and Ziang joined up and dived toward the launch vehicle's positions.

* * * * *

The officer ordered his men to take positions. Gunfire sprayed from the sky. Townsend and his men dug in hard as they heard the metallic sound of bullets hitting steel. Dirt flew everywhere. Unable to resist the urge, Corporal Patrick looked up over the ravine. A stray 27mm bullet slammed into his helmet. Patrick's head disappeared into a cloud of red mist and skull fragments.

Bullets crashed into the Korean men on the roadway. Their chests exploded spreading their innards over the landscape. A Zil 135 truck, at the trail position in the convoy, was the first vehicle to be hit. Rounds tore into the fabric bed cover. Men screamed in pain as they were hammered by gunfire. The gas tank exploded in a ball of flames. Men were thrown out of the truck like rag dolls, their clothing ablaze. What men that were alive, hit the pavement screaming for death as they burned. Rounds pulverized a BRDM-2. The bullets cut into its thin amour, turning the rubber tired vehicle into a ball of flames.

Troops fired AK-47s into the air in a vain hope they could wound the birds of prey. Fires tore through the convoy, bullets easily tore through the thin skinned vehicles. Banking to either side, the jets turned around for another pass at the convoy.

A group of soldiers opened with automatic fire at the incoming jets. Their fellow soldiers readied their SA-7 shoulder fired missiles for the incoming aircraft.

* * * * *

"Come around for another attack, aim for the middle of the convoy!" Chiang ordered. *Fools, here I am coming in around 350*

Unseen Warriors

knots and they think they can hit me with small arms, Chiang thought

Chiang plunged, his aircraft earthward into the direction of the column. Small arms fire flashed ahead like fireworks all around him. Chiang grinned, unafraid of the popping all around him. He opened fire with his cannon with glee. Suddenly his cockpit rattled and shook, the instrument burst into flames. Chiang jerked the stick into a hard left turn. Flames danced all around. His arm immediately became covered with flames. He felt a burning sensation throughout his body. Chiang grabbed the portable fire extinguisher and sprayed his arm and cockpit with dry powder. Thee odor of burning flesh filled the cockpit. His arm felt weak and heavy. Flames raced from the back of the plane into the cockpit. Chiang madly reached down for the ejection seat handle. An explosion erupted, blowing the cockpit section off the main fuselage. Chiang, still strapped in the seat, rode the burning wreckage into the ground. Burning pieces of his plane rained down onto the hillside.

Ziang plunged out of the sky into a steep dive. Transfixed by the column of equipment, he lined his reticule up on the small grey shadows in the road. Before he could fire, a flash blinded him. Two missiles raced to meet Ziang's airplane. Each one found its way into the engine intakes. The missiles
blew out compressor blades, disks, fans and stators. The explosion set fire to the fuel being rapidly fed into the engines. Ziang pulled the airplane sharply out of the dive leveled off. Flames shot from his nacelles like two blow torches as the airplane disappeared into the night and exploded off in the distance.

* * * * *

Townsend looked down at the dazed soldiers. They were bruised and battered, flames burned all around them. Still, they celebrated the downing of the two aircraft. Townsend led his squad down the ridge line to the back of the column. The smoking remains of destroyed trucks littered the roadway.

"Martin, split the team into two groups. I want one flank to go along the river and take out the infantry. Send out another flank to take out the vehicles along the bowl of the canyon," Townsend ordered.

"Goodwin, Constance, Bauer, Diaz, and Olsen, I'll lead you to the right flank. The infantry is priority. We'll attack the vehicles after we clear the roadway. Leduc, you stay here with Lientenant Townsend, and Colonel Pak. Carlson, Williams and Rich, you take the left flank and immobilize those T-55 tanks. Conserve your ammo, use three round bursts instead of automatic fire whenever possible."

Martin and his squad walked to the right flank beside a burning Kraz 25B truck. Nearby, three soldiers in tattered clothing stood. Martin motioned, the team fired a short burst. The three soldiers went down instantly. Walking away, Martin had an inexplicable urge to look into the eyes of the soldiers they had gunned down. He ran across the abandoned roadway with Goodwin and Constance. The two men covered his position. Martin immediately became horrified when he looked down at the faces of three boys, aged 12, 13, and 10. His eyes watered, thoughts about his children filled his mind. He lost all composure and started sobbing.

* * * * *

Gunfire erupted out of the radar vehicle. Corporal Carlson fell to the ground. AK fire slammed into the burning BRDM-2 transporter beside him. The trailing T-55 lay 400 yards ahead of him covered by dozens of troops. *How are we going to clear this area*, he wondered.

Carlson gave Private Rich a twisting V sign. Rich ran to the other side of the transporter and crawled into its ruptured belly. He was about 150 yards from the lead enemy troop concentration. Rich looked to his right, another group of soldiers was closing in from the creek about 300 yards away. Gunfire erupted from both troop concentrations. Bullets rattled the transporter's cavernous interior. Rich realized he was pinned down and there was no possibility of retreat. Rich crawled backed into the transporter. Rich took off his backpack pulled out several grenades. Looking around for a place to place his grenades, His eyes grew wide. A Russian Degtarev machine gun lay half buried in the sand. Three full drum magazines were scattered nearby. Rich fed the linked ammo into the machine gun, snapped the cover over and lay on the ground with the barrel pointed on the oncoming troops.

The North Korean troops eased up on their gunfire. Sighting no return fire, they traveled along the stream bank. Rich opened fire. The gunfire tore into the troop company. Soldiers jumped into the stream trying to escape the murderous gunfire. Rich's bullets continued to target them mercilessly. The water turned red with the blood of the wounded and dead. Several soldiers ran behind a truck, trying to avoid the incoming fire. Rich struck the fuel tank, the truck exploded into a ball of flames. Burning debris and body parts rained down onto the battlefield.

"Click," the machine gun was empty. Rich quickly opened the cover and tore off the empty drum. He hastily grabbed another drum and fed the links. The enemy troops regrouped and fired in his direction. Rounds hit all around the overturned vehicle. Rich could hear the haunting clang of metal on metal. Rich opened fire on the men racing into their direction. The bullets tore into them, shredding their frail bodies with ease.

* * * * *

Carlson became concerned. Rich had been gone for some time. Waves of enemy units continued to flood toward Rich's position with automatic gunfire.

Private Williams, standing by Carlson's side, threw a grenade in the air in the direction of the advancing forces. It exploded harmlessly overhead. The Gunfire failed to ease. Carlson put another magazine into his HK-91. A grenade flew into the crowd of enemy soldiers, exploding in their formation. Several soldiers went down. When the others attempted to regroup, tracer fire tore into the crowd. It easily cut them down until no one stood.

Carlson ran forward toward a burning tank with Williams. When they passed the overturned troop transporter, Rich joined him carrying a machine gun. "I thought you were a goner, where have you been hiding?" Carlson remarked.

"You know me. I like to make a grand entrance. Like my new toy?" Rich said with a wide grin. Carlson laughed and nodded his head.

* * * * *

Martin awoke from his daze. Gunfire was coming from the other side of the stream. Martin called the rest of his team over. They moved around the charred vehicles until they were all behind a T-55 tank. Its engine was still running, no Korean troops were in sight. Bauer opened the hatch and looked. The tank's interior was deserted. He jumped in followed by Constance and Private Olsen. Bauer drove the tank toward the stream. Driving on the muddy bank, Bauer easily avoided the burning vehicles as he rounded the bank. Olsen took up the mounted machine gun.

Flashes blinded Bauer. He saw a couple of old T-55 Tanks and ZSU-23-4 Shilka anti aircraft gun in the distance. The T-55s were firing at him. Carlson and his team ran behind the tank and joined up with Martin's remaining teammates. "Did you clear the tanks?" Martin hurriedly questioned.

"Negative, I couldn't get near them. They've surrounded themselves with troops. They've got a couple of Shilkas over there. We'd get cut up before we even got near them."

Unseen Warriors

"Damn it, Carlson, I gave you an order. Now, we're all stuck here until we can get by that bunch of scrap metal. I swear you're such an idiot sometimes. Go cover my right flank. I hope you can handle that."

Abuse from Martin was not uncommon for Carlson. It sometimes was a daily ritual. Carlson had only been leader of Nishan's squad for a short time. Nishan and company's sudden departure left Carlson with only two other people in his squad. It seemed that Martin had wanted Carlson out of the platoon from the day he arrived. The only saving grace was that Townsend thought Carlson was at least "competent." That was still better than any of Martin's opinions.

Bauer pulled his tank behind another burning hulk, slowing down to a crawl, Olsen and Constance loaded the gun and fired at the Shilka. "Boom," flames raced into the sky. The shell ripped into the Shilka's thin skin, rendering the now blown apart Shilka useless. The team madly reloaded the gun. Several shells landed around them sending debris and shrapnel skyward. Dozens of soldiers charged toward the tank. Olsen jumped on the machine gun and fired bullets wildly into the oncoming crowd. Another shell crashed nearby, dirt, dust and smoke obscured the enemy tanks.

*****

Carlson led his team around some broken equipment. Enemy soldiers ran beside them a mere 100 yards away. Carlson took out his binoculars and scanned the distance. He sighted a cave entrance to the hill just 75 yards forward and left. They made a dash for the entrance, shells rained all around them. Once inside, they were awed by the grand interior. The cave smelled wet and musty. Bats hung from the ceiling. Droppings covered the floor. Dirt and rock rained from the interior as shells continued to smash overhead. Sensing the urgency of their situation, they ran faster and faster to the far end of the tunnel.

The sound of shells crashing around them grew louder and louder with each passing step.

Carlson rounded the corner. He madly stopped, nearly slipping and falling onto the slimy trail. He could see up ahead the officer with a few senior NCOs. Carlson and his team fired a short burst. The NCOs went down grabbing their stomachs. The officer bolted away from them. Carlson put a three round burst into his leg. Bleeding from his thigh, he went down hard slamming into the cave floor. Carlson's team came up to the NCOs who were near death. The team approached the officer. He shouted and screamed at the team. Carlson tied a bandanna around his mouth and silenced him. The other two soldiers tied his arms and legs.

The team walked further and saw light around a bend. Approaching with caution, they found themselves about 160 yards behind the enemy equipment. They watched the tanks pound the friendly tank's position with shells. The team ran toward the closest tank. Sneaking from behind, they climbed up to the turret. Williams expertly opened the hatch. Rich immediately threw a grenade into the opening. Williams slammed the hatch down and gave the lock wheel a quick spin. The team made their getaway to another tank. A muffled explosion occurred inside the tank they left behind. Smoke poured out of the openings, the tank became silent.

The lead tank moved away from the team's direction. Carlson and his team rushed to catch the fleeing tank. They just barely jumped on. The nearby Shilka exploded into a ball of flames. Debris rained from the sky, narrowly missing them. The tank accelerated sharply and turned hard trying to avoid falling shells. The team held on for dear life. The tank turned hard and fired with its main gun. The driver then opened his hatch. Carlson fired automatic gunfire into the hatch as the tank turned toward the river. Williams expertly threw a grenade into the opening and jumped off with the team.

Unseen Warriors

The tank accelerated to full speed crashing into the last Shilka. The Shilka rolled over several times before resting in the stream. An explosion occurred inside the tank, flames leapt into the sky out of the open hatch hundreds of feet in the air.

The soldiers in the overturned Shilka frantically tried to open the hatch, it was jammed. They pried and banged away, but the hatch would not open. One of the soldiers grabbed a pry bar and used it. The hatch opened a crack. Water poured into the tank. The soldiers tried to pull on the bar to get the hatch all the way open. Nothing would work. Water continued to pour in. The soldiers stood on ammo boxes inside the hull, frantically trying to keep their heads above water. The hatch opened an inch more; the water quickly filled the inside of the tank. The soldiers thrashed and shook until their bodies became still.

* * * * *

Watching the enemy tank crash and burn, the tank crew celebrated the joy by hugging each other. Bauer grinned and saluted as Townsend approached. Carlson arrived with his crew. Bauer relaxed, pulled out a cigar and smoked. The fear of combat was over, Bauer felt free, no longer anxious. Constance pulled out a cigarette and joined Bauer.

Olson looked at the two, "Don't you two know smoking is bad for you?"

"What we just did for the last six hours isn't terribly safe!" Bauer replied. The smell of cigar smoke filled the interior of the tank. Olsen laughed, he grabbed a cigar from Bauer's tin box. Bauer lit Olson's cigar. Olson breathed the smoke, his body calmed and relaxed. A missile slammed into the tank, setting the interior ablaze with molten metal. Bauer and his teammates were vaporized by the missiles' impact.

"Get out of here!" ordered Townsend as he ran across the stream to the safety of caves. Two Chinese Mig-29s sprayed the team with gunfire and rockets. Private Leduc crashed into the stream. Bullets tore into his flesh coloring the river red. Williams ran toward the stream, suddenly he was blinded. His ears filled with a ringing sound. He found himself flying through the air, crashing down into the hard ground. He felt his legs turn numb. He looked to the right. His bloody legs wearing boots lay beside his head.

Carlson came and grabbed Williams, trying to drag his body through the mud. Williams grabbed Carlson's jacket, "Go, if you don't, you'll die too, go away!" Carlson ignored him and dragged Williams six more feet. Williams slapped him in the face and smashed Carlson's hand. Carlson fell back, looked into Williams' eyes for a second and ran to the cave. Arriving at the cave he looked back at his friend in ankle deep water. A rocket slammed into the creek, setting the water ablaze.

Watching his friend's body burn, Carlson prayed. "Dear Jesus, please take my brother Jonathan Williams, in his walk to glorify your name. Bless him with all the rewards of walking unswervingly in your path, and always speaking righteously your name. Allow his death not to be a moment of mourning for us, but a time that we may celebrate his taking eternal life serving you forever in Heaven, Amen." Carlson then fell to his knees and sobbed uncontrollably like a baby.

Chapter 5

Black Ops Camp Zulu
07-June-2010
0600 Hours Local Time

JJ quietly ate breakfast at mess building. His leg had healed enough for him to walk without any assistance. But deep inside, he still felt a pain that continued from his le to his heart. "Nice to see you out of the Infirmary, how's your leg doing?" Matthews said before she sat down beside him and started eating her breakfast.

"Fine, my leg hurts a little, but the doctor said the wound is healing fine. In about a week I should be good to go. You seem to be walking well, does you leg still hurt?"

"No, of course I didn't get hurt as bad as you. I talked to the Colonel outside. He says our Purple hearts should be here in about a week. We're going to be decorated soldiers. That's something to write your folks about. I might be able to get Sergeant Zane to send a picture to your folks."

JJ didn't notice he just looked shyly down into his tray, picking at his food. Unable to contain his sorrow, he looked up at Matthews with a glum look. "I left them, I left them behind the other day." Tears streamed down JJ's cheek.

"What do you mean you left them?"

"I was hit, Nishan and Watson stopped to get me. An explosion happened, throwing them in the air. I never saw them afterwards. They fired machine guns and grenades where they were after they carried me away."

Matthews' eyes grew big. Being confined to the Infirmary, she hadn't been able to be part of the defense forces during the attack. After her brief stay in the Infirmary, no one mentioned the missing soldiers, not even Griswalt. She felt betrayed, as if no one trusted her to be rational or calm.

*****

Griswalt marched with Fleming and Walters to Hassan's cell. "Put him into the interrogation room," Walters ordered to the guards posted outside Hassan's cell. The guards opened the cell door. Hassan smiled, and put his hands out motioning to his shackles. One of the guards pointed the barrel of his rifle into Hassan's face. Hassan's smile turned into a frown.

The guards led Hassan, still in shackles, into the cramped interrogation room. Sergeant Walters walked into the room. His guards froze, holding their rifles at waist level.

Walters walked around the room then gave Hassan an evil stare. "Okay Hassan, the game's up! What's Mansoor planning?" Hassan looked on. A glazed look covered his face. Walters walked up to Hassan and stared at him face to face. Looking into Hassan's eyes he said, "I'm not like most Americans you know, I'm as much a ruthless killer as you are." Hassan remained silent, unwilling to speak.

Walters walked away. He ran to one of the guards and ripped the HK-91 out of his arms. Walter pulled the charging handle; a cartridge flew out of the ejection port. Walters ran up to Hassan and pointed the barrel into Hassan's face. "I have had enough of your games. Thanks to your friends' little attack last night, we lost two helicopters and seven of my best men! We killed eighty-five of your stupid fighters. I don't need to deal with you anymore, say goodbye to Allah!" Walters pushed off the safety and put his finger on the trigger. Walters slowly pulled the trigger.

Hassan shouted, "Ok, I'll speak. Please, don't kill me," Hassan cried on the desk, begging Walters to spare his life.

Griswalt ran in with Major Fleming on his side, "Are you crazy Walters, you could be locked up for this!"

"Sir, I don't care. Let's kill him. He's a dog, and a murderer. I'm going to blow his head away!"

"I'll tell you everything I know about Mansoor. Please, don't kill me!" Hassan pleaded.

"Corporal McTavish, get in here!" Griswalt ordered.

McTavish ran into the room, his rifle in hand. "Yes, sir."

"Take Walters away and put him in the stockade and take that damn rifle out his hand!" Walters handed his rifle to McTavish. McTavish swung the rifle over his shoulder and led Walters out of the room.

Griswalt calmly walked over to Hassan and sat down face to face with Hassan. Fleming stood beside Griswalt, a notepad and pen in hand. Griswalt narrowed his eyebrows, looking deeply into Hassan's eyes with a cold stare. "Now, Mr. Hassan, I am very interested in what you have to say. Are you going to cooperate with me, or do I have to call Charles Manson over here?"

Hassan swallowed and spoke. "We were at the castle before your attack the other day. Mansoor came to visit with several foreigners. They were leaders of his cells from across the Middle East. I didn't know all of them but there were representatives from Sudan, Indonesia, Chechnya, Chad, Saudi Arabia, Iraq and Iran. I think there was an oriental man, possibly from North Korea.

"Mansoor came a day early. He said his sources in Chechnya told him that Spetsnaz had been poking around. They had gotten info about our meeting so he changed the time. Not all his leaders would be able to arrive. He thought he might have had a double agent reporting to Spetsnaz.

"Mansoor said in our meeting that he now controlled all of Pakistan. That included its military and weapon development programs. He declared that he was the new strongman of Pakistan. He said Bin Laden had been killed in a bombing raid on the Indian/Pakistan border. Bin Laden was trying to arrange an attack on Indian forces preparing for a major offensive. Mansoor has joined his terrorist forces with Al Qaeda. He said he had a plan to cripple the United States military in a way that had never been seen before.

"Mansoor brought a large bomb about the size of a chesterfield. It had a Pakistani flag and Arabic writing on it. Mansoor said the oriental man was going to take the bomb to use for operations against the US in the Korean theatre. The oriental took the bomb with him on a green six-axle truck. The truck was covered with Oriental writing on the outside. Mansoor said the bomb was part of operation chain reaction. He didn't say what kind of bomb it was, or where the other bombs would be used. That's all I know about, honest!"

Griswalt shook his head. He put his hand on his chin and rubbed his face. "Now, that we're on a roll, I have another question. I have eight soldiers missing. I'll give you their names and you'll tell me what happened to them. Sergeant Richard Stevens, Corporal Jonathan Ortega, Corporal Douglas Schneider, Private Mowia Mohammed, Private Herb Wong, Private Jose Garcia, Private Arturo Sanchez, and Private Maurice Bouchard."

"I remember them vaguely. We caught them several weeks ago and interrogated them hard. One of them finally cracked, he gave us all the info we wanted about this base. We had been keeping them at the castle until Mansoor showed up. He beheaded the Sergeant to rally the troops and took the rest with him. I don't know where the ended up eventually."

"Why did he take my men with him?"

"I don't know. Mansoor often takes captured enemy combatants with him for further interrogation. He says that he has special ways that can draw more information out. Mansoor later ordered me to attack your base the day your people attacked the castle."

Griswalt got up, looked at Hassan and walked away a few feet. Still facing the open doorway, Griswalt said. "You have been cooperative, Mr. Hassan. I will double-check your info. If I find out you've been lying to me, I'll kill you myself." Griswalt walked out of the room with Fleming in tow.

Once outside Griswalt to spoke to Fleming, "Hold him in the interrogation room for a couple of hours, then take him back into the cell. We'll interrogate him some more tomorrow."

Walters approached Griswalt. "Very good Walters, you deserve an Academy award for that performance! Cocking the last bullet out of the gun like that was a nice touch. Thanks to you I got more info out him today than the CIA could have in a year."

"Thank you, sir, do you want to do something like that tomorrow?"

"No, let's not overdo it. I'm going to use the low-key approach for now. If he clams up, we could try another ruse, preferably something original." Griswalt walked away smiling.

Captain York rushed toward Griswalt, almost knocking Fleming to the ground, "Sir, Sir!"

"What is it Captain York?" Griswalt asked in an irritated voice.

"We found Privates Nishan and Watson. They are both ok with minor scrapes."

"Good show Captain York, I want to see them now."

* * * * *

Nishan sat on the bed looking at Watson. Bruises covered all over Nishan's face. His arms were bandaged up, his uniform was in tatters, and his left ankle was wrapped. "So, Watsy, how does it feel like to be a proud owner of a purple heart?"

Watson gave a glum look, his chest was bandaged up and he had two black eyes. "I'd rather have had gotten these in a bar instead. At least I could've said I was trying to pick a girl instead of JJ."

Nishan laughed, "You've got me banged up in a lot of bar fights. This time I got you. It's nice to have some payback."

"Spending a night pinned under rocks while enemy soldiers used my head for a foot rest is a little more than payback. Having our own machine guns firing over my head is a real nice touch. I had bullets land inches away from me."

"It was no piece of cake for me either, Watsy. That bush wasn't much of a bed. Heck, some clown searched me and stole my rifle, ammo, grenades and—what hurt the most—a picture of my mom and dad. If that isn't low, what is?"

"Let me say this, I almost lost my life from our own machine guns. But you're terrified because you lost you folks' picture. You're getting as soft as JJ."

"JJ may be soft, but he seems to get all the sympathy from the girls. You on the other hand are treated like the dirt bag you are. Remember those US Air Flight Attendants in Charlotte, NC."

Watson grabbed a pillow then threw it at Nishan. Nishan ducked, the pillow flew by almost hitting the nurse in the back room. The nurse rushed out of the back room intent on giving the soldiers a piece of here mind.

"What is wrong with you two? Can't you two quit playing infantile games?"

Before anyone could speak, Matthews and JJ rushed into the room. Matthews ran over to Nishan, hugging him and kissing his face. JJ turned red with embarrassment. He quickly walked

Unseen Warriors

over to Watson and shook his hand. "Hey, Nishan, I like your welcoming better than mine." Watson shouted across the room.

"You deserve a spanking not a welcoming they way you just acted!" the nurse angrily commented.

"I missed you, Nishan," announced Matthews. She hugged him in a tight grip.

Griswalt walked in. Seeing Matthews and Nishan in an embrace, he rubbed his forehead and shook his head. He then cleared his throat. "Ahem, Ahem," Griswalt cleared his throat louder. Matthews and Nishan showed no response. Watson grinned ear to ear while shaking his head.

The nurse spoke up, "Oh, Griswalt, can't you see they're in love? Relax, why do you have to be such an old goat?"

Hearing the nurse, Nishan and Matthews quickly broke their embrace and stood to attention, "Yes, sir!" they both proclaimed.

"The reason is, unlike you Captain Taylor, I have to make clear and rational decisions about war every day. I do not have time to spend all day reading romantic novels, fantasizing about men on white horses whisking away love struck women," Griswalt replied.

Griswalt faced the team. "It's nice to see you two in one piece. Major Marsh says you guys should be ready for action in about a week. I am very happy to see all four of you in the room. All of you will be awarded purple hearts for injuries sustained while performing courageous acts in the line of fire over the last few days. Private Nishan and Watson, you two will receive an additional Bronze Stars for valor for your actions during last night's attack. You four have made me proud to have you under my command. I will arrange your transfers to be made permanent.

"Major Fleming and I will debrief you after you get cleaned up. We have a lot to discuss later this evening. Perhaps we can talk over dinner. I will ask the cook to save you some of that steak from the officers' mess. Private Matthews, you and JJ also have a seat at the dinner table. As you were!" Griswalt said before he and York walked out as quietly as they walked.

"You guys are real lucky. I wish the old goat would ask me out to dinner. You're going to have a meal you won't forget."

Watson looked at Nurse Taylor, "I hardly think it is a social call madam! I am thinking if I were going to have the ultimate dinner. It would with a hot blonde, not the Colonel."

"I think the Colonel has another dangerous mission coming up for us, Watsy," Nishan interjected. Watson nodded his head in agreement.

07-June-2010
2000 Hours Local Time

Nishan and company nervously approached Griswalt's boardroom. The aroma of steak seeped through the door. They were all afraid to enter the room, fearing the unknown. "This is crazy! What are we afraid of?" Watson muttered.

"This could the last time were together. We should be shipped off somewhere real hot," JJ meekly spoke.

The door flung open. Captain York waited on the other side. No expression covered his face. "Thank you, for coming, Colonel Griswalt is happy to see you. We have saved a dinner plate for each of you of fresh New York steak with all the fixings. Come follow me," he ordered.

Captain York led the team down the hallway to a large conference room. Colonel Griswalt was seated at the head of the table. To his right sat Major Fleming, to Griswalt's left sat Staff Sergeant Walters, and Corporal Jones. Nishan sat beside Jones, Watson and Matthews followed. JJ sat to the right of Major Fleming.

"Welcome to dinner, I'm sure my enlisted friends here will not object to a steak dinner from the Officer's mess." No one spoke. Their eyes remained transfixed on Griswalt.

"First things first let's pass the wine around. Are there any on who would object to this 1995 Chateau, it's supposed to be from a very fine part of Oregon." Griswalt scanned the room, Nishan and JJ immediately tensed up. "Would you gentlemen prefer bottled water instead?" JJ and Nishan shook their heads in agreement. The tension in the room was thick enough to cut. Griswalt knew it was time to defuse the situation.

"Now that we have our dinner and refreshments in order, let's get on to business. The reason I called you here is not entirely social. I have a special mission planned in the coming days. It is a very dangerous mission and risky. I have chosen you six because you are my finest, and because this mission requires extensive training in the coming days. Not all soldiers are prepared for this rigor. Major Fleming, please give an overview."

"Yes, sir! Ali Mansoor, one of Pakistan's most powerful warlords. He has been under watch for several years by the CIA and Spetsnaz. Seems for the last few months he's been shipping materials on unmarked cargo ships out of Arab countries to various places on the globe. Those places mysteriously have a huge increase in terrorism after the arrival of the ships.

"There is a ship originating from the Sudan on its way to America as we speak. It left about the same time two other ships left Somalia and another left Eritrea. A Saudi shell company known to have links to Mansoor owns all four ships. We believe that there is a major terrorist attack on US soil is in the works and these ships maybe transporting the required goods. The CIA has positively located this ship. They are tracking it with a spy satellite as we speak. Unfortunately we do not have a fix on the other ships yet. Intel does not even know which route they are taking to the US."

"Thank you, Major Fleming. Your mission is simple. You will be flown in the coming days to a friendly nation where you will be based for a couple of days. When the Cargo ship is in range, a helicopter will fly you to the ship. You are to overpower the crew and stop the ship in its tracks, any questions?"

"Sir, isn't this normally a Navy Seal operation?" JJ queried.

"Yes, normally it would be. But with two conflicts in the Middle East and anti-terror operations around the globe, the Seals have lost a lot of good men. The Seals have been working with Army Black Ops on several missions lately. This is very similar to the others. They will assist you with Intel and layout of the cargo ship. When you complete your mission, don't be surprised with having to move on to another ship right away. This is as dangerous as they come for small team missions."

"Sir, what is this friendly nation that we will be based at?" Nishan asked.

"At the moment I don't know, you'll find out on your flight out of here. Tomorrow Staff Sergeant Walters will train you folks further with your HK-91 rifles at 0600 hours, be prepared to leave on a moment's notice. Now let's enjoy dinner." The rest of the dinner went quietly. A somber mood quickly befell upon the team. No one spoke as they contemplated the next mission. Some wondered whether the mission was a dead end, other's thought about death itself.

Finishing dinner, the soldiers left the room. Captain York shut the door and sat beside Griswalt. Fleming peered over to Griswalt and looked at him in the eye with a confused look. "Sir, the Seals lost an entire team last week trying to do this very type of mission near Jakarta. The worst part of it all was that the ship was just carrying toys for Wal-Mart stateside."

"I know, the CIA says it's a 50/50 chance that they even have the right ship. Unfortunately this mission came directly from the top."

"You mean President Hawkins?" Steven Hawkins ran as an independent in the 2008 Presidential election. The American electorate was deeply divided along partisan lines. Neither major political party was able gain the public's trust. Hawkins' middle of the road position politically appeased the grass roots of America. His limited experience in politics was also his biggest handicap. He was unable to work the tough world of diplomacy. Often he would make rash decisions, overruling his experienced advisors. To many in his cabinet, Hawkins was still campaigning for election. To others he was a small state Governor overwhelmed with federal politics.

"It seems that Mansoor blew up another American airliner in Europe. 299 people lost their lives. Add the death of all those Marines in the car bombing in Mosul. Then there was the shooting down the C-17 in Turkey. That all just happened in one week. People in the White House are getting very unhappy with how the war on terrorism is going. They want something quick and flashy to make it look like we're winning," Griswalt said as he shook his head.

"Why don't they announce that we have Hassan? That's got to be worth something?" Captain York interjected.

"The Pentagon is keeping mum for now. Apparently we need something bigger to add to this so it looks like Hawkins is in control," Griswalt shot back.

"Sometimes I wonder if the politicians really have a clue on what it takes to fight a war," Fleming commented.

"Unfortunately they are our masters. Let's get some sleep," commanded Griswalt.

Black Ops Camp Zulu
10-June-2010
1800 Hours Local Time

Training was tough. Walters ran his crew hard, day and night until they were proficient. Nishan and Walters barely had time to heal from their previous injuries, when they received more bumps and scratches from their training. Walters knew that his team had to be ready. The better they seemed prepared, the harder Walters ran them. He knew that his life and theirs would depend on how ell they were prepared.

Nishan sat with Watson on the edge of bench at the rifle range. They took off their boots and squeezed their feet. "Man my feet hurt Watsy! Walters is definitely off my Christmas list," Nishan complained.

"This training is tougher than actual combat. I wonder if it's too late to go back to Townsend's outfit. Heck, they're living it up in Korea while Walters is running us into the ground."

Matthews approached with JJ, carrying sodas. "Walters says these are for you, courtesy of the Colonel."

"The last time the Colonel came bearing fruits we were informed that we had been volunteered to some suicide mission," Watson replied.

"Now Watsy, part of being on the front lines means taking the high risk missions. After all we are the cream of the crop, according to the Colonel."

"How long have we been at this training? Feels like it's been a month," Matthews wondered.

"It's only been five days. At this place a day or a week is all the same. It's all work and no play," complained Watson.

Walter's approached, marching in his distinctive style. "Oh, look, here comes Adolph Walters again! He probably wants us to go for a nice brisk swim in the Pacific," Watson sounded off in a sarcastic tone. "Oh, come on Watsy. That's after we get warmed up with a twenty-mile hike. By the way, where did Corporal Jones disappear off to?" Nishan wondered.

"He probably went for a smoke. The guy has a pack a day habit. He told me yesterday that he wasn't worried about dying from smoking. In the line of work we do, we'll probably get killed by some terrorist first," Watson mused.

"Boy that sounds real reassuring!" Matthews replied.

Staff Sergeant Walters walked up to the team, a clipboard in his hand. "Captain York has given me our orders. Get your gear. We ship out in an hour on the Next flight to Tokyo." The team fell silent contemplating they're next course of action.

Chapter 6

North Korea
07-June-2010
0400 Hours Local Time

Townsend sat down beside Carlson and put his arm around him. "Tim, I know Tom was your best friend in the unit. He died like a hero and refused to live a mediocre life. He chose to make a difference. I know a lot of you guys think I'm a ball buster. I admit I ride you guys hard. I don't do it to be a jerk. When I was in Baghdad during the summer of 2004, I led a platoon on a mission to take out some insurgents. A suicide bomber snuck up and blew himself up behind my team at a checkpoint. After that, I've been a lot tougher on my platoon. I just don't want something like that to ever happen again."

"Carlson stopped sobbing, looked to Townsend and spoke softly, "Thanks"

"No thank you, you brought a little bit more humanity in me.

"Sir, back by the cave we came out of. We wounded a North Korean officer. He's tied up in there. It's about 1500 yards from here," Carlson commented.

"Go get him, take Private Rich with you. Do it quickly, we've got to get out of here before daybreak."

"Yes, sir," Carlson and Rich ran off toward the burning tanks.

Colonel Pak approached Townsend, "We have to get moving soon. The sun will be coming up couple of hours. Northwest of here there are a bunch of caves. We can rest up there until nightfall. I suggest we avoid travel during daylight." Townsend nodded his head in agreement. Townsend looked at his watch. The time was 0400. Nightfall would soon be over. In the distance Carlson and Rich approached carrying a North Korean.

The two men threw the Soldier down at Townsend's feet. Captain Pak spoke to him for several minutes. The North Korean appeared visibly shaken. At times he loudly shouted and pointed to Pak and Townsend. After about ten minutes he calmed down and spoke slowly and deliberately to Pak.

"So, what is he saying?" Townsend inquired.

"He says he was ordered by General Luck to attack American helicopters at will. He met the general a few days ago at a mountain hideout near Hoe yang."

"It's time to move, saddle up," Townsend ordered the Platoon.

The team marched up the steep slopes. The harsh jungle terrain added to the hot humid weather sapped the strength out of the team. Rounding the top of the mountain, the team stopped under the forest canopy. Townsend scanned with his binoculars the battlefield they left behind many miles away.

Colonel Pak spoke up. "The sun is starting to rise over the valley. I can see some activity over the destroyed Column."

"Yeah I see some soldiers gathering around the burnt up tanks. Looks like there's wreckage of one of the downed fighters at the end of the river. I see some thing over there near the horizon. It looks like a slow plane. No, it's not a plane. It looks like a…it's a Mi-24 Hind Gunship! It's headed in our direction. Head for cover!" commanded Townsend.

Unseen Warriors

The team ran through the Jungle canopy, hiding under some thick underbrush and trees. The sound of distant rotor blades grew louder at each passing moment. The Gunship approached slowly. Its chin turret swung left to right like a searchlight in the dark. The gunship came in low, almost at the team's eye level. Martin's eyes grew huge. He was looking straight into the pilots' faces. Martin clutched his HK-91, nervously putting his finger on the trigger. Townsend put his hand on Martin's front sight, pushing down the Rifle. Townsend remained icy cold still, staring into the throbbing beast ahead of him.

Colonel Pak whispered. "He is looking for saboteurs. He has not seen us. If he had, he would have attacked with rockets and machine gun fire. Do not move. We are well camouflaged in the surrounding. He will only attack it he notices movement in the foliage."

Ten tense minutes later, the gunship turned gently to the left. Passing overhead, it followed the ridge line and descended down to the stream. It slowly passed the troops searching below.

"Saddle up," commanded Townsend. The team continued on their search for General Luck. They traveled through the lush vegetation, cutting trails, as they required. After five miles of the grueling terrain, they stopped near a clearing. The sun rose high in the sky, beating down on the team. Townsend looked down on the captured officer. He then looked to Pak. "So, what do you think we should to him when we get to Hoe yang?"

Pak rubbed his eyes; "We should kill him, after we get the general."

Carlson jumped up to Colonel Pak, "That's murder, we're above that!"

Colonel Pak gave Carlson a stern look then began to speak. "Our mission must remain secret. We cannot afford detection. If we let him go, he will report us to the North Korean forces. He has shot down several American helicopters. He has the blood of many Americans on his hands. His actions require a fitting punishment. Death is the only punishment that fits."

"I agree with the Colonel, he cannot be trusted. Nor would it be prudent to allow him to inform other North Korean units about our mission and Colonel Pak's assistance. I will take the appropriate action when the time comes," Townsend commanded to Carlson. "Colonel, how much farther do you think we have to march?"

"Another seven miles, there's a hill we still have to cross. The terrain is much harsher than here."

"We'll stay here and camp for a while. Martin, set up sentries so we don't get ambushed."

"Goodwin, Diaz, I want you two to watch that crest while we eat and rest. I'll send you a relief in an hour," commanded Martin.

"Where are the caves, Colonel Pak?" Townsend asked.

"They're about a quarter mile up the trail. I suggest we stay there until nightfall. Traveling with all these patrols is too dangerous. That Gunship may come back for another look."

"Do you think they're on to us?" Townsend asked.

"I'm not sure. They may have had some infantry escape that alerted a patrol. They don't normally send out a Gunship to investigate unless they think a major threat is lurking in the area."

The team ate hungrily. The lack of sleep did little to inhibit them. The temperature was rising with the humidity. The team's clothes stuck to their skin. The feeling of dampness permeated them through all their layers of clothing. The soldiers drank gallons of water from their canteen. The warm water did little to quench their thirst or cool their bodies.

Corporal Goodwin came running over, Diaz was not far behind. "We've got an infantry patrol coming our way up the hill. They're about 5,000 yards behind us," huffed Goodwin.

"Martin, we need to get over to that wooded ridge line. There we need to setup along the crest with three flanks, each about 275 Yards apart, Saddle up!" Townsend ordered

Unseen Warriors

The team rushed up the ridge line. Hunger and sleep depravation fell to the wayside as adrenaline pumped through their veins. Colonel Pak looked continually back as he hiked the steep ridge line. Men half his age were struggling with their gear, *How can these men be so unfit, yet such as effective fighting force?* he wondered.

The Platoon set up on the ridge line. Martin joined Townsend and Colonel Pak with Diaz in the center. Corporal Carlson stayed on the left flank joined by Rich. Corporal Goodwin with Diaz crouched down on the right just ahead and 60 feet lower from the rest of the team.

"Conserve your ammo! Use short bursts, wait until the enemy gets within one hundred yards or less, before firing," commanded Townsend.

The Korean Patrol approached. There were about thirty soldiers, carrying Ak-47s, hand grenades and ample provisions. They walked slowly, finders on the trigger. The Captured Korean officer loosed the gag around his mouth and he shouted Korean words into the distance.

One of the approaching Koreans shouted something to the team. The patrol immediately opened fire into Townsend's direction. Bullets tore into the officer's stomach and shoulder. His eyes glazed, blood leaked out of his mouth and he slumped over. Martin let out a short full burst. Rounds tore into the trees and shrubs unable to penetrate the dense vegetation.

More rounds crashed into the ridge line. The rocks and soil exploded into dust. Choking dust and dirt rained down on the team. Colonel Pak opened up with a short burst of Ak-74 gunfire. Rounds deflected off trees and shrubs and crashed into unwitting combatants. Several infantrymen were hit as rounds crashed into their arms and legs in strange angles. The men lay helpless bleeding on the ground while they watched their teammates cut down.

A Korean soldier threw grenades at the team. It exploded in mid air and rained down shrapnel and vegetation on the team.

Another grenade flew the air and fell down ten feet from Lieutenant Townsend. Townsend froze in fear. Before he could move, Diaz jumped on the grenade. A loud thud occurred, blood poured out his nose and mouth. Townsend covered his mouth and desperately tried to avoid vomiting.

Carlson sprayed the incoming soldiers with automatic gunfire. The enemy soldiers hid behind trees. After Carlson's gunfire died down, the solders rushed the ridge line in waves. Carlson quickly dispatched them with short bursts tearing their frail bodies into blood and gore. The torn bodies fell down into the soft soil. Their internal organs covered the trees with death. Death filled the air with the smell of blood, gunpowder and sweat.

The last four soldiers turned around and darted down the trail in fear. Corporal Goodwin and Carlson threw grenades at them. The grenades exploded in mid air raining shrapnel on the retreating squad. The soldiers screamed in pain as shrapnel tore into their bodies mercilessly.

Townsend stood up and kicked aside the pile of empty brass shells lying beside his feet. "That was the last of them. Martin, what's our ammunition supply like?"

"I'm down to my last clip, anybody have any ammo left?" Martin asked the team.

Members of the team waved their half empty magazines. Some only had a handful of bullets left. Corporal Carlson pulled out his last magazine. It was empty. He ejected his last round out of his HK-91.

Townsend looked to Martin, "These HK-91s won't be much good without any ammo. We aren't even at the outskirts of Hoe yang and we're already out. Throw the HK-91s away and pick up all the ammo and weapons we can get from the dead."

Martin and his team scoured the bodies for ammo and weapons. Each individual soldier carried a limited supply of ammo. But collectively the enemy platoon's cache was immense. The team was able to round up 40 Ak-47s, several SKS rifles, 3,000 rounds of 7.62X39mm ammunition, and forty Russian grenades.

While the team rounded up ammo, Townsend and Colonel Pak put the Korean officer and Private Diaz into shallow ditch, covering them with loose soil. Martin approached with the weapons cache, "We'll be well equipped, sir. We should have enough ammo to last us through the rest of the mission."

Townsend failed to answer. He and Colonel Pak just stared out to the east. Puzzled, Martin looked over to their direction of sight. Down along the valley on top of a small hill sat General Luck's headquarters.

1600 Pennsylvania Avenue
Washington, D.C.
08-June-2010
0445 Hours Local Time

Every morning President Steven Hawkins had his morning Cabinet meeting at 5:00 a.m. with his trusted inner circle. The meeting was about a little bit of everything...Intel, polls, the economy Foreign affairs and such. Hawkins ran an informal office, which often lead to lot of discussion but very little progress on any issues. Today's meeting would be no different.

Hawkins walked into the White House conference room carrying a steaming cup of tea and sat at the head of the table. Seated in the room were his Chief of Staff, Admiral Chedwiggen, Secretary of State Thomas Bowman, Secretary of defense William Cohen, Vice President William Douglas, Budget director Henry Wu, and CIA Director Henry Lee. Hawkins broke open his briefcase and spread dozens of papers on the table.

"Good morning. What a beautiful day it is today." Hawkins said before he took a sip from his teacup. "Ahh, this Earl Grey is so hot." Hawkins licked his lips for a second and spoke. "I guess we need to get on to business. Henry, what's the story with Ali's cargo ships?"

"We're still tracking that cargo ship. It's probably going to pass through the Strait of Gibraltar tomorrow. We believe it's going to head due west to somewhere near our northeast coast. We have been unable to locate the other cargo ships, but our satellites are looking hard."

"Why can't we find those ships? You know the carrier, you know where they left, how hard it could be to find them? They're in the open ocean," Hawkins said in an irritated voice.

"Mr. President, we only have approximate dates of departure. Heller steamship line has over two hundred vessels. We don't even know the names of the ships. We only know about the Sierra Mist because our mole saw it departing Port Sudan," Lee answered back.

"This better not be another ship carrying Barbie dolls, that incident last week caused me a lot of grief," Hawkins shot back after giving an angry look.

"Sir, that ship's Intel was received through MI-5. The Intel about the Sierra Mist came directly from our mole. His Intel has always been dead right."

"Admiral Chedwiggen, how is the raid behind North Korean lines going?"

"The team deployed sometime last night. South Korean Intel says saboteurs destroyed a North Korean convoy this morning. The location was about five miles from where our team was dropped off. Our team will be under total radio silence until they are ready for pickup. Presently the date and time for extraction is not fixed."

"Does the team have an experienced officer in charge?"

"Yes, he is one of the finest, he's, err…" Chedwiggen dug through a stack of papers read a name out. "Lieutenant Richard Townsend."

Hawkins' eye's grew big as a basketball and turned cherry red, "He is the damn finest, that's my son, you idiot!"

"Sir there's no way General Mackenzie could have known. After all he had a different last name you. If we had known we could have…"

"You idiot, it was Dick's idea to change his name. He didn't want anyone to know or give him any special treatment. I, on other hand think that one tour in Iraq is enough combat duty for one career. The whole idea of sending him to Korea was to give him a smooth ride until he makes captain. I did not intend on having him go on one of the most dangerous missions available in the Southeast Asian theatre. When this mission is over, I want Dick back to stateside, understood?"

"Yes, Mr. President!"

"Now when are you going to attack that cargo ship?"

"A Black Ops team is being flown to Portugal right now as we speak. We're going to let the tanker get no closer than 500 miles offshore of our base in the Azores. That way we will be able to safely scuttle the ship without impacting the civilians in the neighboring islands. The Portuguese government has been extremely helpful. They are providing one of their covert teams to help secure the ship."

"Good, for your sake Admiral, they had better be something on that ship newsworthy. I do not want to be a one term wonder." The rest of the meeting droned on with talk of fact and figures, the economy and taxes. Hawkins was unable concentrate; all he could think of was Richard. For Hawkins, the war on terror had been nothing more than another election issue like taxes or unemployment. Now the war had taken on a more personal tone. Hawkins contemplated the worst-case scenario.

North Korea
07-June-2010
1200 Hours Local Time

Townsend peered through his binoculars. General Luck's headquarters was small wooden building with a rusting roof on a small hill. At various locations around the hill, machine gun nests waited with armed troops. At the base of the hill was a small shantytown of rundown buildings. Fires burned from the village at various locations obscuring sight of the hill. On the north side, a road along a long hill overlooking the village ran straight to the headquarters.

"What do you think is the best way to attack, Colonel?" Townsend asked.

"We need to go through the village, the road has little cover. If we took the road those machine guns cut us down before we got even close to the headquarters. The village is probably full of civilians. We'll incur a lot of collateral damage if things go bad."

"Unfortunately, that's a risk we'll have to take. Martin, do you get any sniper rifles from those Koreans?"

"No, sir, just a bunch of select fire AK-47 assault rifles. We did get a few Simonov SKSs; they're semi-auto fire and have longer barrels than the AKs."

"We're going to need a guy with that SKS to take out the machine gun nests before we storm that hill. We'll proceed through the village. I want him to take the left flank and stay back. He needs to snipe the machine gunners and troops that attack. After the machine gunners are neutralized, we'll storm the hill. I want the sniper to stay back just below the hill's crest. He'll take out any surprise attacks while we're arresting the general."

Townsend led the team down the ridge and through a grass field. They hiked down the steep hill that led toward the village. The smell of rotting garbage and human waste filled the air. The team members covered their faces trying to avoid smelling the stomach turning odors. The team wandered through the tall grass to the outskirts of the village. Black smoke belched from campfires in the village.

Villagers scurried out of their rundown homes to greet the advancing soldiers. The villagers were poor, many malnourished. They tried to sell the foreign soldiers everything from

Unseen Warriors

watches to sheep. Martin pushed aside those who dared to come close. Villagers that failed to heed him, Martin beat off with his rifle.

"These people would sell their kids if they could make a buck," Quibbled Martin.

"Take it Easy, Martin. They're just trying to make a living. We probably eat more at lunch today than they eat in a week," said Townsend.

A woman came carrying a chicken, trying to persuade Martin to purchase it. Martin pushed the women aside. She fell to the ground. Colonel Pak looked on in anger. "They're only poor, they don't mean any harm," Pak lectured Martin.

Martin sighed. "I don't trust any of them. She could have left a hand grenade in the middle of our formation. They're all terrorists as far as I'm concerned!" Pak rolled his eyes. He could not believe such ignorance coupled with anger that filled Martin's mind.

Arriving into the heart of the village, Townsend stopped the team, "Martin, have the sniper set up on the left flank behind the shack with the tin roof."

"Carlson, take the SKS and ammo and get behind that shack," Martin ordered. Carlson grabbed the SKS and dozens of stripper clips filled ammunition. Running behind the shack, he jumped into a shallow ditch. Lying down out of sight, hr placed the rifle's barrel on some packed soil. He dug his elbows in the dirt and lay in the prone position.

Townsend positioned his remaining force behind an old wooden barn, using the frail walls and dirt piles as cover. The team readied their weapons, anxiously waiting Townsend's command. Townsend gave Carlson the signal and shouted, "Guns up!"

Carlson aimed his sights at the lowest machine gun nest. The guard was leaning on the machine gun and smoking. Carlson fired a round from his rifle. The round punched through the soldier's left shoulder smashing the joint into pieces and threw him into the nest. The soldier struggled to get up. Clutching his left shoulder, he cursed at his unseen foe. Another round tore through his stomach spraying the sandbags with blood and internal organs.

The upper machine gun nest opened fire. Unable to see his enemy, the soldier sprayed indiscriminate gunfire into the village. Villagers ran for cover as they were showered with bullets. Men and women went down as the gunfire cut them down in open sight. A bullet slammed into the gunners' helmet. Blood flowed under helmet onto the soft soil.

Soldiers on top of the hillside poured automatic gunfire into the village. Immediately, gunfire erupted out from behind the warehouse. The North Korean soldiers went down like matchsticks. More soldiers continued ran out from a shack on top of the hill firing wildly.

Carlson fired single, measured shots. Each bullet found its mark. The soldiers on top of the hill went down into the mud. Another soldier tried to run to the upper machine gun nest. Approaching within sight of his goal, a bullet from Carlson hit his knee. Cartilage and muscle sprayed into the mud and grass. Struggling in pain to roll out of the incoming gunfire, a round tore into his heart relieving him of his misery.

Townsend stormed with his team from behind the barn. Carlson watched the hillside watched for snipers as the platoon raced up the hill. Townsend stopped the team short of the crest. Using the top of the hill for cover, Townsend signaled Carlson to join the team. Carlson ran up the hill, taking pains to locate any hidden snipers on his way up. Carlson dropped down behind the crest next to Townsend. Carlson noticed a man lurking behind the glass waving his rifle. He steadied his aim and fired a single bullet. The round tore through the glass. Glass shards ripped into the soldier body before the bullet tore into his heart. Blood sprayed the walls. The man's lifeless body fell to the floor with a dull thud.

Unseen Warriors

The team stormed to the building. Townsend was the first to enter. Scanning around the dim, rundown building, he eyed several closed doors leading from the hallway. Townsend looked to Martin. "I need a couple of guards outside while we go into the rooms." Martin posted Carlson and Rich outside. Martin and Goodwin led Townsend and Colonel Pak into the dilapidated building. Goodwin swept the room with his rifle. There was no sight of anyone. All the doors leading into rooms were unlocked except for one.

"Break the door down," Townsend ordered. Martin fired into the lock. The bullets tore out the lock, the door instantly turned into splinters. Martin kicked aside the remaining section of door open. He was the first to run into a darkened room with his gun pointed.

Suddenly lights were turned on. The room was flooded with bright light from dozens of flood lamps. Sitting behind a desk was a Korean four star general wearing fatigues. "Welcome, I am General Luck," he said.

Townsend stepped in front of Martin. "General Luck, I know you've been attacking on our helicopters. Why, what do you gain from this? Answer me! Your game is now over. We are taking you back to South Korea!"

The general gave an evil laugh, "Lieutenant Townsend, or as you are really known Richard Hawkins how nice to see you." Townsend's eyes grew big. He was shocked as much as the rest of his team. "Disturbing isn't it knowing someone knows your most intimate secret? I know your father is the President. I also know you changed your name before going to Iraq. Well, to answer your question, it is simple. It serves my purpose. But first, answer my question. Why did you come here?"

"We came here to stop your attacks on our aircraft along the DMZ!"

"Well, Mr. Townsend now that you've answered my question, I'll answer yours. My goal is to overthrow the central government so I will be the new President of North Korea."

"Too late, we know about you. Your plan's ruined," blurted out Martin.

"Wrong, everything is going to plan."

Colonel Pak raised his rifle and pointed at Martin's head, Martin gulped. "You were far too trusting. Col Pak works for me. Order your men to drop their weapons, if you don't the dear Sergeant dies!" Luck shouted

Townsend put down his AK-47. "That includes the guards outside. I want them here, now!" Luck ordered.

"Carlson, Rich come here," shouted Townsend. Carlson and Rich rain in with their guns pointed. They immediately aimed their rifles at the general upon entering the room. "Corporal Carlson, Private Rich, put the guns down," Townsend ordered. The two soldiers failed to budge. "Do it now, that's an order," Townsend repeated. Carlson begrudgingly put his rifle down, kicking it to the ground. Rich threw his rifle down hard, causing the magazine to fly across the room.

"If this was your plan all along, why did you allow us to slaughter your tank column along the river?" Townsend asked.

"Actually that column was a central government tank group sent to search and destroy me. You and the Chinese Air force fighter planes conveniently took care of them for me. It seems the Central government was bowing to pressure from your father to stop the raids by the 'Raiders' as you call them.

"Now then, Mr. Townsend, I have to do one more thing. Unfortunately I have to turn you over to Mr. Mansoor. He has been anxiously waiting your capture."

"What are your dealings with that terrorist?" Anger filled Townsend's eyes.

"Mr. Mansoor needs some live soldiers for his master plan of some sort. As long as I deliver you to him, he continues the flow of money and arms to me. It's quite a convenient arrangement. Townsend grunted and curled his lip.

"One word of advice, Mr. Townsend, Mr. Mansoor is far less forgiving than me. I would suggest you follow his orders to the word. He has been known to behead people for his own amusement."

General Luck called in some guards. They bound and gagged the team, carrying them off to an awaiting truck. Colonel Pak said one last word before the truck's door closed. "It has been a pleasure working with you Lieutenant Townsend. Mr. Mansoor will take care of you, he is very found of officers." The doors on truck slammed shut. The team grimaced at the thought of being the guests of Ali Mansoor. Knowing Mansoor had recently beheaded several coalition soldiers in Iraq made the team fear their lives would soon be cut short.

Chapter 7

Black Ops Camp Zulu
12-June-2010
1600 Hours Local Time

Walters' team caught a flight from Camp Zulu to Tokyo. Apprehension filled the team as they boarded a second flight to an unknown destination. The war on terror had taken a tone of mobility. For many in the team it was excitement fraught with a new kind of danger. At Tokyo the team boarded a USAF C-5 Galaxy on its way to a USAF base in England.

Nishan sat beside Matthews struggling to start a conversation. "So, how is your leg?"

"Its fine, they said it's only a flesh wound. I guess the bullet just grazed my leg. I was lucky the shooter isn't a marksman."

Nishan smiled, realizing he had finally broken the ice. "You know that night on guard duty we were really worried about you."

"I know, JJ told me. You know Nishan we can be more than squad mates. We can go to the next step." Nishan's eyes opened wide. He became giddy as a schoolboy. He chatted with her through the whole flight opening up to her in ways that he'd never opened up before.

Matthews felt astounded. She had cracked Nishan out of his cocoon, allowing him to be honest with her. Matthews found upbringing in rural Iowa to be boring and constricting. She escaped by joining the Army. Nishan had done the same. Matthews had finally found a common bond. The two held hands through the entire flight. The long journey became a lot shorter for them.

Joining the team was a rugged group of Marines on their way to a deployment in the Persian Gulf. Sergeant Douglas sat beside Staff Sergeant Walters. "Looks like you've got a couple of love birds in your platoon."

"Yeah, those two are real ice couple."

"What's an ice couple?" Sergeant Douglas asked.

"They act like this when they're together on a flight. When they get on the ground, they fight brutally in combat. They're a couple of my best riflemen."

"Sounds like you need a few more like them in your team," Douglas remarked.

"I'd take anybody living and breathing right now, I'm so short handed," Walters quibbled.

"So, am I. Some of my boys are on their second combat tour in three years. Word has it that the Pentagon is going to pull all its troops out of Korea, Japan and Europe. They'll be deployed into various combat units in Iraq."

"What's the death toll in Iraq right now?"

"Now, that the war's been raging for seven years, now the death toll's up to ten thousand at last count. Apparently Ali Mansoor has been orchestrating uprisings all over Iraq. Foreign fighters are flooding into the country to fight us American infidels."

"Why doesn't the President get the guts to take out Mansoor?"

"Hawkins doesn't even know where Pakistan is. He's spending so much time micro managing Iraq and Afghanistan. I'm surprised he gets anything else done."

Walters looked puzzled, "What's he doing?"

"He's giving us targets to attack, areas not to attack, what weapons to use and not to use. Heck it's like having Johnson back in the White House."

"Sounds like a bad situation," Walters muttered.

The plane landed at midnight at Lakenheth airbase in England. Walters rushed his weary team onto a waiting C-17. For the team, the ordeal of air travel was becoming worse than actual combat. The C-17 took off climbing high over the Atlantic Ocean. The team viewed the blue sky with awe as their eyes failed to stay open due to fatigue of the long flights across the Atlantic. The flight went by quickly; sleep considerably shortened the distance to the Portuguese islands.

The C-17 banked over to the approach on Lages field, Azores, Portugal. Clouds that covered the base quickly dissipated as the mighty aircraft broke through the sky and onto a wet runway. Gently planting itself on the ground the C-17 rolled up to a hanger off the taxiway. The rear ramp opened and Walters whisked his people out.

Out of the ramp rolled out thousands of cases of 7.62 x 51mm, and 9x19mm ammunition. More cases of grenades and rifles followed behind. Major Bernier, commander of Black Ops in the Azores, looked on with curiosity. The request for his appearance came from the highest levels in the Pentagon. For Bernier it was a welcomed relief from operations in Afghanistan and Iraq. He was a rough commander who had a different command style than Griswalt. But, for all his preconceived notions, he knew that if Griswalt decided that Walters' team was best. They were the best that Black Ops could offer on short notice.

Lieutenant Sultan approached Bernier, "Looks like they don't pack very light, do they?"

"You got that right! I wonder if they're going to do more that one mission," Bernier replied.

Walters hurriedly rushed his team into the briefing room, Lieutenant Sultan and Major Bernier entered. "Good morning, I trust you had a good flight. I'm Major Bernier. I'll be your commanding officer here at camp X-Ray. Colonel Griswalt and I go back several years, I'm glad to see he sent his best team.

"Your mission is simple. A cargo ship is approaching about 600 miles off the coast of Portugal. We believe it has weapons of mass destruction aboard. Tomorrow morning at 0100 you will ship out on a Blackhawk helicopter to board the ship. A Portuguese Special Forces team will land on the deck first. They'll provide suppressive fire, while you land on the deck. You will infiltrate the cargo hold and engine room. The Portuguese team will secure the bridge. Remember when you are aboard the ship there are no friendly forces aboard other than the Portuguese. Neutralize all occupants with extreme prejudice. You are dismissed."

Bernier watched the team file out, Lieutenant Sultan walked into the briefing room holding a fax motioning to Major Bernier. "What is it Bill?"

"Looks like the weather are going to be very poor tomorrow. Expect high winds, heavy rain and high surf advisory. Landing a Blackhawk on that deck is going to be tough."

Bernier picked up a file folder and read it. "It's going to be even tougher than I thought. I just received Intel from one of our spy satellites, seems that the ship's deck was covered with men carrying AK-47s and RPGs. The CIA says that the crew is probably prepared for an attack."

"Do you think we should consider scrubbing the mission altogether? We could just bomb the ship with an F-16 loaded with a GBU-10A Paveway?"

Bernier shook his head. "The Pentagon says that they want the ship left intact. They want to be able to show the ship was involved in terrorist activities. If we sink the ship in open waters, it would be paramount to declaring war on the nation that it is flagged."

13-June-2010
0100 Hours Local Time

Walters watched a Blackhawk leave with the Portuguese commandos aboard. Overnight, the sky had clouded over. Rain fell hard on the tiny Island as winds whipped up the waves. Walters knew this mission was going to be tough in every way possible. It was a mission he had long trained for but never done in actual combat. Deep inside, Walters wondered if he was up to the challenge. A Blackhawk approached, the door gunner opened the door. On command, Walters' crew rushed into the waiting helicopter, relieved to get out of the high winds and heavy rain.

*****

The Sierra Mist plowed through the Atlantic while waves crashed over the rain soaked deck. Deck crew rushed to assemble a giant scaffold on the pitching deck. Haroon Babajhan, Mansoor's right hand man, looked on impatiently. He finally retired to the bridge where the captain sat watching Al Jazeera while monitoring the ship's navigation equipment.

"You looked perturbed, Haroon. What is it?" the captain questioned in his booming voice.

"The progress on the scaffold is going slowly. We need it done before sunup."

"Have faith, Allah will look kindly on our plight. Start your calculations. We will be within range to launch the missile at our anointed time."

Babajhan looked up the wind conditions of the Azores airport on the Internet. He grinned. *Here the Americans were providing him with details that would ensure their destruction,* he thought. Double-checking his figures for the missile's trajectory, Babajhan plotted the missile's course on a naval map. He corrected for winds and the ships course bearing. He gave an evil laugh, "Perfect, the missile would hit in the middle of Lages field," he loudly proclaimed. Folding up his map, he headed for the cargo hold to check on the missile.

The men on the deck started yelling. They loaded their rifles and RPGs then found places to hide out of sight. A Blackhawk approached out of the distance. The helicopter crossed the bow and took a quick pass around the deck. It slowly approached a large stack of containers near the Deckhouse. Leveling out, it hovered several feet above the ground. The cabin door flung open. Commandos departed the helicopter and set up a perimeter on the containers.

Several RPGs slammed into the Blackhawk causing it to burst into flames. Commandos fled the stricken hull, their clothing ablaze. Another RPG slammed into the Blackhawk; the hull lurched from the force of the impact. It then fell overboard plunging into the murky depth as its hull continued to burn.

Babajhan walked to the top of the container heap where the Blackhawk once stood. Several commandos lay burned, still clutching their 5.56x45mm Heckler Koch 93s. Babajhan gave out an evil laugh and kicked the commandos one by one into the blackness of the Atlantic Ocean. Babajhan watched as the commandos struggled to stay afloat. Eventually they succumbed to exhaustion and hypothermia and disappeared underneath the waves.

The deckhands raced to erect the scaffold. They lashed the crane to the makeshift scaffold. Slowly the crane lifted the scaffold higher and higher until it stood vertical. Cargo hold doors opened, exposing a gleaming tube. The crane swung over to the missile, deckhands quickly lashed chains to the missile while they removed the protective paper covers. The crane lifted the missile until it stood vertical. The crew lashed the missile to the launching scaffold. The cranes then retracted to the stowed position, leaving a Scud missile covered with a huge Pakistani flag and Arabic writing standing in the night.

Babajhan looked at his watch. It was 4:35am, not bad progress. The ship would be in position to launch in half an hour. He walked back up the metal steps to the bridge. Out of the distance the sound of rotors beating in the air echoed through the night.

*****

Walters looked out the window. The rain pounded the skin of the helicopter, obscuring all vision. Winds shook and buffeted the helicopter up, down and side to side while its passengers looked on. Lieutenant Magnason piloted the rotorcraft through the turbulence, expertly controlling the Blackhawk through the rain and wind. Years of training and experience left him unfazed by the violent weather.

Magnason contacted the duty tanker, "Tap water, this is Arc light, we need a fill."

"Arc light 2, this is Tap water, we're pulling into the pattern, angle 7."

Magnason climbed to 7,000 feet, the winds violently shook the Blackhawk as it leveled out. Rain pounded the windshield obscuring what little visibility there was. Magnason extended the boom and turned on his exterior lights. Lientenant Riggens, Magnason's copilot, looked out into the darkness outside. His night vision yielded nothing. Riggens shifted his attention and concentrated on the radar. Riggens watched the tanker displayed as a green symbol slowly traveling to the bottom of his screen. Riggen's grew apprehensive, the range counter continued to count down, "4 miles, I don't see anything out there."

"Relax, bad weather like this is what separates the men from the boys," Magnason assured Riggens.

Unseen Warriors

Riggens peered out into the darkness, like he was trying to wish the tanker from the nights' sky. Suddenly a couple of lights cut through the darkness outside, "Tanker at 2'oclock!"

"Tap Water, Arc Light 2 has visual," Magnason announced to his radio.

"Arc Light2, we're extending the straw starboard side." The C-130's massive props droned through the air. The hose and basket assembly extended between the nacelles into the prop wash.

Magnason gave the stick a gentle tug; the Blackhawk steered into the C130's massive starboard wing. The basket quickly appeared out of the night's sky, bouncing around like a rag doll by the 30 MPH winds. Magnason knew this would be no easy hook up. Magnason held the stick steady. He crept forward to the basket. The closer he came, the more the basket seemed too waved in the air.

Riggens looked down at his fuel gauge. The aircraft was running into its reserve fuel range. "We're at bingo fuel status."

"Relax, I'm almost at the basket. Bingo just means we have ten more minutes of fuel left," Magnason assured Riggens.

"Yeah, but it still makes me nervous when we run the aircraft this low on fuel," remarked Riggens.

"Like I said, this kind of flying separates the men from the boys," Magnason repeated.

Magnason closed in on the basket. He tried to connect with the basket on his first try, no luck. The basket violently swung to the left at the last minute. Magnason allowed the helicopter to fall behind the basket. He attempted to connect a second time and he missed again. Magnason's palms were getting sweaty. Riggens nervously watched the strip fuel gauge descended into the red range.

This can be done, we have no choice, Magnason said to himself as he tried to connect. The basket violently swung to the right at the last moment. Magnason dipped the nose and gently banked to the right. He connected to the C-130. It pumped its lifeblood of fuel into the Blackhawk's fuel tanks. Riggens watched the fuel indicator rise from red to yellow then finally into the green range.

Fuel filled the aircraft's tanks and weighted down the helicopter. Magnason gently applied more torque and slowly raised the nose. The fuel gauge registered full, Magnason reduced the torque, the airspeed bled off. The C-130 disappeared out of view into the stormy night.

Magnason retracted the boom and turned off the external lights. He lowered the nose and continued toward the cargo ship. Riggens looked over to him, "You are too smooth Cool hand, too smooth."

"That's why they call me Cool Hand Magnason. You can do the next fuel stop."

"Naw, I think I'll pass."

"You've got to learn how to refuel in nasty weather sometime. After all you do want to make left seat some day, don't you?"

"Yeah I do, I just don't want to qualify tonight." Riggens looked down on the display in front of him. The range numbers continued to click down to the final way point. Riggens knew that the final way point was the Sierra Mist.

"Arc Light 2, this is Arc Light one. We're a minute from initial contact. We're going to have high surf upon arrival."

"Copy, Arc Light 2 is going to be eight minutes behind you. We had a little bit of trouble getting fuel."

"Copy, we'll board and suppress fire upon arrival. We'll return for some fuel before extraction."

"You know Cool Hand, that refuel show cost us some time?" Riggens reminded Magnason.

"Relax, what are you worried about? Do you think there's going to be no action left for us when we arrive?" Magnason replied.

Magnason checked his position on the navigation page, "Staff Sergeant Walters, we'll be within visual range of the ship in about a minute. Looks like the Portuguese team will have the deck cleared for you."

"Copy, guns up!" Walters shouted and the team members immediately loaded their weapons in preparation for the fight of their lives. The door gunner opened the cabin door, wind driven rain poured into the cabin soaking the team members.

The ships lights broke through the rain, Magnason instantly saw the massive Scud missile standing proud on the deck. Magnason couldn't believe his eyes. The missile mesmerized him. He almost felt drawn to it.

Gunfire erupted from the ship. Rounds slammed into the helicopter's stub wings. Magnason instantly dove toward the water. An RPG flew toward him, narrowly missing him before it plunged into the ocean.

The door gunner opened fire with his .30 cal minigun. Bullets ricochet off containers and steel rails. The deckhands continued their automatic fire unabated. Walters watched a camouflaged figure carrying an RPG. The figure loaded up. Walter fired a short burst. Gunfire tore into the man's chest as he fell down on the railings.

The RPG fired from its launch tube and slammed into a nearby container spraying shrapnel over two deck hands that were firing their AKs. Another man lost his footing sliding on the deck. A large wave came over and swept him overboard. The second deck hand was ejected into the air while still firing his AK full auto. He crashed into a crane, breaking his nose, chin and fell down into the cargo deck.

Magnason raced by the stern of the ship. Gunfire sprayed at the Blackhawk from every nook and cranny from the ship.

* * * * *

Babajhan ran into the bridge, "How long before we are within range to fire at the airbase?" he yelled to the captain.

"Twenty minutes Haroon. Relax. We have time, after all Allah is with us," the captain replied.

"Yes, I know, but we cannot keep that helicopter from landing for long," Babajhan answered back, panic in his voice.

Gunfire erupted into the bridge. The glass windows shattered. The ship's pilot slumped over, his arms and face bleeding. The captain ran to the wheel and freed the stricken sailor. He took control of the ship and steered the massive ship onto its original course.

*****

Magnason pulled the airplane high, climbing up to 2,000 feet. Spotting an open clearing on some containers, he approached and hovered. Walters rushed out of the helicopter while his team quickly followed in pursuit. Bullets crashed into the containers below Walters's feet. Walters dropped down between the containers. The Blackhawk disappeared into the night.

Walter rounded up his troops inside an open container and gunfire erupted all around. "Nishan, Matthews and JJ, I want you to go down and disable the engines. We have to stop this ship! Watson, you and Corporal Jones join me in securing the bridge, we need to find a way to stop that missile from taking off."

Nishan and company jumped below the container. They climbed between the large containers until they found their way to the ship's deck. Gunfire erupted around the corner. Bullets slammed into the container above them stopping the team in their tracks.

JJ and Matthews fired a short burst at their unseen foes. But on every occasion the unknown gunner hid out of sight. Nishan pulled out a grenade. JJ and Matthews sprayed the containers with automatic fire. Nishan pulled the pin, counted two seconds and threw the grenade into the gap between the containers.

Unseen Warriors

A loud explosion occurred rumbled the containers. Metal shrapnel and water peppered the team. Nishan rushed forward, gunfire slammed into the metal deck ahead of him. Matthews looked up and fired a burst into 2 sailors above her on the deckhouse. The sailors threw a grenade. The team dived into a small opening between the containers. The grenade exploded harmlessly in the air above them. JJ opened with automatic fire; a sailor fell over the railing hitting a container. The second sailor responded with automatic fire. Bullets rained down on the team. Nishan laid his rifle on the side of a container carefully steadying it while watching the red dot sight. Another fighter opened automatic fire. Nishan pulled the trigger, rounds burst into the fighters' throat tearing out his windpipe. He fell down onto the deck drowning in his own blood.

Nishan ran forward, running down toward a watertight door. Guns pointed, the team entered the door. The team scanned the area and cautiously proceeded toward a set of steps leading down into the belly of the ship. Gunfire erupted from down below, hitting railings and walls around them. The trio pulled pins and released their grenades, one after one the grenades exploded at different levels. Nishan ran down the steps with his team trailing behind. Fires burned around them at different levels. They continued down to the bottom level and entered the open door.

*****

Walters and Watson walked around to the port side of the ship. They looked over to a gangway that went to the ships' stern. Armed sailors patrolled the gangway around the superstructure. Walters slithered forward on the gangway, stopping short to hide behind a container every ten feet. Jones followed behind to join Watson and Walters. The team continued forward until they arrived at an area where containers were stacked near the missile.

"I'll take that missile on. I figure all I have to do is damage the guidance system, then we won't have to worry about it hitting anything important," Jones whispered to Walters. "Okay but be careful, there are plenty of gunmen around," Walters command, Jones rounded the corner then disappeared behind some containers.

"Watson, I want you to get on top of that container, start sniping those guys on the superstructure while I engage the men on the gangway." Watson crawled up onto a container, using an old metal box for a rest; he steadied his rifle placing the electronic dot on a man on the deckhouse.

Waves crashed into the port side, spraying the deckhouse and the gun toting sailors. A grenade crashed into the crowd. A sailor grabbed the grenade as his mates ran. As reached back to throw the grenade, it exploded severing his upper torso from his body. They instantly fell down, blood splattered the deck railing and walls of the ship.

The sailors on deck house fired automatic gunfire into Walters' direction. Hot lead sprayed into the containers, none were able to find their mark. Watson fired single shots at the sailors on the deckhouse. Bullets tore into a sailor's knee tearing out cartilage and bone. The sailor went down screaming in pain. Hitting the deckhouse floor, another soldier readied an RPG, preparing to fire. A bullet tore into his skull and ripped out his brain. The lifeless soldier slumped over the rail.

A dozen sailors came rushing along the gang way toward Walters firing automatic weapons. Walters threw a grenade at oncoming crowd. Seeing the grenade coming at him, the lead sailor tried to stop. He lost his footing and slid over the rail into the open ocean. The grenade exploded tearing through the column of sailors. The dead fell on the slick gangway. Their bodies washed away in the waves.

"Come on down, we've got to get the deck house," Walters shouted over the sound of waves crashing around him. Watson jumped off the container. The two ran down the gangway toward the deckhouse. Walters looked around and flung the door open. A butt stock to the face slammed into his face.

*****

Corporal Jones snuck through the containers. He sat behind and watched all the guards rush to join the gunfight with Walters and Watson. *Great,* he thought. He ran to the unguarded Scud.

The Scud was surrounded by massive scaffolding. Its ominous body rose high into the night's sky. Jones knew it was ready for launch. He climbed up the scaffold, looking around as he raced up the rungs. Reaching the top, he lay down on the platform out of sight. Jones inspected the aluminum exterior with precision. He rand his hand over the side and found an access panel. He reached down and pulled out his folding pliers.

Bullets tore into the scaffold all around Jones. Immediately Jones' right hand started burning and became stiff. Pain throbbed through his hand as blood poured out of it. Jones reached with his left hand and grabbed his pliers. He pulled out the Philips bit and unscrewed the fasteners securing the panel. Bullets crashed into the scaffold all around him. A bullet slammed into Jones' thigh. Jones felt a burning sensation and extreme pain as blood continued to be pumped out of his thigh.

Jones removed the hardware and the panel. He looked down below. Sailors were climbing up the scaffold toward him. Jones pulled a grenade out and dropped it down. Screaming broke out just before the grenade exploded. Shrapnel sprayed in all directions. Men fell off the scaffold crashing into the steel deck below. The deck became a pool of blood, where men died screaming in pain. Jones shifted his attention to the access opening in the missile. Jones could see wiring and circuit boards. Unable to decipher the transistor based guidance system he tore out the wires one by one.

Gavin Parmar

* * * * *

Nishan slowly walked through the doorway. Fires raged around him, fresh water lines sprayed water onto the floor below. The trio crossed into a huge room. Inside, massive boilers burned diesel fuel, heating water that ran the steam turbines in the engine room. "What if just blow one of these fuel feed lines. We would stop the ship dead in its tracks," suggested JJ.

"We could, but that would create a massive fire we couldn't escape. We need to investigate the turbine room more," Nishan replied. Nishan walked into the turbine room, the massive turbines turned the ship's screws at a dizzying pace. Nishan went down a couple of steps the turbine floor level. Matthews noticed some movement out of the corner of her eye. Suddenly a sailor swung a huge wrench, narrowly missing her but knocking Nishan to the ground. Matthews fired a quick burst from the hip missing wildly. The sailor swung again knocking Matthews to the ground. The sailor swung his wrench for another hit. Matthews stabbed him in the chest with her rifle's bayonet. She pulled the trigger. Click. The gun was empty. The sailor swung his wrench and knocked here rifle into the distance.

Another sailor swung a pipe, knocking the rifle out of JJ's hand. JJ stepped back, away from the sailor. The sailor swung his pipe again. He missed JJ, who jumped onto some crates. Another sailor ran to JJ, grabbed him from behind. The other sailor continually beat JJ. He broke his nose, and punched his stomach and legs until he became unconscious.

The three sailors then surrounded Matthews. She looked around; there were no rifles around. Here pistol was also lost. The three men closed in on her. The lead sailor tore of his shirt, exposing his many tattoos. "Now then baby, you are going to make us very happy tonight," He called out to her. The other two sailors grinned with glee.

Unseen Warriors

* * * * *

Walters fell down with excruciating pain. Blood poured out of his teeth where the stock hit him. Babajhan swung again, Watson ducked. He lost his footing as he fired a short burst at Babajhan. The rounds missed wildly. Watson lost his footing and crashed down onto Walters the corner of the stairwell.

"Foolish Americans! Do you think you really can win? There are seventy of us and only a half dozen of you. Ali Mansoor has commanded us to kill you infidels wherever you stand. Today you will meet your carpenter God. The missile outside is aimed at your beloved airbase. In a short time, your entire base will perish in flames. I guarantee it. Allah Akbar!" He shouted while he beat Walters.

A bullet tore through a window slamming in Babajhan's hand. Glass and bullets showered the room as, Babajhan ran up the stairs into the bridge. "Launch the missile. Destroy the Infidels!" He shouted to the captain as he rushed out of the bridge grabbing his helmet.

* * * * *

Corporal Jones put a fresh magazine into his rifle. He slowly pulled himself down the rungs as he made his way to the deck. Limping along the deck, he dragged his leg while blood splashed into his face. The missile started to rumble, he tried to walk faster, but he was unable to make his leg move quicker. His pain increased immensely. The missile shook as the engines fired up. Flames rushed across the deck burning dead and dying that were lying in their own blood. The missile slowly rose off the deck. It climbed 100, 200, and 300 feet until the flames from the engine cleared the deck.

The missile turned toward the stern. Suddenly it lost power crashing into the sea. An explosion of untold magnitude occurred, waves 500 feet high rushed over the stern throwing containers into the Atlantic. Jones hid between containers on the bow deck, holding on for dear life, trying to avoid being washed away. The massive ship's hull listed up into the air. Holding for a second, it violently crashed down. Cranes, scaffolding and assorted deck equipment was ejected into the mighty Atlantic.

* * * * *

Matthews started to sweat as she pulled back to some railings. The lead sailor approached closer and uttered vulgar things. The other soldiers laughed and jeered. The lead soldier began to swing his wrench when suddenly, the ships hull buckled. Seawater poured into the engine room. Matthews grabbed the rail for dear life. The sailors were washed away into the turbine shafts. They screamed in pain while they were mercilessly crushed. Nishan and JJ came to. They were stuck beside a steel bulkhead 30 feet from Matthews. Seawater was pouring onto floor at an ever-increasing rate. Matthews ran toward the two, "Let's go we got to get out of here. The ship's flooding."

"I guess," said Nishan, his head still in pain.

The trio fought the rising water. They grabbed rails and beams, making their way to the burning stairwell. They ran up the four flights of stairs. The water rapidly followed behind. The team was unconcerned at their lack of firepower. The horrifying sight of water made them ran even faster.

* * * * *

Walters and Watson were thrown across the stairwell as the ship shook then listed to one side. Horrible noises could be heard from the hull below their feet. The ship violently shook and rattled before leveling off. Watson grabbed Walters, "I think Nishan and company took care of the engine room. We've got call the chopper and get out of here."

Walters, still woozy, handed the radio to Watson, "Round the crew up, get that chopper to pick us up at the bow." Walters delicately stood up and ran with Watson.

"Magnason, get us out of here. The damn ship's going down!" Watson screamed into the radio

"Copy, Arc light 2 is inbound," Magnason casually remarked

* * * * *

Nishan's team rushed out the stairwell. They looked around for threats, "Looks like the missile's gone. We need to get to the forecastle before we down," Matthews yelled. Nishan and JJ nodded in agreement, they were still too woozy to argue. The team raced to the bow, crossing between the overturned containers, they ran across a bleeding and bruised Corporal Jones.

"Sarah, give me a hand, we need to get him up," Nishan meekly asked. The two picked up Jones, dragging him with JJ in tow. Crossed between the open cargo deck hold and a mangled crane, they met up with Watson and Walters.

"Watsy, nice to see you, your team did great work getting rid of that missile," Nishan said.

"The pleasure is all mine, you and your girlfriend did a great job stopping the ship."

"Well, err, the ship isn't stopped, it's just going down by the stern," Nishan replied, the feeling of normalcy returning to his mind.

"Can we finish this comedy show when we get to the bow!" interrupted Walters.

Water flooded into the boiler room causing them to crack. Steam sprayed into the air as water hit them. The stern sank deeper into the ocean while the weight of the water inside started the bend the hull at the cargo deck. Watertight bulkheads dividing the cargo bay twisted and buckled under the strain. Finally they burst, seawater rushed into the cargo hold. The stern fell into the ocean while the bow floated for a short time.

The team fell over as the stern began to disappear under the waves. "We've got to get to the bow, before it sinks too," barked Walters.

"First we need a chopper," snorted Watson. The team continued up to the bow, looking back, the aft part of the bow started to slide into the ocean as it filled with water.

Magnason approached, coming around to the bow, he hovered a few feet about the foxel. Watson pushed Walters into the cabin, as Nishan and Matthews pushed Jones into the cabin. The rest of the team jumped in as the bow rose to meeting the Blackhawk. Magnason pulled up on the collective and lifted up off the foxel.

The captain stepped out on top of the bow, not noticing the water flooding all around him. He watched the Blackhawk drift into the darkness. "Allah Akbar," he cried out as the bow disappeared under the water quickly sinking into the watery depths of the Atlantic.

Chapter 8

Lajes Field, Azores, Portugal
10-June-2010
2200 Hours Local Time

Nishan sat back on his bed while Matthews placed a cold compress on his swollen head. The compress helped dull the pain, but he still ached. Across the room JJ sat back watching the two in rapt attention, turning to his right he noticed Watson walk into the hospital room.

Watson quickly opened the curtain separating the adjacent bed exposing Staff Sergeant Walters. His face was swollen around his mouth and both his eyes were black.

"I thought you guys would like to meet your bunkmate. Come on, bunky. Say, Hi, to your friends."

Walters smiled looking over to Nishan and JJ, "I can see that as a squad we took our licks."

Nishan smiled, "That's not true, all of us accept Watsy, all he did was fall down."

The room broke out in laughter as Watson desperately tried to redeem himself. "Hey, Nishan I told you I was going to back at you after that night of guard duty."

"Yeah Watsy you did all right. Too bad you took it out on Walters."

"Watson, next time you want to get even with somebody. You can partner with Nishan. I think I'll be safer with JJ and Mathews."

"Ten hut," shouted a corporal carrying a rifle. The team stood at attention, Major Bernier entered the room. "At ease. Well, it's nice to see my squad together. You folks seem no worse for wear after last night's activities."

"Sir, I have a question."

"Yes, Private Nishan, what's on your mind?"

"What was the missile's warhead? Were they really aiming that thing at us?"

"We don't know. Right now, all we have is Walters' statement. We think they were going to us. But the capital city could also have been a target. Unfortunately all the crew went down with the ship. As for the warhead we won't know until we find some wreckage of the missile. That ship is sitting on the bottom of the Atlantic about 3 miles down. Getting to any wreckage is going to be tough, let alone trying to raise any portions of the hull."

"How is Corporal Jones doing?"

"He was flown to Germany last night. From there he will be sent to Walter Reid. From the sounds of things he won't be joining us anytime soon."

"Is he going to lose his leg?" Nishan mused.

"I don't know. Now for the good news, for your heroism in the face of danger last night, I will award all of you with a Bronze Star. Private Nishan, JJ, Sergeant Walters, I'll have your purple hearts in a couple of days. You guys can have a couple of days off. Enjoy. I believe there's another mission in the works."

1600 Pennsylvania Avenue
Washington, D.C.
11-June-2010
0500 Hours Local Time

"Holy Cow! How did Townsend's squad get captured?" Hawkins shouted on the top of his lungs.

Admiral Chedwiggen shifted uncomfortably in his seat before speaking. "Mr. President, we don't know quite yet. We believe he might have been double crossed by on of our moles."

"So, where is he being kept right now?"

"Not sure, Spetsnaz says their links say they may be in a North Korean prison in an area controlled by General Luck."

"Admiral Chedwiggen I want a team of the best soldiers you have to find Dick. Bring him back alive as fast as you can!" Hawkins commanded.

"Well, sir, that may take a bit."

"What do you mean?" Hawkins eyes grew red with anger.

"Sir, the North Koreans are clamping down on intrusions into their border. We need to find a new way of entering into North Korea."

Hawkins exploded with anger. "I don't want excuses, just get it done. Bill, what did we find out from our boarding of the Sierra Mist?"

"It seems like they were launching missiles from the deck of the cargo ship. We think they were trying to hit our airbase in the Azores."

"What kind of warhead did it have?"

"We are not sure. We think we've picked up traces of nuclear isotopes from the warhead in the atmospheres." The whole room erupted. Cabinet members argued among themselves.

Hawkins tried to calm the room down. "You're saying that the missile may have been carrying a nuclear warhead?"

Secretary of defense William Cohen cleared his throat. He could see Hawkins eyes burning with rage. "Yes, Mr. President, a conventional warhead could not have done that amount of damage to the ship. We picked up trace quantities of fallout radiation consistent with a small nuclear weapon."

"I want all information about this ship classified. I don't want people panicking because of an attempted nuclear attack."

"Mr. President, do you want to raise the threat level?"

"Yes, raise it to orange, also I want more security forces placed around New York, Washington, D.C. and Boston.

"Henry, I want to know more about those remaining ships. We've got to find them before they attack US soil."

"Yes, Mr. President"

Chapter 9

North Korea
10-June-2010
0400 Hours Local Time

Townsend's team felt nauseous after their long road trip along bumpy, windy roads in the hot, cramped truck. Loosening their gags, Townsend and Martin were able to speak.

"What do you think they're going to do to us, sir?" Martin asked.

"I'm not sure. I do know there is a reason we're still alive. They must want something from us, some information that we can't get when we're dead."

"Do you think its info about your dad?"

Townsend fell silent. Suddenly the truck shuddered to a stop. Men grabbed the team, dragging them into a foul smelling building. One by one their gags and blindfolds were removed. They were plunged into a dark cell. The only light was a small window with bars. The cell was constructed of cracking concrete colored with black mold.

Martin, Townsend and Carlson were put in one cell. Goodwin and Rich were put into adjoining cell. Arab voices were heard outside. Shouting and screaming filled the empty hallways of the cellblock. The team members only became more nervous, imagining the worst possible scenarios.

"Sounds like those camel jockeys are really riled up about something!"

"Relax Martin. They want something from us. They'll keep us alive as long as it takes to extract that info from us. None of us should say anything, just name, rank and serial number. If they get what they want out of us, they'll kill us." The rest of the team fell silent contemplating Townsend's order.

The night slowly passed into daytime. The entire team failed to sleep due to apprehension. Fear filled their minds. The beams of sunlight began to cut through the darkness of the cells, daybreak brought on more fear.

Three armed militants approached. They opened Townsend's cell. They grabbed Martin by the collar and dragged him outside. Martin failed to struggle, still groggy. The militants dragged him into a dark interrogation room. Martin looked around surveying the crumbling concrete and dirty floor. They stench of urine and stool filled the air. A militant struck his stomach with the butt stock from his rifle, Martin fell to the ground screaming in pain as the militants stood and laughed. Babajhan walked in, slinging an AK-47. He sat on a chair watching Martin crawling around on the cold concrete floor. "What is your name?" Babajhan asked with a calm voice

"Staff Sergeant Martin, serial number 54216379, US Army."

"I know your name rank and serial number, what is your civilian name?" Martin repeated the standard military reply.

"So, you want to play games do you, I can too," Babajhan angrily replied. Babajhan circled Martin, clutching his rifle. He pointed his rifle's bayonet into Martin's hand and pushed hard. Martin screamed in pain. "Now, I don't want to be jacked around. Are there nuclear weapons at Chinhae Harbor?"

Martin failed to say anything. An enraged Babajhan kicked Martin in the face. Martin went down, pain zoomed throughout his head. He tried to stand up. Babajhan kicked him repeatedly in the face. Martin fell to the ground, blood oozed from his face. Martin's teeth lay strewn on the dirt floor below. Martin kneeled on the cold hard floor.

"You have shown perseverance in the face of pain, I commend you, but you can't win," Babajhan shouted words in Arabic to the guards outside. The guards came dragging a soldier wearing a flight suit. They threw him on the ground beside Martin. The flyer looked up at Martin, blood dripped from his lip. Martin couldn't believe it, "Boxman, what happened?"

"They got me and wingman last night. We got a transmission that sounded like you asking for a pick up, I guess I fell for their bait."

Babajhan gave Boxman a swift kick in the face; Boxman fell back to the floor. Struggling to get us, he got a rifle butt in his mouth knocking out his front teeth. Boxman screamed in pain, blood poured out of his mouth and nose. Babajhan kicked him again on his nose, more blood poured out of his face.

"Now Sergeant Martin, let's try something simple, where did you cross the DMZ?" Martin stayed silent, refusing to speak.

Babajhan pulled out his Makarov and fired a round into Boxman's left palm. Blood poured out of his hand. Boxman screamed in pain lying on the ground.

"Now then, I will continually shoot your friend until you start speaking."

"Chorwan, we crossed at Chorwan" Martin meekly answered

"Very good. Now I want you to write me a set of orders that will allow me to transport some goods, description and signatures have to be realistic." Babajhan threw a notepad onto Martin's lap. Martin wrote quickly making notes about color, paper texture and signatures. Babajhan then ordered his guards to give Boxman medical treatment for his hand.

Martin was lead away back to his cell, thrown beside Townsend. Townsend looked at Martin's beaten body, "What do they want?"

"They wanted orders to transport goods to a naval base."
"Why do they want that?"
"I don't know. They've got Boxman. They shot him down while he was looking for us." Townsend closed his eyes trying to comprehend the situation while he drifted off to sleep.

* * * * *

Staff Sergeant Buckmaster read a letter from his wife; he couldn't believe his children were now teenagers. Buckmaster felt old, he felt that life had just passed him by; Semper Fi he tried to remind himself.

"Sergeant, sergeant!" a young private came rushing in his direction.

"What is it Private Goldstein?"

"Sir we found something near the field!"

"Private, I work for a living. Don't call me, sir. I am a Staff Sergeant. You will address me as Staff Sergeant Buckmaster! Now what did you find?"

"Staff Sergeant Buckmaster. We found a tunnel entrance!"

Buckmaster followed Goldstein to a shallow pit, there, an opening led into a deep dark hole. Buckmaster grabbed a nearby corporal's radio, "Lieutenant Robinson, sir, we found a tunnel going toward the DMZ."

"I'll be there right away, secure the area," he answered in an excited voice. Buckmaster arranged his Platoon to stand guard around the entrance, the troops stood and watched in amazement.

Lieutenant Robinson approached, "Looks like we found on of those fabled tunnels that cross into the DMZ. The raiders must have been crossing through here to shoot down our choppers. Buckmaster, I want a team stationed here 24/7, I'll see about setting up an entrance party."

Unseen Warriors

* * * * *

Light entered Townsend's cell, he shivered in the cold morning light. Looking over, several new soldiers were in the cell next to him. They were dirty, adorning beards, but he could still recognize their tattered US Army uniforms. Townsend leaned over to the nearby Corporal, "I'm Lieutenant Richard Townsend, First of the Ninth, Alpha squad."

The corporal stood up, gave a lackluster salute. "I'm Corporal Schneider, Black Ops, Camp Zulu."

"How long have you guys been here?"

"I don't know, weeks, months. Time stands still here. Only thing that's certain we get tortured every couple of days. They keep asking about naval bases, aircraft carriers, stuff like that. Every time we tell them we don't know anything, they beat us up. They've been giving us a royal going over except for one guy, Private Mohammed. He's joined them. He's been eating well, I even see him walking the compound carrying an AK."

Townsend's eyes grew big, "Do you think he sold you out?"

"We know he did. We were on patrol near the Chinese Border, next thing we know we were surrounded. We tried to fight back; we even called out pick up plane. It was no help."

"Next thing you know we were held hostage at an old castle. All the time, the Arabs are talking to Mohammad, trying to make him comfortable and such. Soon he was wandering around the castle, eating well and hanging around the big cheese. For us it was no food, just dirty water. Just before we moved here, they beheaded Sergeant Stevens."

"Who is was highest ranking soldier after him?"

"That would be me, Corporal Ortega died of his injuries about two weeks ago. He put a hell of a fight the day we got captured. The Arabs refused to give him medical care for his injuries."

"Who are the rest of your team?"

"That's Private Garcia, Sanchez, Wong and Bouchard." The men saluted Townsend and fell into a daze.

An armed guard showed up. He opened the cell door and grabbed Townsend by the sleeve. The man tossed Townsend into the hallway with ease. Townsend fell to his knees. Townsend tried to get up; another guard grabbed him by the collar and dragged him into the interrogation room.

Babajhan walked up to Townsend, "Lieutenant Townsend, it's always nice to moment with the son of the President of the United States. I have longed to meet you face to face. I have many things I want to talk to you about. Let's start with the name of the general who's responsible for Army operations in the Asian theatre?"

"I don't know," Townsend replied.

Babajhan kneeled down to Townsend, "I don't want to play games, now tell me everything I want to know or its lights out!" Townsend remained quiet. Babajhan fired a round into the floor, the bullet ricochet around bouncing off walls. Townsend stayed silent, steadfast.

"So, you wish to play hardball, I can do that too," Babajhan shouted something in Arabic. His guards dragged in Garcia and forced him to kneel down beside Townsend. "Mr. Townsend, you have tried my patience long enough." Babajhan fired a burst of automatic gunfire into Garcia's head. It exploded spraying blood and brain matter over Townsend.

"Now Mr. Townsend, do you have anything to say?"

"You are a heartless barbarian, a cold blooded murderer!"

"You call me a murderer, but you kill thousands of Arabs in Iraq? You call me a barbarian while your planes rain death from the skies onto cities full of women and children. You lecture us about freedom and democracy but you invade our lands to steal our oil, and place puppet governments that only serve your needs. You are a hypocrite like your cowardly father. You sit here like a dog on the floor trying to tell me that I commit murder! But your women run around America naked in the streets while alcohol poisons your bodies. You are infidels, may Allah destroy you with the Jewish state! Enough games, now tell me what I need to know, or I'll execute another one of your toy soldiers," Babajhan called in Arabic to his fellow guard.

"Wait, I'll speak."

"Who is the general of the Asian Pacific theatre?"

"General Lewis Mackenzie."

"Who is your CO?"

"Colonel Stevens."

"Tomorrow we will continue." One of Babajhan's guards dragged Townsend back to his cell, throwing him to the cell floor. Townsend looked up to Martin's swollen face.

Townsend meekly spoke, "I can see what you meant. They play dirty with lives like they play with the truth. They'll stop at nothing in order to get what they want."

"Yes, sir they do, what did they do to you?"

"They executed Private Garcia in cold blood, right in front of me." Townsend shook his head. "He is full of so much hate, so little regard for human life. How can a man be full of so much evil, and do such heinous things in the name of his God? Did you tell him anything?"

"Name, rank and serial number, just like you said." The two men leaned back onto the wall, unable to look at each other; they felt the shame of betrayal inside their hearts.

* * * * *

Buckmaster stood with Robinson, the two felt uneasy watching the tunnel entrance. Robinson finally broke the silence, "How long has he been in there?"

"I'd say about 25 minutes, sir."

"I want you to prepare a rescue party if he doesn't come out in another ten minutes."

Buckmaster nodded his head. Although remaining calm, on the inside he still felt concerned. Suddenly light pierced the darkness from the tunnel's entrance, very weak at first, then it grew stronger and brighter. "Sir, he's coming out!" Buckmaster shouted with excitement. A very dirty Corporal Thomas climbed out of the cramped tunnel entrance. Stretching, trying to loosen up his stiff muscles, Thomas stood at attention and saluted a few feet from Robinson.

"What did you find, Corporal?" Robinson asked with his usual deep voice.

"The tunnel turns around the corner, it then opens up large enough for a man to walk around. There are boxes of AK ammo all around the entrance but no lights; its pitch black in there. I traveled about 200 feet, in several spots the roof is shored up with wood beams."

"Staff Sergeant Buckmaster, set up an attack squad, I want them to investigate the tunnel from entrance to exit. Have them inspect the exit area on the North Korean side, afterwards I want them to set charges and blow it shut."

Buckmaster nodded then called over. "Corporal Thomas, take Hawksworth, Kaa, Howard, Morrison, Johnson, Evans and Bone with you. Weapons are to be a silenced Ruger Mark II and an M-4. Don't use the M-4s in the tunnel unless you have to, the noise will deafen you. Corporal Bone, take some C-4, I want you to blow the entrance when you retreat, Semper Fi."

"Semper Fi" the squad chanted before they entered the tunnel.

Corporal Thomas entered first, using his headlamp to shine the way ahead; he squeezed through the narrow portion of the tunnel with ease. Arriving into the open areas, he got off his knees. The lights from the teams head lamps made the tunnel almost as bright as daylight. Rats ran along the tunnel length, scurrying out of sight from the incoming soldiers.

Traveling down, the opening grew bigger and brighter. After twenty feet, they were able to stand upright. The walls opened up enough that the soldiers were able to march side by side. Corporal Hawksworth came up beside Thomas, "Never thought I'd say it, but this tunnel duty isn't half bad. It must be only 65 degrees F here now."

Unseen Warriors

"Yeah, that's a lot better than that one hundred degree furnace outside; heck just losing the humidity is worth being down here," Thomas replied.

The team continued to march for what it seemed like eternity. Rounding a sharp bend, the tunnel led forward uphill. Standing at the base of the incline, Thomas looked up; light began to break the darkness. Thomas motioned the team to turn off their lights. One by one they turned off their headlamps. Rays of light penetrated the darkness up ahead.

Thomas marched up the incline, closing the crest, he pulled out the pistol, and the team did likewise. Peering into the opening, Thomas watched several North Korean guards roam. They waved their AK-47's mere feet from Thomas' position. Thomas leaned over to Hawksworth, "When I signal, you get the guard to the right. I'll take the one to the left." Hawksworth nodded in agreement.

Thomas used an old packing crate for a rest sighting down his barrel. He squeezed the trigger in rapid succession. The sound of the slide hitting forward was the only sound heard, before the guard could react. A 22 cal bullet hit his shoulder. Flinching in pain, he grabbed his shoulder just before another bullet hit his chest. Another bullet slammed into his head. He fell to earth with a quiet thud, his uniform covered in blood.

Watching his stricken comrade fall, the second guard turned and raised his rifle. A hail of gunfire from Hawksworth's pistol met him. His neck exploded. Unable to speak, the guard clutched his throat and fell drowning in his own blood.

Thomas and Hawksworth quickly grabbed the bodies. They dragged them into the darkened tunnel. Looking at their blood soaked uniforms, Thomas commented, "North Korean irregulars, I think they're part of the raiding parties that have been attacking our choppers."

"How can you tell?"

"Look, their clothes are new, they look well fed, plus, their weapons are Russian AK-74SU's, the best money can buy. Even their ammunition is commercial grade. They're far too well equipped to be in the North Korean Army. The North has barely enough food to feed their conscripts, let alone clothe them with the finest.

Shouting in Korean was erupted up ahead. They looked up to see a soldier screaming while running in their direction. Shining his light at Hawksworth, he fired his Makarov pistol. Kaa returned fire with his pistol, knocking down the soldier with a quick bullet to the head. "I think we've been spotted," announced Hawksworth.

The team slowly entered into the lit tunnel, more soldiers approached firing their AK rifles. The noise deafened the team, Morrison replied with a quick burst from her M-4, cutting the approaching forces down.

"Morrison, you and Kaa watch the tunnel here, kill anybody that approaches. Howard, Johnson, come with me, we'll clear these rooms. Hawksworth, take Evans and Bone and start clearing the tunnel forward. If things get too noisy, fall back here." Hawksworth's team marched forward, M-4's in hand.

Thomas entered a big room with a high ceiling. The electric lights lit it like daytime. Bunks were set up like Army barracks, spare uniforms and boots hung neatly in a closet. "Looks like them Gooks were living pretty high on the horse here," Johnson commented.

Thomas nodded in agreement. Gunfire erupted from a loft on the opposite side of the room.

The team responded immediately with automatic fire into the loft. A body fell out, still clutching a grenade. The team swept the room. Looking around, they found an alcove. Johnson kicked a wooden door in, unveiling a tunnel entrance. The team looked inside. Johnson quietly looked into the adjacent room. Gunfire erupted, knocking Johnson to the ground. Howard quickly pulled out a grenade. Pulling the pin with his left hand he threw the grenade into the entrance as he hid behind the dirt walls. A deafening explosion occurred, walls shook as dirt,

Unseen Warriors

timbers and lights fell from the ceiling. The team members fell to the ground from the force of the blast.

Howard tried to revive Johnson; it was too late, he was dead. Thomas helped drag the body away from the alcove into an open area. "We'll, retrieve the body later. Let's check out this tunnel." Howard nodded in agreement.

The team crawled through the open tunnel into another large room with a high ceiling. Fires raged all around them, officers lay in pools of blood. Kerosene lamps lay shattered all around, their fuel burning everything in sight. Thomas stepped forward to a desk, and rifled through the documents that lay on it. Thomas looked at the strange Korean characters; unable to read any he started to stuff as many as he could into his uniform. "Looks like this may have been their officer's bunk, nice and comfy," Thomas commented

"Yeah, he had first class digs. Look here, it's a radio tuned to Korean Military frequencies. That's how they knew when our choppers were patrolling along the wall." Thomas aimed his M-4 and fired an automatic burst into the radio, causing it to explode into thousands of pieces.

"Let's head back to the main trail," Thomas announced. Howard nodded in agreement.

* * * * *

Hawksworth traveled down the dusty trail of the tunnel as it began to swing to the right, Hawksworth stopped his team. Leaning around the corner, Hawksworth noticed dozens of soldiers loading rifles and pistols. "Looks like they're readying for attack. When I give the signal, we throw our grenades over." Pulling out a grenade, Hawksworth looked over. They shook their heads in agreement as they readied their grenades with their fingers in the pins. Hawksworth pulled his pin and tossed his grenade, immediately diving for cover as his teammates threw theirs. A massive explosion occurred, clouds of dust flew everywhere. Wood beams crashed down all around the team. Gunfire erupted with screams from dying men. Small explosions continued to pop as the dust cleared.

Hawksworth stood up. Brushing the dust off his body he looked around the corner, "Looks like we shut that part of the tunnel up pretty good."

"I never figured a couple of grenades could do that much damage," Evans commented.

"They sure can when they set off ammunition and other explosives like Simtex. We need to back track. We may be able to find an alternate tunnel exit to the outside world."

The team returned to the main trail, the found a small branch tunnel leading to a small wooden door. Hawksworth kicked the frail door into splinters. Looking in he saw a narrow passage leading to a nearby room. Thomas rushed to join the rest of the team.

"Sounds like you guys threw a few grenades and set off a two thousand pound bomb. The roof was shaking in the tunnel way back where Morrison and Kaa were standing guard."

"We set off an ammo cache, like the one back there, I think I sealed up the other branch of the tunnel," Hawksworth answered back.

"It's ok. We've got to stop using grenades down here, and sooner or later we're going to bury ourselves in a cave in." Thomas followed the passage to the open room. The team looked around at a chapel complete with pews and a pulpit. While the team wandered around the room, Hawksworth found a crumbling wall near an alcove. He started punching the wall with the butt of his rifle; the flimsy dirt wall fell down revealing a tunnel entrance leading up a steep incline. "Corporal Thomas, I found something!" Hawksworth shouted in an excited voice.

Thomas crawled into the tunnel. It was very small. A man crawling could barely fit into the small opening. Crawling up a steep incline, Thomas noticed light started cutting through the

Unseen Warriors

darkness. Climbing further, he dug through loose soil. The afternoon sunlight showered him with warmth.

*****

Townsend awoke, he could not tell if it was morning or evening. He had grown weak from lack of food and water. Standing up, he felt dizzy, the afternoon light filled the cell. Babajhan came in, opening Townsend's cell he laughed, "Mr. Townsend, we need to have another discussion." Grabbing Townsend by the collar, he dragged him away out of sight of the prisoners.

Martin yawned. Looking round the room, he saw Boxman asleep beside him. His front teeth missing, his eyes swollen and black, and his hand bandaged with an old T-shirt.

Guards walked in, they clanged metal cups on the bars of the cells, waking the prisoners. One by one the soldiers approached. The guards poured out water into tin cups while passing a plate of steaming hot rice and goat meat. Flat bread topped the makeshift dinner. The prisoners ate hungrily. The Black Ops team showed signs of life for the first time and many spoke amongst themselves.

After the makeshift dinner, the guards shackled up the prisoners, and marched them out of the compound. The team's eyes squinted in pain. They viewed sunlight in its full glory for the first time since their capture. The team stopped in an open corner of the courtyard, the guards arranged them in a line. One of the guards grabbed Private Wong, while the team watched; he took off Wong's shackles and seated him on a chair.

"What do you think they're going to do?" Boxman whispered to Martin.

"I don't know if we received our last meal just now."

"I hate to say it, but looks like you might be right."

A camouflaged militant approached the team and he looked at Private Wong. He shouted some Arabic at the guards. They stood at attention, guns at waist level. Looking over at the team, he spoke in broken English. "I am Ahmed Sadr. I have been sent by the Sheik. The Sheik knows about your capture, he has been busily orchestrating all the events. You have persevered quite well. You have shown great strength while in prison. Alas if you had been Muslims, I would have been given the discretion of freeing you. But, being Infidels, I can only give you one punishment demanded by Allah."

Sadre lowered his rifle and pointed his rifle at Wong. He fired an automatic burst into Wong's chest. Wong fell over with his chair, his heart pumped out the remaining blood onto the ground, as he died with his eyes open. The rest of the team flinched with the sound of gunfire, Martin and Boxman stood terrified with the brutality of the execution style killing.

"You weren't kidding, Hollywood. That was our last meal; it looks like our goose is cooked." Martin shook his head in agreement, so this was how it was going to be, anonymous death in the middle of North Korea.

The gunmen dragged Sanchez forward, forcing him to kneel on the ground beside Private Wong's dead body. Sanchez shouted words in his native Spanish tongue that sounded like prayers, over and over again he chanted while waited. The guards spoke in Arabic, chants of their own for Allah as they prepared. Sadre raised his rifle to Sanchez's head. Sanchez pleaded for his life crying, sobbing for forgiveness. Sadr lowered his rifle pointing to Sanchez' throat, as he shouted Allah Akbar he fired. Sanchez stooped over dead, blood poured out of the base of his neck and skull. The guards pulled off Wong's shoes, then throwing them on Sanchez's face.

They grabbed Bouchand, forcing him to stand up. Sadre removed his shackles. Bouchand darted, running toward the fence. Sadre laughed, watching the unfortunate soul gunned down by guards along the fence.

Sadre shook his head as he announced to the team, "You Americans are fools. Don't you understand you will die?

Unseen Warriors

Resistance is futile; make peace with you Carpenter God. Today you will see him in the afterlife."

A guard grabbed Martin by his neck. They forced him to kneel down. The guard took off his shackles, throwing them on the ground. Sadre looked down to Martin, "have you made peace with your God?" Martin shook his head. "Take a few minutes," ordered Sadre.

Martin thought to himself, *So, this is it! I guess death is the great equalizer. Goodbye Kyle, Christie, I love you. Listen to Mother. Goodbye Boxman, we had a lot of fun together.*

"Time's up, do you have to say anything?" Martin stayed silent.

A guard lowered his rifle to Martin's head. Martin profusely sweated as he looked at the barrel pointed at his head. The guard pulled the trigger. Click. The rifle was empty. The guard pulled the empty magazine out throwing it into the grass. Grabbing a spare, he slapped it into his rifle, pulling the charging the rifle handle, he aimed it at Martin's head.

The guard began to pull the trigger, when a loud bang erupted in the distance. The guard fell to the earth, bleeding profusely from the chest. Gunfire poured into the compound, Sadre and his militiamen returned fire at the unknown source. A bullet slammed into Sadre's hand, blood poured out as he winced in pain. The guard tower exploded into flames and came crashing down. The guard fell to earth, still ablaze. Sadre looked around; there was no sight of any enemy gunmen.

Sadre ran to the prison building with his men. The prisoners remained alone in the compound. Gunfire erupted from the bushes. The bullets slammed into the prison building. Sadre fell to the ground clutching his hand. More gunfire erupted into the prison building, windows shattered from the incoming bullets.

Martin went to a nearby rock and tried to smash his shackles. The rest joined him. Gunfire continued to erupt around them.

Militiamen fired out of the prison windows, unable to see their hidden foes. Leaning out of a second story window, a fighter fired automatic fire. "Click," his rifle was empty. Withdrawing his rifle from the window, bullets slammed into his throat and skull. He went crashed to the floor. Another fighter rushed over to take his place. Before he could start firing, a bullet tore into his head spraying brain matter over the floor.

Another group of fighters crawled along the rooftop, guns in hand. The first gunman hid behind the old brick chimney. As he rested his rifle on the bricks, bullets tore into his chest and skull causing him to fall from the roof. He crashed on the ground, rolling on the grass to a stop, mere feet from the Team. The other fighters continued to fire at the muzzle flashes in the distance. Rounds slammed into the tin roof all around the fighters. The militants fought back, unafraid of the bullets crashing all around them. Within seconds, the bullets had slain each one of the militants.

Witnessing his fighters being gunned down all around him, Sadre ran out the back door. He ran around the corner, crawled under the barbed wire and trudged through a mud filled ditch. He looked back, wiped his brow and crossed a small brook. He ran up an embankment to an awaiting Jeep. He shouted to the driver in Arabic, the driver nodded and drove off. Sadre relaxed, looking at his AK, he pulled out the magazine. There was only one cartridge was left, he threw the magazine on the ground. Then he adjusted his bandage on his left hand, as blood continued to flow out the bandage then onto his leg and the front seat of the Jeep.

The Jeep stopped in front of Martin's team. An infuriated Sadre looked at his driver and screamed at him in Arabic. Sadre stopped speaking when the driver lowered a barrel to his face. The driver discarded his outfit. A smiling Corporal Thomas sat beside Sadre pointing his M-16 at him in a menacing way. "So, Mr. Sadre, we meet again." Sadre shook his head in confusion.

"Let me refresh your memory. In Mosul, Iraq a Marine company caught you for suspicion of setting up roadside bombs. While you were in custody and transported in a Bradley

Unseen Warriors

an RPG attack killed the driver. You escaped by grabbing one of the guard's rifles and shooting up the soldiers before escaping. That was my squad! You killed six of my best men. Today I get to take you into custody, and will not give you any mercy."

Sadre's eyes grew bigger as he looked around. More Marines appeared out of the woods, M-16s in hand. Sadre shook his head at the sight of his Militiamen lying dead and dying on the ground.

"Take the shackles off," ordered Thomas. Sadre complied. Thomas placed a set of shackles on Sadre, extra tight.

Thomas looked around at the dead US Soldiers. Looking to Martin as he spoke, "So, how does it feel like to be rescued by a bunch of Jarheads?" Martin stood dazed, unable to answer, still contemplating his rescue. "Kaa, Hawksworth go into the prison building and clear the area!"

Hawksworth walked in, rifle aimed, Kaa loaded a grenade in his M-203 launcher. Martin watched the soldiers disappear into the prison; looking over to Thomas he shook his head. "Our Lieutenant was hauled off this morning; he wasn't around for execution hour."

Thomas nodded, "We circled the compound soon after they started cutting down your guys. Since then I know that no one escaped." Looking over to Sadre, Thomas put his knife on Sadre's neck, "Where's the lieutenant?" Sadre shook his head, no reply.

Thomas aimed his rifle at Sadre. He pulled the charging handle, a round ejected out of the M-16. "I'm not happy with you. Don't tempt me to do something more serious to you than that wound on your hand!"

Sadre flinched, "Several men from the Al Qaeda took him away. I was given orders to execute everyone here after they left, that's all I know, honest."

Hawksworth and Kaa approached, bearing several AK-47SU's, ammunition, and Russian grenades. Looking to Martin they handed him a rifle and ammunition. "You dogfaces know how to use these?"

"Of course we do, we're not a bunch of stupid Jarheads," shot back Martin.

"Hold it, I'm in command! We're here to rescue you and until we get back to friendly hands do as I say. Do you understand?" Thomas announced

The soldiers nodded in agreement except for Martin, "Listen, Corporal Thomas, I'm a Staff Sergeant in the US Army, no Marine Corporal tells me what to do!"

"Mr. Martin you will do as I say. If you won't I'll shoot you just as easily as I'll shoot Sadre," Thomas raised his rifle to Martin's head.

"Now Lance Corporal Hawksworth, you will give this soldier the respect he deserves. I don't want to hear any more inter-service flame wars, understand?" Hawksworth merely nodded. "We're heading up the hill, saddle up."

The Marines marched in tow, Martin's team slowly staggered, partly from torture and imprisonment and partly from being overwhelmed by the sensation of finally being rescued. The team hiked up a steep hill, fallen twigs cracked underneath their feet. The sounds seemed deafening in the quiet afternoon.

Private Evans stopped, "Corporal, I hear tanks!"

"Keep going to the tunnel, I'll see." Thomas scanned the distant forest with his binoculars, "We've got a tank column coming at us. Look's like General Luck is sending a whole battalion after us!" The team began to run up the hill at full speed. Sadre dragged his feet; Private Morrison poked his back with her rifle to keep him in check.

The sound of the tanks immediately broke Martin's crew out of their daze; instinctively they loaded their weapons and bent their grenade pins. The team ran at full speed up the steep hill dodging low branches and trees.

Artillery shells crashed around the team. Dirt sprayed them as the shell came closer and closer. The sound of the rumbling tanks grew louder and louder.

Thomas ran beside Private Bone, "When we get inside the tunnel, plant the explosive at the base of the tube in the chapel thirty seconds on the timer max. Then drop another just at the entrance to the sleeping quarters."

"Will we have time to get away? After all, thirty seconds isn't very much time."

"We have no choice. If we don't, the North Koreans will overrun the tunnels!"

Arriving at the tunnels, Hawksworth went down the tunnel first; followed by Martin's crew. Sadre next, followed by the rest of the Marines.

"Hurry up, the troops are swarming at us, get in the tunnel and run for your lives." Gunfire erupted all around the team. Thomas and Bone fired suppression fire but the troops swarmed like ants all around the hillside. "Click," Thomas' M-16 ran empty not long after Bone's. "Get out of here, I'm out of ammo!"

Thomas jumped into the tunnel tumbling down the corridor, explosions rocked the tunnel while dirt and dust fell from the ceiling.

Bone watched Thomas fleeing out of the Chapel. Bone set up the C-4. Gunfire tore into his frail body from outside the tunnel. Soldier after soldier jumped through the tunnel opening, stepping on him as they ran toward the fleeing team.

Thomas ran as fast as he could, all the while bullets crashed into the dirt walls all around him. Dead soldiers lay on the floor. Approaching the sleeping quarters his eyes grew big. He tried to avoid his team standing up ahead. "What are you idiots doing? The entire North Korean army is after us, while you are taking a break!" Thomas shouted in an exasperated tone.

"We're just tired, we haven't eaten since…"

"Shut up Martin, get your rear in gear, or I'll shoot you!"

Martin's team got up lazily and ran toward the tunnel exit.

Thomas stopped Kaa, "Give me your rifle, I'll cover you!" Kaa handled over his rifle and ran full speed toward the tunnel exit behind Corporal Schneider.

* * * * *

Buckmaster stood outside the tunnel entrance nervously smoking a cigarette. Pulling out his pack he noticed it was empty. He shook his head and threw the pack on the ground. A pack of Camels suddenly appeared in front of him. Buckmaster pulled it out looking over from the hand, and he noticed Lieutenant Robinson standing there. Robinson pulled a cigarette out. He put away the pack, and gave Buckmaster a light. Lighting his own cigarette he gave Buckmaster a cold stare. "How long have they been down there for?"

"It's been about six hours, maybe a little more."

"They'll be fine; Thomas has a good head on his shoulders." Buckmaster nodded in agreement. Buckmaster flinched for a second. He then looked at the tunnel in amazement. Hawksworth crawled out dirty and black, behind him came out a dazed Martin.

Robinson stepped back at the sight of the Army Sergeant. Later three Army Privates came out of the tunnel followed by a helicopter pilot. Finally a fatigue clad Arab in shackles climbed out with the remaining Marines dragging out Johnson's lifeless body. Robinson gave a stern look to the team, "Hawksworth, where's Thomas and Bone?"

"They're still in the tunnel trying to fight off a battalion of North Koreans!" Robinson raised his eyebrows in amazement.

* * * * *

Thomas looked at his bleeding leg, the blood continued to soak through the bandage dripping onto the dirt floor. Thomas

Unseen Warriors

looked down at his watch, three minutes! He knew Bone didn't set the charge before he was over run. Shaking his head, he loaded the M-203, and pulled up the sights.

Looking through sights he watched as soldiers slowly walked the tunnel, stopping to examine their dead comrades. A soldier looked into the darkness in Thomas' direction. He was carefully looking through his sights and swept with his rifle the darkened area. The soldier's eyes grew big as he noticed the barrel of the M-203 in the darkness. He yelled in an excited tone to his fellow soldiers. Soldiers rushed toward Thomas, guns blazing. They remained unaware of Thomas laying in the darkness.

"Semper Fi," Thomas whispered as he pulled the trigger on the M-203 with his fleeting strength. The grenade flew into the crate of Simtex explosives. A massive explosion erupted filling the tunnel up with fire. Crates of ammunition added to the destruction.

* * * * *

Robinson stood with Buckmaster, shaking their heads at the bizarre tale told by Martin. The ground rumbled like an earthquake and a fireball erupted out of the ground. Flaming debris fell along the DMZ causing mines to explode. Marines all along the DMZ positions looked up at the great fireworks show in awe. Robinson took off his helmet and bowed his head in silence. One by one the Marines followed in a seamless manner.

Corporal Carlson sat on a dirt embankment, looking up at the fire in the sky, he silently prayed. "Corporal Thomas, you died so we may live, may your soul eternally be in heaven with our Father." A tear flowed down his check as he looked up at the flames. Corporal Carlson whispered, "Semper Fi."

Part 2

Urban Chaos

Chapter 10

Oregon Coast
12-June-2010
2300 Hours Local Time

The Christina plowed through the rough waters of the Pacific. Its decks pitched up and down as containers tried to shift on the massive freighter's deck. Captain Santos looked out of the bridge, concern showed on his wrinkled forehead as he smoked a Cuban cigar. "We'll be at the meeting point in about an hour, are you sure the barge will be there to meet us?"

Babajhan shook his head, "Trust me, I have the captain's word. The promise of a large sum of money will curry his favor."

"You know, Haroon, the Sheik is not happy about your failure with the Sierra mist. If you fail again, he may just issue a Fatwa. There is no place in the Arab world where you can hide from such a thing."

"Relax Nestor, our contact will come through, we will be successful. Allah is with us on our attack. The barge captain is weak minded, he only searches for money. His morals are loose like the rest of the American Infidel nation."

Santos shook his head as the big Freighter proceeded to a point slightly north east of Cannon Beach, Oregon. Santos felt nervous, even though he knew that his Philippine flagged vessel was not under suspicion. Customs often failed to inspect his cargo in many US ports. But he felt the mere presence of Babajhan was cause trouble. He knew Babajhan's brutal reputation across the Middle East. Santos knew answering no to him just wasn't an option. Mansoor ordered every one of Babajhan's nefarious activities and there was no place to hide from Mansoor's long reach.

The ship continued to sail in the dead of the night, arriving 300 miles of the coast. Santos looked with his binoculars at the distant lights of the thriving tourist town of Cannon Beach. He ordered his crew to drop the anchor while the high surf continued to pound the mighty ship.

Santos put on his jacket and proceeded to walk out from the pilothouse onto one of the bridge wing. He lit one of his Cuban cigars, absorbing the aroma while continuing to puff. The tension and stress of the day seemed to melt away with each passing puff.

Peering out into the distance, he scanned the open ocean for signs of life. Lights began to appear far off by the stern, very faint at first, then brighter and brighter until Santos could make out individual lights. Santos watched in rapt attention, as the distant ship flashed its signal lights in rapid succession. Slowly out of the darkness, the faint shape of a large barge appeared, stacked with containers and box trailers like cordwood. As the barge approached, Santos could make out a large push boat with deckhands scurrying about on its deck.

Santos threw his Cigar overboard into the open ocean and rushed into the wheelhouse. "Your guest is here Haroon. Do you have the insurance policy?"

Babajhan nodded, "Yes, I have both." Babajhan pulled out a black leather briefcase. Grinning, he pulled his coat aside exposing a holstered Makarov Pistol.

The barge slowly crept toward the waiting freighter, deckhands waited on the barge, ropes ready. The twin screws roared in reverse as the barge's bow approached the ship's stern. The massive barge stopped mere feet from the freighter's starboard side. Deckhands quickly lashed ropes between the ships; the push boat immediately dropped its anchor.

Shutting down the engine, Captain Grote stuffed another Marlborough cigarette into his mouth and lit it. He climbed down the ladders from the wheelhouse to the ships deck. A mean look covered the balding fifty-year-old man's face. Grote gasped for breath as he walked along the deck, taking another long suck from his cigarette.

A rope ladder was thrown from the freighter's deck to the hull of the push boat. Grote looked over to his approaching first mate. "We'll be taking a container on by port side. Get the men ready, we've got be done fast. This has to be totally under the table. If I find out any one of you spoke about this, I'll shoot the whole lot of you myself! Understood?"

"Yes, Captain," the first mate nervously answered. Grote pulled himself up the rope ladder to the deck, and lit his last Marlborough using his burning butt. He threw the old butt and empty package into the open ocean while grunting as a sailor met up with him. The sailor escorted him to the captain's stateroom.

Grote entered the luxurious stateroom. It was decorated with Oak and leather, the carpet was deep plush, and like nothing Grote had seen in a common tramp cargo ship. Captain Santos was seated on a chair at the head of a table. Babajhan stood holding a briefcase. "Where's the money?" Grote grunted to Santos.

Babajhan put his briefcase on the table and opened it up. Grote sifted through the money. He picked up a stack after stack of crisp one hundred dollar bills, carefully proofing each bill until he got to the bottom of the briefcase.

"Now then, Captain, your mission is simple. We have on 50-foot container that needs to go to Pasco, WA. There, a semi trailer truck will arrive to pick up the container. Your job is simple. You are to adjust your load manifest so it looks like the container originated from Port Orford. Mr. Gill will accompany you to Pasco. Treat him like any one of your ordinary deckhands. When you arrive at Pasco, he'll quickly depart and you'll have your million dollars."

Grote grunted in agreement, looking over to Babajhan as he spoke, "Get your rear on my boat." Santos stood up to shake Grote's hand, but Grote shuffled out of the room, while reaching for another pack of cigarettes.

The freighters massive cranes lifted the container off its deck onto the stack of container.

Deckhands rushed to secure it as the first mate recorded the container number. "331679."

Grote met the first mate on the deck, looking at the yellow Post-it note, he grunted and began climbing the steps to the wheelhouse. Babajhan followed wearing a faded cotton loggers' shirt with dirty jeans.

Grote started the massive diesel engines, advancing the left throttle; the barge began to drift away from the massive freighter. Deckhands released ropes as the barge smoothly crept forward.

Captain Santos stood on the bridge wing smoking his cigar watching the departing push boat. Thumbing through his coat pocket, he pulled out his cell phone and dialed a phone number in Berlin. The phone rang several time, then an answering machine beeped, Santos spoke quietly, "The BMW is broke, both the transmission and the differential need replacing, parts are coming by barge. Expect delivery on July 4th, 2010." Santos put his phone in his pocket and took a long puff from his cigar. "Allah Akbar," he spoke as a Port of Portland escort boat appeared on the horizon.

The White House
13-June-2010
0500 Hours Local Time

    President Hawkins sat at his desk eating bacon and eggs; the early hour paperwork wore him thin. Yawning, he took another swig of earl grey tea as he signed another executive order. Hawkins heard a knock from behind the door, "Enter."
    Admiral Chedwiggen walked in. He closed the door behind him and carried a large box. Chedwiggen placed the box on Hawkins' desk and sat down across from Hawkins.
    Hawkins looked up; his glasses lay low on his nose. "This has to be good for you to come this early."
    "Sure is, you have to see this." Chedwiggen put videotape into the TV/VCR combo in the wall and began to play it. The video started with Ali Mansoor sitting at his desk wearing his general's outfit. "President Hawkins, I know you have been worrying about your son, fear no more, he is safe, I may be able to guarantee his release but you must release the people of Afghanistan. Let them go. Return your forces back to America let the role of Islam become the law of the land again."
    "This is going to be aired on Al Jazeera today." Pulling out a photograph from the box, Chedwiggen pointed to a tall pale figure wearing fatigues. "This was taken by a spy satellite after an anonymous tip. I think we've found Dick."
    Color returned to Hawkins' face, closely examining the photo with his reading glasses, he stood still for almost a minute.

"That's him. I see that stupid Eagle tattoo he got on his arm after ROTC." For the first time in many weeks, Hawkins began to smile. "So, why didn't Mansoor say he's got Dick outright?"

"Simple, if he declared that, he knows the sixth fleet would be at his doorstep. This way he gets someone else to do his dirty work. He's a real piece of work."

"How much do you know so far?"

Chedwiggen leaned back into his chair. "Mansoor hangs around the Punjab a lot, he has palaces in several cities; Islamabad, Lahore, Peshawar to name a few. I'm waiting to hear more info from our mole; he supposed to tell to us later tonight to where exactly Dick is being held."

Chedwiggen rubbed his eyes. "There's more Steve. It seems there's also another Al Qaeda in the works. Our buddy Sadr coughed some details about another possible attack on the Azores. The Black Ops team that sunk the Sierra Mist is still on standby we could move them in a flash."

Hawkins grinned. "How prepared is that Marine Force Recon team that you have training in Fort Pendleton? How long would you be able to train them to do a rescue mission in the desert?"

Chedwiggen chuckled. "Something like going into Pakistan to get Dick?"

"Exactly, on short notice."

"You'd be looking at couple of days to finish training, and maybe 2 weeks to setup transport and shelter in Pakistan."

"Start working on it, use whatever resources you need, remember, mums the word." Chedwiggen nodded as he raised his coffee up, Hawkins raised his cup, "let's drink to Dick's safe return, no matter what the cost."

Pasco, Washington
14-June-2010
0600 Hours Local Time

Unseen Warriors

The massive barge docked at Pasco, Washington. The Stevedoring Company quickly unloaded the containers onto the lot, and then cross-matched the numbers with the ships load manifest. Babajhan stood with Grote on the pier watching the activities, soon a large tractor-trailer pull up to the lot.

"Gimme the money," grunted Grote.

"When the container gets on the truck, you will be paid fully."

Grote snarled as he looked down at the briefcase Babajhan carried, lighting another cigarette Grote watched the container being loaded on a tractor-trailer.

"3331679, there she goes on the truck, let's go to my secluded cabin. There you can count your money. Also I have a bonus payment for prompt delivery." Grote grunted in agreement as the two sat into a waiting car.

Driving to the outskirts of Pasco, Grote and Babajhan entered an old farmhouse. Babajhan opened his briefcase on a dusty table, and dumped the contents of his duffle bag on the table. Brand new crisp one hundred dollar bills still in their wrappers covered the table. "You will see there is exactly one million, three hundred thousand dollars on the table, go ahead count away."

Grote grabbed each stack of bills, counting the bills one by one. Babajhan sat back on his chair and watched in glee. Grote turned his back to him and continued counting his money. Babajhan pulled out his Makarov, threaded a silencer on the end. He fired two rounds into Grote's back. Grote instantly went down face first to the wooden floor.

Babajhan picked up the extended casing and put them in his pocket. He dumped the money into the duffle bag and walked. He carried the goods off into the waiting BMW. Sitting in the back seat, he took off his leather gloves and removed the silencer. After unloading his Makarov, he looked over to the man sitting next to him. The figure, wearing a dark suit wiped his forehead. "Have you taken care of the loose ends?"

"Yes, Captain Grote will not be a problem anymore," Babajhan replied.

"Good, I have taken care of our loose ends with the Christina. Captain Santos happened to be smoking on the bridge wing when he slipped off the deck into the Columbia River."

Babajhan smiled as the other man lowered his hat. "Allah Akbar," the two chanted as the BMW drove onto an on ramp to the eastbound Interstate 84 lanes.

Chapter 11

US Marine Corps training ground
Camp Pendleton
14-June-2010
0700 Hours Local Time

Lieutenant Skinner stood at the guardrail watching the troops train below. Back and forth the two squads practiced house clearing exercises; smoke grenades crackled below as the team members shouted at each other.

Major Sweatman joined Skinner to watch the action below. "How long before they're up to snuff?"

"I think they're good right now, I'm just having Sergeant Gibson ride them a little hard to keep their edge."

"Is the word coming down?"

Sweatman nodded his head. "Yeah, I expect orders to ship out anytime. Both squads are going on the mission."

"Do you know what exactly the mission is?"

Sweatman sighed. "It's a high value extraction from deep inside enemy territory, probably in Pakistan or Afghanistan. The mission is top secret. It came directly from the Chief of Staff and the President."

"I hope Hawkins isn't micro managing the war again."

"No, it's bigger, way bigger than that."

Skinner remained transfixed on the action below as Sweatman walked away.

* * * * *

Sergeant Gibson sat cleaning his M-4. The bolt upper receiver was detached on his desk while he cleaned the lower receiver. Completing the cleaning of the lower receiver, he began to disassemble the bolt carrier and bolt head for cleaning. Looking up he saw Corporal Stoner standing in front of him watching him clean his rifle.

"What is it Corporal Stoner?"

"Sergeant, it's been three months since I spoke to my wife, can I take leave?"

Gibson began to frown as stared at Stoner. "No! You signed up and you knew the risks. We all train together, we fight together, and if necessary, we die together. We haven't been training just to lose a few calories, a mission's coming up. Get back into the other room and start cleaning your rifle!"

"But, sergeant, just one…"

"Corporal Stoner, I won't jeopardize my mission and the lives of my entire team because you are lonely. If you don't get your rear next door, I'm going to make sure you spend your entire life in Leavenworth. You'll never see your wife, understood?"

"Yes, Sergeant." The soldier sulked. He turned and walked out to the cleaning room.

Lieutenant Skinner watched the soldier storm away unaware of Skinner a few feet away. Skinner walking into Gibson's cleaning station and cleared his throat. Gibson stood to attention and saluted Skinner. "What was that all about?"

"Oh, that kid is lonely again, wants off to see his wife. Isolation has been hard on the team. They're starting to get a little restless."

Unseen Warriors

Skinner rubbed his chin. "Stuff happens, looks like your doing a good job keeping it in check. Anyways, Colonel Siemienczuk wants us upstairs for a high level meeting in the orange room." Gibson joined Skinner as they made their way up the stairs. Marines saluted Skinner as they went by. Skinner returned the salute, keeping his face straight.

The two finally arrived at the orange room, Skinner knocked. "Enter" was shouted from behind the door. As Skinner entered, Gibson looked around. There was a large table in the center of the room. Seated at the head was Colonel Siemienczuk, to his right sat Captain Watkins. To Siemienczuk left sat Major Sweatman. Skinner proceeded to sit down beside Major Sweatman.

Siemienczuk looked deeply into Gibson's eyes. Gibson could see the veins in his eyes standing up. "Take your seat beside Captain Watkins," commanded Siemienczuk. Siemienczuk looked around the room and spoke.

"Gentlemen, Lieutenant Townsend, a US Army officer was captured while on patrol in north Korea by Ali Mansoor's henchmen. We have orders directly from the president, to rescue him from his captors. Major Sweatman will give you the details."

Sweatman put on his reading glasses and read from a document. "Thank you, sir. Lieutenant Townsend is being held under heavy guard on Mansoor's Palace in Uch Sharif, about 300 miles northeast of Karachi. The building is a large concrete structure. There is a large, flat hill west of the structure. The area around the building is covered with residential homes. West of the Palace there is a small village, sort of a slum.

"The 1st Marine Expeditionary Force will be leaving Okinawa in a couple of days. Sergeant Gibson, your team will fly off the deck on a MV-22 from the USS Tarawa you will then fly low level through Hingol National park west of Moenjodara to the Palace compound.

"The MV-22 will set on a small hill between the Palace and village. One fire team will secure the landing zone and keep the area clear until extraction. The other team will proceed to the Palace and rescue Townsend. After rescue site is secured, the MV-22 will pick up Townsend and team Alpha from the roof. Bravo team will be picked up from the berm. Treat all contacts as hostile. Captain Watkins, give the rest of the Intel.

"Ground forces appear to Pakistani regulars, poorly trained with limited equipment. Intel reports they have neither night vision nor dedicated machine gun emplacements. Enemy air resources are not expected to on alert.

"The MV-22's will circle the sight for limited fire support. If any of the rotorcraft is sighted outside Uch Sharif, the mission is scrubbed.

"Weather is too clear, full moon, night temperature 80F. Intel expects Townsend to be moved to Islamabad on June 27, 2010. Unfortunately, we have to do this mission on a full moon.

"Are there any questions?" Siemienczuk looked around. The room stayed silent. "Alright, Sergeant Gibson you, Lieutenant Skinner, and your team will be transported on a Tower Air flight out of LAX immediately. From there you will fly to Tokyo. You will then catch a military transport to the USS Tarawa docked in Okinawa. Do not reveal any details until you are deployed on the MV-22. We are adjourned."

Gibson stepped out with Skinner. Walking down the halls he whispered quietly, "We're going to risk two full teams for one lousy Lieutenant? Is Hawkins crazy?"

Skinner shrugged his shoulders. "I don't know. I just have a bad feeling about this. Doing a mission like this on a clear night with a full moon is just too risky." Gibson shook his head in agreement.

The team took a transport to LAX. From there they flew on Tower air to Japan. The soldiers relaxed on the flight. The knowledge that they were going to combat relieved their tension. The months waiting for combat had been hard on their moral. The total disconnection from family members and the outside world had left them yearning for a mission. Any kind of mission, no matter what the risk was welcome. Some had even taken to praying for war just so the isolation would end.

From Japan they took a short flight to Okinawa, then a quick ride on a CH-53E to a departing USS Tarawa (LHA-1). The MEU carrier was small. It only carried a small squadron of Harrier jump jets and various helicopters: CH53E, MV-22, AH-1W gunships. Several LCAC's were carried in the ship's hold.

Major Sweatman and Lieutenant Skinner walked out of the CH-53 breathing in the salt air. The two men felt at home. Skinner looked over to Sweatman. "When do we get orders to attack?"

"We'll get coded orders to attack, or scrub the mission in about two days. The ship should be off the coast in about three days."

Skinner nodded in agreement, "The time has finally come."

Skinner and Sweatman walked into their stateroom and unloaded their gear. They changed into their Battle dress uniforms and they sat down on their respective beds. The two men relaxed. A Marine Corporal appeared at the door and saluted. "Sirs, Colonel Somdahl requests your presence at the conference room." The two officers got up and followed the young corporal down the maze of passageways to the colonel's stateroom.

The Corporal knocked at the door. "Enter," shouted a voice behind the door. The two walked in to see the colonel sitting behind a large desk. "You can be seated," Somdahl barked to the two men. Skinner sat to the left of Somdahl, Sweatman to the right.

Somdahl looked to the major, "I want to see your orders." Skinner pulled out his leather bound briefcase and opened it up. He pulled a large folder he handed it to Somdahl. Somdahl inspected the documents, his lip began to curl, the lines in his forehead deepened. His face turned red with anger. Looking up to Skinner, he rubbed his shaved head. "This is the stupidest mission I've ever seen. I have never had a mission full moon with a clear night!" Somdahl breathed in deeply.

"I have 2 MV-22 training right now with experienced crews. I'll equip them in full attack configuration so they can give you some cover after they drop you off at the LZ. Unfortunately, in that configuration they don't have the range to go all the way to the LZ. I'll arrange for a tanker offshore from Pakistan. Expect your deployment date to be 20 June 2010, 22:00 hours local time, dismissed." The two officers walked out, Somdahl continued to shake his head.

CIA Headquarters
Langley, Virginia
20-June-2010
0700 Hours Local Time

CIA director Henry Lee sat at his desk. He continually shook his head as he read the documents. He paused for a second and looked at the picture of his daughter on his desk. In two more weeks she was getting married in Everett. *It was yesterday when she started grade school. If only I had more time with her. Where has the time gone?* Henry wondered. Henry looked up, his assistant Thomas Jeffries, stood in the open doorway. Henry put down his glasses, rubbed his eyes and spoke, "What is it, Thomas?"

"Here is the rest of the Intel about Townsend. Our mole says he will be offline for a few weeks. Townsend is expected to stay at his present location until the first of July at the minimum.

"He also says that there is a major terrorist attack on the US planned for next month. He says he thinks that it may be on the east coast. The end of his transmission got garbled up a bit, and he keeps mentioning a name over Haroon Babajhan. I haven't found anything about such a person in any of our databases."

"When is he going to get back to us again Thomas?"

"Not sure, he did say that he isn't going to respond for awhile. Seems he thinks Mansoor is catching on to him. He's going underground for awhile."

"Thank you, Thomas, I'll review these documents, I have a meeting with President tomorrow."

Unseen Warriors

Henry read the documents some more. *What did they mean?* he wondered. The documents warned of an attack on the pearl of the United States. Henry read a strange passage. It said, *We will attack on the cities that continue to harass the Arab world. We will watch those cities burn and sink into the ocean.* Henry continued to ponder the meaning of these passages. *Could it be that there would be another attack on the Pentagon like 911? New York, Washington, D.C.? Which city was the Pearl?* Henry grabbed the phone. It was time to call Admiral Chedwiggen.

USS Tarawa
Indian Ocean
20-June-2010
2200 Hours Local Time

Lieutenant Skinner rounded the team up in one of the ship's tiny briefing rooms. With Sergeant Gibson at his side, he went over the entire mission. Pick up points, weather and attack plans. Expecting groans and questions, Skinner became surprised as the team stayed quiet, unconcerned above the extraordinarily high level of risk in the mission. The team rushed out of their briefing, they were ready to fight and fight hard. Sergeant Gibson looked to Skinner, "Which chopper do you want?"

"I'll take the wingman. You take the lead, set up your perimeter when you get to the LZ."

Gibson nodded as the team rushed to get into helicopters. Gibson gave Skinner a quick salute as he rushed into the tailgate of the waiting MV-22. Gibson looked out the window as the tailgate went up. He knew the time for action had come. Gibson looked up to the sky. The night sky was bright. The full moon illuminated the sea far into the distance.

Captain Lewis commanded the giant helicopter, he pulled the collective lever up transferring torque from the engines to the to rotor blades. The aircraft began to rise off the deck. Lewis pushed the control stick forward causing the nose to dip down as the massive aircraft began to gain airspeed. The aircraft began to rise as it gained airspeed; soon its airspeed increased enough for him to tilt the rotors forward position allowing the aircraft to transition into fast horizontal flight. The rotorcraft accelerated to 200kts, finally leveling at ten thousand feet in the clear cloudless night. The rotorcraft continued to fly for an hour until it was 250 miles off the Pakistani coast in the Arabian Sea.

Lieutenant Torrance sat in the copilot's seat of the might Osprey. He sat looking at his color displays. He then looked nervously out the window while keeping one eye on his Navigation display. "Two minutes until we make up with the tanker." Lewis nodded his head in agreement. "Exxon, this is Street Gang One-one, we're ready for a fill," Lewis called with his raspy voice.

"Copy Street Gang One, we're at angel ten zero, two hundred knots. You're cleared all the way in, port side."

Just as the call cleared, Lewis saw the distant lights of the massive C-130 tanker in the night's sky. Torrance began motioning with his hands as the call on the radio, "Street Gang One-one has visual on Exxon." The massive aircraft closed in on the C-130, Lewis skillfully guided the five-foot refueling probe into the hanging basket. Lewis watched with a mesmerized look at the massive turboprop aircraft ahead of him. Torrance watched the fuel quantity figures on his display change until they registered full. Lewis reduced the torque on the massive engines, allowing the aircraft to drift several feet behind the now detached basket. Torrance looked over and watched their wingman detach in an almost synchronized fashion.

Lewis continued to reduce torque until the aircraft slowed to 170 knots, The MV-22 plunged earthward, wingman in tow until they were a mere fifty feet above the waters of the Arabian Sea. Torrance nervously looked at the Threat Warning indicator page on his display. There were no radars in the night sky painting them. Torrance began to nervously shift in his seat as they began to fly overhead Hingol National Park. Lewis looked

Unseen Warriors

over to Torrance, bored from the blackness outside the windshield. "What's up Razor, you look like you've seen a ghost?"

"It's too quiet, Grandpa, there's nothing out there. No radar, lights, not even a car is visible on the road."

"Relax, it just means that we got here in perfect stealth. We'll have a smooth ride to Uch Sharif."

* * * * *

Sergeant Gibson looked out into the ground below. There was total and utter darkness, no lights, fires or even vehicles. Nothing seemed to move. There were neither men, nor machine, nor animals in the distance. Gibson wondered what surprises lay ahead in this hostile land.

Bored, he looked over at Corporal Stoner, sitting beside him. Stoner nervously twitched his left hand while clutching his rifle's barrel. Gibson finally broke the tension by speaking up, "What's up Stoner, why so glum?"

"Sergeant, I'm scared, I don't know why but I'm afraid to die. I had a vision while reading my Bible last night. Our aircraft burned to the ground, soldiers lay all around burning while villagers danced around the dead bodies. I lay on the ground bleeding..."

Gibson's temper exploded. "Enough Stoner, those visions are nothing but nightmares. You are a United States Marine equipped with the very finest equipment money can buy. You have been trained to fight in the most elite unit in the USMC. I order you stop speaking of this visions nonsense. I will not have you destroy the moral of the entire squad with talk of visions of doom and gloom. You have a job to do as a Marine and you will do it above and beyond the call of duty, understand?" Stoner reluctantly nodded in agreement. Gibson shook his head, "Religious fools, and next he'll be talking about seeing angels and stars in the eastern sky."

Gavin Parmar

* * * * *

Torrance looked down at his displays. The Osprey had just passed Moenjodaro. They were just a hundred miles from the landing zone. There still was nothing on the TWI. Torrance wondered if it was broken. "Hey, Grandpa, do you think they're on to us, maybe they're planning and ambush."

Lewis snorted and let out a loud chuckle, "Don't you think that if they were onto us, they'd have shot us down by now? After all we're practically in downtown Pakistan."

Torrance felt small in his seat, he had a nagging feeling, but common sense suggested otherwise. Looking down on his display, he checked the clock. They had been in the air almost three hours. The tension mixed with the boredom made the night that much longer.

Torrance continued to look at his displays. They would soon be within visual range of the Palace. Looking through his night vision, he spotted something. "I see the Palace at one o'clock" He announced with renewed vigor and enthusiasm.

"Street Gang One-two, one-one is transitioning. Palace is in visual range, one o'clock." The massive rotor blades rotated back to the vertical position.

"Copy" The wingman answered in a raspy voice.

Lewis slowed the aircraft to 100 Knots as the hill came into sight. The hill was not much more than a large dirt pile covered with rocks and shrubs. About one hundred eighty feet high, eight feet long and about eight thousand feet long it was a perfect landing spot. It had enough cover for the team to avoid detection.

"How much time must we hang around before we have to depart back to the boat?" Lewis asked Torrance

"We've got fuel for about forty-five minutes of loitering time if we keep fifteen minutes of reserve fuel," Torrance nervously answered.

Unseen Warriors

Lewis nodded in approval. He called Sergeant Gibson on the PA, "You've got forty minutes. Any more and we'll swim back to the boat."

"Copy." Gibson pulled his M-4's charging handle chambering a round. "Guns up!" Gibson shouted over the roar of the rotor blades. The rest of the team collectively pulled their charging handles.

"Stoner, Kenyon, Horner, Embry, I want you four to set up a perimeter around the chopper. Clear any unfriendly forces before the next chopper lands. The rest of you, follow me, understood?"

The team gave a collective, "Yes, Sergeant."

"Semper Fi," Gibson announced to the team.

The huge rotorcraft landed on top of the hill, the massive tail ramp dropped open as the rotor blades kicked up dust and dirt into the air. The team rushed out taking positions around the mighty helicopter. Gibson put his night vision monocle on a weaver rail in front of his red dot scope on top of his rifle's barrel. Looking through the red dot, in the prone position, he searched for unseen enemies. Gibson anguished at the lack of any enemy forces, while the sound of rotors beating the air grew louder.

Lewis climbed into the air as his wingman approached gear down. The two helicopters passed each like a couple of elevators. Gibson stepped closer to the edge of the hill, watching the two helicopters pass each other. A flash blinded Gibson's night vision for a second, while recovering his sight he gasped in horror at the sight he viewed. The wingman's cabin exploded into flames. Flames poured through the cockpit windows as the massive aircraft rolled into the wing of Lewis' helicopter.

* * * * *

Lewis struggled to control his aircraft as his EICAS display filled with warning messages. The stricken helicopter continued to roll like a barrel until it struck the ground, cart wheeling again several times before exploding into flames at the base of the hill.

    Lewis struggled to remove his seat belts, frustrated he pulled out his knife cutting off his seatbelts. Freeing himself, he grabbed the crash axe. He shattered the windshield into pieces, and then he grabbed an unconscious Torrance. Lewis madly cut off his seatbelts and dragged his stricken copilot out of the burning aircraft. Lewis tried desperately to revive Torrance, unable he wiped the blood from Torrance's head. Lewis desperately tried to focus his eyes while rubbing his eyes. He quickly pulled his hand back as pain shot through his nose. Lewis looked up at the top of the hill. Flames continue to burn around the hull of the crashed MV-22. He then pulled out his radio trying to call for a rescue plane. Lewis tried several times to raise the USS Tarawa. All he got was static. Growing frustrated, he threw the radio away into the brush. Lewis became tensed up as he heard loud noises in distance. Lewis turned his face toward the village, horror filled his eyes as he watched villagers armed with pick axes and shovels swarm into his direction.

* * * * *

    Gibson grabbed his men as Skinner's helicopter plunged into the ground. Marines jumped out of the stricken aircraft, their bodies covered in flames. Gibson ran to Private Allen, grabbing his radio he called, "Almighty, this is Sleeping King, both transports out of service, please send rescue party ASAP!" The only reply Gibson received was static.

    Gibson frantically led his men to the bottom of the hill. Looking through his binoculars he scanned the compound and its inner perimeter. The troops continued to guard the compound unconcerned with the ruckus in the distance.

    In the background, coming from the other side of the hill, Gibson could hear 9mm gunfire, frantic screams and shouts in

Arabic. Gibson moved his team into a small crevice covered by shrubbery, and tried to calm his troops who became perturbed the background noises.

Gibson peered out with his binoculars looked around and saw the compound. In the middle there was a large concrete two-story building. The rooftop terrace contained several guards patrolling with Heckler and Koch PSG-1 sniper rifles. The palace was encircled by a five foot concrete wall which had breaks every thirty feet large enough for a man to pass through. The Eastern side of the compound, directly opposite of Gibson's position, a small hill overlooked the Palace. There were several machine gun nests and a couple of dilapidated buildings ravaged by the elements. Guards could be seen busying themselves with some meat being cooked on a spit. Others stood smoking while leaning on the mounted machine guns. North of the compound an empty field laid where the ground dropped off into a small valley. On the South side, there was an old single story building. Inside it was dark without any movements.

Gibson dispatched Stoner with his team to the empty building just inside the south wall. Stoner took his team directly to the west wing of the wall. Carefully peering around the corner, Stoner watched several guards lazily watching the burning wreckage from afar. Stoner signaled Kenyon to his side, while Horner and Embry watched their backs. Stoner fired several rounds at the distant guards with his suppressed M-16. The guards looked around unable to discern the direction of the incoming gunfire. Private Kenyon fired a quick shot. The lead soldier grabbed his stomach as he screamed in pain. His buddy began to wildly fire automatic gunfire into Kenyon's direction unable to see their foe. Kenyon fired another precision shot causing the guard's head to explode like a watermelon. Blood and brains sprayed in all directions. Another guard threw grenades at the team's direction. The grenades fell far short of any Marines. Stoner fired a single shot to his chest. The guard fell to his knees when the grenade in his hand exploded leaving the bloody stump of his arm.

*****

Gibson rushed his team to the west wall. Looking around he could not see any guards. Gibson continued to head north until he arrived at the northwest wall corner. Looking north he saw the field spread out as far as the eye could see pockmarked with Tracked SA-15 SAM Launchers camouflaged with brush and netting. Gibson shook his head. *How could have Intel have missed all the SAMs?* Gibson wondered. *The only way was that they had not been there until recently, the Pakistanis had been planning an ambush all along,* he thought. Gibson shook his head in horror as he thought of Stoner's visions.

Gibson continued east along the North wall, carefully looking out for patrols. After walking some two hundred feet, the team found a break in the wall leading to a fortified entrance to the Palace. Several Guards stood in front of the main doors with their Heckler Koch 91 rifles. Above on a second story terrace, snipers stood with their

PSG-1 sniper rifles trained on the distance. Gibson leaned back and pulled out a chocolate bar and began to eat, looking over to Private Taylor he spoke between bites, "Looks like we're going to have to wait for our diversion." Taylor nodded in agreement.

*****

Traveling on the south wall eastward, Stoner closed toward the dark single story building. One by on the team entered a small gap in the wall until they were standing under a glass window on the south face of the building. Just a few feet to the left of the building there was a tattered door that entered into the building. Stoner picked up his grenade and shook it. His team members followed suite. Each team member stood ready with one hand on the pin ready to throw. Stoner threw his grenade into the window, glass shattered as his team mates grenades followed suite. The team hid down, covering their faces as screams and yelling were heard followed by the muffled sound of grenades exploding echoing through the building.

Stoner kicked the door down and rushed his team into the building. In the main room several fighters lay bleeding and dying surrounded by women and children. Stoner tried to look over the mangled bodies while retaining his composure. The rest of the team followed while trying desperately trying to avoid walking near the grizzly scene.

Stoner walked up to small hallway that separated two rooms. One room was on the north side while the other was on the south side of the home. Stoner split his team between the two rooms, he signaled with his fingers causing each team to throw a grenade into their respective rooms before hiding their faces. The building shook as loud explosions erupted in the rooms. Slate tiles fell from overhead as smoke poured out of the doorways. Each team rushed into their respective rooms only to find broken pottery and shredded goat meat everywhere.

Regrouping in the hallway Stoner motioned with his hand to Horner. Horner rushed outside and walked along the south wall until he found a frail ladder. Putting it along the buildings' concrete wall, he climbed up until he reached the red slate roof. He crawled along the roof he got a comfortable spot while using the roof's peek for a cover from inquisitive eyes. He then unclipped his bipod, adjusted the magnification on his scope and trained his cross hairs on the Palace snipers.

Stoner broke out an east facing window with the butt of his stock Embry and Kenyon followed suite breaking the shoulder height windows in the adjacent rooms then training their sights on the distance guards manning the machine guns.

Stoner looked up through the broken roof slates and began to nod his head at Private Horner. Horner propped his shoulders on the broken slates, then fired at a lonesome sniper. The bullet tore into the man's neck. While he grabbed, it gasping to breathe, a fellow guard crouching behind a small rail rushed to come to his comrade's aid. As he approached, a bullet tore into his elbow causing his rifle to fall out of his hand. The man fell to the ground onto the concrete terrace. As he tried to get up, another bullet tore into his skull, easily shredding his plastic helmet. The third guard stood up trying to comprehend the happenings going on, a bullet tore into the base of his skull under his helmet causing him to fall over the concrete rail onto the ground below. The first guard struggled in pain as his comrades died around him until he could no longer breathe.

Horner scanned the area above the rooftop for snipers, unable to see, he shifted his position until he faced the east hill. Slates crashed to the floor from the open roof as Horner signaled Stoner.

Before Stoner could move a muscle, Embry unpacked his M136 anti-tank rocket and aimed at the distant machine gun nest. Embry held still while the three guards continued on their business totally ignorant to the violence just three hundred yards away. The three guards slowly walked to a machine gun nest surrounded by large wooden crates and stacks of open green ammo cans. The three continued to smoke while looking at the palace rooftop with a confused look.

Embry fired. A flash blinded in the team's eyes as the rocket flew across the compound slamming into the cans of linked machine gun ammunition. A blinding explosion occurred while secondary explosions caused the crates of grenades explode, pock marking the east hill with shrapnel. Body parts, Ammo cans and other debris rained down from the sky as the explosion and ensuing fire burned vaporized any soldiers who would be near.

Rounds came slamming into the roof tiles, ricocheting wildly into the night. Horner ducked as slates broke all around

Unseen Warriors

spraying him the ceramic shrapnel. Pain covered his body as it bruised from the ceramic projectiles.

Soldiers appeared from every nook and cranny around the east hill. They wildly sprayed the walls of the concrete structure with bullets from automatic gunfire, unable to see their hidden foes.

Embry fired another rocket into the southeastern side of the hill. Enemy soldiers grabbed their eyes in pain as the rocket went by before it slammed into an old fuel truck. The truck burst into a blinding explosion as flames leapt skywards hundreds of feet in the air. Burning diesel fuel rained down on the soldiers shooting. The Pakistanis screamed in pain as burning fuel set their bodies on fire while shrapnel from the tanker truck tore their bodies open. Blood sprayed everywhere soaking the beige sand, until it turned red.

More troops rushed from around the corner toward the building, the team continued to fire their M-4s at them. The enemy combatants barely were able to raise their rifles until gunfire cut them down. They lay on the concrete screaming in pain, only to be met by more bullets, which put them out of their misery.

* * * * *

A loud explosion shook the ground from the west. The Pakistani guards covered their eyes from the brightness that lit up the sky. They shouted madly to each other, and then they ran into the direction of the east hill leaving the front door unguarded.

Gibson walked forward several feet while being followed by his machine gunner private Taylor, then Private Douglas and Allen. Gibson pointed at the terrace where the snipers lay undisturbed. Gibson pulled the pin on a grenade. After counting for two seconds he threw it up in the air above the terrace. The guards screamed at the sight of the grenade in midair. Before they could move, it exploded. The force of the blast blew the two snipers overboard onto the ground below.

Gibson and his team rushed into the doorway with guns drawn all the while looking for hidden snipers. The doorway opened into a large foyer, concrete steps led up to second story balcony. A darkened hallway led away in the second story out of sight. Sweeping the room with their rifles, Gibson checked every nook and cranny until he was satisfied that the foyer was free of enemy soldiers.

Gibson relaxed for a second; while sitting down on the cold floor he commanded his team. "Douglas, Taylor, go clear the second floor while I try to raise our ride on the radio."

Douglas slowly walked up the steps. Carefully he swept the balcony for shadows or movement. Satisfied, he led Taylor down to the darkened hallway. The hallway was straight. Windows opened up on the south wall, while on the opposite side there were several doors leading into concrete walled rooms. Lighting was minimal. Three lights barely illuminated parts of the wall. The team carefully broke down each of the doors, only to reveal broken pottery and empty ammo cans.

The two slowly made their way the one hundred yards to the third floor steps. The steps now went north half a story to a darkened room. Douglas swept the steps with his rifle, no shadows or movement was seen, and Douglas pained to see around the steps on the third floor.

"Click,", Douglas heard the sound like that of a twig breaking, intense pain came over his throat as he found breathing impossible. Grabbing his throat, he dropped his rifle as he gasped and coughed as blood filled his lungs.

Taylor flinched at the sound, panicking he found himself unable pull the trigger. He heard the same sound again then his throat became covered in intense pain. He tried to scream, but no sound came. He looked around to see Douglas bleeding and convulsing on ground. Taylor fell to the ground, resigned that death soon would be upon him.

Unseen Warriors

* * * * *

Corporal Stoner rushed his team out of the small building toward the south side of the Palace. Quickly rushing around the inner perimeter, he swept the area for any hidden forces lurking among the flames. The team rushed around, carefully walking around the dead soldiers and their pools of blood. Finally locating the main entrance, Stoner stormed in to see Gibson sitting on the ground.

Stoner walked up to Gibson, while unhooking his helmet clasp, "So, how did we do with our diversion?"

"Very good, you cleared almost the entire front entrance. Our Intel was sure dead wrong. I saw SAM launchers in the north field."

"Tell me about it, we had to out gun a bunch of machine gun nests on the east wall. Boy he guys in the CIA really screwed this one up. Lance Corporal Allen, have you been able to raise the boat yet?"

"Naw, I get nothing but static."

Gibson became angry "Keep trying to raise the boat! Embry, Horner you guys follow me. We need to find out what's taking Taylor and Douglas so long." Gibson began walking up the steps while his team followed several yards behind.

Stoner grabbed Allen's radio, "Almighty this is Sleeping King, come in!"

"Sleeping King, this is Almighty, please report."

"Both transports are down! We need pickup ASAP!"

"Rescue will be in the air, what is your position?" Allen began to tug at Stoner's uniform as he pointed with his hand. Stoner looked up at a dark window at top of the roof at the third party. A head seemed to be moving behind the darkened glass.

Stoner heard glass break, then a strange pop. An explosion broke overhead slamming shrapnel into Stoners' team as well as the radio. Gibson lost his balance and rolled down the steps while knocking Embry and Horner off the steps onto the concrete floor below.

Barely conscious, Gibson turned around. His night vision monocle was smashed. Trying to peer through the dim light he looked at his bleeding teammates on the floor. The radio continued to sound, "Sleeping King, what is your position, please contact, we can't send rescue without your position!" A bullet slammed into the radio shattering it as flames briefly shot out of the box. Gibson tried to grab his rifle, the pain raced through his arm. He couldn't move his wrist. He knew it was broken. He tried to move his leg, the pain shot up and down his thigh and knee. Looking up at Horner he saw a large black boot. Gibson breathed in and closed his eyes. The boot swiftly met his face, causing him to disappear into unconsciousness.

Chapter 12

1600 Pennsylvania avenue
Washington, DC
20-June-2010
0600 Hours Local Time

"What do you mean the rescue choppers failed?" Hawkins' face grew red with anger and rage.

"Mr. President, the mission was high risk, any kind of…"

"Shut up Bill, I don't want excuses, what happened to the choppers?"

"Sir, may I interject?"

"Go ahead, Admiral."

"The MV-22 seems to have been shot down at the LZ, the sergeant reported the crash. We didn't get any info about his location nor the status of any other soldiers. Unfortunately, Pakistan immediately tightened up its airspace. Getting a high altitude Recon aircraft would be risky. It would get shot down before it even got close."

Hawkins' anger began to explode into sheer rage that he directed at anyone he saw. He then directed his wrath at the CIA Director's way. "Henry, what went wrong with our Intel?"

"I'm not sure, we haven't heard from our mole for a couple of days. In the last transmission he warned us about a strange Al Qaeda plot. He said something about the burning our cities that wage war with the Arab world. Apparently Townsend's capture was the first step. I'm sorry, sir but that's all I've got to work on."

Hawkins shook his head, this morning's meeting was going to be much rougher than most. Hawkins began to wonder what kind of bad publicity this incident would give him. "Tim, how much information of last night's attack has been spilled to the general public."

Tim Goulet, Hawkins' press secretary, sat nervously, contemplating his next answer. He knew last night's raid was a publicity disaster. Either way, his answer would infuriate Hawkins. "I'm not sure yet, but to be frank, sir, we need to tell the public before the Pakistanis do. Seeing pictures of the burned MV-22s hulls on CNN would bring back a public backlash like Clinton received after Somalia. Our image among the public is already severally damaged because of that suicide attack in Baghdad that killed twenty US Marines."

Goulet's cellular phone rang loudly like a fire truck siren. Hawkins looked at him, anger burned in his eyes as he rubbed his chin. Goulet quickly pulled out his phone and began to speak angrily. "Yes, this better be good, or you just lost your job! Huh, yes, no way, all right I'll tell the President right away. "Sir, our secret raid has been blown wide open."

Hawkins snarled his face, "What does that mean!"

"Al Jazeera just broadcast images about last night's raid this morning. Apparently it shows wreckage of last night's raid plus more."

Hawkins shook his head, "Can this day get any worse?"

"My aid is bringing the tape in right now, judge for yourself, sir." Goulet's aid rushed in, he was out of breath and profusely sweating. He put the tape into the room's VCR. Turning up the volume, he stepped away, fearing the glaring eyes staring at him.

The tape opened up with the burned hull of the MV-22, the words "Marines" was proudly displayed on its aft hull. A large US flag was seen on the aircraft's vertical stabilizer, children threw rocks at it. The camera zoomed out to show the complete blackened hull. Adults were shown looting guns, ammunition and anything else of value from the stricken hull.

The camera panned away to an open field by the hill. Villagers armed with AK-47s dragged the dead bodies of the helicopter's pilots through the streets. Villagers threw their shoes at the bodies while others spit in the airmen's faces. Villagers chanted to Allah as they kicked the bodies, others posed with the dead bodies. Others joyously shot their captured M-16s in the air while burning American flags and shouting "Death to America, death to Hawkins!"

The camera then showed a beaten American soldier sitting on a concrete floor. His uniform was dirt, torn and splattered in several spots with dried blood. A reporter brought a microphone to the face of the beaten soldier. He asked the stricken soldier in a cold, indifferent voice, "What is your name?"

"Sergeant Charles Gibson?"

"What is the branch of service you are from?"

"United states Marine Corps, Serial number 392705163."

"What was your mission in peaceful Pakistan?"

Gibson continued to speak in a cold scripted voice, "We were sent to overthrow the peaceful government of Ali Mansoor and to install a puppet regime of deviants who were to persecute all those who follow Islam." Gibson raised his hand clasping all his hand except for his middle trigger, rubbing his nose and upper lip with it.

The camera slowly panned to a room with Pakistan's chief cleric Akbar Ali. Ali stood wearing transitional robes, running his hands through this way white beard. The sixty-year-old cleric scowled while he spoke in Arabic. The narrator translated in English, "the American infidels have violated our soil, and the land is red with Muslim blood. I declare a Fatwa against the infidel American nation. I command all Muslims across the world to destroy Americans wherever they see them."

The tape ended with more shots of the burned out MV-22s. Hawkins looked to Chedwiggen, "Admiral you have disappointed me for the last time. I want your retirement letter on my desk before you go home. Understood?"

"Yes, sir!"

"Now get out of my briefing, I never want to see you ever again!" A secret service agent came over and stood beside Chedwiggen. Feeling devastated, Chedwiggen got up out of his seat, and he began to walk out the room, a secret service agent in tow.

Looking at the secret service agent, Chedwiggen spoke with a glum face. "I joined the Navy when I was 18 in 1978. Later I got my commission and I learned how to fly an F/A-18. I did my first tour on the USS Forestall. After that my career skyrocketed and by 1996 I was promoted to Rear Admiral. When I made chief of staff, I thought it was the crown jewel in my career. I would put a four year term with Hawkins then retire to a quiet cabin in New Hampshire. I always put the Navy ahead of everything; I never married or raised any children. The military was my marriage. Now I'm a humiliated old soldier. Hawkins didn't even let me stay for the end of the briefing."

Walking out of the White house, Chedwiggen looked at the secret service agent. The agent gave him a cold stare, "Sir there is a car waiting for you." Chedwiggen gave a confused look. A black Volvo sedan pulled in front of Chedwiggen, the secret service agent opened the door. Chedwiggen shook his head then sat down on the black leather seats beside a dark figure.

The Volvo sedan pulled away heading out of Washington D.C., passing the morning commuters. The dark figure turned on his dome light. "Hello, Arthur, how nice to see you again."

Unseen Warriors

Chedwiggen's face became white as a ghost, "James Griswalt, why aren't you at camp Zulu. You deserter, I could have you court-martialed right now!"

Griswalt grinned, "Now is that any way to talk about your brother? Arthur, just because your mom was a billionaire, while mine was a secretary doesn't change anything. We both still had an adulterous father who cared more about him then he did about his own flesh and blood. I know Father loved you more than me. He sure used his connections so you would move up the ranks fast. No sooner did you join the Navy then they warmed up a jet for you to fly.

"I joined the Army so Father wouldn't interfere with my affairs like he did when I tried to join the Navy. Things were going well until you had me shipped to Siberia."

Chedwiggen scowled "I did it because you were a lousy officer, sending you to Siberia saved your career!"

"Arthur Jones, or AJ as you call yourself, are a liar. You sent me to Siberia because you were afraid I would spill the beans about Father. Karen told me about Father's phone call to you. She also told me that you purposely had my leave cancelled so I wouldn't embarrass the family by showing up at Father's funeral last year."

"Karen, my sister spoke to a dirt bag like you. Driver, stop at the next stop, you, Colonel Griswalt are fired!"

"You can't fire me. Thanks to Hawkins you're washout, your career is done. Now if you want to salvage what's left, you will do as I say."

Chedwiggen's face sunk, Griswalt's words cut him down like knife through butter. Rubbing his hand through his balding head, he sighed. "So, what is the plan?"

"First we get breakfast, it's 0700 hours I haven't even eaten yet." Chedwiggen gave a pained look and shook his head. We're going to meet a contact. He's got more details about the plan. For now enjoy the ride. I picked up this 1997 Volvo 850 for five grand. It's only got 100,000 miles, power everything. It's a dream to drive."

Chedwiggen shook his head, "Now today is definitely the worst day of my life."

The Volvo turned onto the I-55, then headed westbound to Virginia pulling off the freeway; the car entered an upscale neighborhood in Fairfax. The car then pulled into a driveway of a plain diner.

"This is it, let's go, Arthur Jones." The two men entered the diner and sat down at an empty booth. The waitress approached, running her hand through her long platinum blonde hair. She poured coffee into two empty cups, "What would gentlemen like to eat?"

"Karla, I want a hot special," Griswalt answered.

Shaking her head, she walked away while running her hand through her hair. "She's old enough to be your daughter, James," Chedwiggen barked.

Breaking out in open laughter, Griswalt couldn't contain himself. "Arthur you are so out of touch. I'll let you in on a secret, that is my daughter and she works for the CIA."

A man followed Karla as she walked toward the two men carrying four plates. Karla placed the plates on in front of the two men, she then she sat beside her father. The man sat beside Chedwiggen, "Hello, AJ, nice to see you again." Chedwiggen gasped as he sat looking into failed 2008 Republican presidential candidate Jonathon Matthews.

"Now that we're all here, here's the plan, announced Griswalt. As you know AJ, the rescue party was captured. Another armed attack would be extremely dangerous. The Pakistani's are fortifying their defenses and cracking down on dissent. The only way we're going to get Townsend and Gibson out is through an inside job. Karla, tell about our options."

"The Pakistani's are funding two large-scale conflicts right now on top of their terrorist activities across the globe. They've been heating up the fighting at the Kashmir border plus they've

Unseen Warriors

been pouring supplies to the Taliban in Afghanistan. Mansoor has been scrambling to get arms and ammunition from all across the globe. If we pose a couple of soldiers as arms dealers, we could get them into Pakistan with free access all over the country. While in their travels, they would be able to free the hostages and their drive back to one of our bases in Afghanistan."

"Listen, missy, I don't think we'll be able to just waltz in like a general into a Colt factory," Chedwiggen cut in with a demeaning tore.

"Of course not, we'll need some Canadian and British passports. We'll also have to set up an office in Lisbon, Portugal. Then we'll ship some arms to Pakistan. That's where we'll need your connections at Heckler and Koch, Admiral.

"Now, we also need a Punjabi speaking soldier to lead the team. He also must be familiar with Muslim custom and religion. He'll be required to play the part of Muslim devout Muslim arms dealer,"

"I have that man." Everybody gasped at Matthews' announcement. "My daughter, Sarah has been dating a fellow soldier. He's an Indian from the Punjab, very skilled and definitely a smooth talker. Maybe one of these days I'll finally get to meet him."

Griswalt laughed. "You must be talking about Private Nishan. They seemed like quite an item when they were under my service. Admiral, in one of your final acts as Chief of Staff you need to transfer Private Nishan, Jonathan Jacobs, Watson and Staff Sergeant Walters at camp Zulu."

"That still doesn't mean anything. We don't even know where the hostages are kept. After all we could spend weeks on this ruse and not..." Chedwiggen protested.

"That's not a problem Admiral. We have a mole in Mansoor's administration. He periodically reports to us through coded messages. He sent a message this morning. Apparently Townsend and Gibson are being held in Islamabad. Mansoor moved Townsend just before the raid. We think he may have been tipped off about the task force heading toward him."

"Fine, but what do I get out of this? After all, even if they get Townsend, all we do is make Hawkins look good," Chedwiggen muttered.

"Simple, after the rescue we come out and tell the media it was entirely your idea, executed by Black Ops. The public will revolt about the incompetence of Hawkins. Hawkins will have to give another more influential post in Washington, D.C. You keep your pension, plus another six-figure salary. I make general with a transfer to the Pentagon. John makes another run for the White house and wins and you get promoted to Secretary of Defense," Griswalt answered in a cold tone.

"There are a lot of ifs in this plan of yours, if we fail…"

"Things would be no different than they are now. Karla will bury the mission in on of those top-secret files. No one will know the difference," Griswalt replied.

"Now Arthur, do you want to end your Navy career in disgrace like this? Think about it, wouldn't Secretary of Defense be the final crown jewel. That's something you could boast about at your Alma Mater."

Chedwiggen sighed; leaning back he watched the ceiling fan spin around and around. Finally he gazed at Griswalt, "Where are we going to get the money for all these weapons?"

Karla gave Chedwiggen an icy stare, "The CIA has plenty of discretionary funds, we have the cash don't worry. Are you in or out?"

Chedwiggen shook his head, "I'm in." He then held out his hand, the four shook hands before quietly departing the diner.

Chapter 13

Islamabad, Pakistan
24-June-2010
1100 Hours Local Time

    Townsend awoke, beams of light cut through the bars into his dark cell. Looking around, the cell was bare except for his tattered hat that lay beside him. He struggled to stand up, while nauseous odors poured in from the outside. *Where am I?* Townsend thought. Townsend stood up and looked out the window. He saw a large Middle Eastern city of concrete homes. Open air markets, crammed streets and Main Square with a set of Gallows. Townsend fell back when he saw the sight of dead men hanging in full public view.
    A guard entered the room. He wore a Pakistani military uniform and carried an MP-5 sub machine gun. "Lieutenant Hawkins, you must follow me," he said in broken English. Townsend followed, while another guard joined behind.
    Townsend walked to a makeshift washing area. The guard handed him a business suit, soap, underwear, shoes and a basic shaving kit. The guard then motioned with his gun for Townsend to enter. Townsend showered in the cold water. The

soap was hard and had a strong aroma. But for Townsend it was the first time in weeks he felt clean. The first time he felt human. Shaving and clothing himself, Townsend couldn't help but look at himself in the cracked mirror. For a brief moment he no longer felt like a captive. Now he looked and felt like a civilian.

The first guard motioned Townsend to follow him. Townsend obliged while the second guard carried his military clothing away. Townsend climbed several flights of steps followed by several hallways around many rooms. Guards appeared all around, their crisp clean uniforms stood out to Townsend. The guards finally came to a couple of double doors.

A couple of Presidential guards opened the doors and Townsend entered a huge room. A huge red rug covered the floor; in the center of the room there was a huge oak conference table. At the head of the table a four star Pakistani general sat.

Looking up he waved Townsend in. Townsend slowly walked in. The general smiled while he rubbing his mustache. The general then motioned to a chair beside him. Townsend silently sat beside the general. "Good morning Mr. Hawkins, I am Ali Mansoor." Townsend stayed silent. "Now Richard, I bring out an olive branch of clean clothes, a shower and upcoming lunch. Yet you still disrespect me this way, why don't you trust me?"

"Simple, I'm your prisoner. I will only give my name rank and serial number."

Mansoor laughed, he then poured tea into his cup followed by Townsend's. "Sir you are my guest, not a prisoner. We have many things in common, many things to speak about, but first let's have lunch."

A white clothed waiter placed a steaming hot plate of Goat Meat and Rice in front of the two. Another waiter placed an orange looking pretzel in front of Townsend. "Eat up, or as you say in America, 'chow down'" Mansoor motioned as he began to eat his rice. Townsend stayed silent failing to move a muscle. Mansoor sighed, and then shook his head. "This is not your last meal. We have plenty to talk about." Townsend remained still and gave a blank stare. "We are both professional soldiers, both officers in our respected militaries. Let's leave politics aside for a second."

Townsend finally relented. The pains of hunger made him unable to resist the sweet-smelling food on the table. Townsend ate hungrily, consuming everything on his plate. Mansoor motioned to his waiter, who quietly brought more food to Townsend. Townsend ate until he was full, wiping off his face he spoke, "Thank you."

Mansoor smiled, "You see, I'm not an evil man like they say I am. Let's go for a walk outside. Mansoor walked with Townsend in tow. A dozen guards armed with HK-91 automatic rifles followed in suit. The procession walked out of the palace into the outer perimeter of the courtyard.

Crowds rushed Mansoor, crushing to get a glimpse as the procession walked into the main square. Mansoor waved his hand in the air as the crowd chanted his name. Mansoor led Townsend to the gallows, waving his hand to the crowds while troops pushed aside the crowd making the square visible. Dead Marine pilots, ground troops, officers and enlisted men alike hung on the gallows with manila rope. Vultures tried to tear off meat from the lifeless bodies. At the base of gallows, debris from the crashed MV-22's was placed all around. Sickened by the spectacle, Townsend vomited on the concrete.

Mansoor nonchalantly handed Townsend a towel as he led him to another one of his Palaces. Entering the Palace, away from the noise of the crowds, Townsend cried. "You seem perturbed Mr. Hawkins. You see your father cared enough to send a rescue party. But for all you high tech electronics and fancy weapons, we are still masters of the desert."

"You're a damn murderer; a cold-blooded killer, a barbarian. You feed and clothe me just to show me your executions!"

"Wrong, I clothed you so that crowd would not kill you. They have lost many of their kinfolk from your bombings in Iraq and

Afghanistan. The mere sight of an American would have incensed that crowd.

"Those soldiers attacked peaceful Pakistan in the middle of the night with guns and airplanes. Their attack was an act of warfare against all my people and me. They were executed like war criminals for indiscriminately killing women and children. I hope your carpenter God can forgive their souls for their sins. Come, I have one more sight to show you."

Mansoor took Townsend and his entourage to another castle looking building. They traveled down a hallway to a dark corner of this castle. Once there they traveled to a dark cramped cellblock. Townsend approached the musty smelling cell. Out of the darkness, Sergeant Gibson appeared. His face was beaten, both eyes were black, and dried blood spotted his face and tattered uniform. Gibson looked up at Townsend with his bloodshot eyes while giving a weak salute. Gibson then spoke in a quivering voice. "Lieutenant Townsend, sir, we were sent to rescue you, I guess we failed you, sir."

Townsend returned the salute. He then looked down at the broken soldier while secretly trying to avoid tears. Finally Townsend spoke in a quiet dignified voice, "No, you did not fail, those who send you failed you." Townsend stood for a moment as the two soldiers looked silently looked at each other while contemplating their futures. Mansoor quickly whisked Townsend off to another stop on his tour of Islamabad.

Gibson sat back down in his cell and curled up into the fetal position as he watched Townsend led away out of sight. A Pakistani officer walked into the cellblock slowly walking until he stopped outside Gibson's cell. He peered in with a cold stare. Gibson hid his face at the sight of Colonel Massoud. "Sergeant Gibson, your illustrious friend, Lieutenant Townsend has spoken. He told us everything we wanted to know. Look at him. He is clean, eats well and dresses in civilian clothing. Mansoor is treating him with the respect the way that Mansoor treats all his guests. Townsend knows America can't win. America has lost the war on terror. Townsend is now reaping the rewards that Pakistan has to offer. We asked him the same simple questions that we asked you. Freedom is there for you, all you have to do is cooperate with us."

"No, you're a damned liar, Townsend would never do that. You're a lying thief. You'll never get any info out of me!"

"Come on Sergeant Gibson, must we go through these silly theatrics every day? Now how do I get into Camp Pendleton?" Gibson hid his face, refusing to speak. Massoud breathed heavily while shaking his head. "You Americans are so stubborn, why can't you do things the easy way?" Massoud motioned with his hands to the guards. He then walked away a few more feet. "I hope for your sake, that you will feel more cooperative tomorrow. I am running out of patience with you."

A large muscle-bound guard rushed into the cell with a large wooden Billy club. Gibson hid his face in the fetal position. A second guard stood watch outside with an HK MP-5 pointed at Gibson. The club wielding guard began rolled up his sleeves. He spit at Gibson while shouting words in Arabic. The guards laughed out loud and pointed at Gibson. The guard then swung his club hitting Gibson in the back. He continued to mercilessly beat Gibson, blow by blow all the while Gibson screamed in pain. His shrill cries echoed through the empty hallways. But no one even noticed. The Guard started to profusely sweat from the b eating. He wiped off his forehead then continued to bludgeon the weakened man until he became unconscious.

Lajes Field, Azores, Portugal
25-June-2010
1200 Hours Local Time

Private Nishan sat on a sandbag while looking out at the airbase. Private Watson sat in the machine gun nest behind the M-60 flicking his switchblade knife open over and over again. JJ ignored the goings around while passing patch clothes soaked with Break-free through the barrel of the mighty machine gun. "This sucks, nothing is worse than two weeks of guard on a stupid island in the middle of the Atlantic." Watson mused. He then jumped off the sandbag and leaned on the M-60s receiver.

"Now Watsy, why do you always want to get yourself killed. Relax; we're finally getting some much-needed rest. After all, Walters said that we should be prepared for another mission at anytime."

"Yeah, that was almost a month ago. Since then all we've done is nothing but louse around."

"I hardly think you trying to get JJ beat up in a bar in Lisbon is lousing around." JJ smiled as he tried to cover the fading bruise on the side of his face.

"With you spending all your free hours with your girlfriend, I need someone to be with during my off hours."

Nishan shook his head, "Why don't you hang around Walters. He seems more your type anyways."

"Naw, he's almost ten years older than me. Also he thinks I'm trying to get him killed after that little show at the cargo ship."

"You should have told him he's got nothing to be afraid of. After all you've been trying to get JJ and I killed for years." JJ and Nishan then broke out in laughter while Watson scowled at them.

JJ looked into the distance, "Look, someone's coming!" Nishan and Watson strained to see into the distance. A Humvee far away approached along the island's perimeter road. At first it was barely visible to the naked eye, but soon, it grew bigger and bigger until it arrived at their machine gun nest. The door flew open, Walters hung out of the door, "Get in, we've got a meeting with Major Bernier!"

The team piled into the Humvee, driving off toward the base headquarters. Watson pulled his Heckler Koch USP 9mm pistol while loading a magazine. "Put that thing away Watson!" Walters shouted as he struggled to drive while trying to fan Watson's pistol at the same time.

Unseen Warriors

"It's just that every time Bernier calls us in it's for a high risk mission. I just want to be prepared for the upcoming action," Watson spoke as he cocked his pistol.

"This mission I'm playing it safe so you're paring up with Nishan." The team broke out into laughter as Watson gave an all too familiar scowl.

The Humvee pulled up in front of Bernier's command building. The team rushed into Bernier's office and saluted. Bernier stood up and returned the salute. "Gentlemen, you four have been picked for a top-secret covert mission. Leave your weapons and uniforms behind. A jet will be here in about an hour to pick you up to a secret location for your briefing. It has been a pleasure for me having you four under my command. You are dismissed."

The four walked out stunned. Nishan gave a lost puppy dog look to Walters. Walters shook his head, "Get into your civilian clothing first. Then you can say good-bye to your girlfriend. She's at the rifle range right now." Nishan ran off into the barracks while trying to fight off tears.

"That's real strange that they left Matthews out of our posse'. I wonder what's going on. After all it isn't normal for Black Ops outfits to split their squads up, is it?" Watson spoke out loud.

"I don't know, I know one thing, if it was up to me, leave somebody behind, it sure wouldn't be her," Walters remarked

"Yeah she's a great shot, and she carries her weight just as good as any man," Watson quietly remarked.

"She never tried to get me killed like you did Watson!" JJ and Walters laughed as Watson rolled his eyes.

*****

Matthews started loading more magazines. The day of automatic fire training had been very exciting as well as tiring. But the minutes of fun were always followed by hours of loading magazines with loose ammunition. Matthews stretched her fingers and hand while she paused between magazines.

"Sarah," Matthews looked up to see Nishan in civilian clothing.

Matthews gave a puzzled look as she put down her magazine and ammunition. "Nishan, what's going on, why are you dressed like that?"

"I'm being transferred out. A plane is coming to take us away in an hour."

Matthews' face sunk, her eyes began to tear up, "But why, where?" She became choked up unable to speak.

"I don't know, Bernier ordered us out with Walters just now."

"Who are you?"

"Walters, JJ, Nishan and Watson."

Matthews shook her head. "Everybody's going except for me. What happened, why didn't I make the cut?" Matthews looked down at her boots as she cried into her hand. "So, are you leaving me for good?"

"No, I won't. I'll write every night, I promise. When we get to our base I'll see if I can call you. I'll miss you, Sarah."

"I'll miss you too. I don't even know your first name."

"It's Gian." Matthews gave a puzzled look. "My first name is Gian." Matthews' eyes lit up. For the first time Nishan had opened up to her in a way he had never opened up to anyone else before.

Out in the background the harsh noise of jet engines began to sound. The two looked over toward the taxiway to witness a large Gulfstream business taxi slowly by the rifle range. Nishan's eyes began to water at the sight. "Sarah, I'll come back soon, I'll come back with an engagement ring."

"Oh, Nishan, I love you."

"I love you too." The two began to kiss. All the troops at the range began to watch while leaning in their rifles. Walters shook his head as Watson broke out in laughter. JJ covered his eyes in embarrassment, causing Watson to laugh even louder.

Captain Driscoll, the aircraft's pilot, stepped out of the plane. He scanned around for his missing team. Seeing Walters and company at the edge of the rifle range, Driscoll became infuriated. "Walters, get your dirt bag friends on this plane ASAP."

Walters snapped out of his daze and began yelling to Nishan. Nishan quickly broke off the kiss while giving Matthews a hug. He grabbed his duffel bag and ran to the waiting jet.

Matthews stood watching as the jet refueled, closed its doors and started up its engines. Matthews took her helmet off then rubbed her sweat-drained hair. The jet slowly taxied to the end of the runway. The engines roared as the plane began to roll. Slow at first then faster and faster until it lifted off the runway and disappeared into the sky. Matthews stayed transfixed on the disappearing sight as he silently mumbled, "Goodbye Gian."

Sergeant Zale curled his lips. "Alright ladies, shows over, get to work. Matthews, this is not high school. You've got a job to do, now get to it." Matthews sighed as she resumed loading her magazines. Zale walked his way to Matthews, his six-foot three-inch stature towered over Matthews small five-foot six-inch frame. Zale looked down into her face with a menacing look, "Private, you will understand that I demand respect. I do not babysit and coddle people like your beloved S. Sergeant Walters. You now belong to me. If you don't perform up to my standards, I will remove you from the Army permanently!" Matthews' lip began to quiver as she watched him walk away.

*****

The Gulfstream G3 business jet cruised at 35,000 feet, the clear night air allowed unlimited view of the open ocean in all directions. JJ was awed at the awesome spectacle in front of his eyes. Watson looked around the leather-lined cabin. He opened compartments and played with the telephones and decks of cards. All the same time he drank the fine wine and ate the steak dinner aboard the luxury plane. Becoming bored with the plush interior, he began to look over to Nishan. Nishan failed to touch his food or any drink, rubbing the tears his face occasionally before continuing to write on a notepad.

"Hey, Nishan you've only been apart from her for about a couple of hours, don't start getting soft on us." Nishan failed to notice, he just kept scribbling into his notepad.

Watson shook his head. Looking next to him Walters ate quickly, devouring his steak. Walters looked up to see Watson staring at him. Curling his lip, Walters swallowed his last piece of steak. "Are you bored already Watsy?"

"Look at him, he just left her and he's already writing her a letter."

"He's in love. I remember when I first began to date my wife Wendy. I always wrote her any time I had a chance. Even on my tour in Afghanistan, I made time to write her once a week. Her beautiful blue eyes, long Blonde hair, and long eyelashes. She is a goddess." Walters got lost in his thoughts of Wendy.

Watson cleared his throat, "ahem, ahem." Walters snapped out of his daze.

"Anyways, I was in love then just like I am now. Wendy has blessed me with three beautiful children. She is so wonderful, the way she patiently waits for me back at Ft. Lewis, Washington."

"You guys are lame."

Walters laughed, "There's more to life than booze and bimbos. One day, Watsy, you'll get bitten by the love bug." Watson shrugged indifferently his shoulders.

Walters just smiled; putting his dinner aside he pulled a sealed envelope, marked secret. Bernier secretly handed it to him before the team had departed. Tearing it open, he began to read the hand written note:

Steve,

When you get to Regan National Airport, there will be a black Saab waiting for you. The driver will hold a sign: Steve and Wendy. Take the car with your team; the driver knows where the destination is. The rest of the preparations are taken care of.

JGG.

Walters shook his head. He wondered who JGG was, and who knew both him and Wendy. Leaning back the seat, Walters closed his eyes and began to sleep.

Bethesda, Maryland
25-June-2010
2000 Hours Local Time

    Chedwiggen nervously fidgeted in his seat while he sat in the front chair in his Bethesda, MD home. Chedwiggen continued looked up at the clock almost wishing time would go faster. "Why are you so nervous Arthur?" Chedwiggen quickly snapped his neck over and looked at Griswalt. "Why don't you have a drink, it'll settle you down." Chedwiggen remained silent.
    The doorbell rang, Chedwiggen rushed to the door, opening it. Karla smiled as she coldly brushed Chedwiggen by while leading an older man to the living room. Griswalt approached with two glasses, putting them down on the coffee table in front of the couple. "Just like you like it dear, scotch on the rocks." Griswalt looked over to the man, "And you, sir?"
    "I'll take a scotch on the rocks" Griswalt passed the other glass to him.
    Chedwiggen sat back down into his chair, giving a mean stare to Karla. The doorbell rang again, Chedwiggen sunk deeper into the chair while continuing to stare at Karla.

A dark suited man entered followed by Sergeant Walters and his team. The team sat down in the sofas. Griswalt handed glasses of cola to the incoming guests.

Griswalt stood up, drinks in one hand, addressed the room. "Now that everybody is here, I'll get started. This is Admiral Chedwiggen, my daughter, Karla—keep your hands off her Watson." Nishan and Walters rolled in laughter, while JJ fell to the floor, his face red with laughter.

"It seems that your reputation with the girls continues to follow you stateside. I guess old man Townsend told the Colonel about your prowess with their fairer sex," Nishan announced while trying to contain his laughter.

Walters curled his lip, "Prowess, I heard he struck out in a Geisha house."

"Let's settle down. Besides being very pretty my daughter is an Assistant to the Director of Middle East affairs at the CIA. Next to here is the Director Hans Huber. Here in the dark suit is CIA special agent Collins, and Private Nishan, Watson, JJ and Staff Sergeant Walters.

"The reason I have you assembled is simple. Pakistani terrorists have kidnaped Lieutenant Townsend. A Marine rescue platoon was intercepted and shot down by the Pakistani's. We believe the Pakistani's hold at least one, possibly more Marines. Our mission is to rescue all our people ASAP, Karla."

Karla pulled out a blue document and red it quickly. Intel says that the Pakistani's are unable to restart the Heckler and Koch plant. The HK employees destroyed much of the equipment before departing. Our job is to buy favors with the government while rescuing our men, Hans."

"AJ will get our weapons, Agent Collins and I will set up a phony arms company based out of Lisbon. Sergeant Walters you and your men will meet with relevant persons of interest. Once invited to Pakistan, you will locate and rescue the hostages and depart the country using whatever means possible. Make no mistake. This is a very dangerous mission. You are officially transferred to us. No other contact is allowed with the US Army or the CIA, is that understood." Everybody nodded, "Nishan, you will be helping agent Collins, here is your passport, you will be now known as Ahmed Ali." The rest stood up picking up their Canadian passports. Sergeant Walters was Wilhelm Hocksteader, JJ was James Eisele, and Watson was Lars Holsheimer. The team members shook their heads at the strange names. Walters tried to practice a German accent, which sounded grossly Australian. The team exploded in laughter.

Griswalt stood up trying to calm down the unruly squad. "Agent Collins we need to get our team going. Collins nodded as he led the team out of the room for another flight. Chedwiggen gave Griswalt a mean stare. "This is a really risky mission. You're risking a lot of good men."

"Arthur, you were always a real hypocrite, your idea cost the lives of sixteen of the finest Marines we have." Chedwiggen sunk low in his chair as he finished his whiskey.

Chapter 14

Lisbon, Portugal
02-July-2010
1200 Hours Local Time

Agent Collins sat back quietly smoking his cigar, Nishan sat across from him at a table. The bustling restaurant area of downtown Lisbon was crammed with office workers streaming in for lunch at the noon hour. Nishan strained to look at the women, hoping one of them would be Sarah Matthews. He felt lonely and anxious knowing that Matthews lay only a quick plane ride away. "Hey, CC, what do you think of me heading to the Azores for a day after our meeting?" Nishan quibbled while fearing the answer.

Collins looked up at the towering Castle Sao Jorge overlooking the city on a distant hill. "Not a chance, we have to look like independent arms agents. Absolutely no contact is allowed with any US Forces. You are to call me Jim Vernier; no actual names are to be used. From now on you will live and breathe your character. Understand Ahmed?"

"Yes, Jim." Nishan began to sulk as he became lost in his thoughts of Sarah.

Collins continued to look around, growing impatient at every passing second. As the time grew closer to one o'clock, the crowds grew thin, ordinary residents continued to dissipate as the sidewalks became bare. Far in the distance, an olive skinned man approached, briefcase in hand. Collins put on his black beret and sunglasses, the man in the distance did the same. "Our contact's coming, look alive." Collins whispered.

The man steeped up to the table, taking off his sunglasses he looked at Collins who performed an almost mirror act. "Mr. Vernier?"

Collins nodded his head, "Mr. Atta, nice to finally meet you in person, please have a seat."

Atta sat close besides Collins while carefully examining Nishan. "Who is your fine friend Mr. Vernier?"

"Call me Jim. This is Ahmed Ali. He had been working for a Heckler and Koch's sister company in England. He is now part of my consortium. Feel free to contact him on any matters of a technical nature. He is well versed in the engineering of the later generation HK products like the G-36, MP-7 PDW and UMP."

"Call me Tariq, Jim Ahmed." Atta shook hand with the two men. He then brought out his briefcase onto the table. "I have talked to my contacts. They are very interested in your proposition. Do you have a sample?"

Collins put his black leather-bound briefcase on the table. "I do have a sample, But I first need to see come collateral." Atta nodded his head then slide his briefcase across the table to Collins. Collins opened the case slowly, cracking it slowly until it was open about four inches. Inside were about thirty thousand crisp US dollars in one hundred dollar bills. Collins rubbed his chin then slowly closed the case. "The collateral is fine," Collins looked around, he then slowly slid the briefcase over to Atta.

Atta carefully opened the briefcase. At first he cracked it, looking around for any suspicious eyes. Atta then opened it up a full six inches. Inside there was an automatic MP-5 submachine gun loaded with a thirty round magazines. Atta carefully ran his fingers on the collapsible butt stock. He silently caressed the trigger assembly carefully touching the bullet diagrams slowly running his fingers along the receiver to the forward vertical grip all the while keeping his eyes firmly on the weapon. Atta slowly moved his eyes at Collins. Euphoria could be seen in his eyes. "Semi, three shot burst and full auto settings, a very nice touch. I especially like the pictograms. The German initials were never really to my liking. S, E, F, what does all that mean?"

Collins smiled at an amazed Atta. "You missed the crowning jewel." Atta looked confused. "Underneath the foam lining, there is a surprise I included especially for you."

Atta pulled the foam away from the top left corner; underneath he saw a long cylindrical object wrapped in a cloth sac. Atta pulled out the bag, grasping the closed end of the back, he slowly withdrew a black silencer, stamped into the outside was "Gemtech."

"I had the barrel threaded to ½ X 28. You'll be able to use any kind of US military accessory like that silencer. Does this sample meet your expectations?"

Atta was overtaken by happiness. He smiled ear to ear while he slowly closed the briefcase. "This more than meets my expectations, how many more samples can you provide?"

"How many do you need?"

Atta nodded, pleased with Collins. "I will need 500 like this one as soon as possible. Can you procure that quantity by tomorrow?"

"Will I get any future orders from you?"

"Yes, but I must test these out for functionality."

Collins confidently smirked. "No problem, I know of a deserted firing range near Alonso on the other side of the Spanish border. I also brought 200 rounds of 9X19 Luger full metal jacket ammunition."

"No need, I wish to test the entire batch of 500 guns at my leisure in a private location. Bring the weapons with you tomorrow at 8:00 p.m. to cargo ramp building C at Lisbon's international airport. I will require the presence of all your associates."

"I will comply, but there is still an issue of payment."

"What is your price?" Atta looked deeply into Collins' eyes.

"I will require twelve million US dollars in cash."

"You will be thoroughly compensated after I test each individual weapon, with your associates present of course."

Collins grew nervous, struggling to maintain his composure. "Why do you require the presence of my associates?"

"I want to meet all the men I'm dealing with, so I don't get double crossed by the CIA."

Collins nervously twitched in his seat, "You're right, I would do the same if I were in your shoes." Atta got up and walked away leaving Nishan and Collins staring at each other.

"We've got an issue here Jim. I think he's onto us," Nishan nervously chatted to Collins

"I'm going to give Hans a call."

Black Ops Camp Zulu
30-June-2010
2300 Hours Local Time

Griswalt sat in his office smoking a cigar while Hans Huber sat back busily scribbling on a notepad on Griswalt's' desk. "You know Hans, this might not work at all. Atta could think that we've set him up"

"I don't think so. Hassan said that Mansoor is screaming for guns and Ammo, especially the HK kind."

Griswalt blew out a deep puff of cigar smoke. "I never thought it would be in our interest to give that barbarian Mansoor weapons. If this plan doesn't work out, those guns could eventually kill some of our boys in Afghanistan and Iraq."

Huber sighed as rubbed his chin. "Unfortunately James that's one of the many risks I have to take every day at the CIA. I've got a lot of American blood on my hands from some of those plans that didn't go the way they were supposed to." Griswalt nodded his head as he looked at Sergeant Steven's dog tags on his desk.

Griswalt's phone rang loudly, thrusting the men out of their boredom. Griswalt looked over at the called id display. "It is agent Collins. He's calling me on my private line."

"Put him on speaker phone, this should be interesting?" Huber immediately ordered. Griswalt pushed the button as the two men began to attentively listen to the telephone. "What's up CC, what do you have to report?" Hans asked calmly.

Collins answered in a panicked voice rushing through his sentences. "We should break the deal, they're on to us?"

Huber rolled his eyes as Griswalt curled his eyebrows. "What makes you think that?" Hans remarked.

"He wants to meet my whole team at the airport to check them out. Also he wants 500 MP5s tomorrow by 2000 hours so he can take us for to the shooting range in some other continent!"

"Relax CC, he's checking you and your operation out. Do you think if he were going to kill you he'd invite you to the airport? He'd invite you to some barren stretch of Portuguese countryside and take care if business. Also, 500 illegal MP5s is a lot of firepower to be packing around when you know you're going to be busted in an airport."

"Ok Hans, but when's the crate coming?"

Huber lit a cigarette and took in a deep puff. "I'll arrange for the Portuguese to truck the stuff out of the FMP plant tonight, where does he want the goods?"

"He wants the goods at the cargo ramp building C at Lisbon International."

"No problem, look for several large crates marked with Volvo Aero Logos. I'll make sure the Portuguese authorities clear you all the way out of town. Bring all your boys like he says, you don't want to show up in Pakistan with extra faces. And one more thing, don't go armed; if he says you packing heat he'll know something's up. He'll panic with that silenced MP5 we gave him."

Huber pushed the end button on the phone. He then gave a strange puzzled look to Griswalt. "What's wrong Hans, you look like your puppy died," Griswalt joked.

"CC's getting nervous, and I don't like the idea of Atta taking him out of the country."

"Atta must think the MP5s are fake, the teams safe as long as CC doesn't panic and call me on this line while he's with Atta."

"James, do you think Atta's brother-in-law downstairs tipped him off?"

"No way, Hassan hasn't slept for almost three days. I've interrogated him hard day in day out for almost two straight weeks. He hasn't been along long enough to brush his teeth, let alone send messages out to the outside world. I don't think he even remembers the day he spilled the beans about Atta and arms shortages in Pakistan."

"Hans I always think of a back up plan. Do you remember the cell phone I gave agent Collins?" Huber reluctantly nodded with a puzzled look. "It's got a GPS homing beacon in it. Griswalt clicked a small desktop icon on his computer. Immediately a map came up of the screen with a flashing star in Portugal. "We can monitor the teams tracks point by point right here. Griswalt zoomed on the star until he was able to pinpoint the exact hotel room Collins was staying.

"Why didn't you tell him about the homing beacon?" Huber asked.

"If he gets caught, that's one less thing for Mansoor to torture out of him." Huber nodded in agreement.

Lisbon, Portugal
31-June-2010
2000 Hours Local Time

Collins looked at the huge number of crates all around him in the cargo building. The wooden crates were stacked on top of each other almost five high. The outsides were labeled "Volvo Aero" just as Huber had promised.

Walters walked in with Nishan and Watson. Looking around Walters became awed at the sight. "Looks like you must have had the FMP factory work overtime for these babies."

"Hey, Mr. Vernier, you have something in say with green furniture, easy to shoot, a light trigger pull. I need an engagement present for my fiancé." Watson and Walters erupted into laughter as Nishan mocked shooting a submachine gun from the hip.

"Staff Sergeant Walters, you need to control your people, this is a very dangerous situation!"

"I though my name is Wilhelm Hocksteader."

"Your name is going to be a slang term for a mule if you keep this up."

"What's the problem Collins, you've been sour faced ever since we arrived in Portugal?"

"It's you. You run your crew in a totally unprofessional manner. You and your crew are a disgrace to the United States military. The only reason you are with me is because Griswalt and Huber picked you. If I had my way, I would have left you and your circus behind at that Siberian gulag you're supposed to be based at."

Walters' face immediately grew a scowl. "You may be the intelligence head of our team, but if we get into a firefight I run the show. You may think my team isn't GI enough for you, but I've fought with these guys on several occasions. If I'd have my choice, I'd take these guys over any of your people in a heartbeat."

Collins gave a scowl as he stood face to face with Walters. "Remember one thing, I run the show on this mission. I'm making the decisions. You follow my orders just like the rest of your monkeys."

Unseen Warriors

JJ came rushing in breathing heavily, "He's coming." The team stood at attention. Atta arrived with two gun-toting bodyguards. Looking at the crates he shouted something in Arabic. The men immediately tore open a crate; looking inside they grabbed one of the submachine guns and handed it to Atta. Atta carefully inspected the gun, and then nodded to his men.

"My men will load the guns into one of our waiting cargo planes, come join me in me in the business jet. The team carefully followed Atta as he led them into a waiting Fokker F100 jet. The team nervously sat down inside the spacious cabin, while the engines whined as they started up. The aircraft rolled down the runway as the engines strained to put out maximum thrust while bouncing down the concrete runway."

The team gazed out into the distance as the aircraft rotated heading toward the sky. Nishan squinted at the window trying to get a view of the distant Azores islands. "I love you, Sarah," Nishan mumbled as Portugal soon became a distant memory while the Fokker cut through the clear night headed toward its unknown destination.

An hour into the flight, everyone stayed quiet, fearing the unknown. Atta, feeling the tension in the air decided to make small talk. "Do you know my brother-in-law Mr. Vernier?" Collins shook his head with a puzzled look. "He was in the business, just like me until he was caught by the Americans." Collins remained stoic, trying to mask his fear. "Look deep into my eyes, are you with the CIA?"

"Do you know how many times you have asked me that question?"

Atta laughed, "You seem evasive, are you an American Mr. Vernier?"

"Of course not, do you know how log an American would last in this business?"

"You are subtle yet mysterious, I will enjoy finding out more of your character Mr. Vernier? Mr. Ali where are you originally from?"

Nishan cleared his throat, caught off guard by the question. "The Indian side of Kashmir, I immigrated with my family to India when I was three years old."

"How is your faith in Allah?"

"I have to admit I have slipped since I moved out of my parent's home."

"You will rekindle your faith in Allah, I will see to it. So, who are you associates?"

Walters cleared his throat. "I am Wilhelm Hocksteader. I'm originally from Germany where I worked for Heckler and Koch on the second generation roller lock type of guns like the HK 33, HK 41, HK 53 and their various incarnations."

"I'm Lars Holsheimer. I specialize in American type weapons such as the M-16, M-4, M-17, AR-18 and such. I guess I am the only non Heckler and Koch weapon's specialist in our organization."

Atta nodded while smiling, "My contacts have been looking for someone who is knowledgeable enough to be able to allow us to exploit the weaknesses of American weapons. They will be very pleased to speak to you." Watson nervously shifted in his seat as he smiled in agreement to Atta.

The rest of the trip went quietly as the plane crossed the Mediterranean into Northern Africa. The aircraft finally arrived at a deserted runway strip in the middle of the Saharan desert. The aircraft slowly circled the runway as it began to line up onto final approach. The speed brake, on the aircraft's tail, popped open as the aircraft immediately fell to earth, a few thousand feet short of the runway. The plane's nose rose high as it crossed the cracked concrete threshold while the engines blew clouds of dust everywhere. The pilot slowed the aircraft by deploying the thrust reversers as it screeched to a halt in the heavily worn concrete runway.

As the jet approached a hard concrete pad beside the runway, the engines whined down as the pilot shut off the fuel. The team soon departed down the steps aircraft's main cabin door. The hot desert sun beat down on their bodies as the gritty sand irritated their eyes. Atta scanned the distant sky then he began to point at a distant contrail. A jet slowly began to appear, very small at once, soon it was large enough to recognize as t-tail rear engine jet. It circled the makeshift airfield several times, before it finally landed on the dusty runway. The deafening sound of the engines shook the ground as the Fokker F-100 taxied up almost parallel to the other aircraft.

The massive fuselage cargo door opened, while men rushed to unload the crates out of the huge aircraft. Slowly the crates were stacked one on top of each other as the desert winds began to pick up.

Atta ripped off the top of one of the crates. He pulled out one of the submachine guns with ease. He inserted a loaded thirty magazine into the gun and pulled the charging handle. Atta shouted in Arabic to his bodyguards. The two men dragged a wooden crate top into the distance. Atta fired the submachine gun in automatic gunfire, empty brass casings flew out of the ejection port barely missing agent Collins. One by one, Atta tested a random submachine gun from each of the crates in semi auto, three shot burst and automatic fire.

After test firing all the weapons, Atta smiled. "You have done well Mr. Vernier, my contacts will be very happy. Atta placed another magazine into his MP-5, and pulled the charging handle. He smiled as he looked over to Collins, "You have also outlived your usefulness." Atta put the gun to his shoulder then pointed the gun at Collins.

Collins gulped. "Aren't we being a little hasty, after all we still have more deals we can make, I get you some USP pistols, G-3 assault rifles…"

"Wrong, I have what I need. I will pocket the twelve million, and you will be dead. No one will be the wiser." Atta placed the gun sector switch to full automatic and signaled his body guards who aimed their guns likewise.

"Wait," Nishan shouted in Punjabi, which was Atta's native tongue. Atta slowly began to lower his gun as looked up. "We know Mansoor is your contact, eventually he will find out you have his money and weapons. When he does, he will issue a Fatwa against you. There is no place on this planet where you will be safe. Arabs will hunt you down. They will come from all over to kill you. You know how long of a reach Mansoor has. I am a Muslim. If you kill me, Allah will punish you for your sin. For that you will suffer all of eternity in Hell. Is it worth risking you place in heaven just for a little money?"

Atta placed the gun selector on safe. He then addressed the team in English. "Your partner has made good sense. I will spare your lives. We must return to Pakistan to deliver the goods."

Chapter 15

Lajes Field, Azores, Portugal
04-July-2010
2000 Hours Local Time

Matthews looked out into the setting sun. The horizon became red as if it were on fire. The ocean shimmered with reflections from the sun. Thee scene was so beautiful yet she felt so lonely. It had been almost one week since Nishan had left, yet for her it felt like a lifetime. For Matthews it was just another dull day of guard duty, while her heart kept longing for Nishan.
"Hey, what's up?" Matthews swung her head over to see Corporal Willard standing a few feet from her. She just shrugged, and then gave him a bored look.
"Guard duty is dull, isn't it? I've been here for the last two years, yet this is the only thing I do."
"I guess I've been lucky, this last week has been the most guard duty I've done since I enlisted. Hey, what's with Zale?" Matthews answered with a monotone voice.
"You mean Sergeant Zale?"
"Yeah, has he always been this rough?"

Willard nodded. "Pretty much, he thinks if he doesn't run you down you won't be tough enough in combat."

"Somebody should run him down back to a Private," Matthews angrily replied

Willard snorted, and then chuckled so hard until he could no longer contain himself. Matthews gave a puzzled look that quickly turned into a frown. "I'm sorry it's just that Sergeant Walters had a reputation of being one of the toughest sergeants in Black Ops."

"He was tough, but fair. He didn't judge people on first sight like Zale does."

"You guys probably got off the wrong foot, after the first mission you'll be one big happy family." Matthews rolled her eyes. A Humvee raced toward their direction kicking up dust as darkness began to fall upon the remote island. "I think I see a mission coming in the distance," Willard announced

The Humvee pulled up locking all four wheels. Dust flew everywhere blinding Matthews and Willard. Corporal Lance shouted out of the drivers' seat. "Get your rears in, we've got a mission." Matthews and Willard rushed into the Jeep like vehicle as Lance revved the engine up. The Humvee rushed through the airbase at top speed until it pulled up to a waiting Blackhawk.

The team rushed into the Blackhawk joining Sergeant Zale and Private Thurston and Zackow already seated in the cabin. The noise of the rotor blades grew louder as they cut into the air straining to lift the aircraft up to altitude. Putting on their night vision monocles, the team looked down as the ground slowly disappeared while Open Ocean began to take its place.

Zale shouted over the whine of the engines. "We've got a merchant cargo ship approaching south of the base. Intel thinks they're carrying some sort of chemical or biological weapon that's going to be used in a terrorist attack on US soil. We've got to go in and secure the bridge and the upper deck. Another

Unseen Warriors

Blackhawk with Portuguese commandos is following behind. They'll land and secure the engine room and cargo hold. The Air force has two F-15E's scrambling to provide top cover. "When we hit the deck, I want you guys to set up a perimeter. The door gunmen will cover you."

* * * * *

Lieutenant Magnason skillfully guided the Black through the clear night. He looked back at Zale's team then breathed heavily as he looked over to Lieutenant Riggens. "So, when do you officially start left-hand seat training?"

Riggens smiled, "Next week, I might not get to stay when I qualify."

"Why, where are they going to send you?"

"Not sure, maybe with an Air cavalry company in Korea, but I'm still hoping I could get on with another Black Ops outfit."

"You like the excitement of this cloak and dagger flying?"

"Yeah, what did the Colonel pull you aside for after the briefing?"

Magnason smiled. "Seems I finally made captain, I get my bars after this mission."

Riggens grinned, "I'll take this refuel."

"Are you trying to make up for the last time when you were too scared to dock?" Riggens grinned as the helicopter continued to pass through the moonless night.

Red and Green Navigation lights immediately began to shine from the distance. Magnason steered toward them while looking at his wingman carefully following to his side. "I'll take the radio, why don't you gas up, left seater."

Riggens smiled as took hold of the stick, "Thanks Captain," Riggens mumbled as he closed in on a silver shape breaking through the darkness.

"Skylark, this is Chicken one, we're ready for a fill."

"Copy, we're leveling off, slowing down to refueling speed. Both baskets are extended. Chicken one the port basket is yours."

Riggens banked the helicopter toward the C-130s left wing as the refueling probe in the nose extended out. Riggens gently lined the aircraft as he slowed to a crawl. Concentrating on the basketball-sized object ahead of him, Riggens expertly slid the refueling probe into the basket with ease. Magnason watched out the right side window as his wingman continued to refuel in almost mirror like fashion. Riggens watched as the strip gauges continued to rise as fuel poured into the helicopter's tanks. Receiving his fill, Riggens slowly reduced the torque on his collective lever. The mighty turboprop transport slipped away into the darkness. Magnason grabbed the control sticks with a firm grip, "I've got them." Riggens reluctantly released the sticks, almost attempting to continue to savor his moment of conquest. Magnason smiled as he steered the helicopter toward their distant threat as he quietly mumbled to himself, "You've a good copilot, buddy."

The helicopters continued to rush through the night's sky as blips on the radar screen continued come closer and closer. Riggens boringly looked down on his displays as the euphoria of the refueling was replaced with the boredom of routine flying. "We're closing in on the intercept point."

"Copy, I'll call the cavalry." Magnason switched frequency while peering out into the darkness as if he was trying to draw the ship into view with his mind. "Mudhen, this is Chicken 1, we're closing on intercept point."

"Copy, we'll be over flying target in one minute."

* * * * *

High above at twenty-two thousand feet Major "Cobra" Holsheimer checked the displays of his F-I5E. The F-15 carried 2 Aim-120E AMRAMM radar guided missiles and 2 Aim-9M heat seeker air-to-air missiles. On its belly, the aircraft carried one two-thousand pound Laser-guided conventional iron bomb. Sitting in the backseat Captain Oropeza sat monitoring his displays. To the right and slightly aft of the airplane, Captain William "Chuckles" Walton flew his F-15E in formation. His Weapons Officer, Captain "Snooker" Meyer intensely watched his displays as a square blip on his air to ground radar rapidly approached.

Holsheimer adjusted his displays until the threat-warning indicator was on the correct display. The other display showed his air to ground radar. Holsheimer rubbed his eyes as he tried to focus on the displays colored like a sea of green through his night vision glasses. "Mudhen 2, one is approaching target. When we get close to the ship, I want you to break off and setup Combat air Patrol six miles off the bow. Two will circle the target and protect the target. If the target launches missiles, chase them down, I'll see about neutralizing the launch area."

"Copy, we will comply. Hey, Cobra, do you really think there is anything going on with this ship? After all, the Intel photos show nothing but a deck covered with containers."

"I know, but the last time Black Ops intercepted a cargo ship, it fired a Scud." Holsheimer continued to look out, seeing distant lights dimly appearing in the ocean ahead.

*****

Riggens looked at his navigation page as he profusely sweats. The tension of the mission began to bear down on him as he approached the ship. "We should be in visual range of the ship in about one minute." Riggens peered deep out into the distant ocean almost trying to wish the ship into view.

"Corporal Lawrence, prepare for boarding!" Magnason shouted in his raspy voice as adrenaline began to rush into his veins.

Lawrence opened the cabin door as he prepared his .30 cal M-60 machine gun while nodding to Sergeant Zale. "Guns up!" Zale shouted as he pulled the HK-91's rifle charging handle. His team followed in an almost choreographed fashion, charging their rifles and turning on their night vision monocles.

Magnason watched the lights grow brighter and brighter until the mighty ship's bow came into view. Magnason's stomach began to tighten as he banked the throbbing helicopter toward the starboard side of the ship. Riggens peered at the deck covered with containers while moonlight reflected of the shimmering waves. As the helicopter rounded the bow, a flash blinded Riggens. "Sam, Sam, one o'clock," Riggens screamed as he rapidly dumped chaff and flares.

Magnason dumped the nose as the helicopter rushed toward the ocean while he pulled max torque into a steep left-hand turn. Magnason watched in horror as the fireball rushed toward the helicopter, undeterred by the falling chaff and flares. The missile slammed into the left engine's exhaust pipe, the airframe began to shake and shudder as the left engine's fire handle began to illuminate while several warning lights on the caution and advisory panel illuminated. Riggens madly pulled the left engine's fire hand while shutting of the left engine. Riggens cussed at the airplane as he watched the fuel flow gauge slowly decrease to zero as the engine starved from the lack of fuel. Riggens fired an engine fire extinguisher bottle. The firelight continued to illuminate.

Another flash blinded the cockpit as another missile slammed into the right engine. The explosion rocked the aircraft. The right engine's exhaust pipe and cowling exploded into pieces as they were ejected into the water. Flames erupted out of the engine hump near the base of the tail boom, as hydraulic and engine oil burned while melting the frail aluminum skin. Magnason pained to gain more airspeed as Riggens struggled to put out both fires in the engine compartment.

Unseen Warriors

"We're going to ditch!" Magnason screamed as tried he tried dead sticking the wounded helicopter toward a smooth landing in the ocean. The APU continued to run providing the only source of power for the instruments as the cockpit's fire-bells continue to blare in the cockpit. Riggens began to brace himself as he began to confess his sins to God while clutching the gold cross around his neck.

Another SAM slammed into the tail boom. Flames showered the ocean as the burning tail boom separated from the aircraft, falling into the blackness of the ocean. The fuselage tumbled, rolling end over end. Guns, ammunition and helmets continue to be ejected out of the fuselage. Matthews tried to grab anything she could see while she and the rest of her teammates crashed and tossed around in the fuselage cabin. The fuselage did a quick barrel roll ejecting Matthews out the open cabin door into the icy water of the Atlantic.

Before the team could mourn the loss of their fellow teammate, the fuselage crashed into the water. Seawater poured into the open door as Willard struggled to stay afloat as his heavy gear dragged him down. Zale pushed Willard aside as he grabbed the machine gun while icy seawater continued to pour and splash into his face. The fuselage continued to sink as the team members madly tried to remove their heavy gear. Yet their struggles were all in vain as the fuselage disappeared under the waves, the team's members soon stopped thrashing as their souls left their bodies.

* * * * *

Holsheimer banked and began flying a large circle in the sky above the cargo ship as he watched the approaching Blackhawk's on his air-to-air radar. He watched the TWI and radar pages while flicking the cover of his master arm switch open and closed, totally unaware of the horrific events about to befall on the fast approaching Blackhawks.

A small square box appeared on his TWI, Holsheimer looked closer at the page when a circle appeared. The SAM light illuminated as well as an obnoxious warning beep. Holsheimer twitched quickly then flung his neck to the left, his eyes grew big and wide as a telephone pole shape with a fireball exhausting from its rear rose toward him. Holsheimer dumped the aircraft's wings over into a steep left turn while slamming the throttles into full afterburner while the missile raced to reach him. Oropeza dumped chaff and flares, as he focused his eyes on the clumpy telephone pole while calling out the missiles' direction. Holsheimer throttled the engines out of after burner as he struggled to maintain the airplane's airspeed at 500 knots. Holsheimer kept one hand on the stick. The other on the throttle as he watched has the round circle close on him on his TWI while anxiously waiting for Oropeza's call.

"Pull up," Oropeza shouted as the missile leveled off while racing at almost three times the speed of sound at the F-15. Holsheimer slammed the throttle to full afterburner while pulling hard back on the electric control stick. The aircraft zoomed skyward as it did a tight vertical turn above the cargo ship, while the last packet of chaff left the aircraft. The missile overshot the airplane, exploding harmlessly away from the fuselage.

Holsheimer struggled to control the aircraft as it racked and shook from the missile's explosion. Wiping his face, Holsheimer looked at the altimeter—30,000 feet. "Mudhen 2, this is Mudhen one, what is your situation?" Before a reply could come in, Holsheimer watched in horror as a Scud missile rose from the cargo ship's deck.

* * * * *

Captain Walton continued to fly a large lazy circle three miles forward from the bow as the clear moonlit night became almost eerie in front of his eyes. The mighty ship sparkled with light as it gently cut through the flat waves of the Atlantic. Walton kept staring at the full moon. He almost felt a magical pull to it as gently banked the aircraft for another trip along the bow. "Hey, Snooker, do you ever wonder what would it feel like to walk on the moon?"

Captain Meyer shook his head, "I guess now you want to be an astronaut?"

"No, it's just that the moon is so calm and gentle, it's almost a magical place. It's a place that we don't travel to anymore, a place that's kind of left in time. It's from a time when we knew our enemies, from a time when we could point to a face and say that he was the enemy soldier. Now days with the war on terror, we don't know who or what is our enemy is. The terrorist could be our neighbor, friend, next of kin, it's like we're fighting a war on everyone yet no one."

"Well, I kind of get what you mean. It is tough doing air to ground combat with a cargo ship carrying toys for Wal-Mart."

Walton leaned back in his seat as he looked at the glistening deck below. A sparkle caught his eye on the deck. Walton peered down trying to see something through his night vision goggles. A flash erupted from the ship, as his glasses immediately became light green. Walton ripped off his glasses to see a fireball rapidly approaching from the ship. He immediately dived toward the ocean while dumping chafe. Meyer watched the fireball closing on the aircraft as the Sam warnings screamed in his ears. "SAM at six o'clock, closing in fast," Meyer shouted as his heart pumped faster and faster, while he began to profusely sweat.

"Pull up, pull up!" Meyer shouted as the missile rushed to close in on the fleeing F-15. Walton yanked the nose straight up. The Sam rushed toward him straining to follow. Walton continued to dump off chafe while his stomach tightened. The missile exploded spraying shrapnel all along the exposed belly of the F-15. The F-15 shook and buffeted as warning lights began lighting in the cockpit. The Engine displays began to fluctuate as a FADEC caution lights erupted all over his EICAS display. Walton struggled to level the aircraft as his control stick became sluggish and Jittery. Walton looked of and saw an FCS warning illuminate on his display.

"Scooter, I'm going to slow this thing down, when we get to the max ejection speed, I want you to punch Elvis!"

"Copy," Meyer shouted as warning bells and tones continued to blare into the cockpit.

Both engine fire warnings began to blare into the cockpit, Walton instinctively shut down the engines and pulled the fire handles. "Eject, Eject, Eject," Walton commanded as fires began to race through the cockpit." Meyer pulled the ejection handle. The canopy blew off into the air stream, immediately followed by him in his seat. The aircraft began to slow down and roll as it quickly approached the ocean. Walton struggled to level the aircraft as his displays turned blank while flames danced around him. Walton held the stick level as the aircrafts fly-by-wire flight control system continued to grow even more sluggish by the moment. Leaning down he began to pull the ejection handle between his feet with the other hand. As he did, the engines exploded hurtling the burning nose section away from the fuselage. Captain Walton began burn alive still strapped in the seat as, the nose crashed into the blackness of the ocean.

*****

Holsheimer slammed the throttles full forward, the afterburners lit off propelling the aircraft to almost 600 knots. He then switched to his medium range air to air missiles. As he continued to adjust his radar in the air to air radar mode trying to lock on the Scud missile while it continued to rush away from him. "Home base, Mudhen 1, you have a scud inbound." Holsheimer throttled back as he watched the missile disappear out of view of his radar. "Home base, Mudhen 1 requires rescue cap at intercept point."

"Copy, we're scrambling rescue chopper."

Holsheimer returned to a lazy circle over the cargo ship. He sat back in seat awe as he watched an orange raft fill with sailors. Holsheimer slammed the stick into a tight turn as he dove faster and faster toward the raft. As if commanded by hidden hands, the raft immediately began to make wild s turns as it tried to avoid the jet screaming toward them. Holsheimer selected his air to ground gun mode on his HUD, then putting a computer generated cross just forward of the raft, Holsheimer squeezed the trigger.

Bullets tore into the path of the fish tailing raft raising huge waves. The raft tried to reverse course with a sharp 180 degree turn. The actions were wasted as bullets tore into the raft, men jumped into the ocean trying to avoid the burning projectiles all around them.

The gunfire suddenly stopped, the men struggled to stay afloat as their poor quality life vests began became damp and heavy with salt water. Looking around, they became exuberant as a bright yellow flash rose in the distant sky. With all their excitement, they failed to hear the whistling sound approaching. A crackling sound broke through the air as a bomb crashed into the water, exploding into a huge wall of water. The exuberant sailors, only a minutes ago celebrated their survival were forced hundreds of feet below the waves to their watery graves.

* * * * *

Major Bernier began to write on his desk, unable to sleep in his quarters. Bernier continued to grow restless, his mind drifted onto thoughts of the lost Navy Seal company only a few months back. Unable to concentrate, he finally put down the pen and pulled out a bottle of Scotch, pouring a double shot into his glass. Bernier looked deep into the son's picture on his desk, he felt pride and sorrow as he looked at the soldier clad in a Navy uniform. Bernier raised his glass to the picture, tears streamed down his check as he spoke in a choked voice. "Here's to you Curtis, you always made me proud to have a Navy Seal in the family, may it never be known that you died in vain." Bernier downed the glass in one shot. His stomach began to burn as the liquor began to fill it.

Air raid sirens sounded as the sounds of fighter jets taking off shook the building.

Bernier wiped the tears from his face, grabbed a coat, and stepped outside the building. Bernier watched patriot missiles rush to the sky as personnel rushed around him all over the base. Three small explosions occurred as popping continued occur all over the sky. More missiles rose to the sky, they're rocket motors continued to light up the night sky.

A blinding flash appeared in the sky from the end of the runway. A 1,000 mph nuclear wind rushed out of the epicenter. Military personnel sat unaware of the explosion for a flickering second before they became vaporized by the nuclear winds. Buildings disintegrated as the winds blew through them while flames continued to consume the walls. The remaining aircraft lined up on the taxiways preparing for takeoff exploded into huge fireballs as the nuclear winds rushed through the base and on toward the ocean. The winds then shifted as they rushed inwards, sucking any solid objects that remained on the island into epicenter of the explosion. A huge mushroom cloud rose thousands of feet in the sky as extinction of all life on the base was completed.

Residents at Ponto Delgado woke out of their beds as the boom of a shockwave shook their homes. The sky lit up like daytime for a second. The Portuguese rushed out of their homes as they grew fearful and somewhat inquisitive of the distant explosion. They stood mesmerized by the sight of a mushroom cloud rising in the sky. Residents rushed into churches trying to

Unseen Warriors

confess their sins to God, as fear of the end times haunted their minds. Priests struggled to control the crowds while residents continued to pour into the crowded Churches. While in other neighborhoods, residents rushed to pray and confess their sins while the streets filled with people trying to find a safe place to pray.

Throngs of people swamped to the airport trying to catch flights to Lisbon, Africa and any other point off the island. Ticket agents tried to calm the people. Butt they continued to panic as stampedes erupted the moment any plane seemed to approach a gate.

Still others rushed to fill any boat, no matter how small or unsafe that would give them passage to the mainland. Crowds swarmed to the docks, pushing and shoving as they threw their suitcases, filled with their worldly possessions, into the Atlantic Ocean in a vain attempt to be able to gain a foothold ant departing fishing boat.

The Prime Minister immediately performed an address on the nation. He plead with the people to stay calm, reassuring the end times were not coming, all the while declaring Marshal Law all across the Azores.

Chapter 16

New York Centre control
04-July-2010
1900 Hours Local Time

    Bill Larsen sat watching his radar screen. As an FAA air traffic controller, he helped guide hundreds of flights on imaginary highways in the sky along the eastern seaboard. He watched a Continental airlines flight heading to Newark, An American Airlines flight from New York to Miami, An Alaska airlines jet from Newark to Seattle all meandering through the shy, while he meticulously arranged their altitudes, spacing and path deviations.

    The twelve hour long shift grew weary. His eyes became dry and red as he stared at the radar screen all day long. Larsen grew puzzled at an inbound flight, an Olsen airways cargo MD-11 jet flying along the US east coast from Panama City to Newark, New Jersey. Flight OA3636 had taken off earlier in the day From Panama, and then over flying Cuba to Miami, the jet continued along jet ways to Newark's cargo ramp.

    Larsen rubbed his chin, and then took a closer look at the cargo planes' flight plan. He checked to make sure that all the way points in the flight plan were filled correctly. Reviewing the information, Larsen still felt at unease even though everything was correct.

The code orange terrorism didn't affect Larsen much. For him it was just another silly bit of theatrics from the department of Homeland security. Every week another warning came out, and always it turned out to be nothing. Larsen, like basically everyone else in air traffic control centre considered the latest warning was just another bump on the road of life. But for all his complacency, Larsen still felt, for some inexplicable reason, unease about OA3636

A FedEx 727-200 cargo jet contacted him as it was handed off by Memphis centre control. Larsen shook his head as he awoke from his ponderings, he then started directing the jet on its slow trip to Newark airport, forgetting about OA3636.

* * * * *

Vice President William Douglas watched out his window as his presidential helicopter continued on its way to the Norfolk Naval Shipyards. Tim Roberts, Douglas' executive aid, continued to cover fine details of Douglas' agenda for the day.

"Bill, can I be frank?"

"Sure, Tim, what's on your mind?"

"Don't you think it's a bit risky having an open air meeting like this with the threat level as high as it is right now?"

Douglas shrugged his shoulders as he smiled while looking over to Roberts. "Tim, we're halfway through our term, we need to remind people about terrorism, and national defense. If we don't, people will start getting back to the issues we're not strong at like health care, the economy. New aircraft carriers create much needed high paying technical jobs while reminding the voters that we're serious about national defense. A Fourth of July christening has all it takes to put us in the spotlight. Plus it'll bury all the bad news that we've been getting on the international front."

"Speaking of bad news, you know the crash of the commandos in Pakistan is going to create a lot of tough questions."

"That is why you are my executive assistant. It is up to you to keep the media at bay while I hammer our point across to the media."

Tim shook his head as he watched the city of Hampton pass by as the mighty UH-60. The helicopter then passed over Norfolk as it settled along a path straddling the Norfolk/Portsmouth city lines. Finally they broke through the dark clouds, the mighty machine slowly descended and landed beside a Navy pier near Davis Avenue. Secret Service Agents rushed out to secure areas around the pier, while snipers and military police watched with their fingers on their triggers.

Douglas walked out helicopter. He looked around then stood confident, undeterred by the rain pelting him from all directions. A Navy Admiral quickly rushed up to him, he then saluted him before escorting him to a building overlooking the pier. Roberts rushed behind, using his briefcase as an umbrella as he tried to dodge the pounding rain.

Finally in shelter, Admiral Reardon sat on a conference room, while providing Douglas with a steaming cup of coffee. Douglas wiped his dripping face and hair with a towel and then began to drink with one eye on Reardon. "Admiral, what preparations have you made for tonight's christening?"

"I'll have a crowd one hundred sailors and hundreds of support workers the pier while sailors will encircle on the deck as The USS George W Bush when you deliver your speech. Later an entire squad of FA-18's to do a fly over as you finish your christening. I will get maximum effect for your national security message, sir."

"Good, I will make sure that I have the appropriations' committee run that request you have for another three Reagan class aircraft carriers. Most importantly Admiral, President Hawkins assures me you will be his next Chief of staff."

Reardon smiled, "You won't be disappointed Mr. Douglas, I will make sure I do the best job I can do for you and President Hawkins."

"I don't doubt that, but remember we want results, Chedwiggen was unable to deliver, and that is why he was allowed to retire." Reardon shook his head in agreement.

*****

Major Mueller sat at his desk reviewing notes about another terrorist attack warning from Homeland security. Mueller knew he was going to spend another boring night of patrolling the empty sky. Captain Taylor walked up to Mueller's desk and sat down on a chair beside him. "So, Snake, are you ready for another patrol of keeping America safe from terrorism?" Taylor stood up and mocked a British salute while whistling Yankee Doodle.

Mueller rolled his eyes while shaking his head. "Goose, sometimes you can be a real jerk. How did you survive in the Air Force this long?"

Goose gave a smirk. "My uncle is Admiral Reardon."

Mueller buried his head in his hands for a minute then looked up at Taylor with a frustrated look. "Let's get going Silver Spoon."

The two pilots continued on to the ramp where their F-22 Raptors lay waiting. The massive aircrafts stood on the wet ramp while winds continued the blow rain sideways. Mueller looked at the sleek airplane. Its smooth wings and strange angular lines only interrupted by two two 600 gallon external fuel tanks hanging of the inboard wing station pylons.

Mueller continued his walk around of the lower fuselage. He slowly covered the airplane inch by inch as he checking the gear for missed pins. Mueller ran his hands along the smooth tires as he looked up into the aircraft's belly. Its bay doors lay open exposing six Aim-120E AMRAMM missiles.

Having completed his walk around, Mueller sat in the spacious cockpit. Securing his seatbelts, he then passed the ejection seat safety pins to the ground crew while he lowered the canopy down. Mueller then signaled his ground crew for a start. The ramp coordinater stepped twenty feet back, and gave a signal to start engines. Muller placed the battery switch to on, he then placed the auxiliary power unit momentarily to on, he then placed both throttles to idle. The APU roared to life, soon after the aircraft automatically started up the main engines right to left in a mere 30 seconds.

The aircraft came to life while the APU shut itself down. Mueller scanned his displayed making sure that all the avionics were configured to his preferences. Mueller shook his wrists pointing his thumbs out. The ramp coordinator rushed to pull out the chocks from the nose tires.

Mueller looked to his right at Taylor's aircraft. Taylor gave him thumbs up, then another mock British salute. Mueller felt a headache coming on as called for clearance to taxi.

The two jets slowly taxied through the east ramp until they arrived at the end of runway 26. Mueller pushed the throttles to the max afterburner detent. The engine whine as it raced to max rotational speed as a huge orange flame poured out of its tailpipe. The two aircraft began to rush down the runway in perfect formation while the F119-PA-100 engines screamed into the nights.

Mueller pulled the stick back, causing the nose to quickly rise, while the exhaust nozzles matched the requested angle of attack with vectored thrust. Mueller quickly raised his gear as the aircraft rushed to 20,000 feet where Mueller leveled out at 400 knots. He watched his displays with a bored look as Taylor quickly joined up.

"Wow, wasn't that a rush snake!" Taylor shouted in an excited voice.

"Yeah it was just too exciting Goose," Mueller casually replied.

Mueller had been one of the first USAF pilots to begin training in the F-22. It was at first a technical marvel that overwhelmed him. But as time went on, he had grown bored of his high tech toy just as he had lost the novelty of his F-15 many years ago. For Mueller, flying had totally changed from his days of piloting an F-15. Everything was now automated. Engineers had been so successful in reducing his workload, that in peacetime he was no more than just a passenger on the flight. Mueller used the long night of flying to contemplate his future.

The twin F-22's flew north to Washington, D.C., then northeast to New York and Boston, then south again along the Eastern seaboard. They finally passed over the Norfolk shipyards to complete the loop. From there the pair would continue the loop, refueling where required until the end of Independence Day festivities.

* * * * *

Captain John Harris yawned as he stared out the multi function display counted down the range to Norfolk high altitude VOR. The 2100 mile flight from Panama had been boring and routine. Harris struggled to stay awake as his thoughts of drifted to being able to enjoy spending the Fourth of July weekend with his wife and grand kids. Despite the orange level terror alert Harris felt unconcerned as he wondered if this Fourth of July weekend would be memorable.

Harris' first offices, William Stull spoke into the radios and he contacted New York center control. At 43, Stull was ten years younger than Harris. He was a good pilot, but felt inpatient in that he still had not made captain. He felt singled out and bitter toward Olsen airways, as many pilots junior to him in seniority had moved on to a captain's rating. "I hate flying flight 3636, this is the worst paying long haul flight there is."

Harris awoke out of his daze, where he smiled, "Patience Bill, remember the worst paying routes allow you to get your captain's rating the fastest."

"It's been thirteen years, yet I'm still a flap operator."

Harris laughed at the remark, "Next time a captain's slot comes open, I'll write you a personal recommendation. You should be a shoe in. Don't you think so Cory?"

Corey Dillon smiled and nodded in agreement. Dillon was Olsen airways' only mechanic in Panama City. He needed to do some advanced maintenance training at Olsen's main repair hanger in Newark. For Dillon, this would one of his first flights in several years from Panama back to his Native New Jersey. Dillon had specifically asked for the jump seat in this flight. Trying hard to hold costs down flight Ops agreed, allowing Corey a rare glimpse of the cockpit in-flight.

"Hey, Carey, what's that huge cylindrical thing in the upper deck?"

Dillon fidgeted in his seat as his back began to ache from the stiff jump seat. "It's an airplane engine in a special shipping container."

Harris raised his eyebrows in surprise, "That's a big engine isn't it, Bill?" Stull failed to answer still sulking in his seat while staring out into the distance. Harris shook his head at the pathetic sight of his first officer.

"So, John, when will be over Norfolk?" Carey anxiously asked.

"About ten minutes."

"Are we going to be able to see the Navy docks where Vice President Douglas will be doing his address?"

Harris smiled. "There's no chance of that Carey, that whole airspace is restricted. As we close in on Norfolk, they'll direct us east over the Atlantic. I guess they're afraid that someone might try to crash an airplane into him or something." Harris then shook his head as he continued to glimpse at his FMS computer data.

Unseen Warriors

Dillon got up from his seat, stretched his back, and walked out the cockpit door. The cockpit door had been lazily left open through the long flight. Dillon mimicked going to the lavatory, instead he snuck out to the cargo deck. He continued to walk down the centre of the fuselage, sneaking between several narrow covered containers until he reached a massive iron cylinder. Dillon looked around then lifted a small steel plate near the bottom of the container. Exposing a keypad, Dillon punched several buttons until a timer began to count down from ten minutes. Dillon pulled out a large knife from behind the cover, carefully checking its sharpness by scraping it along his fingernail before folding the knife up before hiding it in his pocket. Dillon reinstalled the cover onto the keypad before heading for the lavatory.

* * * * *

Stull rubbed his watering eyes as he watched the aircraft come closer to the Norfolk airport way point. "I'm going to do the call of nature, okay?" Harris nodded as he donned his emergency oxygen mask, while staring out to the blackness in the distance.

Stull walked out the narrow corridor out of the cockpit toward the lavatory. Stopping short of the lavatory, he began to look around for Dillon. Stull rubbed his head, and looked forward. A hand grabbed him on his face. Stull struggled and fought as he tried to scream, but he was unable as the hand closed tighter around his mouth. Stull frantically tried to tear the hand off his mouth as he waved his arms grasping for anything nearby. A sharp pain ripped through his back before it spread into his chest. Stull struggled to breathe as his lung collapsed while his chest began to fill with blood. Stull violently waved his arms as he struggled to make noise, but Harris continued to stare out into the sky, still wearing his headset a mere fifteen feet away. Stull continued to cough up blood all over the floor, as a knife plunged into his heart, Stull lost all energy as his heart pumped out his remaining blood over his white shirt. Soon his body became still as his soul soon departed while his body gently fell to earth without making a sound.

Dillon wiped the blood of his knife blade and hands on Stull's coat. Dragging the lifeless body into the cargo deck, Dillon looked around. He nonchalantly walked into the lavatory, washing the rest of the blood off his hands and face, and then carefully combing his hair. Dillon then walked into the cockpit sitting in the jump seat and putting on his observer's headset.

"Carey, where were you?"

Dillon cleared his throat, "I had an extended visit in the lav. I saw Bill rush in after I walked out."

Harris snorted, "Yeah Bill ate too much Chinese food before we left Panama City. I think his body is rebelling at the lack of steak and potatoes."

"Can you see the shipyards from here?"

"Not really, there's too much overcast, anyways we'll probably have to do a course correction soon. New York center will soon ask us to fly east over the Atlantic Ocean in a couple of minutes."

Dillon's eyes grew red as opened his automatic knife, "No, we won't be traveling east over the Atlantic." Dillon cut the wire of Harris' headset. Harris immediately swung his head over, his eyes huge. Dillon lunged onto Harris, grabbing his head with one hand, while repeatedly stabbing Harris with his knife. Harris raised his hands trying to block the knife as it slashed his arms. Harris struggled as he pulled the yokes back and forth while he screamed for Stull as he tried to fend off Dillon's attack.

Dillon grabbed Harris' neck as he plunged the knife. Harris swung his arms as the knife plunged into his wrist. Blood sprayed all over his shirt and Dillon's arm. "Are you crazy, what's wrong with?" Dillon stayed silent as he pulled out the knife. Harris continued to fight back; punching Dillon in the stomach. Dillon fell to the ground fell to the ground. He wiped

Unseen Warriors

the blood from his face. He then charged as Harris frantically tried to level the aircraft and place it back on course. Dillon crashed into Harris struggled as Dillon's knife dug itself into Harris' stomach. Harris grabbed his stomach as he screamed in pain. Dillon rammed the knife into Harris' lung. Harris gasped as he tried to breathe as Dillon plunged the knife into his heart.

* * * * *

Larsen watched as OA3636 start to weave on his screen while losing thousands of feet of altitude. He quickly grabbed his radio, "Olsen cargo 3636, this is New York center." There was no reply from the jet. "Olsen Cargo 3636, you are violating FAA air regulations, please contact." Still no reply, Larsen began to panic. "Olsen 3636 please contact New York center control immediately, if do not answer we will send fighters to intercept you." The silence on the radio was deafening.

Larsen tore off his headset, "Bob, Olsen3636 is a no contact!" Robert Stacy looked at the radar screen, giving it a quick glance. He picked up the phone and called Homeland Security.

* * * * *

Mueller passed over Washington, D.C. The last hour's worth of flying was starting to make him sleepy. The radio began to fill with panicked voices. "Air force 705, New York center, we have an Olsen Airways MD-11 performing unlawful course and altitude deviations. The aircraft is headed toward Norfolk, traffic is being cleared, you are cleared to engage and neutralize the aircraft immediately."

"Copy," Mueller wiped his forehead as his gut tightened up. "Okay Goose, its show time." Mueller slammed the throttles full forward. He then pulled the F-22 into a tight 8g turn. Reversing course as the afterburners roared to life. The jets raced toward Norfolk, screaming through the air at almost 650 Knots. Mueller watched his range indicator quickly tick down as the distant lights of the coast line city came into view on the horizon. Muller knew that in short time they would be able to intercept the jet. Deep inside he wondered if he would arrive in time to prevent a disaster.

* * * * *

William Douglas stood in front of a large crowd of Navy support staff. In the back, a huge aircraft carrier stood docked. Sailors in their finest white uniforms freshly cleaned and pressed encircled the deck.

Douglas stood up to the Podium, while photographers continued to flash their cameras all around. "My fellow Americans, we are at the cross roads in the war of terror. We must continue to put pressure on terrorist nations that ship their attackers all across the globe. America requires a strong defense to protect us from these assassins.

"Many of our detractors claim that we are spending too much money on defense, that we are diverting resources from the war on terror by building cold war relics. Let me tell you this, myself and President Hawkins are committed to making America a formidable fighting force. This fighting force will be capable of defending America from terrorism all across the globe. We will have an ability to strike at the hearts of those terrorists who wish, before a single innocent American ever dies on the soil of this great nation.

"We are determined to keep all of our brave Service people safe with the most modern fighting equipment that we have available here in America, so that the war on terror may be won with their courage, determination and skill. Today I formally declare CVN-77, George H W Bush, our newest arsenal in the war of terror, officially in service with the United States Navy. May this mighty ship serve our nation well, ensuring the safety of our children and grandchildren."

Unseen Warriors

Air raid sirens began to sound as sailors rushed around the dock. Secret service agents quickly rushed to Douglas' side as a black limousine pulled up a few feet from the podium. "Good night and may God bless you," Douglas declared as he was quickly rushed into the awaiting limousine. Several secret service agents rushed into the awaiting motorcade as the vehicles rushed away from the adoring crowd.

* * * * *

Mueller watched his radar as the rapidly descending blip on his radar began to close in while he switched his radar to the 40-mile range. Continuing at 20,000 feet at full military thrust, Mueller selected his medium range radar missiles. A giant circle appeared on his Heads up display, a small square appeared at the bottom. Mueller anxiously rubbed his sweaty hands as he waited the missile to lock. "Goose, when you get a lock on, fire the missile ASAP," Mueller calmly commented.

"Copy," Taylor exuberantly replied.

Mueller watched as his aircraft rapidly closed into the MD-11 while he sped at Mach 1.1 without any afterburners. Finally, at 25 miles, a flashing diamond appeared over the square, while the words "Lock" flashed across the HUD. Mueller flicked his master arm switch to arm. Shortly afterwards the bomb bay doors quickly opened in the aircraft's belly. Two shimmering Aim-120E glistened in the night's sky as they waited for their command to leave the airplane.

"Fox 3," Mueller shouted as he depressed the fire button on his control stick. The two missiles began their freefall to earth as the attach clamps in the bomb bay released. Falling a mere fifteen feet from the jet's fuselage, the rocket motors fired off in a flash. Hurtling the missiles off into the night's sky, while the missiles' internal radar continued to guide them to their unseen prey.

"Fox 3," Taylor shouted as two fireballs raced by Mueller's starboard wingtip.

The MD-11 began a steep dive toward earth as it closed in on the navy shipyards. The aircraft continued to fall faster and as its airspeed continued to increase while winds buffeted its mighty fuselage. Mueller's missiles slammed into the fuselage, separating it into two pieces. Contents of the cargo pit spilled earthward as the two sections began to tumble and burn in midair as containers free felled to earth. Taylor's lead missile crashed into the aft fuselage section, skin sections tore like paper as cables, hydraulic lines and rivets snapped of the aircraft's thin aluminum hull. The Tail section, still intact with its rudder and elevators tumbled through the air as the number two engine sandwiched between the two continued to provide thrust as it consumed the last remnants of fuel in the lines.

The forward fuselage section began a steep fall to earth, while Dillon remained looking out the windshield, still strapped in the First Officer's seat. As the nose section passed below five thousand feet, Taylor's remaining missile slammed into the back of the fuselage, shredding the fuselage section. The debris fell like confetti over the docks as sailors rushed to dodge death from the sky.

Sailors stood on the docks, watching the light show in the sky. Explosions occurred all around them as two twin afterburner flames rushed across the sky. Many watched curiously as debris continued to rain down into the water, while fires burned in the sky.

A blinding flash raced through the air, shock waves blew out of the eye of the explosion a mere thousand feet from Douglas' podium. Spectators and media were blinded by the fly, before they were able to contemplate the horror in the sky. 1,000 MPH winds rushed through the docks instantly vaporizing them. Radioactive winds rushed passed the George Bush, the ship rocked and shook as the sailors and ground equipment vaporized from its deck. Slowly the ship began to roll until the hull finally slipped under the waves.

Vice President Douglas looked out of the port window of his UH-60. His eyes grew big as a giant fireball rushed toward him as the helicopter strained to escape the death approaching him. Nine hundred miles per hour winds raced through helicopter, the rotor blades broke away as the fuselage exploded while the nuclear winds incinerated the hull into ash and dust.

The winds continued rush north and east from the Elizabeth River. Naval vessels, cargo ships, and pleasure craft burned in the river as their crew's vaporized before they were even able to scream. At Norfolk's airport, aircraft burned on airports tarmac, gates and on the runways. Aircraft and body parts rained down from the sky as Far East as Virginia Beach as the winds reversed course and rushed into the epicenter. Men, women and children still left alive in burned out terminal building screamed in pain as their burned bodies oozed with bodily fluids from open sores. The smell of burned flesh filled the terminal buildings as dying people prayed to their various Gods for immediate death.

Burned out cars lined Interstate 464 from as far south as Essex Meadows as far north of Willoughby Beach. Office buildings in downtown Norfolk stood hauntingly empty as the winds stripped the mighty buildings to nothing more than concrete shells.

The nuclear winds finally slowed after crossing eastern fork of the Elizabeth River. Residents as far as West Virginia beach Boulevard stood in awe as the massive mushroom cloud rose in the sky. Night became day.

As the mushroom cloud began to slowly dissipate, the remaining residents wandered dazed and confused through the barren streets unable to fathom the holocaust that had just occurred. Anarchists quickly grabbed their firearms while rushing through burned sections of the city looting at will. Gun shops fought pitched battles with the attacking mobs as hundreds of victims, some still with untreated burns, rushed the gun shops trying to obtain weapons and ammunition to protect themselves from the looters. Gun battles between rival factions occurred all over the empty streets, as those without weapons became victims in the deadly crossfire.

*****

Governor Gary Larkin sat back in his plush chair watching his children play. His wife Sheila came and gave him a steaming cup of hot chocolate. "There you go, Gary."

Larkin smiled as he watched his two boys play with their Lego. "I can't believe Ryan and Dennis are seven now. It seems like yesterday when they were born. Sheila, I've decided, I'm no going to run for a second term. I spend all my time running the state it leaves me with no time for the twins. I'm tired of playing politics while ignoring you. I want to spend more with you."

Sheila smiled as she gave him a hug. Tears flowed down her cheek as she became choked up. "But Gary, you start out in politics to make difference, and you have. We still spend time together, maybe it isn't as much as I would like. But you try your best, the twins sure aren't suffering." Larkin gave a serious look as he looked into Sheila's eyes. Shelia gave Larkin a deep look into his eyes in return. "If you don't want to run again, do it because you want to. Don't do it because you feel guilty about missing time with the kids. Anyways, the fireworks will be starting soon dear. I'll turn on the TV."

Larkin smiled as helped Ryan with his Lego as the phone rang on Larkin's private line. Larkin answered, his smile soon turned to a frown as Sheila looked on with a puzzled look. "Of course, send the National Guard out, I want them to shoot on site. Also, I want martial law declared with an immediate curfew!"

Sheila looked with a sorrowful look. "What is it dear?"

"Norfolk naval yards was hit by a nuclear attack. The naval works plus large portions of Norfolk, Chesapeake and

Unseen Warriors

Portsmouth crew wiped out. Looting has broken out, as well as mass panic. I guess it's too early to get out of the Governor's mansion just yet. Sheila looked with a shocked look.

* * * * *

    Cars clogged the highway trying to escape the devastation. US 13, US 17, I-58. I-664, and US 258 filled with cars whose owners carried their worldly possessions as they escaped the ruins of the nuclear holocaust. State police officers vainly tried to control the mayhem on the roads. All their efforts were futile as cars crossed mediums and emergency lanes undeterred by the heavy Police presence on the roads.
    Hospitals filled with burned and blinded people while their staff broke under the crush of people. Doctors, nurses, even orderlies tried to deal with the horrifying injuries of the incoming people. Death filled the air as the masses too sick to walk died in the hospital parking lots, waiting rooms and even in the cafeterias while waiting for medical care that would never come for them.
    National Guardsmen fought pitched gun battles in the streets with looters and militias armed with shotguns, assault rifles and even hunting rifles. The vastly outnumbered Guardsmen fought with all of their might and courage wile watching their numbers dwindle further as radiation sickness soon began to conquer even some of the many mightiest of men. For the brave Guardsmen, Armageddon had come and the anti-Christ had finally delivered his blow. They prayed for Jesus on his white horse to come deliver them from this Hell on Earth.

Chapter 17

Madras, Oregon
04-July-2010
1400 Hours Local Time

    Babajhan looked at his four associates. They wore authentic US Army uniforms, down to their ranks and insignia. Babajhan felt proud speaking in confidence, "Gentlemen, our associates on the eastern seaboard will begin their phase of the attack in about a couple of hours. Here are your dog-tags, from now on only speak English to each other with your assumed names." The men looked at their names on their dog tags: Lieutenant Townsend, Private Wong, Private Bouchard and Corporal Schneider.
    The men grabbed their dog tags and put them on. Babajhan looked at the men, "Allah Akbar." The men returned the saying before entering their trucks.
    The men posing as Lieutenant Townsend and Private Wong pulled out of the rural Madras, OR. They headed on US 26 westbound to Portland.
    Babajhan looked at the remaining men. "Do your attack at

Unseen Warriors

7:00pm. I need to go back to Pakistan. Babajhan disappeared into a black BMW that drove off into the distance. The two remaining men inspected their green six axle US Army truck transport truck mentally preparing for their grizzly duty.

The Lieutenant looked at his map while the Private drove. "Don't drive too fast. We don't want to arouse suspicion." The private nodded in agreement. They continued on its way through the picturesque cascade mountain range. The bright summer shown down on the faded truck while it passed by Mt. Hood. Slowly the truck wove its way through the windy roads passing by small towns such as Welches and Sandy.

Residents watched and waved at the truck as it passed through downtown Sandy. The two camouflaged clothed men in the cab continued, unconcerned by the attention they attracted. The truck passed through the congested streets of Gresham. More of the local population waved flags and cheered at the vehicle, unaware of its deadly cargo. The truck continued through the heavy traffic until it finally made its way to Interstate 84 on ramp.

The Private spoke as he continued on the road ahead. "There's a lot of police on the roads ahead, maybe we should take an alternative route."

"No! We need to time our attacks, if we are late, we aren't going to have our element of surprise," the officer snapped back

"We are taking a big risk," the Private replied in a worrying tone.

"Don't worry, I will detonate at will if required," the officer said as he handled a small control panel connected by wires directly to his dangerous payload.

* * * * *

The Corporal and Private entered their Green military transport truck. They followed the same path the first truck took, exactly three hours to the minute later. They traveled a brisk pace, carefully driving below the speed limit until they reached Portland. The truck soon arrived in Portland. Traveling along a side road along the Airport, the truck soon arrived at the Portland Air National Guard base.

The Private became anxious as he approached the main gate. The truck pulled up slowly. A young entrance guard looked inside while he spoke, "Your military identification cards and orders." The Corporal and Private passed their fake ID cards and travel orders. The guard looked at their id cards then he stared hard into the orders. "I have to check something." The guard went back to speak into the telephone. He spoke softly while nodding his head while and over at the waiting truck. A scowl began to cover his face as he looked in the cab of the waiting truck.

"Floor it!" The Corporal shouted. The trucks' engine raced. The massive weight of the vehicle bogged it down as the Private floored the gas pedal. The truck tore through the gate, shattering the block into pieces. Guards rushed in shooting at the fleeing truck with their M-16's.

The truck rushed around between buildings as machine guns opened fire, tearing holes in the truck's thin sheet metal skin. The Corporal reached down under the seat and pulled up an AK-47 with a hundred round drum. Leaning out the window he fired automatic gunfire at the rapidly approaching vehicles behind him.

Air raid sirens sounded as the truck rushed toward the waiting F-15s. Humvees filled with troops rushed to close in on the truck. The Private wove the truck left and right on the airport ramp. The Corporal continued spraying gunfire in the direction of the approaching vehicles. Rounds tore into the lead vehicle's windshield. The driver slumped over as brain matter and blood sprayed over his passenger. The steering wheel jerked to the right. The Humvee rolled several times, ejecting bodies, guns

Unseen Warriors

and magazines over the ramp. The trailing Humvees slammed on their brakes, blue smoke poured out of their tires. The drivers madly tried to avoid the damaged Humvee ahead of them. The trailing vehicles slammed into the vehicle rolled on its side. Flames erupted through the two vehicles. Injured soldiers unable to move burned alive.

The truck continued to rush through the ramp, sideswiping F-15's in the process. Military police officers fired their automatic rifles before rushing to avoid the fast approaching vehicle. A rooftop sniper on one of the hangers fired his Remington 700 at the fast approaching vehicle. The bullet tore into the man's chest, shredding his lung in the process. The truck crossed through ramp, crashing into the ditch along the taxiway.

The bleeding corporal watched the approaching vehicles spray the truck with gunfire. Chanting, "Allah Akbar with his last breath, he pressed a red button on the keypad. A click occurred followed by silence.

Armed soldiers approached, guns pointed at the overturned truck. Sergeant Dempsey signaled to Private Ryan and Private Hayden. The two men walked the back of the truck. Ryan grabbed one door handle, while Hayden grabbed the other door handle. Dempsey nodded his head. The two quickly pulled the door open to reveal a ten-foot long cylinder.

The soldiers slowly walked through the tight cargo hold of the truck before making their way to cab. Inside the cab lay two dead men wearing US Army combat fatigues. Dempsey slowly inspected the soldiers with extreme caution.

* * * * *

Airport officials quickly ordered all aircraft into gates. TSA and Port of Portland Police frantically tried to evacuate the terminal building. Crowds quickly gathered outside the terminals. Dazed and confused people tried grasp the enormity of the situation. Overwhelmed Police tried to contain the growing chaos. They pushed the overflowing crowds into the roadway. Drivers in cars shouted and screamed in frustration, unable to depart the maddening gridlock. Airport way became blocked with vehicles unable continue forward or reverse in order to escape the roadway. Army helicopters flew overhead as chaos rained supreme. Baffled police tried to combat panic and hysteria among the general populace.

Portland's light rail train, MAX, continued on its regular schedule from the Columbia street station on toward the airport. Passengers riding the train watched in confusion as the train arrived at its station mere feet from the hysterical crowds. A man wearing a dark suit walked out of the train, carrying his bulky suitcases. He looked up at the ornate glass above him. Smiling, he continued to drag his suitcase until he stood in a crowded section of roadway.

Carefully, he looked around at the terminal building full of shouting and screaming patrons. He slowly worked his way through the heart of the crowd, remaining apologetic at all times. Looking around one last time, he left his heavy bag among many. The crowds continued to pour out of the terminal building, pushing their way further and further into the roadway's extremities. The man slowly walked back, unnoticed by the crowds all around him to the waiting train. He watched the crowds of people continue to panic, closing in on the large suitcase in the middle of the roadway.

The shadowy figure rode the max train until he arrived at Columbia station. Nonchalantly, he walked up to his car, waiting in a public parking nearby. He drove his Black BMW the short distance to Mt. Tabor. Getting out of the car, he adjusted his hat and coat. The man pulled out his binoculars. He carefully scanned the airport from his hilltop position. Blackhawk and Huey Cobra helicopters circled the airport overhead. Airport way was a solid mass of cars in both directions. Small clouds of tear gas rose slowly rose from the terminal buildings. Smiling, he pulled out his cell phone and dialed a 503 area code phone number.

* * * * *

Bomb squad members entered at the overturned truck. They attempted to understand the inner workings of the control panel attached to the strange cylindrical object. An Entire Army platoon stood guard around as they prepared for a secondary attack at any moment.

The head bomb squad member pulled aside a cover to look at a key pad attached to an alarm clock type digital display. The numbers appeared to be slowly increasing. His curiosity perked, he continued to look around the box for wiring while keeping his eyes on digital display. The digital display turned to four numbers: 66:66 then stopped it froze.

The truck exploded into a huge fireball. Axles, fenders, engine parts pounded the soldiers before hot winds incinerated them. Airmen as far away as F-15 ramp screamed in pain as steel nails tore into their frail bodies as the ground around the truck disappeared into dust.

Huey Cobras helicopters hovering above violently swayed as flames rushed by them. Instantly, the hot winds turned the complex mechanical machines into burning metal dust. Violent winds blew through the frail metal hangers housing F-15s. The jet fighter exploded inflames with the disintegrating hangers. The violent winds quickly shifted, sucking in any solid objects still remaining at the Air National Guard base. A giant mushroom cloud rose from the ground. Dying men, their shin burned of their flesh, lay all around the outskirts of the base. Burning buildings echoed with their moans, but no one was able to tend to their wounds.

The sound of the loud explosion and mushroom cloud in the

sky caused chaos outside the terminal. People began to trample each other as they rushed to run away. Crowds raced to pack into the waiting max trains. Jamming into the open doors, people tried to force themselves in. Innocent passengers at either end of the train cars struggled to breathe as they were forced harder and harder into the walls. Cars lay abandoned all along Airport Way. People struggling to enter the crowded roadway with their precious vehicles, now ran away, terrified of the rising cloud in the southern sky.

    Corporal Cook, a Port of Portland police officer, noticed an orphaned boy crying in the middle of a stack of abandoned suitcases. Taken aback by the plight of the lonely boy, he approached the crying child, unconcerned with the utter chaos break out all around him. Approaching the lost child, he knelt down speaking in a childlike voice. The child wiped his eyes and walked toward Cook, falling over a large suitcase. Cook grabbed the child, wiping the tears from his face. Cook looked at the strange suitcase, noticing a silver tag attached to the handle. Looking further, he realized the tag was a US Army dog tag for a soldier the name of Mowia Mohammed. Cook called in, reporting his find. His sergeant replied back, warning him not to inspect the bag. A bomb squad dog would come quickly. Cook agreed, he grabbed the boy and walked away still sneaking peeks at the suitcase. Cook sat down inside, the now abandoned, airport terminal. The empty hall echoed with the sounds of distant footsteps. Cook played with the child while still keeping an eye at the distant suitcase.

    A huge explosion erupted out of the suitcase. A flash blinded the crowds in the roadway and parking garages. Hot winds quickly swept the terminal, parking garages and gates while incinerating people trying to outrun their deaths. Fireball winds rushed along Airport way, the massive traffic jam disappeared into a fast-moving fireball. Aircraft at gates exploded one after the other as the winds tore through aluminum hulls. Dying

Unseen Warriors

National Guardsmen received their dying wishes. Firestorm winds rushed through the base, homes business as far as Columbia Blvd. succumbed to burning winds. The winds quickly reversed direction, concrete, rocks, steel all rushed into the burned airport building. A huge mushroom cloud rose boldly in the sky.

Cars packed Interstate 5, 90, 205, US 26, and 30. The frightened general population packed every car, motorcycle and ATV they had. Any vehicle which could provide transportation was used to escape the Metro region.

Standing on Mt. Tabor, the dark suited man smiled at the rising mushroom cloud in the sky. He looked at his watch, waiting ten minutes he then dialed another 503 area code phone number. He closed his phone while giving an evil laugh. Shaking his head, he drove off into the sunset.

* * * * *

The green army transport truck continued to drive along the Interstate 5. Clunking and shaking as it ran out the concrete expansion joints. Arriving at the I-405 interchange, traffic slowed to a standstill. The impatient driver looked at the officer. "This is slowing us down; we won't make our 7:00pm appointment."

The passenger looked over. "Relax Amoud, Allah will be with us." Traffic continued to travel slowly, inching its way through downtown Seattle. Looking at his watch again, the driver impatiently left the freeway at the 7th avenue exit. The truck then took a hard right turn onto Madison Street. The rear wheels slid across the slick wet roads narrowly missing a Volkswagen bus stopped in the westbound lane. The truck continued to race eastbound on Madison, spinning the tires through intersections.

Corporal Davidge sat in his Seattle Police department patrol car in the Swedish medical center parking lot. Davidge tried to drink his hot coffee. He curled his eyebrows as he burned his roof of his mouth with the hot coffee. "Damn it!" Davidge shouted as he tried to cool his coffee.

The truck roared through the red light at the Boren avenue intersection. Davidge threw his coffee out the window and turning on his lights simultaneously. He sped off out of the parking lot, eastbound on Madison Street Davidge raced toward the speeding truck, confused drivers tried to pull over in the heavy long weekend traffic.

Davidge closed toward the truck accelerated forward, narrowly avoiding sideswiping cars stopped all around him. "Dispatch, 13-622, I'm in pursuit of speeding military transport truck eastbound on Madison, crossing Broadway right now."

"Copy 622, we'll send backup," the dispatcher replied. A King county sheriff pulled off Broadway joining Davidge on the pursuit.

The truck continued to rush down the street increasing speed at every moment. It smashed through cars waiting at the Pike street intersection, weaving through the lanes.

A westbound Ford truck crashed head long into the fleeing truck. The truck shoved the vehicle aside into oncoming cars. Davidge and the County sheriff carefully wove through the mess of wrecked vehicles undeterred by the carnage around them

Two Seattle city police cars raced off of 23rd avenue. Their rear tires smoking as they cut in front of Davidge. The two cars pulled up, side by side, to the speeding truck. Officer Daniels drove the car at left flank Officer Witt drove on the right flank.

The truck jerked to the left, slamming into the police car. Daniels hung onto the steering wheel for dear life as he fumbled for his Glock 17 Handgun. Daniels pulled out his gun, narrowly missing oncoming traffic. The canvas back cover of the truck quickly opened. A camouflage fatigued man pulled out an AK-47 and began to fire at Daniels. Bullets slammed into Daniels' windshield and right fender. Daniels tried to cover his head behind the dash, barely able to see the road. Glass shattered all around him.

Daniels slammed the gas, accelerating to an almost parallel position beside the truck. He harshly jerked his steering wheel to the right. His car slammed into the truck's front tires with a loud crunch. The truck shook and swayed, almost uncontrollably. The driver slammed the wheels to the left trying to counteract the rising left wheels. The truck swung around to a harsh ninety degree turn. Westbound cars smashed into each other, madly avoiding the massive truck crossing ahead of them.

The driver stormed the vehicle north along East Interstate Blvd. in Washington Park. Daniels pained to stay behind the truck, fighting to gain control along the narrow windy road through the park. The gunmen appeared occasionally to fire a short burst of rounds at the approaching police cars. Often he wildly missed the swerving vehicles.

The truck raced around the corner toward Lake Washington Blvd. A police road block appeared up ahead. Officers fired their AR-15 rifles at the fast approaching vehicle. The truck increased speed, undeterred by the gunfire erupting ahead of it. Police completed laying a spike belt at the road block. They rapidly jumped out of the way of the truck rushing toward them.

The truck tore through a point of the road block at the far right edge. Stunned officers rushed into their cars. The truck rocked its sides, lifting its left wheels off the ground as raced onto the eastbound S20 highway on ramp.

Steam rose out of the trucks' radiator. The driver, unconcerned, continued to drive onto the floating bridge. Truck raced at full speed, its his windshield too fogged up. The driver wiped the glass with his bloody hand. He looked to his passenger for a fleeting second. The passenger held a torn T shirt onto his bleeding shoulder. An Ak-47 lay on his lap. Daniels raced along the side of the truck's passenger's side pulling out his Glock. He held it steady as he approached the cab. Witt continued behind the truck, holding the steering wheel stiff. Officer Ault, Witt's, partner pulled out his Glock cleared the shards of glass around him. Ault held his gun steady on the dashboard, aiming at the truck ahead.

The gunmen appeared from canvas. He fired automatic gunfire at Witt's patrol car. Ault quickly fired three bullets in rapid succession. The gunmen froze for a second. Ault rapidly fired five more bullets. The gunmen dropped his gun on the pavement. He grabbed his chest, and then fell to the street. The police cars violently swerved to avoid hitting the bleeding body in the roadway.

Daniels fired his Glock at the trucks' spinning tires. The truck slammed into the police car. Daniels fought to regain control as the car. The vehicle careened over the guard rail crashing into lake Washington.

Witt slowed down his patrol car as the truck continued to weave back and forth between lanes. Ault loaded another magazine into his pistol, he continued to fire at the rushing truck ahead of him until the magazine was empty. The truck's aft tires exploded. Rubber shrapnel sprayed into the pursuing Police vehicles. The truck spun around the wet pavement, rolling end over end. Parts peeled of its frail skin. The truck came to rest, wheels up on its crushed roof. A fire burned from its engine compartment. The Pursuing police cars slammed on their brakes, trying to dodge the assortment of truck parts scattered along the roadway.

Witt and Ault rushed out of their cars, guns pointed at the truck. Corporal Davidge quickly joined in with Sergeant Roberts—a fellow King County Sheriff officer. The sound of sirens grew louder and louder as more vehicles continued to approach. The bridge gently swayed side to side in the breeze. Emergency vehicles rushed toward the wreck in both directions. A final count, there were thirty vehicles parked all around the disabled truck. Firefighters sprayed down the burning truck while several Police helicopters circled from overhead.

Sergeant Roberts grabbed his AR-15 and aimed it at the back truck. More officers grabbed whatever weapons they had. The officers followed Roberts' lead, their fingers waited apprehensively on their triggers. Corporal Davidge ran to the cab, inside a dead man wearing standard US Army Camouflage fatigues lay twisted and torn across the front seat.

Witt ran the back door and held. Davidge rushed to position himself nearby. Witt flung the door open. Davidge rushed forward with his bright flashlight in one hand, his gun in the other. The flashlight pierced the darkness, unveiling a horrifying sight. A large green cylindrical object lay strapped to a wooden pallet. A small makeshift electronic control panel was attached at the top of the cylinder.

Roberts put his rifle down and approached forward toward the strange object. Barely in view, a cheap cellular phone was attached to the control panel. Roberts flinched as the phone began to ring. A nanosecond later, a bright flash occurred.

Immediately the truck, surrounding people and pieces of debris on the roadway vaporized. Nuclear winds rushed out of the epicenter into the distance. The bridge shook for a second before disappearing under the waters of Lake Washington. Huge tidal waves rushed out from the center of the explosion, ever increasing in size as they covered the Lake. Boat and rafts bobbing in the lake were quickly incinerated just before the huge waves rushed unabated toward the lakeshore.

People playing at Edgewater Park grabbed their eyes as the flashed blinded them. They soon screamed in pain as the radiation burned off their delicate flesh before the tidal wave swamped them.

Students at the University of Washington hid their eyes where they stood at the shores of Union bay. The giant tidal wave crashed into the lakeshore, destroying everything in sight. The waves raced to Pacific Street, washing cars from the roadway. The waves the rushed over the 24th Avenue Bridge, washing any vehicles that dared to cross its deadly path into Portage bay.

The Nuclear wind quickly changed direction. They then rushed back into themselves and formed a missive mushroom cloud in the sky. People as far away as Everett, Tacoma, Kent and even Bremerton stood in awe and shock. Paralyzed by fear by the haunting sight, vehicles plugged the main arterial highway out of Seattle; Interstate 5 and Interstate 90 became huge parking lots as the fear struck population scrambled to escape their nightmare. Flights became stranded as toxic clouds of radioactive debris dumped their deadly cargo all around the Puget Sound area. Looters, in all their ugliness, rushed through the empty city blocks, uncaring of the radiation burning off their skin.

Washington, D.C.
04-July-2010
2200 Hours Local Time

Steven Hawkins and his wife, Mary, stood on the lawn of the White House. He prepared to start the Fourth of July fireworks celebrations. Hawkins smiled, stepping up to the podium to make his speech.

Smiling and laughing he cleared his throat. "Gentlemen, today we celebrate our freedom. Our nation was born fighting for freedom from tyranny and oppression. Over the last 279 years we have fought nations who have held definite borders, definite names and are definite plans for their attack.

But today, we fight an enemy who larks among us. An enemy who hates us for the very freedoms we have. I will fight every day that I'm president, so that Americans will never have to live in fear. I promise that as long as I am president America will be safe from terrorist attacks."

Reporters rushed foward, rushing to Hawkins' podium. Secret service agents rushed forward shielding Hawkins. Hawkins formed his ranks, the secret service agents quickly relaxed. Hawkins stepped forward to the microphones being forced to his face, cameras flashed all around him. "Mr. President, what are you doing to do now that the naval yards at Norfolk have been destroyed by the terrorist nuclear attack?" Hawkins eyes grew huge as he removed his spectacles while unable to speak.

Chapter 18

1600 Pennsylvania Avenue
Washington, D.C.
20-June-2010
0600 Hours Local Time

Hawkins rushed into the White House conference room, madly calling in his trusted inner circle. David Wolf, homeland secretary was the first to rush to the makeshift special session. "Good morning Sir." Hawkins remained silent, giving a cold stare while he fathomed the events of the last few hours.

Secretary of defense William Cohen and secretary of state Thomas Bowen jointly appeared. Their hair was unkempt and they wore civilian clothing.

"Where the hell are Douglas and Dave?" Hawkins barked while curling his lip.

Wolf meekly stood up. "Sir, Vice President Douglas was in Norfolk at the time of the attack. We believe that Mr. Douglas may be a casualty." Hawkins tried to wipe the tears that began to drip from his eyes. "CIA director Henry Lee was in Seattle for his daughter's wedding. No one has been able to contact him, at present he is presumed missing." Hawkins lowered his head on the conference as he tried to ponder the events. Hawkins thought of his seven year plus relationship with the two men.

"Mr. President, sir." Hawkins flinched.

Wolf spoke again. "Shall we continue?"

Hawkins nodded, still in deep emotional depression.

"There were four attacks today. The first attack occurred in the Azores. The launch vehicle was a scud missile carrying 2.5 megaton yield thermonuclear device. The transport means was via a merchant cargo ship. It seems the ship was probably highjacked soon after it left South Africa. It later docked at an unknown port, then continuing directly to the Azores."

"How do we know the ship was highjacked, it could have been run by a rogue shipping line," Bowman rudely interrupted Wolf.

"Not possible, the shipping line is owned by Vice President Douglas!" Voices were heard from the room as Wolf tried to keep everyone the room calm. Wolf shuffled through more papers, trying to keep his reading glasses from falling off. "The ship was armed with one nuclear tipped scud and seven surface to air missiles of an unknown manufacture. We lost one F-15E and at least one Blackhawk. The Portuguese are attempting to rescue our downed airmen. Is there anything you wish to add Mr. Cohen?"

Cohen stood up buttoning his coat. "From the reports I received, the ship had quite a sophisticated tracking radar system. Our F-15's didn't even know the ship was preparing to launch the missiles until the aircraft were practically right on top of the ship."

Hawkins waved his hand, he trying to rush the briefing along. Wolf stood up again. "A cargo aircraft attacked our Norfolk ship yards. It was shot down by our combat air patrol aircraft. Unfortunately a very large bomb, almost seven megatons, exploded in mid air before the aircraft was totally consumed by the fire and explosion."

"Mr. Cohen which ships were destroyed in Norfolk?" Hawkins quibbled with a mixture of anger and depression.

Cohen shuffled through a pile of papers until he found the list. "This is an incomplete list at this time: USS George Washington (CVN 73), USS George HW Bush (CVN-77).

"As for attack subs that we lost: USS Oklahoma City (SSN 756), and the USS Scranton (SSN 756).

"The loss of frigates would be: USS Carr (FFG 52), USS Kaufman (FFG 59) and the USS Klakring (FFG 42).

"Finally for Arleigh Burke Class destroyers we lost: USS Barry (DDG 52), USS Gonzalez (DDG 66), ant the USS Mason (DDG 87)."

"Mr. Cohen, just tell me how many ships in raw numbers," Hawkins complained in a bored tone.

"Confirmed losses were as follows: two carriers, two submarines, two fighters, and three destroyers. Like I said, this is only a partial list."

"Mr. Wolf what is the death toll?"

"Sir, I'm not sure exactly but our best estimates seem to be." Wolf dropped a file folder onto the floor spilling papers everywhere. Hawkins rubbed his face as Wolf frantically tried to gather his papers together.

"I want to know now!" Hawkins' voice boomed through the room.

Wolf grabbed a piece of paper from the floor while profusely shaking and sweating. "From the Azores, the death toll is 5,000. Norfolk is 120,000, Portland Oregon, 1700 and Seattle Washington's toll is 900. So, the total is 127,600 civilians and military personnel."

Hawkins sank back in his chair as his eyes glazed over. "Almost three times our death toll in Vietnam." The room became eerily quiet at the sound of the massive death toll. Hawkins looked at Richard's wedding photo on the conference table surrounded by papers. Hawkins shook his head as the horror of terrorism continued to sink into his head.

Unseen Warriors

"On top of that Mr. President, I the center for disease control figures that at least 40,000 more deaths are expected in the next three years from radiation poisoning," Wolf spoke meekly to the President.

"What's our situation on the ground in Norfolk?"

"Norfolk is in total anarchy." Hawkins listened intently, his face remained emotionless. "Most of the police officers are either dead of wounded. The governor called out what little national troops he has. Far away states, Pennsylvania, Connecticut, North Carolina even Georgia are sending troops to help combat the looting and violence.

"The city of Portsmouth is in total lawlessness right now. Armed bands of thugs carrying rifles patrol the streets, killing and looting at will. Right now weapon equal power, we don't have enough law enforcement resources for police to make a difference."

Hawkins tapped his nails, "Is the situation improving at all?"

Wolf shook his head, "It is getting worse, and most of downtown Norfolk is a no entry zone for Police day or night. The no entry zones are spread across the city."

Hawkins stormed out of his chair, "Damn it Dave, I'm tired of hearing about this doom and gloom. Cohen, I want you to find the bastards who did this attack. Then nuke them with every damn bomb we have. I don't ever care if they just claim responsibility. Just nuke them, anyway that you can!

"Bowman, get Henry's assistant, I can't remember his damn name. Make him the acting head of the CIA. Tell him to find our attackers ASAP." Hawkins looked out into the room, "Is this understood?"

The entire room answered in one complete "Yes, Sir." Hawkins stormed out of the room.

Islamabad, Pakistan
05-July-2010
1200 Hours Local Time

Townsend sat in his jail cell. The noise of the marketplace woke him as the sun strained to rise into the horizon. Townsend tried to see what time it was. But for him there were no clues in the way of clocks or calendars. It was almost as if time didn't exist here.

A disruption down the hall could be heard. The sound of banging of bars and shouting disturbed the silence. Townsend sat back, analyzing his situation. The noise continued became louder. Babajhan arrived, carrying an MP-5 sub machine slung on his shoulder. He looked deeply at Townsend. Rage could be seen burning in his eyes. "Townsend follow me!" Guards quickly unlocked the cell door for Babajhan. Townsend failed to move a muscle. Babajhan stormed into the cell then beat Townsend with his guns' collapsible stock.

Blood tore out Townsend's forehead as he tried to stand up. Babajhan grabbed Townsend's epilate. Babajhan proceeded to drag him up the stairs to an awaiting Mansoor. Mansoor sat back in his chair as Babajhan threw Townsend on the floor at Mansoor's feet. Townsend looked up at Mansoor's face, "Why are you doing this?"

Mansoor gave an evil laugh then stood up, walking to edge of his desk, he sat on it mere feet from Townsend. Townsend struggled to get up, "The reason will be quite clear in a few minutes, Mr. Hawkins. Babajhan curled his lip as he looked down on Townsend. Mansoor looked coldly at Babajhan, "Now is not the right time." Babajhan kept a mean stare at Townsend.

Colonel Massoud stormed into the room, dragging Sergeant Gibson by his tattered shirt. Massoud looked at Mansoor for a brief second. Mansoor nodded slowly, still maintaining a cold stare at Townsend. Gibson screamed in pain as his broken wrist crashed on the concrete floor. Massoud gave a swift kick to Gibson's ribs, Gibson screamed in pain as he gasped to breathe through his broken ribs.

Mansoor raised his hand at Massoud. "Stop! We are not barbarians Colonel." Massoud stepped back, unconcerned with Gibson reeling in pain on the floor. "I have brought you two here as witnesses to life and death. The birth of a great new Islamic Empire which will be dominate in the Middle East. And death of a corrupt infidel empire, the likes of which have never been seen before."

Mansoor gave Townsend a hand. Townsend got up and stepped to a large window overlooking the street. Townsend's eyes grew huge. An entire battalion of soldiers stood in the main square. Bell Huey Cobra gunships hovered overhead. F-16 flew over deafening all those below with the roar of their engines.

Townsend looked over to Mansoor with a puzzled look. "Your American forces are quite out matched in the deserts of Afghanistan. Many of their air assets are tied up in the civil war and strike in Iraq. Soon I will send my troops through Khyber Pass and take Kabul. Another battalion will march from Quetta to Kandahar and join forces with the Taliban. With our combined forces, Afghanistan will fall and so will your puppet region of Hammed Karzai."

"Why, what do you gain by this anyways?"

Mansoor laughed at Townsend. "Have you ever heard of the Trans-Afghanistan pipeline?"

"Yeah, it's a pipeline that some conspiracy buffs claim is being built to feed Israel."

"Wrong, it's a spider web of pipelines being built from Karachi to Iran, Tajikistan and Uzbekistan. You see Saudi Arabia and the other Gulf States have been making far too much from their oil sales. Once we get our pipeline done, the massive oil fields south of Kandahar and Laskar Gah will be mine. Through the help of the Iranians, I will be able to feed the worlds' massive appetite for oil. The Iranians will help of course, for which they will receive a cut of the profits.

"Then Mr. Babajhan and friends with cripple Saudi Arabia and Kuwait's oil production. The United States will be stuck in

Iraq where oil wells will be regularly destroyed. My consortium of countries will be richer than all of Gulf States."

"You're mad. There's no oil in Afghanistan, not would my father allow you to ever attack," Townsend protested.

"Wrong again," Mansoor shook his head. "The oil field has always been there, the stupid Taliban never realized it. Osama Bin Laden knew about the oil. He started some crude exploration when George Bush attacked in 2002. That halted his exploration, but not my will to explore further. But luckily for me, your occupation allowed my geologists not only verify the true existence of oil fields, but to calculate the size." Mansoor shuffled to his desk and pulled out a piece of paper. "It seems there's almost 10 percent of the world's proven oil reserves.

"As for your dad, watch this." Mansoor placed a videotape into a nearby VCR. Images flashes of burning aircraft carriers sunk in water. Empty burning buildings were all over. The camera flashed to a hospital where men, women and children all screamed as their burned skin was treated.

Mansoor turned up the volume, a news anchor read the news. "The state department reports that the death toll stands at 135,000 from yesterday's nuclear attacks. Radiation burn cases continue to flood into Hampton City hospitals. The Center for Disease Control reports that all the soil within thirty-five miles of the attack is contaminated. Much of the running water is also unfit for human use. Please, stand by for more instructions from homeland security."

Mansoor turned off the T.V. and gave Townsend one last stare. "You see, I don't joke around, I'm deadly serious when it comes to politics." Townsend fell to his knees, contemplated the events on the television screen.

"Now Mr. Hawkins, you and Sergeant Gibson have outlived your usefulness. Colonel Massoud will escort you to your new home."

Massoud shouted several words in Punjabi. Two guards rushed into the room, guns in hand. Townsend looked up at the guard, and nodded his head. The other guard grabbed Sergeant Gibson and dragged him away. Townsend looked back at Mansoor. "It has been a pleasure having your company Mr. Hawkins. Townsend slumped over and walked ahead of the guard, Colonel Massoud followed behind."

Babajhan curled his lip as he looked over to Mansoor. "You should have let me kill him."

"No, Haroon. Now is not the right time." Babajhan gave an angry look. "Hawkins will be going to a place where he will suffer for more than anyone has suffered. By the time I finish with him, he will wish he was dead." Babajhan grinned in pleasure.

Part 3

Desert Seige

Chapter 19

Islamabad, Pakistan
05-July-2010
1200 Hours Local Time

Nishan looked out his window. Islamabad was beautiful with ornate buildings, green trees and the Indus River flowing through the center of the city. Although he felt apprehension on his coming adventure, he also felt at ease at the site of the beautiful city below.

Collins looked at Atta. The long flight had worn him with fatigue. But he felt wide awake as the airplane banked its left wing as it lined up for final approach. "So, do we get to meet Mansoor when we touch down?"

Atta shrugged, "I'm not sure. You will meet my contact first, from there you will follow up higher up the chain of command." Collins nodded as the aircraft landed along the runway before coming to a stop. Atta led the team out of the jet. The harsh noise of the airplane's APU cut through the air. The concrete under the team's feet vibrated with passing of a dirty Pakistani airways jetliner.

Collins looked around, armed Cobra gunships took off and landed like charging bees above the airport. Collins looked to Atta, screaming over the sound of jet engines all around him. "Hey, Tariq why are their gunships flying all around the airport?"

"Mr. Mansoor ensures security at all his airports just like you do. Homeland security reins with an iron fist." Walters rolled up his sleeves, the hot sun burned his skin with pain.

The team relaxed, entering the air-conditioned terminal building. Collins became nervous seeing Pakistani soldiers wandering the building armed with HK-91 rifles. Atta led the team to an Immigration queue. Atta nodded to a mysterious Colonel waiting just outside the waiting area. Soldiers immediately rushed in, surrounding the team. Walters raised his hands, the rest of the team followed. Collins stood, confused, unwilling to budge. Walters leaned over to Collins and whispered into his ear. "So, what's the next step in your plan?" Collins gulped, nervously looking around.

Colonel Massoud rushed into the crowd and looked at Atta. Atta raised his briefcase, carefully opening it for Massoud. Massoud inquisitively looked at the MP-5, delight filled his eyes. Massoud swung his head to the team. He harshly barked several orders in Punjabi to the soldiers.

A Pakistani Sergeant yelled several words in Punjabi to Collins. Collins gave a puzzled look to the soldier. The Sergeant grew agitated, now screaming at Collins.

Nishan leaned over and whispered into Collins' ear, "He says, 'Follow me.'" Collins begrudgingly nodded to the Sergeant.

The Pakistanis rushed the team into waiting cars outside the terminal buildings. Nishan, Collins and Walters joined in on the lead Mercedes. JJ and Watson followed behind in a separate car. Gun tooting soldiers filled the remaining seats of each car. Nishan sat uncomfortably between Walters and Collins. The two men continued to give each other dirty looks through the long trip. Nishan could feel the hostility grow at each passing moment. Walters finally broke the silence, "Great plan, so now what are you going to do to get us out of this mess!"

Collins exploded with anger. "I suppose you would have done things differently if you were king?"

"We wouldn't be off to our execution, that's for sure!"

A soldier from the front seat angrily shouted to the men. Collins' anger continued to grow, but before he could speak another world his cellular phone rang. The ringing continued for a short time with the sound of the theme song of Star Trek. All those in the car looked at Collins with puzzlement. Embarrassed, Collins slowly pulled out the phone of his coat pocket. The soldier in the front seat turned his attention away to the road ahead.

Collins flipped open his phone and began to speak in a strange language. The language sounded like a strange compilation of Japanese and Korean. Those seated in the car, sat in amazement, unable to decipher what was being spoken.

Nishan leaned over to Walters, "I know our problem. We are being led by a Vulcan." Walters burst out laughing. Collins continued to speak, unconcerned by the conversations going on all around him.

The vehicles continued to work their way through the crowded streets of Islamabad. The typical evening traffic continued all around unabated. The cars slowed down the main square. Nishan and Walters' eyes grew huge and their skin turned white as a sheet when they looked out. Collins continued to speak into his telephone unabated. His conversation only broke when he looked outside the window to see a horrifying sight. Three bodies hung from the gallows. The only identification was their olive-drab Marine uniforms. Their rotting flesh continued to be eaten by vultures. Collins covered his mouth, trying to keep from gagging.

Collins hung up his phone, Nishan gave a strange look before speaking to him. "Nice, are you going to tell us who called you before our execution date?"

Collins scowled, "Everything in due time." The vehicle made a sudden stop in front of a large Palace. A soldier opened the passenger door and motioned with his rifle barrel to Collins. Collins stepped out of the car in confusion, Nishan and Walters quickly joined. The second vehicle pulled up, soldiers quickly forced out JJ and Watson. The team looked around nervously. No one dared to speak or move.

A large Pakistani soldier shouted words to Collins. Collins shrugged his shoulders in confusion. The soldier shoved his rifle barrel into Collins back. Collins nodded in agreement, following Colonel Massoud. The rest of the team followed suit, climbing up several flights of stairs in the Palace. Ornate paintings covered the wall, complemented by rich Persian rugs on the floor.

At the end of a large hall, the team reached a pair of double doors. Two immaculately dressed guards stood at the double door. The two slung their MP-5 machine guns over their shoulders. They, in perfect harmony, opened the double doors. Colonel Massoud marched the team into the luxuriously carpeted room. The two guards closed the entrance doors behind the team with quiet precision.

The Team looked around at the beautiful teak furniture, complemented by the ornate brass chandelier that hung from the ceiling. Massoud shouted several words to the soldiers standing with him. The soldiers removed their helmets, Massoud followed by removing his beret.

A well-dressed man in a general's dress uniform stepped out of an alcove in the corner of the room. His hair was short and neatly trimmed, gold clusters on his shoulder shone with a freshly polished brilliance. The general sat down on the leather lined chair behind the teak desk. The general coldly spoke, "Gentlemen, I am Ali Mansoor." No one spoke nor moved a

Unseen Warriors

muscle in the room. Mansoor looked around the room. He casually waved his hands at the soldiers in the room. The soldiers immediately relaxed, but still kept their HK 91s pointed at the team. Mansoor looked down at some documents. He slowly shuffled through them, carefully, unconcerned by the goings on in the room. Mansoor looked at Collins, speaking in a careful deliberate tone. "So, Mr. Vernier, it seems that you delivered quite a prize to my grocery clerk."

Collins stood steady fast, refusing to speak or show emotion. Mansoor sighed, carefully putting his documents to one side. He stared into Collins' eyes, "You Canadians are so suspicious. You are my guest, just like the rest of your team. If I suspected you of being a hostile agent; I would have killed you before you ever entered the Palace." Collins allowed his brow to curl.

Mansoor shook his head in frustration. He shouted several orders to the gun toting soldiers in the room. The soldiers quickly disappeared from the room, closing the double entrance doors behind themselves. Mansoor shifted his attention to Nishan, looking deeply into his eyes. "So, you are the only fellow Muslim in Mr. Vernier's operation. Where did you grow up?"

Nishan surprised by the question, quickly blurted out his answer, "Vancouver, BC."

Mansoor smiled, "Did you grow up by Main Street and 49th Avenue."

Nishan feeling more relaxed quickly answered back, "Close, between Knight and Victoria Drive on 45th Avenue."

Mansoor smiled ear to ear, he then shifted his attention to Collins. "See it's simple, I respect you, you respect me, then there's no problem. Now shall we talk business?"

Collins cracked a smile, "Yes, I would like to discuss over some Hal Lal goat and rice."

Mansoor broke out a wide grin. He gestured for the team to sit alongside his desk. The team nervously walked forward, several of Mansoor's guards entered the room with beautifully hand-carved mahogany chairs. The team sat down, still apprehensive. Waiters rushed into the room, serving hot spicy goat meat, rice and flat bread.

The team ate heartily. Their apprehension quickly melted away with each and every bite. Mansoor ate slowly, carefully watching the team and Colonel Massoud at the same time. Mansoor finally broke the sounds of the feast, "Mr. Vernier, where did you procure that rare MP-5 Submachine gun?"

Collins quickly swallowed his food, "Mr. Hocksteader would be better able to answer that question."

Mansoor shifted his attention to Walters, giving him an icy stare. Walters cleared his throat, "The MP-5 you say is very similar to the version we sell to the US Navy Seals as well as several US law enforcement agencies." Mansoor listened intently, captivated by Walters' speech. "Everything from the Navy lower to the 1/2X28" threaded barrel is manufactured to allow the maximum number of US military accessories."

Mansoor rubbed his face with a silk handkerchief before looking at Collins. "I will require a large quantity of complete weapons, parts and ammunition from you. It will take several days to give you a complete tally for my order." Mansoor nodded to Massoud. Massoud quickly walked forward and placed a briefcase in front of Collins. "Now that I am assured that you are not a spy, here is the payment that you were supposed to receive from Mr. Atta." Collins opened the briefcase. Inside there were millions of dollars in Euros. "You see Mr. Collins, I never send my grocery clerks with the real cash. You will find exactly 12 million Euros, enough to cover the first shipment plus this sample model." Collins put down his silverware and nodded his head in agreement.

Mansoor looked Collins directly into his eyes, "I will arrange accommodations for you and your group at respectable Hotel. I trust you very much Mr. Vernier. If you do anything to betray my trust, you and your entire team will hang from the gallows in the center of town. Do you understand?" Collins nodded in agreement.

Mansoor called out several orders in his native tongue. Several well-dressed guards appeared. The team stood up. Collins stepped forward and shook Mansoor's hand. "It has been a pleasure doing business with you, General." Mansoor quietly nodded in agreement as the team was lead away out of the room.

Mansoor walked up to a window overlooking the Mercedes parked outside. Massoud quickly walked along side, his face curled with displeasure. "General, I do not trust them." Mansoor watched the team climb into the waiting vehicles and drive off into the disappearing sun.

Mansoor stepped back from the window and looked at Massoud. "I do not trust them either Colonel, perhaps we need a backup plan to take care of things." Massoud nodded in agreement.

Chapter 20

Pakistan
05-July-2010
2100 Hours Local Time

    The team looked around in awe at the posh five star Hotel. The huge building was lined with marble floors and ornate Persian rugs. Beautiful rare wall hangings lined the walls of each room. Fine wood furniture filled each room with elegance unseen by the team before.
    A bell boy led the team to a large Suite on the top floor. Out the window, the dazzling sights of Islamabad could be seen in the distance. Collins tipped the bell boy, who quickly disappeared from the room. Walters jumped on the posh bed, the softness quickly relaxed his tight muscles. Nishan jumped on a nearby bed with Watson, the two struggled in a juvenile manner on the huge king-sized bed. JJ picked a luxurious chair and gracefully sat in it despite all the commotions caused by Watson and company.
    Collins loosened his tie and glumly spoke to the team. "Gentleman, unfortunately I received a very sad phone call

from Colonel Griswalt and Hans Huber before our arrival at Mansoor's Palace."

"We didn't know Griswalt spoke Klingone!" Watson ruefully interrupted. The rest of the team broke out in hysterical laughter.

Collins tried to stay dignified while he continued. "Griswalt and I both speak Klingone. It is the only way we know no one can eavesdrop on our communications over the telephone. Anyways, US soil was attacked in four separate terrorist bombings last night. Our base in the Azores, Norfolk Naval shipyards, Portland Oregon International airport, and downtown Seattle, Washington were all attacked by several devices of nuclear origin."

Collins paused for a brief moment. The room quickly fell quiet and somber. Collins looked around, cleared his throat and continued to speak. "Hans says there is a great likelihood that the Nuclear weapons originated from Pakistan. Coalition forces including India and Israel will be joining in on a full scale attack of Pakistan in as little three days. We need to find Townsend immediately. Hans says that Mansoor has a large number of small nuclear weapons still in country that will be shipped out very soon. He plans to use them in multiple terrorist attacks on US soil. We need to help neutralize those weapons before we leave the country. Griswalt will be sending me a text message very soon on our next step. Right now, we need to get some sleep. Tomorrow morning we move out at 0600 hour.

Nishan's heart sunk, grabbed his head and began to cry. Watson hugged Nishan, "Don't worry buddy, I'm sure Sarah got out alive. She's a survivor just like you and I."

Nishan sniveled, looking up at Collins, he began to speak. "Is there a chance that she…"

Collins shook his head, "I'm sorry, the whole base is destroyed. There were no survivors except for a handful of flight crews. Shortly before the missile attack one of the pilots says he saw Major Bernier standing outside his door. Not long after there was nothing left but a large crater at the end of the runway, not a single building was left standing." Nishan shook his head, trying the grasp enormity of the situation.

Walters wrestled with his thoughts before he finally spoke up. "So, what is the death toll?"

"It's only approximately 140,000 and rising," Collins answered.

Walters rubbed his chin, anger burned in his eyes, "According to conventional military planning, The Air force and Navy will pound Pakistan with aerial bombing continuously for a week before a land invasion. We need to find Townsend quickly, before his position gets bombed."

Collins nodded in agreement, "I'll arrange for a meeting with one of our contacts first thing in the morning."

A knock came from the door. Collins rushed to the door, cracking it at first to see who was outside. A bell boy tipped his hat. Collins nodded and opened the door wide open. The bellboy pushed his cart into the middle of the room. The team looked in confusion at the strange guest. The bellboy put his finger to his lips and whispered "Shh," he quickly locked the entrance door. Slowly, meticulously he swept the room looking under table lamps, behind window shades and behind picture frames. Carefully one by one he pulled out several hidden microphones strategically placed in the room.

The Bellboy removed his while clothes and hat to reveal combat fatigues. He put on a black beret securely on his head and spoke. "Gentlemen, I am Agent Rabin of the Mossad. Your lives are in great danger, follow me." Rabin threw off the white sheet placed on his trolley. The trolley was loaded with several automatic Uzis, grenades and several fully loaded 32 round magazines. Rabin carefully handed out loaded weapons as well as spare magazines to each one of the team members. "Mansoor's people have been listening on all your conversations. We must leave immediately, follow me and shoot anyone that gets in your way," Rabin said in a quiet, deep voice.

Unseen Warriors

Rabin cracked the entrance door open. Gunfire tore into the door, sending splinters flying into the room. More gunfire from the outside tore into the windows. The glass windows exploded all around the room. The team instinctively ducked, hitting the floor. Gunfire from the outside continued to pound away into the windows and doors.

Rabin held still, impervious to all the happenings around him. He grabbed a grenade, delicately holding the pin. Lying low on the ground, he shouted to the team, "After this explodes, we all rush out firing automatic fire. Don't worry about civilian casualties, fire at will!" Rabin pulled the pin. He counted "One-one thousand one, one-one thousand two, one-one thousand three." He threw the grenade, bouncing it off the walls down the hallway. Screams were heard shortly before the grenade exploded. Rabin bolted from the room firing automatic gunfire. The rest of the team rushed behind, frantically trying to follow behind.

Rabin raced down the hall firing at will at the dazed soldiers. The Pakistani soldiers struggled to regain consciousness. Rounds tore into their bodies, spraying blood over the walls and rugs.

The elevator doors opened, two soldiers walked out, their HK-91s at shoulder level ready to fire. Walters rushed up to Rabin's side. The two sprayed the elevator shaft with gunfire. Rounds slammed into the nearest soldier's head. Rounds tear out his brain, spraying brain matter and blood all over the elevator shaft. The dead body slowly fell to the floor. The other soldier opened with automatic fire, bullets tore into vacant rooms and doors in the hallway. Walters fired a short burst. Rounds tore into the soldier's shoulder, blood muscle and bone blew out of his arm. The soldier struggled to hold his arm still, his arm motionless.

Walters and Rabin rushed by the wounded soldier, not even noticing his stricken body bleeding into the floor of the elevator. Nishan rushed into the elevator and jammed his bayonet into the dying man's stomach. The soldier screamed in pain. Nishan twisted the bayonet connected to his rifle several more times before withdrawing. Collin's eyes grew huge at the gory sight that occurring in the elevator. JJ rushed to the elevator, and pushed the button for the first floor button. The doors solely closed, JJ quickly threw a grenade into the elevator before the doors closed. JJ rushed to join the rest of the team a mere twenty feet away.

Rabin ran forward, stopping short just behind a corner. Rabin removed his beret and jammed in onto his Uzi's bayonet. Pushing it around the corner, gunfire erupted from beyond the corner. Wood and plaster sprayed the team like shrapnel. Rabin threw on his bullet ridden beret. Looking to Walters, he spoke with a calm serious tone. "Keep these men at bay while I neutralize the rest of the floor." Walters nodded in confusion.

Rabin signaled to Nishan. Nishan rushed to Rabin's side, struggling to speak over the sounds of gunfire all around him. Rabin raised his hand, speaking in a slow polite manner, "There is one more elevator shaft we need to neutralize, prepare a grenade!"

Nishan nodded in agreement, pulling out a grenade from one of his bulging pockets.

The two rushed down to the other end of the hallway to a pair of elevator shafts. Nishan placed a finger through the pin, anxiously awaiting the command to engage. The familiar ding of the elevator occurred seconds before the door cracked open.

"Ready," Rabin shouted. Nishan instinctively prepared to throw the grenade. The elevator door opened almost eight inches. Bullets tore out, crashing into the hallway ahead. Nishan quickly pulled the pin and threw the grenade into the opening door. Rabin and Nishan jumped into an empty utility room. The elevator shaft rumbled with a deafening explosion. Screams were heard followed by the loud thud of bodies hitting the floor.

Rabin and Nishan rushed out of the room to witness the elevator doors stuck open halfway. Alarm bells continuously rang inside, unnoticed by a squad of dead soldiers inside. One of the men moaned, Rabin fired several short bursts. "Click," the Uzi failed to fire. Rabin pulled out his magazine, no bullets remained. Rabin threw his Uzi away in disgust. Rabin quickly searched through the dead bodies, removing and ammunition, rifles and magazines that lay. Nishan helped with Rabin with the munitions. Rabin spoke in his usual polite tone, "We have to help your friends back at the corner!"

*****

Walters fired another short burst. Gunfire erupted from the corner, hitting closer and closer to Walters' position. "Anybody have any grenades?" Walters shouted, barely audible above the gunfire. JJ, Watson and Collins shook their heads.

Walters fired another short burst followed by silence. Walters flinched, pulling out the magazine from his rifle. Walter found it empty. Walters threw the magazine down the hall, pulling out another from his pockets. An explosion occurred nearby; splinters of wood and masonry peppered Walters.

Rabin ran to Walters' position, barely standing under the weight of ammo and weapons. Rabin handed out the grenades, loaded magazines and rifles to each of the team members. Immediately, Walters' Uzi failed to fire. Walters pulled out the empty magazine and threw it away. Walters searched his pockets. There were no more loaded magazines. Looking back, Walters looked at Rabin smiling at him. Rabin passed Walters an HK-91 rifle with several loaded magazines.

Rabin fired a small burst of gunfire into a door across the hallway. Rabin kicked the door open and the team rushed into the darkened hotel room. A frightened elderly couple rushed out, still in their nightgowns. Screaming at the team in French, they rushed down the hall. Intense gunfire erupted followed by blood curling screams.

Unconcerned with the goings on around him, Rabin smashed out the glass windows with the butt of his rifle. He tied a large rope to the window frame, throwing the remaining rope out the window to the dimly lit ground below. Rabin looked to JJ, "I'm going to climb down the rope to the second floor below. I'll clear the room of any hostile personnel. I want you to grab Walters, throw the grenades down the hall to cover our retreat." Rabin pulled out several grenades, giving then to JJ quickly before disappearing down the rope into the night.

Rabin skillfully lowered himself down the rope despite the weight of his rifle and ammunition. Rabin stopped just short of the top window, he pulled out a grenade. He pulled the pin and threw it into the open window below. Shouting and screaming erupted from the room, followed by a loud explosion. Wood and glass blew out of the open window, violently shaking Rabin's rope. Rabin expertly climbed down the rope into the second floor room. Only to be welcomed by the sight of bleeding children lying in pools of their blood.

* * * * *

Walters continued to fire at his unseen assailants, unafraid of the bullets ricocheting all around him. Walters looked at Collins motioning to him from a room across the hall. Walters looked back to see Pakistani troops trying to flank him from the other side of the hall. The troops hid behind an open doorway, using it for cover while they continued to fire at Walters. Walters placed a fresh magazine into his rifle. He placed the selector to full auto. Walters rushed across the hall while he fired automatic fire at his hidden foes. He dived headlong into the bedroom, grenades continued to explode in the distance behind him.

Walters looked up, only to see Collins disappear into the bedroom window. JJ provided Walters with several loaded magazines and grenades. The sound of gunfire grew louder and louder. Walters pointed to the window several times.

Unseen Warriors

JJ quickly climbed down the rope with all his strength and courage. Arriving in the second floor room, JJ covered his mouth at the ghastly sight below. He carefully stepped, terrified at the shattered bodies all around him. Rabin stood at the end of the hallway with the rest of the team. JJ rushed to the rest of the team, trying to block out the haunting image of children.

Rabin looked around to do a quick head count. He spoke in his usual calculating way to the team. "When we exit this room, we need to find a way through a back exit. We're probably going to exit through the kitchen to the loading dock. Mansoor has a whole battalion stationed at the front lobby entrance. Follow me. Remember to use anything for cover that you can find. Above all trust no one!"

* * * * *

Walters looked down at the rope, thoughts rushed through his mind. He positioned himself behind the bed using the night stand as a rest for his rifle. He concentrated on the front sight of his rifle, his finger anxiously hung on the trigger.

The door violently flung open. Several huddled Pakistani soldiers slowly walked, firing the automatic weapons wildly. Walters fired several carefully aimed bullets at the huddled mass of soldiers only thirty-five feet away. A bullet tore into the lead soldiers' upper leg. His hip socket exploded into dozens of broken bones. Blood and muscle sprayed over the while walls of the room. The soldier fell down, screaming in pain and wildly firing his rifle into the ceiling. Plaster pelted the soldiers below. The chandelier came crashing down on the second soldier. The heavy glass shattered, sending deadly projectiles into the two soldiers. The Soldiers screamed in pain. Blood flowed unabated over the plush carpeting.

Walters jumped into the window with a rope tied around his waist, a rifle slung on his shoulder and a grenade in his left hand. Walters heard loud more sounds in the hallway. The sounds of boots hitting the ground, orders being shouted and of guns being cocked did not faze Walters. The noises abruptly stopped, Walters knew the soldiers were nearby. He pulled the pin and threw the grenade into the open doorway.

Walters fell straight down, almost past the second floor window before bouncing up and down between the second and first floor windows. Watson and Collins rushed to pull the two hundred pound Staff Sergeant through the window. Bullets from the outside slammed into the walls all around the window frames. Distance muzzle flashes continued pop all around in the darkened night. Watson rushed forward and fired several short bursts at his hidden foes. Walters struggled to free himself from the rope tied around his waist.

Rabin cracked the door open an inch and looked around. Rabin hurriedly signaled to the team as he rushed across the hall. Watson and Nishan quickly followed behind. The trio quickly rushed into an alcove furnished by a vending machine, twenty feet away from the rest of the team. Rabin pulled out his knife, he signaled to Watson and Nishan. The two men walked slightly toward each end of the hall and raised their guns.

Rabin stuck his knife in the tumblers of the dead bolt lock. Using the fine dexterity of his fingers, Rabin carefully rotated the tumblers with almost magical precision. "Click," the deadbolt unlocked. Rabin opened the door. "Let's go!" Rabin shouted at the remaining team members across the hall.

Nishan stood still, strange sounds came from the end of the hall. Nishan raised his rifle, peering through the sights. He saw several dark shadows in the distance. Gunfire erupted form the end of the hall. A hail of bullets crashed into the walls all around the alcove. Nishan, instinctively, hit the floor into the prone position. He fired several short bursts at the hidden shadows in the distance.

Collins hurriedly rushed across the hall. JJ followed behind, providing covering fire at his unseen foes. Walters followed behind JJ, providing relief fire while JJ madly reloaded his rifle.

Bullets crashed into the floor and walls, spraying Walters with splinters and masonry.

Rabin held the door open, urging the team to enter. Nishan and Watson dove for the door. Walters dutifully continued to provide covering fire. "Click," Walters' rifle was empty. Walters fumbled around for more magazines. Gunfire continued to tear into the walls all around him. Masonry fell down, crashing to the floor. "We don't have time, just get in!" Rabin shouted over the murderous gunfire. Walters dove into the door. Rabin slammed the door shut and stuck Walters' empty rifle across the door handle and wall.

Rabin methodically walked down the dimly lit stairwell. The sound of butt stocks hitting steel continued to ring from the door above. Walters ripped the rifle out of Collins' hand. Collins lip curled, a scowl formed on his face. Walters stood up face to face to Collins speaking slowly and deeply, "You haven't even fired a shot, this kind of hard fighting is my arena, not yours!" Collins stayed quiet, Walters removed the rest of his magazines. Walters handed Collins a Heckler and Koch USP pistol and spoke, "This is all you need, leave the heavy fighting to us professional soldiers." Collins continued to give Walters a cold stare.

Rabin carefully walked down the steps of the stairwell to the first floor entrance door. Rabin cracked the door an inch, inside several gun toting soldiers walked around chatting and smoking. Rabin silently closed the door and placed a crash axe through the door handle and wall.

"We have to go a different way," Rabin whispered. Rabin slowly led the team down to the basement level. Here only one exit remained at the bottom of the stairwell. Rabin crawled to a set of double doors, he rose up until he could see through the crazed windows. Cooks prepared food in massive steel pots. Waiters and waitresses carried around huge steel plates of steaming hot food. Soldiers wearing camouflage fatigues wandered through the crowds of workers. They carried their

MP-5 submachine guns at waist level unconcerned by the activities several floors above them.

"Sergeant Walters, come here," Rabin spoke in a hushed voice. Walters crawled along the cold concrete floor to Rabin's side. Walters looked through the frosty glass, grunting at the sight of the soldiers wandering the kitchen. Rabin whispered again to Walters, "I will take Mr. Collins and Watson to the left to the bar. I want you to take Nishan and JJ behind the stoves to the stock rooms on the south side of the kitchen. I will attempt to clear the troops at the bar and restaurant. If I don't get clear of this area, take your men east down the corridor where you will find a freight elevator. Take the elevator up to the lobby level where you will find your freedom."

Walters nodded in agreement, placing his rifle into automatic. He gave Rabin a quick handshake and spoke quietly, "thank you, for your help, I hope that you can explain all of this at the end of the day."

Rabin smiled, "Everything will become very clear in a short while. You fight hard, God has given you the skills to survive." Rabin looked back at the team, "Mr. Collin, Watson, follow me."

Rabin crawled through the double doors until he reached a large table between the bar and the entrance doors. Collins and Nishan silently joined up, unseen by the restaurant workers scrambling around them.

Walters waved to Nishan and JJ. The two followed Walters as he scrambled around on all fours. Walters carefully hid in the shadows of the kitchen, finding a large stack of pots to hide his team behind. A female waitress walked to stack, sifting through the pots until she found her chosen one. Picking up the pot, she saw Walters hiding below. She screamed, dropping the pot to the ground.

The Women's scream resonated through the restaurant and bar. Soldiers rushed in from the bar at a frantic pace. Bar patrons dived to the floor at the sight of the menacing soldiers rushing in their direction. Rabin sprayed the incoming soldiers with automatic fire. Three soldiers dived to the ground, using overturned tables as cover. Gunfire crashed all around, turning innocent glasses and bottles into dangerous projectiles. Bar Patrons screamed in horror, trying to escape the unfolding gun battle. Rabin sprayed rounds at the overturned table fifty yards away. Watson pulled out a grenade and threw it at the table.

Seeing the grenade rushing at him, the lead soldier ran away from the table. Rabin's .30 cal bullet slammed into his shoulder. The soldier grabbed his arm, trying to control the blood pouring out of his shoulder. The soldier tripped on a bottle on the floor. He crashed backwards into his fellow soldiers screaming in pain. His two mates tried to get up, they had no luck, being entangled in their fellow soldier's limbs. The grenade exploded, a massive thud shook the table. Shrapnel cut into the soldiers. Blood sprayed on the floor as they screamed in pain.

More soldiers came rushing toward Rabin's position, madly firing their MP-5s toward the kitchen. Pots and pans clanged with the sound of ricocheting bullets. Horrified kitchen staff rushed out of the kitchen, screaming for the nightmare to stop. The soldiers stopped in the middle of the bar, unable to decipher their foes from the stampede of onrushing cooks and dishwashers. Watson expertly picked off the soldiers one by one through the maze of civilians.

*****

Walters heard the gunfire erupting in the bar. "Saddle up," Walters shouted to his team. The trio rushed toward the east hallway. Gunfire erupted up ahead, Walters and his team crashed to the ground. Poorly stacked pots crashed down everywhere through the hallway. Sacks of rice exploded all around the team from gunfire.

"Grenade!" Walters screamed to his team. A grenade sailed through the air above the teams' heads. The team rolled into the fetal position trying to shield themselves from the blast. An explosion resounded through the kitchen. Pots and pans immediately became airborne, scattering throughout the kitchen. Gas stoves exploded into flames, spreading fires through the kitchen. Flames jumped from the stoves to furniture as burning oil sprayed all over the kitchen. Black acrid smoke spread through the hallway and kitchen.

Walters covered his face with a handkerchief, trying to breathe through the thick black smoke. Gunfire continued to pour from the freight elevator, unabated. Walters pulled out a grenade and threw it at his unseen foes. A loud thud shook the distant elevator, silencing the distant gunfire. Flames started to fall from the ceiling into the hallway, taunting the team.

"We've got to get to that freight elevator ASAP!" Walters shouted. His voice was barely audible above the distant gunfire. The team rushed down the hallway, barely navigating through the thick black smoke. Walters casually walked by the dead soldiers on floor. JJ quickly removed their loaded magazines before rushing into the elevator. Walters slammed the gate down and pulled the lever to go up. Smoke continued to fill his lungs, despite his improvised smoke mask.

Reaching the lobby level, Walters pulled aside the metal gate. He inspected the deserted lobby level for hidden foes. JJ handed Walters loaded magazines in preparation for another assault. Walters walked down the brightly lit hallway to the loading dock. The air was quiet. The only sound was of a distant breeze swirling around the empty loading dock. Walters stopped short of a darkened room a few feet from the loading dock. Standing to one side, Walters silently turned the doorknob. The door was locked. Walters relaxed for a second.

The door violently opened. Commandos rushed out of the room and from behind large crates on the loading dock. The lead commando pointed his MP-5 at Walters' head. Walter threw his rifle to the ground. JJ and Nishan kept their rifles high, ready to shoot at any time. Walters gave the two a serious look and

Unseen Warriors

motioned with his face. JJ and Nishan gave an exasperated look before throwing their rifles to the ground.

The lead commando motioned with his rifle to the open room. The exhausted team complied walking into the dimly lit room and sitting down on a splintered wooden bench. The commando shouted orders in Punjabi to his men outside. The team meticulously arranged themselves around the elevator, guns ready to fire. The lead commando stared down at Walters with his bloodshot eyes.

* * * * *

Rabin loaded his last magazine. He swung his head over to Watson. Watson showed his last loaded magazine. Rabin nodded in agreement, Collins sat huddled, still clutching his HK USP 9mm pistol. Gunfire continued to pour from the freight elevator. More soldiers slowly advanced from the restaurant, their guns blazing away.

Rabin looked to Watson, the two nodded in conjunction. They slowly started to walk toward the freight elevator. A huge explosion ripped through the kitchen. A huge flame, fed by natural gas from the ruptured stove, rose violently in the air. Food, oil and even tables immediately erupted into flames. Another stove exploded, mere feet from Rabin. Rabin crashed to ground, flames erupted all around. Rabins' ears rang violently, the room took on a strange blurred shape. He tried to stand up stand up on his wobbly legs. Watson and Collins rushed to Rabin's aid, dodging burning piles of oil all around. Gunfire slammed into the kitchen from the distance. Collins fell to floor, screaming in pain.

Rabin tried to regain control of his legs. The ringing in his ears dissipated with every passing second. Rabin looked to see Watson dragging Collins, blood pouring out of his lifeless leg. Rabin tore open the elevator gate. Watson struggled to drag

Collins's heavy body through the hallway. Choking smoke filled the narrow hallway end to end.

Gunfire erupted from the bar, smashing into the walls and fire extinguishers all around Watson. Watson no longer had strength in his muscles. He crashed to the floor, succumbing to the thick smoke all around him. Rabin ran toward Watson. He used his superhuman strength to drag the two men to the elevator. Bullets continued to crash all around him in the narrow hallway.

Rabin slammed the gate down while madly pushing the up button. The elevator lurched, and then slowly rose. Rabin fired off his last magazine at his unseen assailants. Watson placed his last into

Rabin's hip pocket. Rabin pulled the pin from his grenade, throwing it with one last weak throw. Rabin fell to the floor of the elevator. He watched the next floor appear from the darkness, life-giving air cleared the black smoke. A loud thud shook the elevator stranding it halfway from the dock level.

* * * * *

The lead commando pulled off his black balaclava. He exposed a rough sunburned face, covered with three day stubble. He spoke in a deep, raspy voice. "Your mission is over; tomorrow you will die in the main square with your Marine friends!" He grabbed a cigarette out of his pocket and put it in his mouth. Pulling out a match, he stuck JJ's face. The match immediately lighted, JJ grimaced in pain.

The commando looked down at JJ, cigarette smoke oozed from his nose and mouth. "You don't like that pain little boy?" JJ remained silent. The commando blew smoke directly in JJ's face. JJ coughed, gasping for breath. The commando laughed in sheer joy. He grabbed JJ's face and spoke to him eye to eye. "I am Captain Sharif, the most feared commando in Pakistan's Army. I was hand picked to capture your children!" Sharif threw JJ aside. He pulled out a large knife from his waist. Sharif watched the dock's lights shimmer off the blade. He taunted JJ and rest of the team with his weapon of death.

Gunfire erupted from the elevator shaft. Sharif's men fell to earth, screaming in pain from their wounds. Sharif switched his attention to outside the door. JJ lunged onto Sharif. He grabbed Sharif's knife and rammed it into Sharif's stomach. Sharif screamed in pain, begging JJ to stop. JJ twisted the knife several times. Walters ripped off Sharif's MP-5, spraying the hapless commandos with 9mm gunfire.

JJ continued to struggle with Sharif, blood pouring out of his stomach. Nishan jumped up, kicking Sharif several times. JJ struggled with the bleeding man, pulling out the knife and burying it into Sharif's heart. Sharif crashed to the ground, screaming in pain. JJ looked down at the helpless man lying in his own blood. He gave the knife one last twist.

Walters rushed to the elevator shaft. He strained to pull out Collins and Watson. Rabin pulled himself out, throwing his empty rifle aside. Walters looked to Rabin, "thank you, very much, for a minute I thought our goose was cooked."

Rabin smiled, "Mr. Walters, you must have faith. God will always reward those who depend on him not themselves. Come, we need to collect the weapons for our next mission."

Walters chuckled at first. He then broke out in laughter. The rest of the team stood in silence, trying to fathom Walters' strange thoughts. Walters finally contained himself, still unable to hide his smirk. Walters looked to a confused Watson. "Well, Watsy, you didn't like the confusion and disarray of the first mission I led you on. What do you think of your first mission with Rabin?"

Watson snarled his face, anger burned in his forehead. "Frankly Staff Sergeant, I kind of wish I was back in old man Townsend's outfit. At least I would be home right now, instead of here in this dump!"

Walters laughed and shook his head. "I have to give you credit, you didn't try to get me killed this time!" Watson grunted a reply, embarrassed by Walters' comments. Collins cracked a smile out of the corner of his mouth. That soon disappeared into a snarl when Rabin started bandaging his leg.

The team collected all the guns and ammunition off the dead soldiers. Meanwhile, Rabin tore off the clothing from the soldiers. Walters gave Rabin a confused look. Without even turning his head, Rabin spoke to Walters, "We need this clothing, trust me."

A large 5-ton truck backed up to the loading dock. Several camouflaged fatigue wearing soldiers rushed out of the truck. One of the men stepped toward Rabin. He pulled of his ski mask and spoke. "Ariel, we must leave, more troops are arriving by helicopter and truck!"

"Yes, Yitzhak, we shall move," Rabin said in his usual polite tone. Rabin led the team to the back of the truck. Yitzhak Levi closed the roll up door and drove on. The truck passed by several large troop trucks brimming with soldiers. Pakistani soldiers anxiously waved the truck away as the continued to storm the hotel. Huey cobra gunships hovered above, patrolling the sky above Islamabad.

The truck left the city limits, approaching a highway leading south to Multan. Sharon looked to Levi, "This is very strange, we have yet to see a roadblock. All of this is happening too fast!"

Levi smiled, "No, it is not. I see a roadblock ahead." The traffic snarled to a stop. Pakistani regulars searched the stopped vehicles for their foes.

The soldiers came up to the truck and peered in. The lead soldier spoke to Levi, "Where are you headed and why?"

Levi stayed calm, speaking in a polite tone, "We have an important mission in Karachi. It has been given to us directly from General Mansoor. We are not at liberty to discuss it with you or any other common soldier."

Unseen Warriors

The lead soldier angrily replied to Levi, "We will determine how important your mission is. Get out and open the back door."

Levi and Sharon marched out walking slowly and calmly. Levi and Sharon stopped at the door. Levi looked at the lead soldier. "When Mansoor finds out what you have done, you will surely be sent to the Kashmir front."

Anger burned in the soldiers eyes, "I don't want to hear your lecturing anymore open the door or I'll shoot you both dead on the spot!"

Levi shook his head and opened the roll up door. The soldiers froze in fear. Five commandos pointed their guns at the Pakistani soldiers. Their eyes burned with rage through their balaclavas. The head commando wore a pair of captain's clusters on his sleeve. The name Sharif was sewn onto his blood stained uniform.

The Pakistani soldiers slammed the door shut, fear filling their eyes. "Go!" The soldiers ordered with a sharp wave. The truck rumbled along, bypassing the hordes of traffic jammed ahead of it.

Inside the truck, Rabin tore of his balaclava, wiping the sweat off his face. Walters followed suite, a grin covering his face from ear to ear. Rabin spoke in his usual polite way, "Mr. Walters, now that you have tasted the entre, would you like to try the main course?"

Walters chuckled while replying "Is it as hot as this?"

"It can be much hotter," replied Rabin with a smile.

Chapter 21

Pakistan
06-July-2010
0400 Hours Local Time

Nishan rubbed his face as he awoke. The long night's drive had been bumpy and rough. Even with all the distractions, lack of sleep and fatigue had still overtaken him. The truck continued to shudder and shake. Nishan pained to see through the dim light. Dirt and sand crusted the corners' of his eyes.

"Ahh," screamed Collins. His terrifying scream pierced the darkness.

"Relax," Rabin spoke in his usual gentle manner. Nishan stood up to witness Rabin carefully bandaging Collins' leg.

Nishan stood up and walked over to Rabin. The truck continued to shake and rattle along the bumpy road. Nishan sat beside Rabin and looked into his face. "How is he doing Agent Rabin?"

Rabin smiled at Nishan, "He has lost a lot of blood. I don't think he will be able to continue with us on our next mission."

The truck shuttered and shook, the driver's side rose up high sending the team crashing to the passenger side. The truck left side crashed to the ground, slamming the tires hard into the pavement. The rest of the team immediately woke up to the sound of crashing wheels and tires. The truck slammed to a hard stop, brakes screeched in pain under the weight of their load.

The roll up door shook and rattled. The team instinctively grabbed their weapons, preparing for combat. Three quick knock, one after the other was heard. Rabin lowered his gun. "It's Yitzhak," he announced to the team.

The door rolled open, darkness could be seen all around the outside of the Truck. Sharon and Levi helped the team members out of the. Everybody quickly rushed into an old concrete building.

Upon entering, the team showered in cold water. The feeling of wetness against their skin washed away the sweat and filth of combat. A change of clothing brought renewed vigor to the battle weary soldiers. Rabin provided for men Israeli military rations, goat, unleavened bread and lots of kosher vegetables. The team ate heartily, filling their stomachs with the wonderful Jewish food. Rabin's teammates continued to tend to Collins' injured leg.

Rabin broke the eerie silence, "So, Mr. Walters, what is your mission here in Pakistan?"

Walters gulped down his last bite, "It is to rescue one of our officers, Lieutenant Townsend. Apparently Mansoor is holding him in one of his gulags here in Pakistan."

Rabin patiently listened, "Has you mission changed since the nuclear attack on your nation?"

"Yes, we are supposed to stop a nuclear weapons shipment out of Pakistan."

Rabin seemed mesmerized, trying to picture something in his mind. "Are you part of the CIA?"

Walters fidgeted, becoming uncomfortable with the line of questioning. "Mr. Collins is our liaison agent. We are part of a US Army counterterrorism team."

Rabin's eyes lit up, "Ahh you are part of Black Ops. I can see that you deserve your reputation of being stellar soldiers across the globe." Walters' eyes grew huge with Rabin's quick assessments. "We have several goals in common with you Mr. Walters. We were sent to stop the same nuclear weapons shipment as you. Like you, our intelligence is very sketchy. We all have a common goal, come join my team and together we can help you get your officer."

Walters nodded his head in agreement, "We must get Lieutenant Townsend immediately. We think they'll kill him."

"No, they won't. Everybody knows your President is going to send a naval task force to attack Mansoor very soon. Mansoor is using Townsend as a human shield. There's no way President Hawkins will attack with nuclear weapons as long as Mr. Townsend is still captured. I would guess Townsend is most likely kept at a high military target."

Walters listened intently, forming a clear vision in his mind. Walters knew that at this phase of the operation, he would be led by professionals with far more experience than him. Rabin continued to speak, "We must first attack a nuclear armed missile being readied for launch to Israel."

"How are we going to destroy it?" Walters inquired.

Rabin laughed, "Not quite they way we plan it. If we destroy the missile after launch, the Pakistanis will just build another one in short time. But if we sabotage it, causing it to hit local soil, the Pakistanis will spend years trying to figure out what went wrong"

Walters nodded in agreement, "So, what is your plan?"

Rabin smiled, "Agent Sharon and I will take your team to the launch location about 100 miles southwest of here near at Rahimyar Khan. We will wear these commando uniforms, infiltrate the base and adjust the missiles' flight plan way points in its guidance computer. The missile will launch normally and crash somewhere in country. Agent Likud and Berg will watch over Mr. Collins until we get back."

Unseen Warriors

Walters looked around to his team with a cold look. Walters pondered his thoughts for a second then spoke. "How are we going to stop the nuclear weapons shipment?"

Rabin cleared his throat, "The shipment is not due out for at least a week. We need to act fast on other mission goals. I expect your Navy will do its airborne attacks in less than three days. A carrier battle group is steaming into the Arabian Sea as we speak."

Walters nodded, "when do we deploy?"

Rabin chuckled, "The missile launches tomorrow morning at 0600 hours. We need to leave here tonight at 2100 hours. You and your team has six hours to get some sleep."

"That much?" Walters answered. The rest of the team and Rabin broke out laughing.

06-July-2010
2000 Hours Local Time

Nishan walked through the tall green. Yellow dandelions littered the field as far as the eye could see. The sweet smell of roses and marigolds filled the air. Nishan felt free, the soft grass folded under his bare feet.

Sarah Matthews held out her arms, her sandy blonde hair blew gently in the wind. Sarah's bare feet stood firm in the lush green grass. Nishan rushed to Sarah, running faster and fast. The harder Nishan ran. The further away Sarah seemed to drift away. Nishan tripped over some roses, blood poured out of feet. "Sarah!" Nishan cried. Sarah stood, unmoved by Nishan's cries. "Sarah, don't leave me again!" Nishan cried. Matthew stood, emotionless, disappearing into the distance.

"Nishan, dude it's time to get going!" Watson called out while shaking Nishan.

Nishan rubbed his face, "I'm awake you clown," Nishan answered in an irritated tone. Nishan stood up, still groggy from his nap.

Rabin gave Nishan a serious look, "Good morning Mr. Nishan. Please, take your weapons. Nishan nodded in agreement receiving an HK-91, seven loaded twenty-round magazines and an IMI SP-21 9mm Barak pistol.

"We must leave." Rabin announced to the team. Rabin rushed the team into a six-axle military transport truck. Walters, Sharon, Watson and JJ hid into the back. Rabin opened the drivers' door, motioning for Nishan to sit down. Nishan complied, still groggy. Rabin sat in the passenger seat, looking over at Nishan, studying his movements. Rabin looked into Nishan's eyes, "I have chosen you to be our driver because you can speak the language far better than anyone of us. At the check point, don't act overly eager; stay cold and calm. Remember our lives depend on you."

Nishan stayed quiet, concentrating on the lonely road ahead. For all his concentration, thoughts of Sarah Matthews continued to fill his mind.

06-July-2010
2300 Hours Local Time

Collins pulled out his phone, trying to dial it. He was unsuccessful as every attempt. The phone just beeped and chirped before going dead. Collins shook his head and sighed in frustration.

Likud walked over carrying a plastic cup of orange juice. Collins curled his lip at the sight of the beverage. Likud smiled, continuing to point at Collins then the cup. "You must drink Mr. Collins, you have lost much blood," Likud spoke in a deep, slow voice. Collins relented, drinking the sour beverage. Pain continued to travel through his leg.

Likud smiled at Collins' face, "Mr. Collins, who long have you been a CIA agent?"

"It's been about twelve years, and you?"

Likud ran his hand through his graying hair, "I've been in the Mossad for about fifteen years. Unfortunately, I've been doing my job too well. Soon I will retire from my duties as field agent to a desk job in Tel Aviv. I don't know if I will be able to survive the dull repetition—as you call it in America—of nine to five."

Collins smiled, "I know what you mean. I have seen a diminished number of field assignments in recent years. I used to do field assignments all the time. Now I rarely do one more often than one every six months. For me, desk duty is a certainty that will befall me very soon."

Likud poured another cup of orange juice for Collins. "I guess we will be going to the old spies' home very soon." Collins laughed, for the first time the pain in his leg lessened.

Agent Berg walked in, his eyes read and watery from lack of sleep. Likud looked up, "Relax Aaron, you need to get some sleep, I will go outside and stand watch." Berg thanked Likud, lay down beside Collins. Unable to keep his eyes open, sleep befell him immediately.

Likud walked to the door, reaching to open it. The door flew open, knocking Likud to the ground. MP-5 gunfire erupted into the room, tearing up Likud's chest. Collins and Berg flinched, struggling to get up.

Colonel Massoud walked in, a silenced MP-5 in his hand. Commandos rushed behind, each carrying a signature MP-5 like Massoud. Massoud gave out an evil laugh then spoke in his booming voice. "Agent Collins, It is nice to see you again." Collins grew agitated, trying to stand up. Massoud poured a burst of gunfire into Likud's chest. Likud fell to the ground, blood poured out of his chest. Massoud lowered his rifle, smoke exuding from its silencer. Massoud looked down to Collins, "Do you like my new toy; it is one of your fine deliveries to Mr. Atta."

Collins struggled, the pain tore through his body. Massoud grinned. His commandos rushed through the building, thoroughly searching each room for any evidence of the location of the inhabitants.

Collins shifted his weight, unable to speak. Massoud looked down at Collins. "I will find the rest of your men. I also have double my guards on Mr. Townsend. Your plan is doomed to fail." Collins gulped the futility of the situation left him exhausted. Massoud continued to laugh at Collins. "So, Mr. Collins, are you a Christen?"

Collins meekly answered, "Yes, I am a Catholic."

"Have you renounced your sins to a priest lately?" Collins frantically shook his head violently. "Good," Massoud immediately poured gunfire into Collins' chest. Blood soaked into the sofa.

Massoud picked Collins' bloody cell phone. Looking at it, Massoud pondered for a second, he then threw it at the wall, shattering in into hundreds of pieces.

* * * * *

The team loaded in the truck rounded over a hill. Looking down about a mile away, the base lay in a valley sprawling over thirty acres. An eight foot high electrified fence encircled the base. In the center of the base, there was an L shaped command building. On the north side, a concrete launch pad was connected to a two-story control building. On the southeast an ammo dump dotted with machine nests looked down on the compound. On the southwest, a large metal warehouse building stood, trucks and Jeeps scurried around the nearby roadway.

Rabin looked to Nishan, "Go through the main gate, head east along the roadway to those containers on the east side of the of the control building." Rabin handed Nishan papers written in Urdu. "Tell the guard you're with Colonel Massoud. I will take care of the rest."

Nishan drove on, failing to even acknowledge Rabin's order. Thoughts and doubts raced through Nishan's mind. "What if the guard doesn't cooperate?" Nishan inquired

"Don't push the matter. I'll just have to find another way," Rabin replied.

Nishan pulled the truck up the gate. A guard rushed out of the shack, his rifle at waist level ready to fire. "What is your business here?" The guard angrily questioned.

"I have orders from Colonel Massoud to deliver these goods before the next missile launch."

The guard looked suspiciously into the cabin. His lip curled as he scanned Rabin. "Who is your passenger?" The guard demanded to know.

"I am Captain Khan, personal assistant to Colonel Massoud!" Rabin answered in a belligerent tone.

The guard's anger exploded, "I do not know of any such person. Where are you're..."

"You will treat me with the respect an officer deserves. If you do not cooperate, I will personally tell General Mansoor about you insolence. I will make sure you never see the light of day ever again," Rabin angrily replied.

Stunned by the officer's belligerence, the guard madly read the orders written in Urdu. Shielding his eyes from Rabin, the officer spoke to Nishan. "This signature is very difficult to read, who is the author?"

Nishan gave an icy look while answering. "Ali Mansoor." The guards' eyes grew huge. He fathomed the consequences of defying one of Ali Mansoor's direct orders. The guard madly opened the gate and waved the truck through. Still shaking in his boots, he rushed back to the shack.

Rabin cracked a smile from the corner of his mouth. "If you weren't a Christian, you would make a splendid Mossad agent," Rabin announced.

Nishan continued to look ahead. He answered in a deep serious voice, "I'm not a Christian; I am a Hindu." Rabin remained silent.

The truck rounded a corner until it was between the command building and the control building. "Park the truck over there," Rabin ordered. The truck pulled up slowly. Threading a fine line between the crates and containers sloppily stacked around the building. The dark shadows of the control building hid the truck out of site.

Nishan and Rabin jumped out of the truck. They ran into the back of the truck and donned their night vision monocles with the rest of the team. Rabin carefully checked everyone to make sure their equipment was in working order. Satisfied, he rubbed his blood shot eyes and addressed the team. "Agent Sharon, Nishan and I will enter the control room and attempt to sabotage the missile's guidance systems. Mr. Walters, you will lead Mr. Watson and JJ to the Ammo dump. I want you to set some remotely operated explosives on the south side near the fence. If our plan becomes complicated, I may require you to detonate the explosives. Return to the truck, in which we will depart before sun up." Walters nodded in agreement before charging his rifle. "Remember this is a stealth mission. The best way of getting out of here in one piece is by not firing a shot, understood?" The team nodded in agreement.

Rabin was the first to exit the truck. Sharon and Nishan were quick to follow behind. The team rushed between crates and containers until they reached the launch pad. A tall chain link fence encircled the launch pad. Rabin shook his head, "Looks like the only way in is through the control building." Nishan and Sharon remained silent. Rabin rushed toward the darkened building, Nishan and Sharon followed scanning for hidden foes.

Rabin continued along the control building, feeling and inspecting. Rabin abruptly stopped. He found a large steel door. Rabin pried the door lock with his crow bar. The lock easily pulled away, allowing access to the darkened building. The trio rushed in, Sharon dutifully closed the door behind to prevent suspicion.

The team walked down a darkened hallway, the empty building creaked. Rabin stopped at another steel door midway down the hallway. Sharon silently opened the unlocked door.

Unseen Warriors

Sharon stood in awe at the mighty sight of two intercontinental missiles standing proudly in the night's sky. Sharon looked to Rabin, "I will take care of the missiles."

Rabin put his hand on Sharon's shoulder. "May God's will be with you," Rabin silently whispered. Sharon nodded in agreement before disappearing behind the steel door.

Rabin looked to Nishan, "We need to see if we can find some documents about the weapons transfer." Rabin rushed down the hall to a set of steps. Nishan struggled to follow, his mind still wavering between thoughts of the mission and Matthews. Rabin rushed up the steps to a second floor office. Rabin entered the office and scanned around the desks, looking for anything of importance. Nishan looked through the darkened glass to see both missiles illuminated by bright lights.

Nishan rushed back to Rabin, pointing to several dark shadows behind frosted glass doorway at the end of the hall. Rabin grabbed Nishan and dragged him underneath a large desk covered with computer equipment. Footsteps behind the door grew louder and louder. Nishan's heart raced with anticipation.

The lights in the office immediately came on. The room flooded with fluorescent light, illuminating every corner of the office. Rabin and Nishan pained to shield their eyes from the bright light.

A scientist wearing a white coat, followed by several fatigue clad soldiers entered the room. The soldiers spoke in hushed words while their footsteps grew louder. Rabin pulled out his silenced 9mm Barak pistol. Remaining silent and preparing to take aim at a moment's notice.

The scientist sat on a chair between Rabin and Nishan. His shoes shone with a bright glimmer. Nishan could smell the fresh shoe polish inches away. The scientist put on his glasses and loosened his neck tie.

A soldier with brass stars on his sleeve looked down at the scientist's computer screen and spoke. "Dr. Mahmood, The

American fleet is almost in position. We need to launch the missile before they begin launching their aircraft!"

The scientist spoke to the general in an exasperated tone, "General Majeed, this is the only high yield nuclear warhead we have left in stock. I still haven't properly tested the guidance system on a live missile."

Majeed curled his lip in distain, "If we don't fire and destroy the American fleet, there won't any more missiles left to test. Is the other missile loaded with the low yield warhead ready to be launched to Tel Aviv?"

"Yes, they will be both ready very shortly. All I have to do is upload the navigational data into the guidance computers."

"Do it! General Mansoor expects a launch as soon as possible."

Mahmood sighed, "Seal the perimeter fence, I'll launch in about an hour." Majeed walked away in silence, leading his troops out the door they entered. Mahmood continued typing into his keyboard.

Rabin looked to Nishan and grabbed his throat. Nishan gave Rabin a thumb up.

* * * * *

Sharon silently walked through the shadows the massive missile. Lights in the second story control building came on. Sharon flinched, he then ran behind some scaffolding near the eastern most missile.

Sharon inspected the surroundings. The missile remained unguarded. Sharon climbed the long distance to the top. Lights shone on the missiles top half, blinding him. Sharon slithered along the catwalk toward the missile body. Pulling out the Philips screwdriver, he unscrewed the quarter turn fasteners. Sharon gently pried the panel off, exposing a maze of wires and circuit boards running the length of the missile. He pulled open a main wire conduit, exposing hundreds of multicolored wires. Sharon methodically cut several wires with his wire cutters.

Alarm bells rang out along the launch pad. Lights illuminated the remaining dark shadows of the launch pad. Armed troops swarmed over the launch pad. Sharon looked down at the unfolding sight below with horror.

* * * * *

Walters marched his team around the control building. Walters looked into the roadway at the activity picking up. Vehicles and troops ascended toward the roadway. Walters looked to Watson, "The heat is on, we've got to do something fast!" Watson nodded, pointing toward the ammunition dump.

Walters knelt down, allowing the traffic around the compound to subside. Walters stood up and scanned the roadway for soldiers. Seeing none, Walters ran across the compound to the north side of the ammo dump. Walters hid behind several crates, watching an approaching guard.

The guard stopped, he looked out to the distant launch pad illuminate with powerful lights. Sirens blared in the distance. The guard watched the distant missiles with a hypnotic stare.

Walters silently crawled closer to the guard. He pulled out a black nylon cord and wrapped each end of the cord around his leather gloves. Walters pulled the cord tight, watching the guard only a few feet away. The Guard slung his rifle on his shoulder. Parched, he pulled out his water canteen and took a long gulp. Walters lunged up, wrapping his rope around the guards' neck. The guard dropped his canteen to the ground. Walters pulled the rope tight, forcing it deep into the Pakistani's neck. The Pakistani struggled, he tried to scream, but no sound came out of his mouth. The guard continued to struggle for a few more minutes before life left his body. Walters let the body quietly fall to the soft soil below. Walters dragged the body behind several crates.

Walters signaled to Watson. Watson and JJ rushed across the compound, taking care to stay in the dark shadows. Walters searched through the dead body, removing all the loaded magazines and loose from the dead soldier.

Walters put on his binoculars and scanned the compound. The Pakistanis had moved several trucks and Jeeps into the roadway in front of the control building. More troops patrolled the compound with dogs. Walters rubbed his face, contemplating the tough situation ahead around him. He spoke to his team members, "On the southwest side of the compound, there is a warehouse. Watson, set up the explosive around the south wall. When we get across the west side of the compound, I want you to set the explosives off. Hopefully that'll draw fire away from the launch pad. Stay here, I'm going to scout around the corner."

Walters screwed a silencer onto his pistol. He crawled along the soil, taking pains to stay in the dark shadows. Walters navigated through the maze of crates and ammunition cans. Looking back at JJ, Walters' foot caught on several out of place ammunition cans. He fell to the ground. Ammo cans came crashing all around him. Several cans fell on Walters' wrist, cutting his frail skin behind his leather gloves.

Several soldiers rushed to the back of the dump, sweeping their rifles, trying to peer into the darkness. Watson and JJ immediately hid behind a large crate. Meanwhile, Walters madly tried to bandage his wrist. The lead soldier silently walked through the soft dirt, waving his rifle. His finger lay on the trigger ready to fire at a moments notice.

Walters froze in fear. The soldier walked by his bleeding wrist, unaware of the injured man mere inches from him. A dog barking in the distance charged the fence snarling and growling at the soldiers.

The soldier beside Walters laughed. He raised his rifle, and fired. The bullet tore into the dog's hind legs. Instantly the dog went down. Yelping and barking, the dog's hind legs became unusable. Another bullet tore into the dog's skull smashing it into pieces. The nearby soldiers laughed at the sight of the stricken dog.

The two soldiers by the west side of the ammo dump walked back to the guard shack. The lead soldier impressed with himself, placed his rifle on safety and lit a cigarette. He dropped the lighter on the ground. He fished for several minutes in the soft dirt before putting his boot on Walter's bloody wrist. Grinning and smiling, he stared right into Walters' eyes.

*****

Rabin carefully cocked his pistol. Above, the scientist madly typed into his keyboard, unaware of the two men beside his feet. Rabin grabbed a ball bearing out of his pocket and threw it on the floor. Mahmood flinched, swinging away from his desk to look at the source of the curious sound.

Rabin lurched from the desk, immediately hitting Mahmood with the butt of his pistol. Mahmood became unconscious. He fell out of his chair and crashed to the cold floor below. Nishan jumped up barely able to stretch his achy joints discomforting him.

"Get on the desk and open that ventilation vent!" Rabin shouted while madly altered Mahmood's entries into the computer.

Nishan put several boxes onto a nearby desk and looked down at Rabin. "Do you know what you're doing?" Nishan inquired in confusion.

"Never mind what I'm doing, get that shaft accessed," Rabin snapped back at Nishan.

Nishan carefully removed the grill, pushing the away into the empty shaft. "Ready to go," Nishan meekly spoke.

"Good, get up in there, I'll join you in a few minutes," Rabin replied while still concentrating on the computer screen.

Using the crates to hoist himself up, Nishan dragged himself up into the empty shaft head first. The inside of the shaft was dark and dusty. The opening was a mere 4 feet by 4 feet.

Rabin finished typing then pressed enter. Footsteps and shouting could be heard from outside the room. Rabin climbed on the boxes. His 5ft 7in stature was unable to reach the duct. Shouting grew louder from behind the door, Rabin began to sweat. Rabin stepped back from the duct. He ran toward it and jumped. Nishan grabbed his arms and pulled him up. The stack boxes fell from the desk to the ground.

The entrance door flew open. General Majeed and a dozen armed troops rushed into the room. Majeed quickly grabbed Mahmood and revived him. His soldiers secured the room. Mahmood regained consciousness. A migraine headache throbbed through his head. "What happened to you Doctor?" Majeed asked in panic stricken voice.

Mahmood shook his head, paining to remember his recent activities. He tried to stand, steadying his balance to avoid falling over. Looking down on his screen his eyes grew big. The launch counter read ten minutes to launch.

*****

Sharon continued his work, unconcerned about the activity below. He methodically inspected the small circuit board on the missile's guidance computer until he knew which components to remove. He snipped and bent resistors, capacitors and transistors from the circuit board. Successful, he skillfully reinstalled the board with all its attaching components back into the missile with ease.

Sharon looked at the crowds below began to thin. Slowly rung by rung, Sharon descended down the scaffold ladder. Soldiers stood in the bright lights smoking and chatting amongst each other.

Unseen Warriors

Sharon crawled on his belly toward the west missile while staying in the darken shadows. He pulled out his automatic knife and placed it into his mouth. He slowly crawled behind the missile's scaffold. A guard lazily smoked, mere 6 feet away, his glance fixed on the missile above him.

Sharon opened his automatic knife. He avoided allowing the stainless steel blade any contact with light. The bored guard stepped back into the darkness, trying to light another cigarette. Sharon grabbed his mouth and buried his knife deep into the soldier's heart. The soldier struggled and shook. He tried fight off the unseen attacker. Blood poured out of his heart as Sharon twisted the knife back and forth until his life force left him.

Sharon dragged the body into the maze of scaffolds and exchanged clothing. Sharon casually walked toward the awaiting missile, several soldiers stood ahead busily in conversation. Sharon placed a cigarette in his mouth he approached the troops. A nearby Sergeant shouted in Punjabi, "Private!"

Sharon walked to the angry Sergeant, lighting his cigarette. "Yes, Sergeant," Sharon confidently answered.

"I need a light!" The Sergeant barked in a menacing tone. Sharon lit the cigar with his lighter while the sergeant madly sucked on the cigar.

The sergeant continued in busy conversation unaware of Sharon casually disappearing toward the missile. Sharon slithered between the scaffolds. He quietly walked up the steps to the second floor level. Looking down to the ground, the squad of soldiers continued their conversation unaware of his presence on the second floor level. Sharon walked on the deck, taking pains to stay in the dark shadows. Sharon lay on his stomach and slithered on his belly to the missile. He opened an access panel by depressing the quick release fasteners.

Sharon looked inside to find a maze of aluminum tubes and wires running lengthwise. He pulled out his pliers and snipped several wires. He placed the serrated portion of the pliers over some tubing. Sharon squeezed with all his might, the tubing slowly deformed until it kinked. Sharon continued with several other tubes, kinking them in a similar manner.

Sharon reinstalled the access panel to original condition. He silently descended down the metal steps to the soft soil below. Sharon carefully inventoried his ammunition. He walked off through the shadows toward the squad of soldiers busying themselves with gossip.

Activity in the second story control room rapidly increased. Several people looked out of the windows, others rushed around in the background. Sires rang out through the night. Loudspeakers loudly proclaimed, "Saboteurs in the compound!"

The Sergeant yelled to soldiers, "Get your rears in gear, we have to kill the invaders!" The squad rushed to the Sergeant's direction. Sharon lurched out of the shadows, seamlessly sliding into the formation. Collectively, the team stormed into the control building, their guns ready to fire.

* * * * *

Nishan crawled through the dusty ducting. His mini flashlight provided the only illumination in the darkness. The dust continually fell down, wild sounds of gunfire and human voices could be heard below. Nishan sneezed several times. The dust continued to fall from the ceiling. Nishan came across to a point where the duct diverged into two. "So, which way do we go now?" Nishan asked.

"Wait," Rabin whispered. Rabin pried the duct joint open enough to peek below. "Go to the right" Rabin whispered.

Nishan continued for seven feet. Tears flooded his eyes in a vain attempt to wash the quickly accumulating dust. A ventilation grill appeared ahead, casting dim beams of light into the darkness. Nishan crawled up the grill, horror filled his eyes. "We have problems," Nishan said in a panicked voice.

"What is it?" Rabin replied.

"There's a crowd of seven Pakistani soldiers below!"

"Do they know where here?" Rabin casually remarked.

Nishan sighed, "No, I think we have the element of surprise at this moment."

Rabin remained silent, assessing the situation in his mind. "Hold still," Rabin ordered. Rabin crawled backwards through the ducting until he arrived at the previous junction point. He crawled to the left about twenty feet to another junction point. Rabin shined his flashlight to the left. The duct connected to another vertical duct. Rabin crawled to the right. The duct led to a ventilation grate. Rabin closed in, below a dozen guards stood watch with automatic weapons.

Rabin backtracked to Nishan's position. Rabin whispered to Nishan, "I want you to throw a grenade at the troops below, than follow me back."

"Understood," Nishan replied. Nishan pulled out a grenade and placed it to one side. Nishan smashed the plastic grate with his rifle.

The soldiers below flinched at the sound of plastic falling down to their heads. They looked up to see a grenade fall to the ground in front of them. They stood in fear, paralyzed by the sight of the grenade. The grenade exploded, spraying the hapless soldiers with shrapnel.

Nishan rushed back down the duct, following Rabin to the next junction. Gunfire broke out behind Nishan. Rounds tore through the thin galvanized steel ducting. The duct rattled and shook, raising choking dust from every nook and cranny. "Go down the duct, I will follow!" Rabin shouted over the sound of gunfire.

Nishan rushed forward, disappearing into the darkness below. Rabin crawled forward to the right. He smashed the ventilation crate with his rifle barrel and fired several short bursts of automatic fire. Hot spend shells bounced around, ringing at the point of contact with any metal surface. Rabin feverously shifted, trying to avoid the burning casings.

Soldiers below rushed to avoid the gunfire raining down from above. The soldiers grabbed their rifles for return fire. A grenade fell out of the grate and exploded in mid air.

Rabin madly backtracked to the vertical duct and dove down, head first. Grenades exploded inside the ductwork behind Rabin. Huge sections of ducting crashed to the ground on the second floor. Enraged soldiers fired hundreds of rounds into the mangled steel in vain, trying to kill their unseen enemies.

Rabin fell thirty feet to the lowest floor. His head pained with his limbs. Rabin scampered around in the darkness for his missing flashlight. He reached out ahead, feeling for any clues. A hand reached in and grabbed him by the wrist. Rabin struggled through the tiny duct, being dragged with immense force. Bright light flooded his eyes. Another hand grabbed his coat and dragged him into a brightly lit room. Rabin hid his eyes, madly trying to shield them from the painful light flooding into the room. The bright light penetrated deep into his skull, causing his migraine to grow deeper and harsher.

Slowly, Rabin's eyes focused, only to see seven Pakistani soldiers standing in front of him. Nishan looked badly shaken. A Pakistani Sergeant stood in front of Rabin. The Sergeant looked deep into Rabin's eyes and spoke in broken English. "Are you ready to die?" Rabin shrugged his shoulders. The soldiers in the room raised their rifles to his head.

* * * * *

Walters grinned, looking into the barrel of a 9mm pistol. The soldier motioned with pistol for Walters to get up. Walters raised his hands and rose from the soft dirt. The soldier stood, still pointing his gun.

The Pakistani soldier grinned, reaching for his radio. "Bump," the soldier fell onto Walters. Blood poured out of the back of his skull. Walters lowered the dead body aside and madly removed the dead man's ammunition and pistol. JJ joined up. Smoke lazily rising from the end of his silencer. Watson followed in tow.

Sirens blared in the distance. The main gate guards tightened up and became tense. Walters looked to JJ Watson, "I'm going to take care of the guards. When I'm done, I'll flash my light three times. Set the C-4 with a ten minute charge then get back to the guard shack." Watson and JJ nodded. They both pulled out several charges out of their backpacks.

Walters crawled through the grass along his stomach. He followed a zigzag pattern from bush to bush, staying in the dark shadows of the compound. The two guards in the shack looked into Walters' direction, the brush slowly swayed back and forth in the wind. One of the guards walked out toward the tall grass. He looked around at, kicking the bushes in various places. He stared at the ground, trying to peer through the dark vegetation.

A large truck pulled up to the guard building. The two guards shifted their attention to the main gate. The guard in the brush pulled out a cigarette and lit it. Smoking, he watched the large truck idling thirty feet away. Walters jumped up, wrapped a gag around the guard's mouth. Walters dragged the man down into the grass and fired two shots into his chest. Walters dragged the body and hid it in the brush.

The truck drove off toward the control building. The remaining guard looked around for his lost comrade. Getting frustrated, he called for his lost gent, there was no reply. He pulled out his flashlight and scanned the dark corners of the brush. He walked into the waist knee grass, his rifle ready to fire at a moments notice.

Two bullets tore into the soldiers' stomach. He shook in disbelief, trying to contain the blood in his body. Arms grabbed his legs and tripped him to the ground. A knife plunged into his heart, shutting down anymore movement.

Walters got up and ran into the guard shack. He looked at the horizon turn ominously red. Morning was arriving very soon. Walters knew the team was running out of time. Walters flashed his light, Watson and JJ rushed through the grass then dived into the shack.

*****

The Pakistani sergeant curled his upper, looking to a Private beside he spoke, "Take these dogs to General Majeed. The private nodded his head and pointed his rifle at Rabin's head. Rabin walked forward with his hands high in the air, Nishan slowly followed behind. The trio marched 20 feet ahead, the private stopped the two. Nishan and Rabin looked into each others' face in bewilderment. The Private placed his rifle on full auto mode and looked behind his shoulder at the crowd of soldiers. Rabin gulped. The soldier lowered his rifle to his chest level.

The distant sergeant angrily spoke to the Private, "Why have you stopped? Do your duties now or I'll shoot you myself!" The Private nodded in agreement then motioned to the two men to start walking. Nishan and Rabin slowly walked forward, almost out of sight of the crowd behind them.

Rabin fell down while reaching for his boot. The Private lunged on Rabin, madly swinging his rifle. Nishan stripped the soldier's rifle and fired several short bursts toward the team of soldiers. Gunfire broke out from inside the ranks of the soldiers. The men fell to the ground, blood dripping from their bodies onto the clean white floor.

The Pakistan soldier fumbled for his pistol, his other hand squeezed Rabin's throat. Rabin buried his knife into the soldier's throat. The soldier fell back gasping, blood filled his windpipe.

Nishan pulled another loaded magazine from the dying soldier and pointed at the crowd of dying soldiers at the end of the corridor. A Private, in a blood stained uniform, remained

Unseen Warriors

standing among the carnage only 60 feet away. The soldier pulled off his beret and smiled. He looked at Nishan, he spoke. "It's me, Agent Sharon. Don't you recognize me Mr. Nishan?"

Nishan lowered his weapon and wiped the sweat off his brow. He proceeded to remove the remaining magazines from the dying soldiers beside him. Sharon walked to several more dead soldiers. He stripped the bodies at will until he had enough ammunition and guns for the trio.

Rabin smiled at Sharon, "I adjusted the guidance system way points, both missiles with crash into the ocean after their launch. We have only a few minutes until launch time!"

Sharon nodded, "No, I damaged the wiring of both missiles one will explode on the launch pad, the other will explode after a small flight. Either way, we need to get out of here and find Staff Sergeant Walters' crew right now!"

Rabin nodded in agreement, loaded a fresh magazine and ran down the hall to nearby door. He cracked the door open and looked inside. The hallway was clear. The team rushed down the hall to an exit door. Rabin looked around. He was at the west side of the control building. The early morning light shone through the compound. Rabin hid his eyes in pain. Two hundred yards west of the building sat a green three axle truck. Two guards with dogs guarded it. Rabin looked to Sharon with as sinister look. The two men nodded in agreement and gave their weapons to Nishan.

Nishan marched the two at gunpoint toward the truck. Immediately at the sight of the men, the dogs barked loudly. The soldiers pained to hold the dogs back, yet still the dogs became more ravenous at each passing moment.

The forward guard raised his head. His team mate struggled to contain the dogs. Looking to Nishan, he spoke in an angry tone, "What is this all about?"

Nishan confidently replied in Punjabi, "These men are saboteurs. My orders are to take them back to Captain Sharif!"

The guard curled his lip in disgust, "We do not recognize Sharif and his band of Pirates. We only take orders from General Majeed!"

Nishan raised his eyebrows and flared his nostrils. "Captain Sharif's commandos are hand picked by Ali Mansoor to do his most dangerous assignments. Your general is a mere grocery clerk who only follows routine orders."

The guard boiled with anger, squeezing his rifle hard, "When the American dogs invaded our soil, we captured then in the old castle. We still hold their leader there to this day."

Nishan looked into the guard's eyes while he stood face to face. "Several Americans have invaded our sacred land while posing as arms dealers. We have been tasked to get them.

A huge explosion rocked the compound. Flames and smoke rose high in the sky. Ammo cans and spent cartridges rained down on the compound. Secondary explosions continued popping all over while the smell of burned cordite filled the air.

Nishan swung his rifle firing a long burst of automatic gunfire. The two dogs immediately died. Bullets tore through their bodies while their handler looked on helplessly. Nishan slammed his butt stock into the guard's face breaking his nose and lips. Rabin pulled out his pistol and fired several rounds into the other guard.

The three men jumped inside the truck. Rabin drove, Nishan sat next in the passenger seat of the open roofed vehicle. Sharon jumped into the open back of the truck. Rabin frantically started the ancient vehicle. He raced the engine before engaged the stiff clutch. The truck lurched forward with every one of Rabin's rough gear shifts.

Sharon inspected the back. His eyes grew huge at the sight of the cache of weapons strewn about. Rocket propelled grenades, belt fed HK 21 machine guns, HK 91 rifles and scores of ammunition belts and cans. Sharon excitedly clipped several belts together and charged an HK 21.

Unseen Warriors

Nishan smashed out the remaining pieces of windshield in front of him with his rifle. Sharon madly handed over a machine gun. Nishan grabbed the machine gun and laid it on the hood of the truck. Nishan attempted to organize massive belt strewn around the trucks cab.

The truck raced toward the command building. A nearby 6x6 truck started up, troops rushed into the idling vehicle. Sharon loaded an RPG and fired it at the idling truck. The RPG slammed into the truck's right-hand fuel tank. The tank exploded into a massive ball of fire. Truck parts, bodies and rifles rained down on the compound. Rabin instinctively drove around the burning debris.

Machine gun nests on the corners of the compound opened fire on the fleeting truck. Nishan lined up his sights and fired several quick bursts at the southwest nest. Rabin continued to perform sharp s-turns to avoid the incoming gunfire.

In the southwest machine gun nest, bullets crashed into the ground level. The Pakistani soldier continued to fire, unafraid of the .30 cal bullets raining down all around him. The soldier stopped firing and madly clipped several more belts to the short links dangling from his gun. More rounds tore into the nest, bouncing and ricocheting all around. A round ricocheted of the soldiers' helmet. The soldier was thrown back into sandbags. Dazed and confused, the soldier lifted his head up. More rounds tore into his chest, spraying the sandbags with blood and tissue.

Rabin jerked the steering wheel to the left. Nishan lost his grip on the machine gun and crashed into the passenger door. The truck's aft wheels skidded out, spraying rocks and gravel. The left wheels rose for a second before crashing to the ground. Sharon crashed around the bed. Spend cartridges and links dumped on the roadway below.

A Jeep overflowing with soldiers pulled forward, rushing headlong toward the oncoming truck. Nishan sprayed a long burst of automatic fire at the speeding Jeep. The Jeep violently jerked, dumping dead soldiers overboard. Nishan continued to spray the Jeep with gunfire, his pulsing increasing with every passing second.

Another Jeep full of soldiers pulled behind the truck, spraying gunfire with violent rage. Sharon loaded an RPG and fired. The Jeep expertly swerved, avoiding the RPG and continuing to follow, unabated.

Rabin allowed the oncoming Jeep to close in. At the last second he spun the steering wheel hard left. The trucks rear wheels strained to turn with the nose. Sharon held onto the box for dear life, the G-forces threatening to eject him.

The two Jeeps slammed on their brakes. The wheels locked up, plunging the vehicles headlong, out of control toward each other. Clouds of dust rose, blinding the drivers. In the confusion that followed, the two vehicles sideswiped each other.

The driver of the eastbound vehicle rotated the steering wheel back and forth. The Jeep continued out of control toward a crowd of soldiers. The soldiers immediately dropped their weapons and ran. The Jeep drove over the running soldiers. One by one, the tires drove over bone and cartilage, instantly cracking it into pieces. Terrifying screams drowned out the sound of the engine. The rear tires drove over the final body before coming to a halt.

The westbound Jeep flipped, rolling end over end. Bodies, guns and parts were ejected over the compound. The vehicle rolled over several more times, coming to a rest, wheels down and the engine still running.

Rabin plunged toward the guard entrance, adrenaline still pumping through his veins. Walters jumped out of the guard shack, waving his arms at the fast approaching truck. Rabin slammed on his brakes, locking up all six brakes. Dust and blue smoke erupted from the tires, blinding Walters. Walters jumped into the back of the truck. JJ and Watson soon followed, their feet barely clearing the ground when the tires started rotating. The truck started rolling faster and faster. Walters and Sharon madly dragged their teammates into the back.

A Jeep approached at high speed from the distant road. Sharon loaded and fired an RPG with his usual calmness. The RPG slammed into the drivers' chest, killing him immediately. The drivers' body slumped over, pulling the steering wheel into a hard right turn. The Jeep performed a sharp right turn, colliding into a pursing Jeep. The two vehicles rolled off the road into a shallow ditch, trapping the surviving soldiers underneath.

Rabin passed by the carnage, Sharon firing another RPG into the wreck behind them. Nishan leaned over to Rabin whispering into his ear, "I like your driving. You're almost as good as Watson." Rabin laughed giving Nishan a playful punch to the stomach.

* * * * *

Dr Mahmood madly typed into the computer, desperately trying to halt launch sequence. General Majeed rushed to his side, the look of fear and anger filled his eyes. "Doctor, we must stop this launch, if we don't. Mansoor will personally execute us both!"

Mahmood stayed focused on the computer screen, "I know General, and I'm trying my best."

The computer counted down to zero. The eastern missile's motors fired off. Soldiers and ground crews rushed away from the awakening giant. The missile rumbled and shook, its huge motors spewed white smoke around the launch pad. The concrete pad shook and vibrated. The huge missiles body rose into the sky, slow at first, then faster and faster. The missile soon disappeared into the morning sky with a cloud of smoke.

Mahmood's eyes grew huge, "That missile's headed for Islamabad!"

Majeed flinched, "If that thing hits, the high yield nuclear bomb will take out the whole city!"

Mahmood paused his typing into the computer, "General, if Mansoor is still in the city, he will be killed. You could take the throne of power and declare yourself the leader."

Majeed grinned from ear to ear. He put his hand down on Mahmood's keyboard. "That is enough, we will let Allah decide destiny."

Mahmood pushed himself from the desk. Leaning back into his chair, he put his reading glasses away. "If Mansoor survives, we can blame the Americans."

Majeed nodded, "Doctor, when I become president, you will get all the funding you need to destroy the Jewish state." The two men stood and peered out the window, still congratulating each other.

Outside soldiers stood, frozen in fear at the silent monster above them. One by one, they approached the missile, trying to inspect its fault from outside.

The missile rumbled and shook, its rocket motors fired off. The huge machine rose high into the sky and departed into the northern sky. Several minutes later, it exploded, destroying large parts of Quetta with a thermonuclear blast.

Mahmood looked to Majeed, "Most of our Army divisions are presently based at Islamabad and Quetta. Thanks to these missiles, the Americans will roll across our country at will. They will destroy any remaining forces in no time. We will suffer a loss far more humiliating than the Taliban did ten years ago!"

Majeed put his hand on his hand on Mahmood's shoulder and spoke in a sad tone. "Doctor, there is nothing that can do about that now. The only thing preventing the Americans from destroying out cities with nuclear blasts is their search for their captured officer. If their sabotage team rescues him, nothing will be left of cites but ruins in a very short time. I must get back to Uch Sharif and move him to different location."

Mahmood looked to Majeed, "Go, may Allah be with you."

Chapter 22

Pakistan
07-July-2010
0900 Hours Local Time

Rabin continued west on the bumpy road. The bright morning sun hurt his eyes. Looking to his side, Nishan lay asleep on the machine gun's butt stock. "You have done well Mr. Nishan, may you be blessed in all your future endeavors," Rabin whispered. The lack of sleep continued to make his eyelids heavy. Rabin struggled to stay awake. The hot sun rose higher and higher in the sky.
In the back of the truck, the rest of the team slept blissfully in the morning light. Sharon lay beside his beloved machine gun. Belts of ammunition lay piled around him. Watson and Walters lay against both corners of the aft ends of the truck's box. Their uniforms were dirty covered with dirt from the night's adventures. JJ leaned against the front of the box. His had stopped aiming his rifle several hours ago. Sleep was slowly trying to overcome him. He was too tired to sleep, but too tired to keep his eyes open. Still every bump and clang, really every noise kept him from falling to sleep.

A strange noise echoed through JJ's head. JJ immediately opened his eyes, the sound continued unabated. "Watson, I hear something. Something's coming our way!"

Watson moaned with pain. He rubbed the dirt from his eyes. He pained to focus through the choking dust around him. "Do you know you're violating the dead JJ?"

JJ gave a puzzled look, "No, really Watson I hear…"

"Damn it JJ, you're always hearing things. Leave me alone, I want to get some sleep!"

Sharon woke up from the back of the truck. Grabbing his binoculars, he looked into the distance. He meticulously scanned all corners of the horizon. Sharon took another swig out of his canteen. A few drops of water wetted his dry tongue. Sharon threw the canteen on the truck's bed in disgust. Sharon scraped the dirt out of the corners of his eyes. He put on the binoculars and continued to scan the sky for the mysterious sounds only heard by JJ. Sharon flinched and rubbed his eyes. He put on the binoculars and looked deeply through into the distance. Sharon gasped and shouted, "Helicopters on the horizon!"

Rabin Madly shook Nishan's shoulder. Nishan gradually opened his eyes, still groggy. "Helicopters inbound!" Rabin commanded. Nishan lurched out of his seat and rapidly attached more belts of ammunition.

Walters and Watson each loaded an RPG and aimed at two peanut sized shapes in the distant northern sky. The sound of rotor blades grew louder and louder, unnerving the two men.

Rabin made a sharp turn to a westbound road. The two helicopters changed direction and started their attack run from the back of the truck.

Sharon rested his machine gun on the truck's tailgate. JJ madly dumped out more belts from the ammunition cans. Waters and Watson stared through the sights, wishing the airplane closer. "Do not fire until I order you to do so," Sharon commanded over the noise of the truck and distant rotor blades.

The two Cobra gunships circled in the sky, maintaining a constant distance from the fast rushing truck. The two helicopters looked menacing with launch tubes packed with 75 mm rockets under each stubwing. Under the chin, a pair of machine guns panned back and forth, following the trucks route along the road.

The lead helicopter pulled out of formation and dived toward the truck. Salvos of rockets sprayed out of its wing one after the other in a blinding flash.

Sharon watched the airplane break out of formation. At that exact moment he shouted, "Rabin, now!" Rabin jerked the steering wheel hard to the left. The trucks body angrily resisted following the front tires into a dirt field. Rockets crashed all around the truck. Explosions sprayed dirt, grass and scrub brush over the team.

Rabin turned sharply again onto the main road. Rabin shifted the truck into high gear and sped forward toward the onrushing helicopter.

"Fire!" Sharon shouted on the top of his lungs. Watson fired an RPG immediately. Walters joined in, firing several seconds later. The first RPG rushed headlong toward the Gunship. The helicopter violently swung to left. The RPG passed by harmlessly. Walters' RPG slammed into the left stubwing. The stubwing immediately disappeared into a ball of flames. The Gunship shook and rattled. Smoke poured out of the remaining charged pieces of metal hanging on the helicopter's side.

Sharon opened fire with his machine gun. Bullets and tracers crashed into the helicopter's skin. The helicopter shook side to side. Smoke poured out of its engine compartment. The gunship stood still, almost motionless in the air. Walters and Watson fired off another pair of RPGs in rapid succession.

The RPGs crashed into the cockpit. The whole front of the helicopter erupted into flames. The fuselage spun out of control, rotating in an opposite direction of the rotor blades. The helicopter fell to earth, flames covered the sky. Black smoke followed by small secondary explosion rose from the stricken fuselage.

Rabin wiped the sweat of his brow. The last few days of combat had aged him greatly. Nishan madly attached the remaining belts of ammunition to his machine gun. Nishan looked over to Rabin, "I'm glad it's over,"

Rockets exploded ahead. Rabin jerked the steering wheel hard right, narrowly missing the craters ahead of him. Rabin slammed on the gas while doing a series of sharp S-turns along the roadway. Machine gun fire tore into the ground all around the truck. Rabin grabbed Nishan's head and dived under the dashboard. Bullets shredded the windshield into glass confetti.

Rabin pulled of onto a bumpy road. Ammunition and spent casings bounced and shook in the back. JJ madly added the last belt of ammunition remaining in the back of the truck. Sharon looked down at JJ, a solemn looked covered both men's faces.

"Here he comes again!" JJ shouted while diving for his rifle. Gunfire erupted into the ground. Rabin violently jerked the steering wheel. The whole set of driver's side wheels rose high in the sky. The team in the back clung onto the sides of the truck for dear life. Expended casings and empty ammo cans poured of the trucks' side.

Rabin straightened the wheels up for an approach into a tunnel. The left side of the truck fell several feet to earth. The team members were ejected up, out of the truck several feet before crashing down to the bed. Upon entering the tunnel, Rabin locked all wheels up. Smoke poured out of the tires. The choking stench of burnt rubber filled the air. Rabin madly performed a three-point turn. Rabin pulled up, thirty feet short of the tunnel entrance. He madly revved the engine in anticipation.

The Gunship dived over the hill toward the roadway. The pilot's eyes grew huge at the sight of the hidden tunnel entrance. He jerked the stick back hard, terrified at the sight of the hill closing in on him. The gunship pained itself to rise above the

Unseen Warriors

landscape. The tail boom crashed into the hillside, shearing off at the fuselage connection point. The helicopter shook and vibrated, falling onto its back. The rotor blades blasted off into the distance. Engines screamed at top speed, unaware of the dead crew in crushed the cockpit. The cracked fuel lines sprayed fuel on the fuselage, dousing the jet fuel with an explosive mixture. The helicopter exploded into a ball of flames. Flames shot out on the roadway and beyond. Aircraft parts littered the surroundings, oily black smoke rose high marking the grave.

A loud noise filled the air, the tunnel shook for a brief second. Rabin harshly engaged the clutch and drove out. Aircraft parts burned on the roadway, the smell of burning jet fuel filled the air. Rabin easily dodged the carnage around him, driving back to the main roadway.

The team stayed quiet, the excitement of victory soon became a letdown into fatigue. The hot sun and windy road combined to exhaust the soldiers. The celebration of victory soon became a distant memory. Rabin looked around, everybody had fallen back into deep sleep, and his eyes were getting equally heavy. Rabin fought sleep, his eyes closed for a second. Rabin immediately awoke violently steering the truck back onto the roadway. The truck drifted side to side, sometimes nearly crossing the roadway into the dirt fields nearby. Rabin forced himself to stay awake by praying, singing and even pinching himself. Butt all was in vain, he was fighting exhaustion that was much more powerful than him.

Rabin pulled the truck over into a lightly wooded area half a mile away from the roadway. Sharon awoke, rubbing his eyes and shielding them from the bright sun.

"Have we arrived?"

Rabin yawned. Dark circles now appeared underneath his eyes. "We are about seven miles from the safe house. I cannot safely drive anymore."

Sharon picked up a rifle and several loaded magazines, "Go to sleep, I will stand guard." Rabin nodded in agreement and quickly fell into deep sleep. Sharon walked out of the truck and cut several branches and leafy twigs. He placed the vegetation all around the truck. Concealing as much of truck's body he could.

Sharon painted his face and proceeded to hike up a knoll several hundred yards away. Dehydration and lack of food slowed Sharon's advance. The hot sun beat down on him, making each and every step an ordeal. Sharon soon arrived at the crest. The trek from the truck had sapped much of his strength.

Sharon fell to the ground. He dug into the ground in the prone position, rifle in hand. Sharon looked around, the beautiful blue sky extended to all four corners. The roadway was barren. It seemed as if the whole country side had taken the day off.

Sharon put on his binoculars and scanned the cloudless sky. High above blue contrails circled into a spaghetti pattern. Sonic booms crashed all round, flares popped around high in the sky. White contrails rose vertically into the sky, mysteriously ending as fast as they began. Sharon wiped the sweat from his brow and placed his binoculars down. The invasion of Pakistan had begun.

Sharon placed the rifle on semi-auto, checked the magazine and stared out into the roadway. Heaviness filled his eyes, Sharon struggled to stay awake. Thoughts of Tel Aviv, Gaza and Jerusalem filled his mind. Sharon fought sleep hard like generations of soldiers before him. Sleep fought back, drowsiness filled Sharon's body. Eventually sleep won its battle.

Sharon was in Jerusalem, its streets quiet of its usual business and traffic. The terrorism was no more. Jews and Arabs lived side by side in harmony. One of Sharon's childhood Arab friends waved to him. Sharon laughed and hugged Pervez. Pervez picked up a newborn lamb. The lamb was white as snow, its hair soft as soft as silk.

Sharon motioned for the lamb. Pervez handed the lamb to Sharon. Sharon hugged the lamb, joy filled his heart. Suddenly, Pervez pulled out a knife. He plunged it deep into the lamb, twisting back and forth while withdrawing. Blood sprayed on the lamb's skin and Sharon's fine white clothing. Sharon screamed in horror at the sight.

Sharon awoke from his nightmare. Despite the 100F degree outside air temperature he was covered in a cold sweat. Sharon looked at his watch, it was 1600. He had been sleeping for almost three hours.

Sharon grabbed his binoculars and scanned all around. The roadway had stayed empty, a hot breeze howled through the empty hills around him. In the sky, fresh contrails crossed overhead.

Sharon heard rumbling sounds in the distance. He looked into the area where the truck was park, nothing. He scanned toward the safe house, dust clouds rose from the distant roadway. Several large transport trucks filled with troops rumbled along the roadway toward his direction. The transport trucks continued until they stopped about a quarter of a mile from Sharon's position.

Sharon slithered back into the brush, hiding his watch and rifle from the bright rays of the sun. He cursed himself for falling asleep. He knew any movement now would be spotted by the nearby troops. Jets above high did high speed passes, the sky rumbled with the sound of sonic booms. Sharon rotated his rifles rear drum side to the 400-meter setting. Sharon dug his elbows into the ground and rested his barrel on a smooth rocky outcropping.

Dozens of soldiers poured of the truck, taking up positions along the roadway. A Colonel walked out of the truck, he sniffed the air. His lips curled, anger filled his eyes. The Colonel grabbed his binoculars and scanned around the roadway and hillside.

He shouted orders to his men in an angry tone. He remained peering through his binoculars, stopping at point where he looked directly at Sharon. Sharon's stomach tightened. He held still, willing to hold his breath if required. The Colonel put down his binoculars down.

Sharon slowly slid another loaded twenty round magazine to his side. Sharon peered through the rear sight and placed the front sight on the Colonel's chest. Sharon concentrated on thoughts of attack and exit strategies that rushed through his head.

The Colonel pulled out a scoped PSG-1 and stared into Sharon's position. Sharon breathed heavily and placed his finger on the trigger. A Private ran out of one of the trucks and brought it to the Colonel. The Colonel ripped the radio out of the Private's hand. He spoke slowly and deliberately into the radio.

The Colonel waved his hand in an irritated way. The Colonel and the rest of his men jumped into the waiting trucks. The trucks started up, wild noises and dirty black smoke exhausted from their tail pipes. The trucks took off, disappearing into the distance.

Sharon breathed deeply and placed his rifle on safe. He stood up and collected his items and ran down the trail toward the truck. Sharon huffed and puffed, exhaustion bit onto his lungs. Sharon crashed through the brush and crashed into the truck. Inside the truck, the team silently slept. They had been unaware of the recent events.

Rabin jerked, screaming loudly in terror. Sharon ran to Rabin's side, shaking him awake. Sharon shouted to Rabin, "Wake Ariel, you're having and nightmare!"

Rabin opened his eyes, looking to Sharon, he spoke. "Yitzhak, my dream was terrible. I dreamed that I was back in Tel Aviv. I was with my childhood friend. We were laughing and playing in the streets. My friend gave me a lamb. It was white and beautiful, perfect for sacrifice. My friend handed me the lamb. The lamb nestled in my arms and slept. My childhood friend pulled out a gun and shot the lamb. Hot blood sprayed over my white shirt, the lamb cried in pain." Rabin wiped the tears from his face. The horrific dream shook him down to his heart.

Sharon spoke in a deep soft voice, "When I was on the hill, I had the same dream. It is no coincidence that we had the same thoughts. Just as God spoke to Abraham in a dream, he surely has spoken to us."

"I agree Yitzhak, God has given us a vision. We must not disgrace him by ignoring it."

Nishan awoke, his eyes were dirty and his hair was mess. The bright sun made opening his eyes painful. Rabin looked to Nishan, "You fight hard and sleep just as hard." Nishan gave a confused look.

Rabin stood up and announced to the slowly waking team. "We must return to our safe house, Mr. Collins must be getting lonely." The rest of the team gave a weak thumbs up, unfazed by Rabin's joke.

Sharon jumped into the truck's box. Rabin jumped into the drivers' seat and started the truck. The truck drove off into the distance toward the safe house.

Rabin rounded the top of the hill. Deep down in the valley, the safe house lay, tucked away in the brush. Rabin stopped the truck and peered with his binoculars at the distant sight. The house seemed untouched. The 5-ton truck the team originally used for transport remained where they left it the day earlier.

"Prepare for combat," Rabin casually remarked. The team immediately readied their weapons for combat. Rabin pulled off to the road side. He casually drove through brush, maintaining sight of the safe house at all times. Rabin pulled the truck up to a stopping point three hundred yards away. "We will disembark here. Take only the weapons you can carry," Rabin said.

The team picked up their HK-91 rifles. Sharon looked to Rabin, "I will secure the perimeter."

Rabin nodded in agreement, "Take Nishan and JJ." Sharon disappeared into the brush around the corner, JJ and Nishan in tow.

Rabin led Walters and Watson to the front door of the safe house. Watson grabbed the doorknob, it was unlocked. Rabin and Walters readied their guns. Watson flung the door open, Rabin and Walters rushed forward.

Inside the safe house Likud, Berg and Collins hung from the ceiling. Walters rushed forward to the dead men, knife in hand. Walters madly cut down the dead men and attempted to resuscitate them.

"Don't bother!" Rabin spoke. Walters looked up. "Colonel Massoud did this to warm up. We need to collect all the food we can and evacuate ASAP!"

JJ rushed in out of breath. "Tanks are coming from the valley!" The four rushed out of the safe house, they headed east to the knoll overlooking the roadway and valley.

Out in the distance, six tanks rolled out of the vegetation toward the roadway. Shells pounded into the soil around the safe house. Soil, rocks and vegetation exploded all around the safe house. The teams' truck exploded into a ball of flames. The tanks raked the area around the truck with machine gun fire.

Rabin scanned the roadway and valley with his binoculars. Tanks, armored personnel carriers and helicopters scanned over the valley toward the roadway. Helicopters, gunships continually fired rockets into the safe house. Flames engulfed the building, sending burning debris airborne.

Rabin put down his binoculars, "We need to get out of here now!" Rabin said. Rabin led the team east over the bare ground to the other side of the hill. The sounds of gunfire and explosions echoed from the other side of the hill. They rushed through the scrub brush and soil. Fear and adrenaline pushed them to run farther and faster. After many hours of running, the team collectively stopped, unsure of their next course of action.

Unseen Warriors

Rabin wiped his face. The hot sun pounded his skin. Sweat provided little relief. Watson looked to Rabin with a helpless look. "Do you see anything in the distance" Watson asked with a quivering voice.

Rabin looked into the distance with his binoculars. Three miles in the distance, several small buildings lay. Beyond, Rabin could see the fringes of the Thar Desert. Rabin put his binoculars down, "See those buildings ahead," Rabin spoke while pointing at the distant buildings.

Walters tried to focus with his tired eyes before speaking. "Yeah I do, they look like a bunch of rundown shacks."

Rabin's eyes lit up, "That's about three miles from here. We need to get there before the sun goes down. We'll get some sleep and maybe find a plan to get ourselves some transportation."

Walters nodded, exhaustion filled his eyes. Walters opened his canteen, and rotated a single drop dripped out onto the parched ground. Rabin pulled out his canteen and handed it to Walters. Walters took a long gulp of the hot water before passing it to Watson. The rest of the team gulped the remnants of the water. Their thirst remained unquenched.

The team continued on, the hot sun slowly drifted toward the horizon. The distant buildings grew larger and larger. But for all the team, the distance seemed to grow longer and longer.

JJ fell to the ground with exhaustion, his skin hot and clammy. Watson picked up JJ and carried him the remaining distance to the abandoned shack. Rabin and Sharon meticulously inspected each of the musty old wooden buildings for signs of life.

Satisfied, the team rushed into the largest building. The inside was bare except for the cracking concrete floor. Frosted glass allowed small peeks of light, illuminating the interior with red rays.

Rabin pulled out several small candy bars from his backpack. He handed one to each of the team members. Rabin looked to

Watson, "We need to stand guard." Watson nodded. The cool air of the setting sun slowly blew in providing some relief.

Rabin climbed up a rusted ladder on the outside of the building to the flat roof. Rabin found a comfortable spot and lay down, Watson sat beside Rabin, marveling at the panoramic site of the desert.

Rabin scanned the westerns sky with his binoculars. Watson watched in total despair.

Watson broke the silence, "Where are we?"

Rabin pointed north and slightly west at some distant hills. "That is Bhawalpur. We're about forty miles from the Indian border."

Watson shifted uncomfortably, "Are we ever going to get out of here? After all, we have no food or water. No transportation and a shanty for shelter."

Rabin smiled, "Mr. Watson, you are not a God-fearing soul are you?" Watson shrugged. "We in the Mossad plan for my unexpected occurrences, unfortunately, many disasters can not be planned for. Sometimes faith is the only thing that can save a stranded soldier."

Watson fell into despair, "You mean we're supposed to hang out here until we die. You're even crazier than…"

"Relax Mr. Watson," Rabin interrupted. "The Pakistanis think we're dead. They're not chasing us. We just need a way to gain transport out of here."

Watson slid back, believing with Rabin's speech. Thoughts of home filled his mind. Soon sleep overtook Watson. Rabin shook his head at the sight of Watson sleeping. Rabin picked up his binoculars and scanned north western sky contrails out through the twisting and turning in the sky.

The night air-cooled Rabin, he shivered. The lack of food and sleep started to take effect on his body. Rabin looked at his watch, it was now 0400hours. He must have fallen asleep for a couple of hours. Sharon stepped up to the rooftop, Rabin barely acknowledged his presence. Sharon looked at Watson peacefully sleeping next to Rabin. Sharon whispered to Rabin, "How long did your mighty friend stay awake?"

Rabin answered, "Half an hour at tops."

Sharon smiled, "And you?"

Rabin shook his head, "You always knew everything I did, Yitzhak." Rabin paused for a moment, "I slept for about four hours."

Sharon picked up his binoculars and scanned the blackness to the east. "How has Watson's moral been?"

Rabin guffawed for a second, "His moral has hit an extreme low point. He thinks we will die in the desert."

Sharon breathed deeply, "Is that Watson's moral or yours?"

Rabin sighed, "Both of us, except Watson is willing to admit his hopelessness."

"Yitzhak, great leaders admit when they are wrong. But fools show weakness to their troops."

Rabin looked to Sharon, "I feel I have failed the mission. Three of our team members are dead. We're stuck in the middle of the desert without provisions."

Sharon ran his hand through his hair. "No, we did not fail. We prevented the attack of a nuclear missile onto our homeland. That alone saved thousands of lives. You did the best anyone of us could do. You have failed no one. Do not worry. Our forefathers wandered the desert for forty years until they reached Israel. God was with them on every step of their journey, just as God is with us right now." Rabin pulled out his candy bar and ate. Sharon's comments raced through his mind.

Hours passed by, the two men stayed silent. The Angry red sun slowly rose from the east, illuminating the darkness of the desert. Sonic booms broke the silence. High overhead, jet fighters rushed through the sky toward the heart of Pakistan.

Sharon peered through the binoculars. Dust rose up in the eastern sky. Sharon cleaned the dust and debris from his eyes before looking again. Clouds of sand and dust continued to rise from the east.

Sharon put down his binoculars and looked to Rabin. "How far is the border from us?"

Rabin shrugged, "Fifty, maybe sixty miles. Why do you ask?"

Sharon fell into deep thought for a second. Contrails high above continued to streak the sky.

Sharon peered deeply into the binoculars. The dust gave way to a tank column. A hundred tanks lined up side to side crossed the open plane. Helicopter gunships passed overhead, sweeping the sky from side to side. Sharon jumped, flashing his light at the approaching gunships.

A Mi 34 hind gunship straightened its course and headed straight for Sharon. Rabin woke up out of his slumber. The beating of rotor blades shook the wooden roof below him. Rabin stood up to see an Indian army gunship hovering overhead.

The rest of the team rushed out to see a wall of tanks, armored personnel carriers and dozens of support trucks and Jeeps approaching. Rabin and Sharon rushed off the roof to greet the incoming warriors. Watson awoke to find he was alone on the roof. He quickly ran down, struggling to keep from tripping over the rocks on the ground.

The massive wall of armor stopped about twenty feet from Rabin. The sound and smell of a hundred diesel engines idling filled the sky. A large truck pulled up to Rabin. A tall, well-groomed man walked out, one gold star ran along each his epaulets. The general looked at Rabin and Sharon, "I'm Brigadier General Jaswal of the Third heavy infantry Battalion, Republic of India. Who are you gentlemen?"

Rabin spoke up, "I am agent Rabin. This is my fellow agent Sharon of Mossad. These gentlemen are members of elite US Army counter terrorism team."

Jaswal smiled. "What are you folks doing in this part of the world?"

"We're here to rescue a captured American officer," said Rabin.

Jaswal gave a serious look, "Where is this officer kept?" Rabin hesitated for a second.

Jaswal jumped on Rabin, "Agent Rabin, you are not being completely honest with me."

Rabin spoke, "I'm sorry, lack of water and food is having an effect on me. He is being kept in a palace at Uch Sharif. The US Marine corps staged a rescue attempt weeks ago. The rescue party was captured and ceremonially executed in Islamabad's main square. Our secondary mission is to find a shipment of nuclear weapons. It's being shipped out of country for terrorist attacks across the world."

Jaswal listened intently, "What about the nuclear missile that crashed into Islamabad."

Rabin reluctantly answered, "The missile was aimed at Israel. We then changed the coordinates for the guidance computer before it was launched."

Jaswal nodded, "Thanks to you, a large proportion of the Pakistani army has been destroyed. That has helped us greatly!" Rabin gave a confused look, Jaswal continued to speak. "A coalition of countries has joined American to avenge the nuclear attacks on US soil. My battalion is going to storm Bhawalpur this morning.

"American and British air assets are bombing major targets in Pakistan as we speak. Another Indian army battalion will attack the outskirts of Lahore within a few hours.

"Come, join my trucks, we need to get you to my command center." Rabin agreed, Sharon and the rest of the team staggered into the 6x6. The truck drove past the massive battalion. Large numbers of supply trucks crisscrossed to the awaiting tanks with much needed supplies.

The truck arrived at a makeshift base camp several miles from the main attack force. Jaswal escorted the team to a hastily erected tent. The team ate the hot spicy food voraciously, unwilling to stop until they had their complete fill.

Jaswal looked to Rabin and laughed. "Your men have been without food and water for some time." Rabin nodded, eating mouthfuls of food at the same time."

Jaswal pulled out a large laminated map of Uch Sharif. Rabin stepped up with Walters, both still munching their food. Jaswal marked several positions with his felt pen on the map. "The palace is in a small field surrounded by hills on both sides. An area of the field north of the Palace contains a radar vehicle and dozens of long range SAM launders.

"Recon photos show that the Pakistani's have been building forces in that area. They probably expect you to come by a surface route. Large numbers of infantry line the roads on the outskirts of the palace. Strangely, there are no anti-aircraft guns or any low altitude SAMs."

Walters gave Jaswal a puzzled look. "Are you suggesting a helicopter insertion?"

Jaswal opened his eyes wide. "Yes, in a way. South of the palace, there is a huge wheat field."

Rabin looked closer at the map, "The original American assault team entered from the west and landed on the west hill. Sam launches shot down the aircraft at very low altitude."

Jaswal nodded in agreement. "The hill they used for landing made them vulnerable to the concentration of surface to air armaments. I'm sure someone heading west would immediately be seen approaching by the palace guards.

"I could send a squadron of fighter aircraft to knock off the SAM launchers with my main assault force. The Pakistanis would think that the attack was part of the main siege into Bhawalpur. They would shift their forces east. I could transport your team with a dozen of my crack troops in by helicopter to the wheat field. Your troops would be able to storm the palace before the main battalion would be able to launch a counter offensive."

Walters inspected the map running various scenarios through his mind. Breathing heavily, he spoke to Jaswal, "It is possible General that many of your men will die in this attack."

Jaswal stayed fixated on him, "Many more of my men would have died if you hadn't wiped out that battalion in Islamabad."

Rabin gave Jaswal a stern look. "Are there any other forces attacking from the west?"

Jaswal pulled out his clipboard and he scanned through pages and pages of text. Jaswal looked to Rabin and Walters, "American and German forces will advance from Kandahar to Quetta within the hour." Walters remained silent. "Gentlemen, your teams need to get some sleep. At 2100 we will attack." Walters, Rabin and Jaswal shook hands.

Chapter 23

Pakistan
08-July-2010
2200 Hours Local Time

Walters awoke. The sounds of rotor blades beating the air shook the ground around him. Walters rubbed his face and yawned loudly. The few hours of sleep had done little ease his fatigue. Walters tied his boots and staggered out of the dimly lit tent.

Outside, Helicopter gunships raced in. Crews madly refueled and rearmed the idling weapons of war. The gunships immediately pulled power after being services. Clouds of dust rose up. The might machines disappeared into the darkness of the night. The ground crews partook in a rest, anxiously awaiting the arrival of the next wave of warriors form the sky.

Walters covered his face from the choking dust. He tried to focus his eyes. The bright lights blinded him, the sharp light penetrated deep into his skull. Deep inside Walters cursed the light and prayed for the darkness of night.

Escaping the bright lights around, Walters staggered into the command tent. Jaswal looked up, his eyes were red, dark circles

Unseen Warriors

lay underneath. "Welcome, Agent Rabin will be here in a short while," Jaswal spoke, unmoved by the stress of war all around him. Walters sat down, longing for caffeine to alleviate his fatigue.

Rabin walked in with the rest of Walters team, each member clutched a large coffee cup. Behind the team, several Indian Privates entered with an Indian Army Sergeant.

Jaswal raised his attention to the team. He took a long sip of his steaming hot tea and spoke. "Now that we're all here, I'll begin. This is Sergeant Gupta. He will be assisting your team. S. Sergeant Walters and Agent Rabin, you will fly in the lead Gunship. Sergeant Gupta will take the trail. My air assets have been bombing military sight in the Multan, Bhawalpur, and Uch Sharif triangle continually for the last twelve hours. Most of the Pakistani defense forces have shifted location to Bhawalpur. You should meet minimal resistance at your landing zone."

Walters took a large gulp of his coffee, "Is there any chance of the front moving?"

Jaswal looked deeply into his map, "Probably not, the Pakistani forces are putting up heavy resistance at Bhawalpur right now. The front should be stationary for at least the next twelve hours."

"Mr. Walters, Rabin, do your teams wish to keep their captured weapons?" Walters and Rabin nodded. "Good, let's deploy." Jaswal rubbed his eyes one more time, thoughts blazed through his mind. Rabin turned around and began to march out of the tent. "I have one more thing, Agent Rabin." Rabin flinched and looked straight into Jaswal's bloodshot eyes. "Don't trust anyone, especially Pakistanis claiming to be double agents. In the Kashmiri conflict I ran across many Pakistanis helping the Indian cause, their true intent lay otherwise." Rabin pondered Jaswal's word for a second. He gave Jaswal a formal salute and walked out.

Rabin led his team to a waiting Mi-34 Gunship. One by one, the team members jumped into the waiting Gunship. Walters remained outside, watching Sergeant Gupta rushing his team into the trail Gunship. Gupta looked gave to Walters a deep look and a thumbs up. Walters begrudgingly returned with a thumb up.

Walters jumped into the cavernous interior. The fuselage rattled and shook with the beating of the rotor blades. The fuselage gently rose into the sky. To the right, the trail helicopter rose, leveling slightly below the lead's altitude.

In the cockpit Major Minhas sat in the pilot's seat. His years of training and experience with minor skirmishes at the Kashmir front had left him lusting for a full-scale attack. For Minhas the time had come for him to show his stuff.

Minhas cruised along two hundred feet above the ground. Below, he watched huge numbers of supply vehicles snake along in mile long columns. Dust and dirt rose, blocking what little moonlight there was. Minhas could see tanks and artillery firing shells into the distance. Clouds of black flak erupted. Minhas dived toward the ground. Tracer fired erupted around gunship.

Minhas' gunship raced around through the sky above the columns of tanks. Hapless infantrymen hid in their foxholes. Mortars exploded on the ground. Pockets of black smoke billowed up all along the front.

JJ looked down in awe. He had envisioned the front being a large wall of armor and troops. But here it was a loose collection of tanks, artillery and infantry. Stationed at staggered points some were on hilltops, others behind concrete homes. Still others stood on the plains, dug into wheat fields that hid their dangerous foes.

Minhas slowed the gunship and stopped behind a small hill. Flak bursts jarred the aircraft. Minhas rose a few feet. "Tiger 310 is unmasking," Minhas announced over the radio. His wingman replied with a click on his microphone.

Minhas rose a few feet above the hill. His threat-warning indicator exploded into lights. Tracer fire erupted over the hill.

Missile tones filled the cockpit. Minhas dropped the collective while madly dropping chaff and flares. The aircraft plunged to earth. Missiles and tracer fire raced overhead. Minhas wiped the sweat from his face and announced over the radio, "Lions den, Tiger 310 need Sam suppression at map grid hotel 17."

"Copy," a voice coldly answered.

*****

High above at 13,000 feet, twenty miles away, Captain Dange raced through the air with his Dassault Mirage 2000 fighter-bomber. The veteran airframe had recently received its final upgrade. Dange longed for his next replacement aircraft. He had become bored with the new avionics. Dange's wingman, Captain Baines, flew alongside. Baines' eyes were red from fatigue and exhaustion.

"Elephant 1, Eagle."

"Go ahead," Dange replied.

"Air cavalry requires SAM suppression at Hotel 17."

"Copy, will comply!" Dange replied. Dange throttled the jet forward and changed heading. "Elephant 2, did you copy Eagle's last transmission?"

"Copy, let's get some action!" Dange excitedly replied. The two jets raced along to Minhas' location. Combat exhaustion and fatigue was washed away with excitement and euphoria.

Dange approached the attack way point. His TWI remained strangely quiet; no radar points providing emissions. Dange checked the status of his KH-58 anti radiation missile on his display pages. He only had two and knew he couldn't waste them. Dange spoke in his mike, "I'm climbing to angel one-five. I'll put on some music when I crest, let go a missile at the first radar you see."

"Copy," Bans replied.

Dange throttled his engines up and climbed to 15,000 feet. Instantly his TWI filled with numbered squares. The airplane's missile tone screamed into his ears. Dange looked out of the canopy. A large fireball raced into the sky. Dange banked the aircraft, keeping the rising fireball on his right wing. He steered toward the missile, dumping chaff in the process. The missile turned sharper and sharper, trying to track the fleeing aircraft. Dange turned hard right into the missiles path. The missile passed harmlessly below and exploded a short distance away.

*****

Baines rubbed the trigger with his thumbs. Sweat ran down onto the joystick. Baines' moved his cursor on the missile's tracking page until he locked on the main radar transmission station. Bain's pressed the trigger, firing off a KH-58 missile. The missile fell off the pylon and disappeared into the distance. Baines lined up his cursor and another radar target and fired. A minute later it disappeared alongside several other secondary radar targets.

Feeling confident and impressed with himself, Baines joined Dange's airplane. The two pilots selected their cluster bombs and set the way points for the AAA position on the ground radars.

Dange slowed the aircraft in preparation for a dive. Looking down, his eyes filled with fear. A pair of AIM-9 sidewinder missiles raced to his positions from the ground below.

"Sidewinder inbound!" Dange shouted while diving away from the fast approaching missiles.

Baines jerked the stick to the opposite direction. He dived to the ground while dumping loads of flares at the same time. The missile turned hard toward the ground trying to chase down the fleeing aircraft. Baines continued to dump flares. The missile closed in closer and closer, undeterred by the ground clutter. Baines jerked the stick back at the last second while dumping his last flare.

The missile exploded, spraying the rudder and exhaust pipe with shrapnel. Caution and warning messages filled the cockpit display panels. The stick became sluggish and unresponsive. "Elephant 2 needs a rescue chopper!" Baines screamed into the mike. Baines pulled the ejection seat. The rings at the base of the seat pulled Bain's legs in. The canopy violently blew off, sending the ejection seat high into the air.

The ejection seat jerked several shaking and jostling Baines. A parachute automatically deployed, the ejection seat fell into the darkness. The parachute jerked Baines conscious. Pain raced his shoulders and face. Bain wiped his face, his nose stung with a sharp pain. He looked down at his gloved hand. It was covered with blood.

A loud explosion erupted below. Baines looked down to see a fireball on ground. Tracers and fires raced across the dark ground below.

Baines drifted down for what felt like an eternity. Out in the distance, three distance lights approached him. The ones on the right and top were red. The left was green. Baines felt relieved, he knew an airplane was approaching. He drew a big smile. It felt good to be alive. Baines smile became a frown when tracer fire erupted toward him.

* * * * *

Captain Dange zoomed at the speed of sound at full military trust. The sidewinder missile exploded above him in the distance. Dange jerked the stick to the left and pulled hard. The airplane pulled a bone crushing 8gs around the corner. Dange selected the radar to track while scan mode and selected his AA-12 radar guided air-to-air missile. Dange raised his aircrafts radar dish, scanning for his unseen enemies.

The radar dish hummed, as it swept back and forth. Dange watched his radar display. Apprehension filled his mind. Two small diamonds appeared in the middle of his display 9 miles away and 7,000 feet above him. Dange selected the nearest blip. A square box appeared on Dange's HUD. Dange throttled up, closing on the nearby threat. A diamond super imposed on the box followed by the words "Lock" appeared on his HUD. Dange launched a missile. Dange locked on the second blip and fired off his last remaining air-to-air missile. The closest blip rotated and turned in the sky. Dange witnessed a flash in the sky. A burning fireball fell from the sky.

Dange closed in the remaining blip. It turned and twisted before diving toward the ground. Dange dived toward the ground closing in the twisting aircraft. Through the darkness, he closed in on at the fleeting target. Dange selected his guns, and strained to peer through the darkness struggling to gain a sight of his unseen foes.

The darkness lifted to reveal a Pakistani Air Force F-16 twisting in the air. Dange fired several short bursts with his cannon. Bullets tore into the fuselage. Airplane parts and smoke poured out of the stricken fuselage. The F-16 exploded into a burst of fire, followed by its tail spinning into the ground. Dange threw his throttle into the afterburner detent and raced away into the darkness.

* * * * *

Minhas heard distant explosions. Bright flashes erupted from the other side of the hill. Over the radio a voice spoke, "Tiger 310, Wild Weasel flight has completed its mission."

"Copy," Minhas replied. Minhas raised his helicopter above the hill and peered into the distance. The TWI stayed silence, hiding its secrets in a cloak of darkness. Out in the plains, several tracked vehicles lay on their sides and burned with bright yellow flames. Infantrymen lay dead, strewn around the plain. Minhas climbed over the hill, staying low to the ground. His wingman stayed close, hugging the terrain and Minhas' side.

Through his night vision, Minhas could see the dead bodies glowing in the darkness.

Minhas watched his way points change on his display. He was now headed straight for the palace. Minhas' family had live in Amristar several years ago. Pakistani insurgents sneaked across the border and exploded a bomb in the holy Sikh shrine at Amristar. Minhas' wife and three kids all died that day with 90 other civilians. From that day on, Minhas swore that he would get revenge. Today his urge for bloodlust would come. The sight of the dead soldiers strewn about excited him. For Minhas, the bloodletting on the battlefield became his drug. The way point markers on the navigation display counted down to less than 4 miles. Minhas changed his scowl to a grin. The slaughter was about to begin.

The TWI chirped. A strange radar identification appeared on his display. Minhas instinctively hid behind a nearby hill and hovered. The diamond shape on his TWI performed several sharp S-turns. The threat was getting closer to Minhas. The feeling of euphoria was about to go through his veins. Minhas turned in place until his helicopter's nose pointed at the incoming threat.

Minhas' chin gunner, Lieutenant Mukherjee watched the rapidly twist object in rapt attention. His hands became sweaty as he stroked the fire button on his stick. The twisting diamond circled several more times in the northern sky. The radar ID suddenly extinguished. The northern sky exploded into fire. Huge clouds of smoke rose high into the sky.

Minhas rose to thirty feet above ground level. The mighty helicopter crept forward toward a nearby northern hill. The TWI remained quiet. The silence disturbed Minhas. The helicopter crossed over the hill, the stillness of the night contrasted deeply with violence all around. Burned trucks, tanks and assorted tracked lay scattered around the hillside. Dead men, still clutching their rifles lay along the helicopter's path.

Minhas approached the wheat field. Sporadic fires burning the lush wheat littered the landscape. Minhas touched down at the center of the field. His wingmen did the same fifty feet away. Walters' team stormed out of the helicopter and ran to a location 2000 yards away from the rumbling beasts. Gupta's men joined seconds later.

The massive helicopters throbbed. The rotors beat the air, lifting the mighty fuselages into the air. Watson watched in excitement, sweat rolled down his brow. The helicopters shook and rocked, disappearing into the sky.

The team hiked up the field to the ridge line. The soft sounds of wheat being crunched echoed through the night. Arriving at the crest, the team hid in the shrubbery. Walters and Gupta scanned the area with their binoculars. To the north lay the Palace. Its former brilliance was now greatly tarnished by the ravages of war. Flames blackened the concrete sides. The ornate stained glass windows were smashed out. The great barrier wall that encircled the Palace was in ruins. The east hill burned with explosive yellow flames.

The two men looked to each other. Emotions, a mixture of and confusion filled their minds. Walters was the first to speak. "It looks like General Jaswal took care of the heavy artillery for us."

Rabin immediately joined the discussion, "We must clear the perimeter. Sergeant Gupta, head north to the house on the south side of the Palace. Continue east to the hill, clear any remaining Pakistani combatants. Meet us at the entrance. Do not enter until we join you. We'll clear the west flank and join you at the entrance.

"Once we meet up at the Palace entrance. Call the rescue chopper. We'll rescue Townsend and assemble on the terrace roof. That'll be your signal that mission is accomplished. If you don't see us on the Terrace, evacuate on the chopper without us." Gupta agreed and disappeared to the house in the distance.

Rabin's team ran west to the base of the hill. The odor of burning flesh filled the air, sickening the team members. The team continued north along the base of the hill. Explosions in the distance thundered away. SAMs rose into the air and exploded. Sonic booms shuddered in the sky.

The team continued until they were directly west of the Palace. Walters picked up a burned Marine helmet. The 1st Lieutenant Rank insignia was still visible. The thought of the dead Marines saddened the men. Watson picked up some shiny objects from the dirt. Most were expended 5.56mm shells. One was flat and blackened. Watson scraped the carbon off and read the Inscription. "Charles Skinner, USMC." For the team the dead men no longer were just uniforms. They now they had names.

Rabin picked up a skull from the soft soil. Vultures and dogs had chewed the flesh from it. Teeth marks defiled several parts of the skull. Rabin said a silent prayer and placed the skull in the ground. He covered it with the soft soil, and spoke another silent prayer. The rest of the team members looked in confusion and awe at the spectacle. Rabin smiled, "Your men died here. This is now their graveyard. They deserve the respect that all soldiers are given when they die in foreign lands."

A rustling sound came from a portion of the battered wall. Walters raised his rifle and aimed. A helmet rose above a section of stone wall, unaware of the team's presence. Nishan quickly pulled out a grenade and threw it behind the wall. A loud explosion erupted, followed by a large dust cloud. Nishan and Walters ran behind the wall and inspected their work. A lone soldier lay dead. His rifle was empty, his clothing burned off his flesh.

Nishan looked to Walters, "He didn't seem like much of a fighting force to me," Walters snarled and waved the rest of the team over. The Team members nonchalantly walked over, unconcerned about enemy threats.

The once might wall that stood for almost a century, now lie in ruins. Decades of invaders had done little to damage to the stone fortress. One aircraft with a few bombs had destroyed the ancient monument in a matter of minutes. The only reminder of the walls former glory was several small solid sections and hills of colored sand.

The team headed east along the north face of the ruins. To the north, the field burned with fires. Massive numbers of tracked vehicles, trucks and Jeeps burned. The smells of burning rubber, diesel oil and gunpowder choked the air. Hundreds of bodies burned in the raging inferno. Walters covered his mouth, the smells and sights made him nauseous.

The team walked for a few more minutes and arrived at the Palace entrance. The wall remained intact at this position. Walters lay down, his back to the wall, and breathed deeply. Rabin looked into Walters' eyes and gave him a sorrow look. Walters returned with a sigh and spoke. "What is your plan now, agent Rabin?"

Rabin pondered for a second and spoke. "For something like this, there is no plan."

Walters shook his head, "It's eerily quiet here."

A tank nearby exploded into a giant ball of flames. The bright light shone into Rabin's face. Rabin spoke in a deep monotone voice. "This is a graveyard for Americans and Pakistanis." Walters shrugged his shoulders. His eyes remained transfixed on the burning bodies in the distance.

Sharon came to Rabin and whispered several words into Rabin's ear. Rabin nodded and waved his hand. Sharon disappeared into the darkness. Walters spoke up, his eyes still transfixed on the burning bodies in the distance. "What caused all of this?"

Rabin looked at the fires and spoke, "Cluster bombs, maybe even napalm. Those tanks were taken out with some sort of a dedicated antitank missile like a Maverick or Hellfire." Walters remained transfixed on the fires in the distance. The smells, sight and sounds made him think deeply about his future.

*****

Sergeant Gupta and his team rushed to the south house. Its ornate slate roof lay in pieces scattered over the floor. The intense fires blacked the concrete walls. Expended 5.56mm shells were littered all over the floor. Gupta's team swept all the interior of the house. The rooms were hauntingly quiet. They lacked any presence of human habitation. Gupta walked to the east-facing window. He put on his binoculars and peered east into the distance. The eastern hill was deserted. Fires burned from overturned vehicles.

Gupta led his team out of the house toward the hill. Craters pockmarked several places where the mighty wall had once stood. Vegetation burned in scattered fires all along the roadway.

The team reached the hill in a relatively short time. An armored personnel carrier burned explosively with bright orange flames. Suddenly, bullets crashed all around the team. Gupta led his team behind the burning amour. More gunfire erupted, crashing mere inches from Gupta's feet.

Gupta motioned with his hand. Private Singh ran up to Gupta's side bearing his M-203 grenade launcher. The remainder of Gupta's team set their rifles to auto, anxiously awaiting the command to fire. The enemy gunfire continued for several seconds, then stopped. Gupta and his men rose up and sprayed automatic fire into a machine gun nest. Expending their magazines, they dived to the ground. Singh fired a 40mm grenade and dove for the dirt.

A loud explosion rocked the hill. Small secondary explosions popped and crackled immediately afterwards. Gupta's men reloaded and waited. A flare rose into the sky and exploded in the distance. Gupta and his men charged up the hill, sporadic gunfire emanated from positions nearby the machine gun nest. Gupta and his men fired several more short bursts, silencing the gunfire. Gupta's men then charged the hillside.

Gupta was the first to reach the hilltop. Inside the machine gun nest, several dead women wearing torn civilian clothing lay. Empty MP-5 submachine guns lay strewn across their laps. Gupta turned his face in disgust. The grisly sight turned his stomach. Gupta looked to the northern flanks of the hill. What little brush that had grown was burned off. More dead women lay strewn, their clothes burned off by the napalm.

Gupta put on his night vision binocular and inspected the Palace rooftop. There were no snipers. The rooftop seemed devoid of human life. Gupta tried to peer into the windows. Strange movements occurred inside. Gupta removed his binoculars and pondered for a second, thoughts raced through his mind.

"It's time to meet Rabin's team!" Gupta announced to his men. The team raced down the hill, taking pains to avoid stepping on the dead women. Gupta's team ran across the compound to Rabin's position. Gupta stood puzzled at the long faces of Walters' team. Gupta looked to Rabin and spoke, "Where is Agent Sharon?"

"He is doing a little scouting for us," Replied Rabin. "We'll go in first, watch the exit for intruders. I want you to call the rescue chopper now. Have it land right here, we'll be ready." Gupta agreed and ordered his radioman.

Rabin and Walters burst into the Palace's entrance. The followed a darkened hallway into a large foyer. Concrete steps led into the second floor. The rest of the team followed behind.

Walters immediately ran to a shiny metal object on the floor. He picked up and read the raised writing out loud. "William Stoner, Catholic, 376-09-5321." Walters raised his face and looked at Rabin. "The original rescue party made it this far, what happened?"

Unseen Warriors

Before Rabin could answer, Nishan fired a burst of automatic fire at the top of the steps. A woman wearing civilian clothing fell to the ground with a rifle in her hands. Rabin shook his head in disgust, "It seems our enemy is short on troop."

Walters rolled his eyes, "Let's clear the rest!" Walters ran up the steps, Nishan followed, Rabin and JJ came behind, and Watson covered the rear. The team entered the second floor. Each member kicked one of the doors down exposing torture devices using water baths.

One room contained several car batteries connected to a strange table. Walters inspected the batteries and table, Rabin walked in, his eyes grew red with anger. "They are torturing people with electricity. I have seen these rooms used by Hamas in the West bank."

Walters lip curled, anger filled his eyes. "Let's kill all of them, men and women!" Walters marched into the hallway, his rifle selected to auto. He kicked the door open and arrived at another set of steps. He walked up confidently up the steps to another wooden door. Nishan kicked the door open. The two men filled the hallway with indiscriminate automatic gunfire.

Walters ran down the hallway. Rows and rows of cells lined the distance as far as the eye could see. A couple of cells down, a shattered figure lay on the cold concrete. His legs were wrapped in crude bandages. Blood crusted the open sores on his face. Many of his teeth were gone. His clothes were torn and dirty. The stench of urine and stool emanated from his body.

"Free him now!" Walters screamed at Rabin. Rabin quickly pulled out a knife and slid it into the cell lock. Rabin twisted the knife several times. "Click," the lock released. JJ and Watson frantically charged into the cell. Watson looked into the man's stunned eyes. "Hey, soldier, I'm from the US Army. We're here to rescue you." The dirty individual stayed stunned, unable to speak. Color returned to his face. He tried to move his mouth, but confusion and disbelief filled his eyes.

Watson moistened a rag with water and wiped the soldier's face. He spoke again, this time softly. "What's your name soldier?"

The man touched Watson's hand. Tears flowed from his eyes. "I'm Sergeant Gibson, US Marine Corps, Force Recon." His voice quivered, his eyes filled with fear. "How are my men?"

Watson breathed deeply and hesitated for a second before answering. "We believe you're the only survivor."

"God, I hate you!" Gibson screamed at Watson. Gibson cried out loudly and fell to the floor. Watson picked up Gibson and hugged him. Gibson continued to bawl like a baby.

Walters marched forward unabated. Anger filled his eyes. In a nearby cell another man lay. Burns covered his arms and hands. The man stood up and walked to the cell door.

Walters kicked aside several dead men. He picked up a set of keys from one of the dead. The keys shimmered in the night, blood dripped from their tips. Walters wiped the blood off on one of the dead bodies and madly attempted to unlock the door. The door unlocked with Walters second choice of key.

Walters kicked the door open and stared into the eyes of the man. "So, you must be Lieutenant Townsend," Walters said in an angry voice. Townsend nodded with a sorrowful look. A scowl covered Walters' face, "Do you know how many people died to save you?" Townsend's eyes grew huge. Before he could speak, Walters interrupted and continued to lecture Townsend. "Two squads of Force Recon Marines and the crews of two transport helicopters died to rescue you outside this very building. One of my men, two Mossad agents and countless Indian soldiers died for your rescue. Thanks to you, the sin of all the carnage outside is on my hands!"

"Can I say anything in my defense?" Townsend asked. Walters nodded while breathing heavily. "If you want to be angry with anyone, be angry with my father, Steven Hawkins." Walters' anger subsided for a second. Confusion covered his face.

"My father is the president, that's why there was all the pressure to rescue me. Look at me!" Townsend pulled up his pant legs and sleeves. "They've been electrocuting me for what seems eternity. The pain was horrible. Many times I wished I were dead. They kept asking me questions about a Black Ops camp, Camp Zulu!"

Walters flinched, "What about Camp Zulu?"

"They wanted to know what its defenses were. The type of its nearby terrain and what kind of aircraft was stored there," Townsend answered.

Walters' anger subsided, now it was replaced by confusion. "Why did they want to know that?"

"Because you have Hassan in your custody," answered a voice from an unknown corner. Walters raised his rifle, the rest of the team followed suit.

A door at the end of the hallway opened. A Pakistani general entered and stopped short of Walters. Walters continued to aim at the generals head undeterred. The general smiled and shook his head. "You don't remember me do you Staff Sergeant Walters?"

Walters eyes grew huge, his anger overtook his confusion, "Who are you, how do you know my name?"

The general answered, "My name is General Majeed. I was at the missile base when you did your little sabotage show a couple of days ago."

Walters curled his lip, "You still didn't answer my question General!"

Majeed laughed, "You and me served together. You used to know me as Private Mowia Mohammed."

The revelation stunned Walters, thoughts raced through his mind. "That doesn't change anything. You're a traitor!"

Majeed smiled. "After we were captured at the Chinese border, I infiltrated Hassan's cell. Since then I've been sending coded messages to the CIA, I am your mole. My recognition code is Parrot 1967."

Walters lowered his rifle, the rest of the team followed suit. "How did you get this high up in the Pakistani army?"

"Mansoor knew I had inside knowledge about Black Ops. The ruse in North Korea was a plan on luring your team into our trap. Townsend turned out to be an unexpected prize for Mansoor."

Walters breathed deeply, "What is so important about Hassan?"

Majeed rubbed his neck and spoke, "Hassan was one of Mansoor's planners for July 4th Attacks. Sadr, who you captured in North Korea, is another. The final mastermind is a Saudi named Haroon Babajhan. He is a brutal terrorist. He'd kill Mansoor if it suited him. His only allegiance is his cause to kill American. He's a religious zealot."

"Did you know about the July 4th attacks?" Walters asked.

Majeed raised his eyebrows. "I spent the last month on Mansoor's nuclear missile project. The Intel I got was that he was aiming to do the attack with an intercontinental ballistic missile. I thought Mansoor was going to attack the sixth fleet in the Persian Gulf with one large nuclear warhead."

Walters fell into deep thought. "The CIA would like to talk to you about Mansoor's associated plans. Will you come back to camp Zulu with us?"

"No, I can't go with you. Your missile sabotage caused one of the missiles to destroy Islamabad. Mansoor and Babajhan are both dead. Colonel Massoud is now the ruler of Pakistan. Once the Indian forces overrun the country, there'll be a power vacuum. I need to stay behind and assume the presidency."

Walters curled his lip. "Yes, but the Indian forces have lost a large number of forces in Kashmir. Revenge runs deep in their blood."

Majeed put his hand on Walters shoulder. "When I was in Black Ops, I had plenty of altitude problems. I got myself in lots of fights. I was in the Army almost seven years, and I got busted down to Private twice. My fitness reports were poor. I just didn't fit in. Heck, I never fit in with civilian life.

"Here in Pakistan. I have a purpose and a place. No one knows about my tortured past. I've got a fresh start here and I plan to make the most of it. I want to make Pakistan great, like America."

Walters walked to the jail cell and helped Townsend out. Townsend walked slowly, the burns covered huge sections of his body. Fluids oozed from open burns on his legs and arms.

Watson and JJ brought out Gibson. Gibson floated back and forth between consciousness. A mixture of disbelief and excitement filled his mind. For Gibson it seemed an endless nightmare was over, but the long road to recovery had yet to come.

Walters led the team down the hall through an open door to the concrete terrace. Majeed trailed the team. The clear night's air felt good in Townsend's lungs. The sight of burning tanks helped quench the need for revenge in Townsend's heart. Explosions continued to pop in the distance. Sonic booms thundered above. Townsend knew that the war was on in earnest.

Rabin looked to Majeed, "Mr. Majeed, where is the remaining storehouse of backpack nukes?"

Majeed hesitated for a second then spoke. "There is an airbase near Multan. It is controlled by Colonel Massoud. The nukes are presently stored on a Boeing 737-200 cargo aircraft. Mansoor planned on smuggling them out tomorrow before the Indian forces get near the outskirts of Multan.

"Do not try an attack from the air. The airbase is far too heavily defended by SAMs and AAA. Even an F-117 Stealth would have a difficult time surviving the onslaught. A commando raid is your only way penetrating the perimeter defenses."

Rabin looked to Walters, the two men nodded and winked once. Sharon lunged out of the hallway onto the rooftop. Gupta followed shortly afterwards. Sharon looked at Gibson and Townsend. Sharon shifted his attention to Rabin and spoke in an emotionless tone. "I see we've achieved our primary mission objective."

"Yes, we have," Rabin Replied.

The air began to vibrate with the sound of beating rotors. Out in the distance, two Mi-35 gunships approached from the southern sky. Walters looked to Gupta, "Get your men onto the lead gunship. I'll get my men on the trail. Get General Jaswal to medevac my men to a US military hospital ASAP."

Gupta shook Walters' hand and spoke, "I'll make sure your men receive the best medical care possible."

The group of men marched through the Palace down to the outside courtyard. The morning sun broke over the eastern sky. The sky turned blood red as if angry that it had to reveal the nights carnage.

The lead gunship landed in front of the Palace entrance. Clouds of dust rose into the dim morning light. Gupta's men rush in. Gupta walked to the entrance door slowly, he turned back to Walters and gave him thumbs up. Walters smiled and gave him his Hawaiian salute. Gupta walked in the door closed. The massive helicopter lifted into the sky, dust clouds erupted all around. The gunship rose high and departed into the sunset.

The trail gunship landed into a cloud of dust. Nishan and Watson carried Gibson into cavernous interior. Walters led Townsend inside and sat him beside Gibson. Walters went to the cockpit and spoke to the pilot. The two shook hands.

Walters stepped up to Townsend and spoke over the noise of the rotors. "Sir, the Indians will take good care of you. When you arrive in Germany, you need to contact Colonel Griswalt, at Black Ops camp Zulu."

JJ, Watson and Nishan walked into the cabin and saluted Townsend. Townsend saluted the men and spoke. "I was wrong about your guys. You guys are crack troops. If you ever want to come back to my squad, you're welcome."

Nishan smiled and shook Townsend's hand. "Thank you, for the offer, sir. We've got a home now and we like it." Nishan stepped back and gave Townsend a salute.

Watson walked forward and spoke, "Sir, I couldn't be part of your squad. You were right. There isn't enough action in your squad for me." Watson saluted Townsend and stepped away. JJ stepped up and saluted Townsend.

Walters yelled out to the pilot something. The team ran out of the helicopter. The helicopter shook and rose into the air. Townsend rushed to the open door and yelled at the team. Walters and the rest of the team stood and saluted. Townsend stood yelling at the team while the gunship took off into the sunset.

Sharon pulled up in an army 6 x 6 truck from the burning field of tanks. Rabin looked to Walters, "Shall we continue onto our secondary mission goal?" Walters curled his lip and nodded. Sharon stepped out of the cab and held the door open. Nishan begrudgingly stepped into the driver's side. Rabin sat in the passenger seat, the rest of the team piled into the back of the truck.

The truck headed west on the roadway. Burning vehicles lined both sides of the roadway. The acid smell of burning diesel and rubber filled the air. Nishan wove through hills to a village on the west side of the hill. Fires burned through out the concrete walled homes. Burned and dazed villagers flooded the roadway in a vain attempt to secure medical aid. Nishan drove on through, ignoring the pleas of the civilians all around him.

Nishan pulled onto the main highway and headed north. Crowds of refugees flooded the streets. Men, women and children rode cars, motorcycles, bicycles and even oxcarts to escape the advancing Indian forces. Bombs exploded along side the roadways. Indian fighters twisted and turned in the sky, dog fighting Pakistani F-16s. Building alongside the roadway disappeared into clouds of dust and rubble without warning.

Nishan slowed down, he wove his way between crowds of donkey carts. Nishan's eyes grew huge. Just off the distance near the Indus River a B-52 burned. Villagers ransacked the bodies of the dead airman. Vultures flew in and tore flesh from the dead men. Nishan gripped the steering wheel tight. "Continue on your mission, don't get disturbed. We cannot help them," Rabin announced.

The truck continued north along the roadway. Above, two Huey Cobra gunships twisted in the air. Indian fighter planes dived to the ground, spraying gunfire at the twisting rotor craft. The crowds on the roadway fled for cover. Bullets and expended shells rained down on the ground, injuring innocent civilians.

The fighters launched air-to-air missiles at the helicopters. The first helicopter immediately exploded. Chunks of burning debris rained down on the ground. Civilians screamed in pain as burning jet fuel set their skin on fire. The second helicopter dumped flares and chaff while twisting in the air. A missile followed behind hunting down the helpless helicopter. A Flash blinded all who watched, fire fell from the sky. Large numbers of trees burst into flames.

The crowd grew hysterical. Team members beat away civilians trying to board the truck. Nishan floored the gas, weaving through the legions of cars, oxcarts and mobs civilians clogging the roadway.

The truck continued several miles north toward the distance landscape. The noisy engine drowned out the sound of the crowds in the distance. The sun crawled high into the sky. The heat and lack of water parched the team. The excitement felt by the team after Townsend's rescue soon led anxiety and distraught thoughts. The sight of the civilians clamoring for safety brought a new human face to the war on terror.

Walters leaned forward to speak to Rabin. The crashing and shaking of the truck upturned his normally placid stomach. "What is your plan on extracting us out of this crazy country?"

Rabin failed to look up at Walters' direction. He continued focusing in the dirty worn out map on his lap. "We have two options. We could travel east to Lahore and cross to India through Amristar. We could also continue north Peshawar, and then travel east to Kabul."

"Which one do you recommend?" Walters asked with hint of doubt in his voice.

Rabin pondered for a second. He lifted his eyes to the rising sun and gazed into the clouds. Contrails from high-speed jets crisscrossed the cloudless sky. "Indian and Pakistani forces are probably fighting pretty hard at Lahore. The route to Kabul is much longer, and more dangerous. The American forces are probably marching east from the Khyber Pass as we speak. I'm sure the Pakistani forces have withered away from the northwest region. There is too much mountainous region to guard against American air and ground forces. We should take the Khyber Pass; your forces will protect you from Pakistani gunships. Anyways, the distance from Multan is only 500 miles max. Well within a days drive."

Walters nodded in agreement. He knew Rabin was in control. Though, deep inside, Walters wondered whether any logical reasoning was possible in the chaos of this battlefield.

The truck approached the outskirts of Multan. The nearby village was empty, devoid of life. There were neither fleeing crowds here nor graveyards of wreckage. For the team the only sign of war was the thundering sound of jets taking off in the distance. The truck continued to close in the airport. Dozens of trucks loaded with troops raced by at high speed. The sidewalks and concrete buildings remained devoid of civilian activity.

Nishan turned on the final leg to the airport. The airport was now in full view. Fighter planes thundered into the sky, their blue afterburner flames still visible in the noon sky. Fleets of helicopters rose in the sky. Missiles ominously hung from stub-wings on their fuselages.

Nishan approached the airport's main gate. His pulse raced with anticipation. A stern faced Corporal walked up to the Nishan's window. An angry scowl covered his face at the sight of the dirty soldiers in the truck's cab. "What is your duty here?" he barked to Nishan.

"I have several commandos on a high risk mission. We need to get some fuel before we continue," Nishan casually remarked.

The Corporal became perturbed, "Who authorized your mission. This is a high-level military base, not a gas station!" He shouted into Nishan's face.

Rabin slid out of the truck's cab and approached the corporal. The corporal immediately raised the rifle to eye level and aimed it to Rabin's head. "Stop!"

Rabin waved his hand, "Relax Corporal, I have something for you." The corporal failed to move from his menacing position. Rabin held out a paper bag shaped like a wine bottle. The corporal lowered his rifle and waved Rabin closer. Rabin smiled and handed the bag over to the soldier. The corporal held the bag by its base. He peered inside at its cap and label. A smile befell the soldier. He continued to peer into the paper bag, taking pains not to revel its contents.

Rabin spoke to the corporal in a low and deliberate voice, "We have a very important mission. Our mission could change the very course of the war. We need your cooperation, take this as evidence of our sincerity."

The corporal continued to stare at the bottle. Abruptly he tucked the bag away out of sight and spoke to Rabin. "You may pass. There is a fueling station about 1200 meters away. Take the first left after this gate."

"Where are the cargo planes kept?" Rabin casually inquired.

"They are about 500 meters from the fueling station. You should see them on your right beside several warehouses," the corporal replied.

"Thank you," Rabin replied with a salute. Rabin walked back to the truck, the gate immediately opened. Nishan passed onto the perimeter road with out incident. Several trucks loaded with bombs hurriedly passed by on their way to the waiting fighter planes.

Nishan looked to Rabin, "How'd you get that guy to change his mind so fast?"

Rabin smiled, "A bottle of Johnny Walker can do amazing things to lonely soldiers."

Nishan gave a confused look, "Where did you get that from?"

Rabin's eyes gleamed, "General Jaswal, it was a parting gift. The six of us were supposed to drink it when we got back to the base in one piece."

Nishan shook his head, "Now we have generals providing liquor to us. It's not like we don't have enough problems with alcoholism in the ranks as it is."

"Relax Nishan, Yitzhak and I don't drink, so it's no skin off our noses. After all we won't be celebrating when we get back anyways."

Nishan swung his head in surprise. "What do you mean we won't be celebrating together?"

Rabin gave a stern look, "Mr. Nishan, we must stay anonymous. The Mossad does not allow any intimate knowledge of its agents by outside agencies."

Nishan rubbed the sweat of his forehead. "Are Yitzhak and Rabin even your real names?"

Rabin shook his head. "No, your team is full of very good men. But we must maintain our secrecy."

A tear slowly worked its way down Nishan's cheek. Nishan madly swatted it before Rabin could take notice. "I was hoping that after…"

"I understand, many times I have wished I could become personally in touch with those who I have met on my foreign missions. Alas, it's a lonely profession that we practice in the Mossad."

Nishan focused on the last bit of roadway ahead. Thoughts of Rabin, the mission and Sarah raced through his mind. Breathing heavily, Nishan wished he could stop everything and have time absorb the shock of all the events of the past few months.

Nishan slowed the truck. A large rusty pump station was ahead to his left. Nishan pulled along side the decrepit station and began refueling the trucks massive fuel tanks. Rabin stepped into the pack of the poorly covered truck bed. Nishan immediately jumped into the truck, his heart a mixture of sorrow and excitement.

Rabin spoke to the team in a hushed voice. "Look at the northeast." The team madly hovered to the trucks passenger side and peered through the green canvas. Behind the cargo warehouse stood a dirty Pakistani Airways cargo Boeing 737-200. The rest of the cargo apron was devoid of activity. A lone 6x6 truck stood nearby. Rabin pulled the team back into a huddle and spoke. "Agent Sharon and I will disable the crew and evacuate via the jet. Through the chaos, the tower will clear us to take off with the rest of the military traffic.

"Mr. Walters, you are now in command of your team. Take the truck and head to Kabul immediately after we depart your vehicle."

Walters gave a confused look to Rabin, "Are you crazy? We could storm the airplane with your..."

Rabin immediately interrupted Walters. "Mr. Walters, the nukes are our primary mission objective. Agent Sharon and I are easily capable of flying the airplane out of a here. The plane is unguarded. A massive show of force by us would only arouse suspicion on the part of the Pakistanis."

"What if you need backup, we could provide covering fire..."

"No, Mr. Walters you are quite a strong-willed man. That makes you an excellent soldier. But sometimes you can be far too stubborn." The gas pump clicked, the fuel tanks were now full. "The two of us will seem just like a couple of pilots preparing for a normal flight. We could be on our way in only thirty minutes. Any sighting of your men by the local forces would lead to a complete shutdown of the airport. By splitting up, we also increase the chances of our parties surviving. The outside world must be told of the Pakistani weapons of mass destruction. We do not want our soldiers to be second guessed for generations because the media never found their smoking gun."

Walters remained in deep thought for a few minutes. Walters raised his eyes and pulled out his right hand. "It has been a real pleasure working with you. You men have saved us from certain death several times. I hope we meet again under better circumstances."

Rabin smiled, "You helped us destroy that missile. Without your help, thousands of Israeli civilians would certainly have died. Thank you, for your help, that mission went very smoothly."

Watson grunted, "You jokers think a smooth mission is one that we have to almost get killed."

Rabin shot back, "Any mission we walk away from is a smooth mission." The team erupted into laughter. "We must leave Mr. Walters, remember secrecy is utmost." Rabin shook hands with all the team members, Sharon quickly followed suit. Immediately the two departed from the truck.

Walters stepped outside and looked around. The two men had vanished into thin air. Walters shrugged off any notions and sat into the truck's passenger seat. Nishan disconnected the fuel hose and entered the driver's seat. Nishan started the truck, immediately the gas gage rushed over to the full mark. Nishan rolled the truck forward, just short of the perimeter road. In the mirror, a lumbering convoy of transport trucks rumbled. Nishan waited for the last truck to pass and he casually pulled behind the trail vehicle. The vehicles sped up, turning toward the airport exit. The corporal immediately opened the gate, a silver flash in his right hand. The convoy raced through the gate.

The corporal watched the green trucks go by, unconcerned by the vehicle count.

The immense convoy of vehicles immediately turned north on the main road toward Sargodha. Other trucks loaded with food, fuel and ammo intermingled. The drivers paid no attention to the team's vehicle in the middle of the pack. For the next four hours the vehicles raced along. They only slowed for trucks loaded with terrified conscripts rushing toward the front at Lahore. High in the sky contrails twisted and turned. SAMs raced to the sky, chasing down their elusive prey. Clouds of chaff and flares fell from the sky. Indian aircraft quick changed from the hunters to the hunted in the hot summer sky.

Nishan slowed the truck. The huge supply column had now grown to almost sixty vehicles. The road was clogged with a sea of olive drab vehicles. Nishan squeezed the steering wheel. The traffic jam had changed his thoughts from fear to wonder and bewilderment. Nishan looked over to Walters, "Do you think will see them ever again?"

Walters shrugged his shoulder, "I don't know. They're the first Mossad agents I've ever met. I going to guess we got a lot closer to them any other ordinary soldiers before."

A sonic boom shook the truck. High above a contrail twisted side to side in an imprecise manner. The lead truck turned right onto the main road to Lahore. Nishan pained to drift off away from the main convoy unnoticed. Nishan gripped the steering wheel. The slow progress tested his patience.

The lead truck exploded into a ball of flames. Several other trucks exploded nearby. Small shrubs and grass planted along the roadway exploded into flames. Fires danced from vehicle to vehicle with ease. Nishan slammed on the brakes. Horror filed his eyes as he watched a huge fireball race toward his direction.

* * * * *

Unseen Warriors

Rabin stared through his binoculars. Sharon kept tugging at his shirt like an impatient child. "Where are they Ariel?" Sharon queried.

Rabin continued to stare out into the distance, unmoved by Sharon's pleading. "They have managed to infiltrate a large truck convoy heading north. I am quite surprised by Mr. Walters' willingness to leave so quickly."

"Mr. Walters is a professional soldier. He knows sacrifices must be made during times of war." Sharon rubbed the stubble on his chin, "Did Mr. Nishan put up much of a fight?"

Rabin lowered his binoculars. "He is a much more sensitive man than Mr. Walters. The horrors of combat have not hardened his heart yet."

Sharon smiled, "I hope he won't be badly scarred after the war. I've seen many much weaker men than him lose their sanity."

"It is time for us to deploy," Rabin announced. The two men climbed down from the container they were using for a vantage point. The two men shed their rifles and traveled to the waiting jet. The APU's exhaust cut through with a harsh, high-pitched wine. Rabin plugged his ears with his fingers.

Two Privates stopped the approaching men. "Who are you?" The leader demanded to know.

"We are pilots sent by Colonel Massoud on a top secret mission," Rabin shot back in an arrogant tone.

The Private curled his lip. "Show me your documentation!"

Rabin nodded in agreement. "We can only show our paperwork in a secure location. I will show you everything you need to see in the cockpit. Take your partner along."

The four men walked up to the airplane and walked up the steep entrance steps. The mighty upper cargo deck extended the length of the fuselage. Small pallets of containers were stacked on end to end into the distance. Rabin pulled out some documentation and laid it on a container. The Private walked up and started rooting through the stack of documents.

Sharon pulled out his silenced pistol and fired two shots into the Private's back. Silently, the Private flinched for a second and fell to the floor below. The second Private fired his handgun several times. The rounds missed Rabin wildly. Sharon grabbed the man from behind and choked him with a nylon rope. The Private struggled for a few minutes before falling to the cold floor below.

Rabin threw the top open of the nearby container. Sharon pulled out a small suitcase-sized object. Rabin carefully inspected the object. His eyes grew huge with horror. "I think we have found our stash of nuclear backpacks," Rabin spoke in a horrified voice.

"Yes, you have!" A voice boomed from behind a container in the cargo deck. Alarms rang all around the airport. Hundreds of armed soldiers encircled the aircraft. Colonel Massoud stood up, an MP-5 in his hands at waist level. Massoud walked up, twenty feet short of Rabin. "I have finally caught you. My plan is complete." Massoud let out an evil laugh. Rabin and Sharon looked at each other with a confused look. "Early in February we suspected that there was a mole in our organization. Too many of our plans were being foiled by the Americans and Russians. Boarding parties would appear at the exact moment of our planned raids. That is why I planned the charade to capture the American officer. I figured I could easily find my mole by luring him to a rescue attempt in Uch Sharif. Unfortunately things didn't go as planned when those stupid Marines tried to perform a rescue attempt.

"Luckily, I had a backup plan. That is why we had Atta bring in the American's masquerading as arms dealers into the country. We wanted to flush you out. I was waiting for you with a whole Battalion at the hotel. Your fellow Mossad agents died far too quickly. You two will suffer far more for your crimes against the Muslim nation."

Rabin's anger grew, "So, this was all a ruse. You have made one mistake. My American friends are free. They will soon be back in India, ready to plan another assault against your beloved homeland."

Massoud gave out an evil laugh, "The Americans are fools. They are too busy bogged down in battles in Iraq and Afghanistan. I will kill that weasel Majeed and become the President of Pakistan. The desperate American forces will be more than happy to sign a peace deal with me."

Sharon grinned at Massoud, "Is your soul saved for Allah Colonel?"

"Why do you want to know?" Massoud barked back.

"My soul and Agent Rabin's are ready for our trip to heaven."

Massoud broke out in laughter. "You and Agent Rabin? Agent Guerin, don't you mean you friend Agent Vanunu?"

Rabin's face sunk, "How did you…?"

"I know you real names from a mutual friend of yours," Massoud rudely interrupted. Footsteps thumped up the metal steps leading into the airplane. Rabin's skin sweat with anticipation and fear, thoughts raced through his mind.

Tariq Atta entered the airplane, "Hello, Yitzhak, Ariel," Atta called out in a calm voice. Rabin and Sharon's faces became white with fear. "I see you remember me from the days when I used to spy for you in the Gaza. I had to stop that because I got a much more lucrative offer from Colonel Massoud. I delivered him the American officer, the team sent to rescue them and now you. I am going to be a very rich man."

Anger filled Sharon's eyes. "Really Ahmed Hassan. Do you know the Americans still hold your brother in jail?"

Atta laughed, "Yes, and Colonel Massoud is going to help get him out after I get rid of Jewish vermin like from Pakistan!"

Sharon smiled and looked to Rabin. Rabin winked his eye at Sharon. Sharon spoke up, barely able to contain his glee. "Colonel, is that one of the MP-5s that the Americans brought into the country?"

"Yeah," Massoud grunted at Sharon.

"It is not going to do you much good any more," Rabin shouted, he pressed a button on the suite case like object behind him. Massoud fired automatic gunfire at the two Agents.

The aircraft vaporized into a wall of flames. A nuclear blast wave raced out of the cargo ramp. Mass numbers of troops, building and aircraft being serviced disappeared into a wall of fire. The high-speed winds quickly rushed through the airport. Aircraft taxing, taking off and landing immediately disappeared into huge balls of fire.

The nuclear winds slowed their trek outward. In a matter of nanoseconds, they changed direction and rushed headlong into the epicenter. Frail metal shelters disappeared into piles of scrap metal. SAM, AAA and other anti aircraft defenders rolled and crashed into the building epicenter.

A huge mushroom cloud towered into the sky. Indian forces fighting in Bhawalpur danced in joy at the distant sight. An aide rushed into the command building and immediately gave General Jaswal the news of the Atomic blast. Jaswal cringed at the thoughts rushing through his mind. Colonel Shanker put his hand on Jaswal's shoulder. "I'm sure they got out alive. They are tough willed soldiers."

Jaswal cleaned his reading glasses. The stress of battle was beginning to take its toll on him. "Yes, they are strong-willed soldiers. Send the bombers in. I want every Pakistani troop concentration, land convoy and airfield destroyed from her to the north. Tomorrow morning we march into Islamabad and take what ever is rightfully India's. Shanker saluted and disappeared, Jaswal remained concentrating at the laminated map of Pakistan."

* * * * *

"Abandon truck!" Walters shouted to the team. Nishan and JJ jumped out of the truck's left side and ran into water filled ditches. Walters and Watson did the same on the opposite side.

Unseen Warriors

The fireball raced through the convoy, destroying the trucks in a quick fell swoop. Burning diesel fuel and debris rained down on the roadway. High above, two fighter planes finished circling one last time before departing into the distance.

Walters stood up from the ditch. The team's vehicle burned with black smoke. Expended 20mm shells lay strewn about the roadway. Nishan and JJ slowly wove between the burning vehicles to make their way to Walters' position. Walters shook his head, "Looks like we're out of wheels. We're going to have to make it by the old-fashioned method of the shoe leather express."

The team marched down the highway toward the junction. Trucks were filled with dead and dying men burned. The sounds of flames were the only thing that could drown out the moaning and crying of the wounded. The injured men begged for aid from the team, Walters pushed aside the men. He took pains to avoid any eye contact with the wounded.

The team arrived at a strange highway junction. A huge sign hung above, it was written both in English and Urdu. An arrow pointed to the right, followed by the words Islamabad. Another arrow pointed to the left, followed by Kabul. Walters stared at the sign for a minute. He headed toward the west for a few feet. The team waited for a second and looked on, confusion and fatigue filled their faces. Walters looked back at the weary men, "The sign says it's the right way, come on. What are you guys waiting for?"

"So, we're going to walk all the way to Kabul. No food or water, in the middle of summer. We'll die before we ever get near the border from this Godforsaken country," Watson wined.

Walters laughed, "After all we've been through. I can't believe you still have doubts." The rest of the team stayed quiet, Walters curled his lip. "Don't worry, we've survived this long, an opportunity will present itself."

The rest of the team begrudgingly followed suite. They walked rest of the day, the hot sun continued to bear down on them. Mirages on the asphalt met them every mile they walked. The roadway was completely devoid of life. No cars, trucks or even a bicycle could be seen. It was as if they had stumbled onto a place where extinction of human life had finally occurred.

The team marched into the early darkness of the night. The hot sun was now gone, the cold air befell upon the desert. The moon shone high in the air, illuminating the distance as far as the eye could see. Walters stopped the team and marched them into an area off the highway. Walters scanned the distance with his binoculars, grunting several times. Nishan and JJ tried to make a fire.

Watson watched him in rapt attention. He felt unconcerned with the goings on around him. He ignored Nishan's coaxing to join in the fire building. Watson finally spoke up, "So, Walters what do you see?"

Walters continued scanning the distance, "I see a road sign a fair distance away. It says 'Kabul 250 Km'. I say we're on the right track"

Watson rolled his eyes. "So, at our current pace, we should be in Kabul in a month." Watson said sarcastically.

"Go have a nap," Walters ordered. Watson grunted once, walked to the fire and lay down beside JJ.

Nishan smiled and walked up next to Walters. Sensing his presence, Walters put down his binoculars and turned to Nishan. "I can't believe Watsy some times. You'd swear he was a walking raw nerve."

Nishan smiled, "Don't worry about him, he's just grumpy because he needs his baby sleep." Nishan gave out a laugh for a second. Walters immediately gave a confused look. "It's kind of funny to hear you call Watsy a raw nerve. I remember our last Sergeant saying the same thing before we were thrown out of the Platoon."

Walters gave a snort, "So, how'd you guys deal with all the time?"

Nishan gave a strange look, "I don't know either. Watsy's desire for excitement can get real annoying when the action dies down. He'd drive JJ and me up the wall when we'd be put on guard duty. Sometimes I think he'd get us in bar fights just because he was bored."

Walters laughed, "Well, Nishan, you and him still make quite a pair." Walters looked at JJ sleeping peacefully on the ground, "So, what's his story?"

Nishan gave a strange look, "He needs to get out of his shell. I've been trying. Unfortunately bar fights with Watsy always happen at the wrong time."

Walters placed his left hand on Nishan's shoulder. "Nishan, do you know what his favorite hobby is?" Nishan gave a confused look. "Its dirt bikes, he's into riding dirt bikes. You see Nishan, in order to connect with people you need to know the basics. Then you can bring them out of their shells."

I guess that is why you are a leader and I am a follower," whimpered Nishan.

Walters sighed. "Not quite, it comes from years of experience. I didn't get to be a Staff Sergeant just because I can shoot guns and fight with knives. I did because I understand people, and I know how to use their weaknesses and strengths. I can integrate them into a team, so their strengths will make them strong fighters. Their weaknesses will never be a hindrance when they fight. If I can do all of that as a boss, can you imagine what you can doe as a friend?"

Nishan nodded a few times and rubbed his puffy red eyes. "I'll get some sleep," Nishan announced to Walters. Walters nodded silently. Nishan walked to the burning campfire and lay down. Thoughts of home, combat and Sarah filled his mind. Soon sleep overcame him.

Walters shivered in the cold night's air. He warmed his hands by blowing on them, little comfort came. Walters looked to the fire and put it out with a boot. The smoke slowly rose from the burning coals. Walters set his rifle's rear drum sight to the 200 meter range. Walters leaned against a large nearby rock and scanned the desert in all four directions with his binoculars. The desert was empty; Walters couldn't even see any insects or snakes in the distance.

Walters put down the binoculars. Thoughts of home made him feel lonely. Walters shook his head, his eyes became heavy. Walters tried hard to fight back. Emotional and physical exhaustion fought equally hard back to control his mind, and body. Walters drifted in and out of sleep seconds at a time. He cursed himself for being weak in the face of his battle with his enemy. Walters finally relented. He was exhausted from fighting sleep itself. Walters fell to the ground, lost in deep sleep.

10-July-2010
0600 Hours Local Time

JJ rubbed his eyes, the morning sun penetrated deep into his skull. JJ struggled to stand up. The night's sleep on the hard ground made his back stiff and painful. JJ looked around, Watson and Nishan peacefully slept around the charred remains of last nights' campfire. JJ turned his face to the blue sky in the west. Faint mechanical sounds emanated from the distance. JJ ran to Walters and shook him, "Sergeant, sergeant, something's coming from the west!"

Walters jumped awake with a mixture of embarrassment and excitement. Walters madly reached for his binoculars, throwing aside the equipment he had huddled next to his feet. Finding his binoculars, Walters scanned the western sky. A grin quickly fell upon his face. Walters ran to Nishan and Watson, he shook the hard while yelling, "Get up, it's party time!"

Watson opened his dirt-encrusted eyes, the morning sun made him cringe. "What's up, JJ hear another sound?"

"Get up, there here. We're saved!" Walter screamed into Watson's face. Watson covered his ears with his jacket.

Nishan stood up. He cleaned the dirt from the corners of his eyes and squinted at Walters. "What's up Walters?"

"Our camping in the desert is over. The boys have come to take us home!" Walters shouted out in excitement.

Nishan looked into the western sky. Dust clouds rose high from the distant roadway. Apache gunships circled high above. A huge column of M1 Abrams tanks thundered into view. Walters ran into the roadway and waved his arms at the fast approaching vehicles. The rest of the team staggered behind, wondering if the sight was a mirage.

The ground shook with the sound of dozens of turbine engines filling the air. Tanks rumbled by, barely acknowledging the team's position. Walters stood confused at the mighty armor column rumbling by at a leisurely pace.

A Bradley Fighting vehicle stopped and pulled aside from the roadway. A full bird Colonel stepped out of the vehicle. His desert combat fatigues were freshly ironed. The Colonel stepped up to Walters. Walters immediately saluted. The Colonel returned with a lazy salute. "I'm Colonel Peace, what are you gentlemen doing out here in the desert?"

Walters relaxed and spoke in a humble tone, "I'm Staff Sergeant Walters of Black Ops, Camp Zulu." Walters waved his hand to the dazed men in the background. "These are the members of my team."

Peace broke out a smile, "You must be Griswalt's boys. You did a great job getting Townsend and Gibson back. Bring your boys inside. I'd like to debrief you before we continue on our mission." Walters followed the Colonel into the massive vehicle.

Nishan, JJ and Watson followed behind. Their faces were dirty and dusty as their uniforms. The sights and smells of the wall of armor brought relief and a mood of somberness. JJ was the first to break the silence. "So, it's over, were finally going home."

Nishan smiled, "First thing when we get back, you owe me a ride on your dirt bike." JJ smiled and shook his head.

Watson snorted, "First it was his girlfriend, now it's dirt biking. Nishan, you're unbelievable." Nishan ignored Watson and continued to chat with JJ.

Overhead, fighters boomed in the cloudless sky. Helicopters roamed just above the ground. The soldiers in the tank column madly sent messages back to each other. Black Ops had another successful mission in Pakistan.

Chapter 24

Black Ops Camp Zulu
Main Conference Room
13-July-2010
0600 Hours Local Time

Griswalt sat down for his morning meeting. His eyes were bloodshot red, and dark circles lay underneath. The last few months of stress and intercontinental travel had taken its toll on him. He took a sip from his coffee cup, the sweet taste and warm aroma calmed him. Major Fleming and Captain York sat on either side of them, steaming coffee cups in hand. Griswalt cleared his throat and spoke, "I trust you both have read the transcripts?"

"Colonel, I have several issues with Walters' account of his adventures abroad," Fleming blurted out.

Griswalt grinned, "What would that be?"

Fleming's face turned red, "Where do I start? Do you really believe his accounts about Pakistani double agents? Then there is the Mossad aiding him in sabotaging the Pakistani nuclear program. Also, how was he able to run around with impunity?"

Griswalt shook his head and had a large sip from his cup. "Relax Fleming, all will be explained in a few minutes." A knock sounded from the entrance door. "Enter!" Griswalt spoke with a commanding voice.

Walters entered the room followed by JJ, Nishan and Watson. The four men looked confused. "Sit down!" Griswalt barked. The four men sat down in a chair facing Griswalt. The men became tense, fearing Griswalt's angry wrath.

Griswalt loosened his tie and rolled up his sleeves. "I have read the transcripts of your debriefing. Do you have anything to add Staff Sergeant Walters?" Walters shrugged his shoulders in silence.

Griswalt rubbed his face. Thoughts raced through his mind. "Were Agents Rabin and Sharon helpful to you?"

"I didn't know you knew about them," Walters answered in a quivering voice.

Griswalt grinned, "I'll explain everything to your crew, among others." Griswalt gave Fleming a fleeting look. "Agents Rabin and Sharon have been our moles for the last two years. They were able to penetrate the deepest levels of the Pakistani government. They had been providing us with Intel about Mansoor and Hassan's organization.

"Your meeting with them was no accident. The telephone Agent Collins carried contained a GPS locator. Using it, we were able to locate your position."

Griswalt looked deeply into Walters' eyes. "Did you provide any sensitive information to General Majeed?"

Walters' face became horrified. "No, sir, everything I said was included in our debriefing."

Griswalt rubbed his chin. "Good," Griswalt pulled out a photograph and placed in front of the team. "Do you recognize this photograph?"

Walters peered into the photo for a second and spoke. "Yes, that is General Majeed!" The rest of the team nodded in agreement.

Unseen Warriors

Griswalt pulled out a document from his file folder and silently read it. "This photo was taken by a security camera at Portland Oregon International airport. General Majeed left a suitcase loaded with a small nuclear bomb outside the terminal building. The bomb detonated and killed scores of people.

"A body was found by US forces near Kabul last week. The finger tips were cut off and the jaw was smashed. DNA tests confirm the identity to be that of Private Mowia Mohammad." The team gasped at the revelation. Walters' face sunk with anger.

Griswalt continued to speak. "The backpack nuke shipment was a trap set by General Majeed. A nuclear explosion was detected by Indian forces shortly before your rescue. The Mossad informs me that both Agents Rabin and Sharon are both presumed to be dead."

Waters hung his head low, a mixture of anger and grief filled his mind. Walters longed for a simpler time when the enemy wore black clothes. A time when enemies were separated by uniforms, language and geography.

Griswalt sighed, "All is not lost. Majeed has been spotted by Spetsnaz by the North Korean border. Majeed and a few of his closest contacts escaped out Pakistan about the same time you did. Staff Sergeant Walters, take you're team to interdiction point. Spetsnaz will meet you there, together you will storm Majeed's compound. I want Majeed, dead or alive!"

Griswalt called his phone and spoke in a hushed voice. Two men immediately entered the room and stood to attention. Griswalt looked at the men, inspecting their attire before speaking. "Corporal Patterson and Private Marsh, you will be joining Staff Sergeant on this mission. Look alive and fight hard. If you don't, I'll personally ship you out on the first plane to Iraq!"

Griswalt looked to Walters, "Get you men debriefed, you ship out in a half hour!"

Gavin Parmar

* * * * *

Aircraft 507 sat at the end of the ramp. Its engines whined and hissed. The APU blasted hot air out the exhaust with a sharp shrill. The twin engine turboprop had been completely rebuilt since its last sortie in the spring.

Walters led his team into the massive turboprop. The ground underneath their feet shook from the twisting props. "Get in!" Walters shouted at the two new hapless troops. The soldiers piled into the aft entry door, the props blasting them with a deafening wind.

Walters walked down the narrow fuselage and sat beside Corporal Patterson. Patterson was nervous and clammy. He gripped his rifle hard. A strange look covered his face. Walters rolled his eyes at the bizarre sight next to him. Unable to contain himself, Walters spoke to his nervous teammate. "Why are you so uptight Patterson?"

Patterson nervously twitched. "I'm not uptight. This is how I get warmed up for every combat mission."

Walters put his hand on Patterson's shoulder. "There's nothing wrong with being scared." Patterson grunted an inaudible reply.

The engines hummed and roared with take off. Rooster relished having his old plane back. Rooster looked over to his copilot, Captain "Speedster" Swisher with glee. Swisher looked back with a confused look and spoke. "Rooster, you look like you just swallowed a catfish."

Rooster laughed, "Speedster, this is my plane. I've had it ever since I came to Black Ops. That is why my name is painted on its side." Swisher rolled his eyes. "501, 505, 507 and 504 just don't compare. Each one of these things flies differently, they're like leather gloves. Some you grip, others you wear. This one fits perfect!"

Swisher chuckled, "Rooster, you've finally gone off the deep end. These buckets of bolts are nothing but oversized eggbeaters. They all shake, rattle and roll like they have square tires. I can't see how any of these beasts could fly differently."

Rooster rubbed the throttle. "Flying is not a science, it is an art. When you get to be in the left seat, you'll find that flying one of these planes is like making a painting. They all look good, but the artist gave each one his own special touch."

Swisher rolled his eyes and looked out on the scenery racing by below. The Siberian terrain dashed below at a dizzying pace. Streams, rivers, forests and hills all disappeared under the plane as fast as they appeared.

Rooster dived to treetop level, turned south and straddled the Russian/Chinese border. The plane raced up hills and plunged down valleys. The tall grass in the placid fields parted with the rushing airplane's prop wash.

Swisher calmly stared at the TWI and navigation pages on the instrument panel. The lack of activity on his TWI made him feel safe and secure. But deep down, he was apprehensive about crossing deep into North Korea. The way points on Swisher's navigation page changed. A faint red line running across the page slowly approached. "Fifty miles to the North Korean border," Swisher announced.

Rooster replied with a grunt. He advanced the power levers and descended ever so closer to the ground. Winds and vortices shook the airplane. Rooster tried to hold the yoke stiff with all his strength.

The North Korean border raced below the plane. Swisher's stomach tightened. He focused on the TWI and held the condition levers tight. The plane continued southwest, 35 miles inside the Korean border. The final way point flashed on the navigation page. "We're there," Swisher announced.

The plane circled a flat plain about 30 miles from Puryong. Rooster examined his map and compared it to the field below. Steep canyons rose high on each side, obscuring visibility in key area.

Rooster dived toward the field and slowed as if approaching to land. Pink smoke rose from the field a mile into the distance. Several colored lights flashed nearby in a pattern similar to Morse code. Rooster flashed his landing lights repeatedly. The lights flashed again, mimicking Rooster's reply. Rooster gained altitude and circled near the opposite end of the field. He slowed to 130 knots and turned around toward the field. Swisher lowered the flaps and slapped the gear handle down. The gear lowered, shaking and rattling the aircraft. Rooster smoothly retracted the throttles with graceful ease

The aircraft smoothly descended to the ground below. The main wheels hit the muddy grass, bumping and shaking. The ground spoilers rose high into the sky. The aircraft shook and rattled on its quest to stop. Several thousand yards down in the distance, green smoke rose high in the air. Rooster immediately steered the lumbering plane into the distance. Nearing the position, a camouflaged soldier stood, a rifle slung across his shoulders. Rooster stopped the aircraft 200 yards short of the figure.

"Saddle up!" Walters shouted to the team. The aircraft's front door popped open, Walters led his team out of the idling airplane. Patterson closed the cabin door and ran behind the team to their unknown location.

Rooster spun the airplane around and raced down the grass field. He jerked the nose, the airplane rose high into the sky.

Walters walked up to the fatigue-clad soldier a head and spoke. "My goat needs to be milked."

The soldier answered in a heavy accent, "My sheep needs shaving."

Walters' face became relaxed "I am Staff Sergeant Walters, Black Ops."

The soldier replied, "I am Sergeant Vladimir Kotov of Spetsnaz." It is a pleasure to finally meet you. Kotov held out his hand both men shook. From the distance several move soldiers walked forward bearing AK-74SUs.

Walters looked of the men approaching. A smile covered his face, "How far away is the camp from here?"

Kotov smiled, "A half day's hike. If we start now, we should be there around 1800 hours."

Walters gave Kotov a harsh stare, "How hot is it?"

Kotov laughed, "About as hot as any place a foreign commando can be in North Korea!"

Walters understood Kotov's humor and cracked a grin for a second. "Saddle up!" He commanded to his team. The two teams joined up and hiked single file through the woods. Dried twigs and branches cracked underneath. Deer darted away out of sight from the incoming invaders of the jungle.

The trails climbed steeply through mountain passes. Kotov led the way, hacking through the jungle with his machete. The forest was alive with the sound with the sounds of birds, coyotes and other animals. The sounds of nature allowed Walters to delay exhaustion that much longer.

At 1300 hours, the team stopped for food and water. The cool morning breeze had departed leaving a hot humid sun. Humidity penetrated through the men's clothing, sapping their strength. Sweat made their clothes hot and sticky.

After lunch, Kotov lay out his map and arranged the team in a circle. Kotov spoke in his thick accent. "We rest here for a bit, the camp is beyond those hills." Kotov pointed to a small batch of heavily forested hills nearby.

Walters inspected the map. Thoughts raced through his mind followed by apprehension. "What is that flat area east of the camp?"

Kotov looked closer at the map. "That is the airstrip that the Muslims us to fly personnel and supplies in. It is small, about 6,000 feet in length, and heavily guarded by anti-aircraft missiles. We almost lost an SU-27 reconnaissance fighter plane last week." Walters rubbed his forehead. The horrors of war in Pakistan continued to remain in his mind. Anger swelled from his heart, he ground his teeth tight together and stared coldly into the map.

"Staff Sergeant Walters, Staff Sergeant Walters!" Walters awoke from his daze. Kotov was staring at him, "Corporal Koslov is my sniper. He carries an SVD Dragnov rifle. We could position him on a small hill northwest of the main road. From there he could target the snipers on the nearby hills."

Walters breathed heavily, "Other than the main road, is there any way of entering the camp?"

Kotov nodded, "The camp and airstrip are set up on a large flat hill. Steep ravines and cliffs encircle the hill on the south, West and east sides. A large mountain range restricts access to the north. The roadway travels from the east to west, slowly gaining altitude. In the southwest corner, the road heads north through a very narrow cutout of the rock formation formed by two very large hills. The road then travels east to the camp along an open field. Several thousand yards east of the main entrance through rock, there is a steep trail that we could hike to the airfield altitude. One of our captured soldiers claimed there was a tunnel from the base of the east hill. It ends at the northwest corner of the west hill."

Walters surveyed the map one more time. He looked at his team in apprehension. Despite a weeks reprieve from fighting, JJ, Nishan and Watson were tired and exhausted. Patterson was still nervous. Marsh stared at the sky in some sort of transcendental meditation.

Walters shook his head and a snap decision came to mind. "Take your men to the main entrance and wait to fire. I will take Corporal Koslov with me through the tunnel. He can wait hidden on one of the small hills on the northwest corner. I'll take my team through the north and head through the forest to the west side of the camp. Corporal Koslov can engage the snipers. When they are dead, that will be your signal to go through the main road. Whoever of us gets through first must secure the airfield first."

Kotov nodded, "You have an excellent plan." Kotov and Walters shook hands. Kotov looked at his watch, "We must get going."

"Saddle up!" Walters commanded to his team. Kotov yelled several Russian words to his men. Immediately the two teams joined up and began the long march to the hills ahead.

The team continued the long arduous hike for five more miles. The humidity continued to sink through their clothing. Spots of skin that were at one time uncomfortable were soon the beginnings of rash. Mental exhaustion added to Nishan's physical exhaustion. His mind wandered between the horrifying combat in Pakistan to thoughts of Sarah. Deep inside, he felt Sarah was still alive. She would come back to see him.

Watson remained mentally exuberant despite his physical fatigue. Thoughts of combat fueled his physical energy. Adrenaline pumped through every one of Watson's veins. For Watson combat was his drug, and a fix was soon coming his way.

The team marched through a valley. Walters stopped the team and scanned the distance with his binoculars. The faint sight of a roadway cut through the heavily forested ahead of him. Kotov pointed to an overgrown trail rising up the hill. The team marched up, loose branches, rocks and soil fell below.

Kotov held out his hand, the team froze. Kotov scanned with his binoculars and dove for cover. The team instinctively followed. The sounds of wind swaying trees and running water filled the forest. The distant sound of a diesel engine echoed through the air.

Kotov pulled out his binoculars and scanned the hill. A dust cloud rose from the southeast. He continued to look, mesmerized by the growing dust cloud. The faint shape of a truck appeared, very small at first, but it grew larger and larger.

Kotov was soon able to discern the distant object as a transport loaded with dozens of armed men.

Kotov signaled with his hand. Private Alexandrovich, armed with an Rpk-74, ran to his side and dug his elbows into the ground. Alexandrovich cocked the belt fed machine gun and looked through the sighs.

The truck rounded the corner and rumbled slowly along the roadway. Walters' stomach tightened. He moved his guns to the automatic setting and concentrated on the lumbering truck ahead. The truck slowed near the team's position. The armed men in the trucks' bed angrily peered angrily into the vegetation along the roadside. The driver stared out ahead into the windshield and drove off past the team's position. He remained unaware of the armed men that had lay mere feet from his truck moments ago.

Kotov raised his stance and scanned the distant roadway. Followed by the team, he ran across the open roadway into some heavy brush along the hillside. The team settled into a rough cut trail that headed west. The steep trail paralleled the nearby roadway.

Walters looked down at the eroded roadway below. Deep ruts collected dirty water in several points. Thoughts raced through his mind. Walters found himself daydreaming of Pakistan, the old castle and the mission in hand. Walters tripped on a large rock buried in the dirt and awoke from his daze.

Kotov stopped the team pointed above. Walters scanned the two towering peeks ahead. Both peeks were guarded by a sniper lazily smoking. A Dragnov rifle lay in their laps. Walters lowered his binoculars and turned to Kotov.

Kotov turned and spoke. "Those snipers are watching the roadway. They can't see us because of the heavy underbrush. I'll take my team east to the base of the hill. We can get to the roadway and subsequent camp level from there.

"Private Koslov will lead you to the tunnel. We will wait and watch the snipers. When they are both neutralized we will attack."

Unseen Warriors

Walters nodded, looking to the team, he shouted. "Saddle up!" Koslov lead the team to a heavily wooded depression in the ground. He kicked aside the debris and revealed a tunnel entrance. The team gasped at the size hole. It was barely large enough for a man to crawl on his belly. Koslov slung his rifle across his shoulders and turned on his night vision. He crawled in and disappeared into the ground. Walters followed with the team in perfect order.

* * * * *

Kotov lay motionless, his mind drifted to Moscow. The sights of red square were as fresh in his mind as the first day he saw them. Kotov longed for normalcy. His proud motherland of Russia had now become a bankrupt relic of the cold war. He had watched the Soviet states separate, followed by a mass exodus of the finest minds in Russia. The best and brightest now found home in the west. Kotov wondered if he guarded nothing but a hollow country, a shell of a nation whose pride had been stripped away.

Kotov flinched out of his daze. The distant sound of rotors beating the air echoed through the sky. Kotov flipped his rifle's selector to automatic and scanned the sky with his binoculars. Out from the western sky a North Korean Mi-24 Gunship appeared. Its stubwings bristled with rockets. Approaching Kotov's position, the gunship slowed. The chin turret swayed left to right on its quest for hidden foes. The gunship slowly passed over Kotov's position. Kotov peered up to see grease stains running along the machine's belly.

Alexandrovich gave Kotov a confused look. Kotov answered, "General Luck has come for a visit." Alexandrovich and Kotov smiled and rubbed their hands together.

* * * * *

Koslov slithered through the darkness. Mice and rats scurried ahead of his in fear. Despite the heat and humidity above, the tunnel remained cool and dry. A distant light broke through the darkness ahead. Koslov pulled out his silenced Makarov pistol and cocked the slide. The light darkened and distorted several times before disappearing. Koslov approached the tunnel exit and fired several shots at the darkness ahead. A thud came from ahead followed by rising dust. Koslov continued forward. He pushed aside a dead body and exited the tunnel.

The team followed Koslov out the tunnel to the brilliance of the late afternoon sun. The team members hid their eyes in pain. The bright cut through to their skull. Walters scanned around with his binoculars. They were now on the north side of the west peek. High above, a sniper sat on the east peek lazily watching the roadway.

Koslov pointed to a nearby hill several hundred yards north of the team's position. "I will cover the snipers."

Walters nodded in agreement, "Attack in half an hour. We should be in position by then."

Walters led his team east through a deeply wooded region. They walked about 2000 yards to a rocky outcropping. Walters stopped the team and checked his watch. Koslov would attack in ten more minutes. Walters looked to Patterson, "Take marsh with you and cover the flank by that rock 60 yards ahead." Paterson and Marsh ran forward.

Walters looked to Nishan, "The camp lies about another 1000 yards away. I want us to split up into two teams. You will take the north side and flank around to the runway. You have to prevent the aircraft from taking off. Sabotage them with any means possible. Take JJ and Watson with you. I'll take Marsh and Patterson with me and head directly east into the camp and secure woods. One more thing, don't leave cover until you hear Koslov fire his second shot. Understood?"

Nishan gave a strange look, "Patterson out ranks me. He should lead the team."

Walters coldly answered back, "You three out experience him!"

An explosion rocked the ground. Dirt, branches and leaves crashed on the team. Patterson madly sprayed the forest with automatic fire. Automatic gunfire tore into his chest. Blood sprayed over Marsh's face and arms. Marsh immediately ran back toward Waters' position. A grenade exploded behind him. Marsh's body was launched into the air and crashed down beside JJ. Marsh flinched for a second, automatic gunfire tore into his head and chest.

The team hid down behind the large granite rock. Bullets crashed into the rock and ricocheted into the surrounding trees and soil. JJ pulled out his grenade and threw it over the rock. A dull thud echoed through the air. The automatic gunfire continued unabated.

Walters huddled the team together, "I want everyone to follow m with a retreat back to the tunnel." His teammates nodded in agreement.

A clanging echoed from the rock. A Russian grenade rattled off the rock and landed ten feet behind the rock. The team's eyes grew huge at the sight of the destructive device near them.

JJ ran out and grabbed the grenade. He ran away from the rock and threw the grenade in the air. The grenade exploded in midair. Shrapnel radiated out of the explosion and tore into JJ's body. JJ fell to the ground, his body covered in blood.

* * * * *

Koslov walked to the top of the hill. Lush vegetation carpeted the hilltop. Koslov looked around, the view was magnificent. For a second, combat seemed like a distant memory. Koslov lay into the soft soil. He dug the bipod and elbows into the soft soil.

Koslov threw branches and leaves over his rifle and clothing to break up his profile. He zoomed in his scope on the nearest sniper. The sniper was still unaware of his position. Koslov calculated the range with his rangefinder and adjusted his scope elevation. Koslov checked his watch one last time, the time to attack would be soon.

The sound of machine gun fire echoed through the air. Koslov scanned the distant forest with his binoculars. The muzzle flashes of several distant machine guns erupted from the dense forest.

Koslov switched his attention on the nearby sniper. The enemy sniper was scanning the forest with his binoculars. Koslov steadied his rifle and fired. The bullet tore into the sniper's head. The sniper rolled over, the rifle falling out of his lifeless body.

Koslov scanned the east hill, the other sniper was gone. Koslov madly scanned the roadway, forest and nearby hills. There was no sight of the sniper. It was as if he just disappeared.

Koslov steadied his scope on the muzzle flashes in the distance. He could see soldiers spraying automatic gunfire from his RPK-74 at Walters' position. Koslov reached for the trigger and pulled. A bullet slammed into Koslov's elbow and shattered the joint.

* * * * *

The sounds of bullets echoed in the distance. Sergeant Kotov checked his magazine and selected the gun to automatic. "Let's go!" he announced to the team. Kotov ran up the hill. Automatic gunfire erupted from the roadway. Kotov hit the ground. Androvich lay down next to him and opened fire with his machine gun. Deadly gunfire raced over Kotov's head at a frenzied pace. "Conserve your ammo, use short burst!" Kotov yelled over the noise.

Unseen Warriors

Private Zuzik crawled up and threw a grenade at the source of the incoming tracer fire. An explosion rocked the distance. The tracer fire ceased.

Kotov ran up the roadway. A truck loaded with troops raced from the camp. Alexandrovich sprayed it with machine gunfire. An explosion rocked the truck. The vehicle swerved and shook. Burning troops fell out of the careening vehicle. The truck rolled several times and crashed into a ditch. The burning troops screamed in pain. Kotov quickly gunned down the hapless soldiers. Alexandrovich looked to Kotov and gave a dirty look, "They are murders of mother Russia. They are lower than dogs, you should have let them burn."

Kotov curled his lip, "I do not want dying men attracting unnecessary attention!" Kotov marched his men along the south edge of the roadway. A bullet tore into the Private at the end of the formation. The Private hit the pavement grabbing his throat. "Get into cover now!" Kotov screamed to his men. The men ran behind a large rock outcropping east of the roadway. Another bullet slammed into the stricken Private, killing him instantly.

Kotov scanned the distance with his binoculars. *Somewhere in the distance there is a sniper*, Kotov wondered. A bullet slammed into the ground next to him. Kotov darted out of the brush with his team in tow. Another bullet slammed into a trail Private, the bullet shredded his chest. Blood sprayed on the soft ground. The Private immediately fell to earth

Kotov led his team until they were about 1000 yards from the camp. He pulled out his binoculars and scanned the area ahead. The camp sprawled around almost thirty acres. There were six two-story wooden. East, there was a steel deck airstrip. On the taxiway two Canadair 600 business jets sat with their APUs running. In the nearby mud an Mi-24 gunship sat quietly.

Kotov ran his hands through the stubble on his face, a plan of attack ran through his mind. Kotov led his team through the brush and down a steep ridge. They continued east, using what little vegetation and rock there was for cover. Kotov peered through the brush with his binoculars. At the end of the runway lay only 1000 yards away. Kotov looked to Private Zuzik, "Do you have the explosives?" Zuzik silently nodded in agreement.

"Alexandrovich, cover us with the machine gun! Zuzik, Kovalev come down with me!" Kotov ordered. Kotov led his team down to a ridge by the runway. The area was eerily quiet. Kotov ran across the open field to the southern business jet. A shot rang out from the distance. Kotov scanned with his binoculars, there was no sight of the gunmen.

Kotov made his way around to the aircraft's nose. He looked around and opened the aircraft's avionics bay door. Inside, dozens of computers lined each side of the belly. They hummed with a high-pitched noise barely audible above the APU. Kotov looked to Zuzik, "Set the timers to thirty minutes." Zuzik complied, placing the explosive as far back as possible. Kotov closed the door and shifted his team to the next aircraft.

Zuzik performed the same operation while Kotov inspected the aircraft's wheel wells. Kotov gave Zuzik a cold hard stare and a nod. Zuzik, Kovalev and Kotov ran across the open field to a small rocky outcropping. A bullet tore into Kovalev's chest, destroying his lungs. Kotov and Zuzik froze in fear. A second later the two men darted toward a ditch.

An explosion rocked behind the two men. Kotov found himself being propelled into the air and crashing into the ditch. Dazed and confused, Kotov struggled to gain his balance. Kotov's hands and arms were bloody. Kotov rubbed his face. The pain rocketed through his head. Zuzik lay 60 feet away, bloody and motionless.

The dirty water in the ditch shook with a smooth harmony. Kotov looked up out into the distance. A T-70 tank crawled out of a building. Its turret swept the runway looking for hidden foes. Automatic gunfire tore out between other buildings into Kotov's position. Zuzic's body exploded into cloud of blood and tissue. Kotov reached into his pack and grabbed his radio. All that remained was broken plastic and a bunch of wires. Kotov shook his head. He knew he had fallen for a trap. A nearby explosion sprayed Kotov with loose gravel. Kotov looked up. Horror filled his eyes when he saw the approaching tank.

* * * * *

Koslov inspected his bloody arm and shook his head in displeasure. He inserted another magazine loaded with ten rounds of 7.62 x 54R ammunition. Using his good arm, he wiggled the rifle to a position where he could see the three gunmen firing in the woods. Koslov held the shaking rifle still and fired with his left hand. The bullet missed wildly. Koslov cursed himself and endured great pain to steady the cross hairs on the enemy soldier. Koslov dug his good arm into the mud and fired. The soldier fell to the ground clutching his bleeding leg.

Koslov lined up the cross hairs just ahead of another enemy solder. Koslov breathed in deeply and relaxed. He steadied the rifle and fired a second shot. The soldier stopped firing and slumped over dead onto the ground.

Koslov moved the heavy rifle to a position where he could see the third and final gunman. Koslov breathed out slowly and reached for the trigger. A bullet slammed into his face and shattered his skull.

* * * * *

Nishan dragged JJ's body closer. JJ's arms and upper torso were covered in blood. JJ screamed out in blood cursing screams at the top of his lungs. Pain shot through his body at lightning speed. Watson madly tried to apply field dressings to JJ. JJ madly screamed and thrashed about every second in a made attempt to fight off pain. Nishan held JJ down in a mad attempt to assist Watson. Walters coldly dragged JJ's rifle away in silence.

Watson looked up at Walters with an angry look. "We need to medevac him his ASAP!"

Walters look coldly at Nishan. "Stay here with him. When you see my flare, bring him to the airstrip!"

Watson curled his lip in disdain, "He could bleed to death right now as we speak!"

"A lot more people will die if Majeed gets away!" Walters angrily replied. Watson gave a dirty look to Walters. "It's time to move, saddle up Watson!"

Watson angrily grabbed his rifle from the soil. "You are a bastard!" Watson angrily shouted to Walters.

JJ screams died down. He now just shivered and shook. Nishan held on to him tight, tears rolled down his cheek. Walters leaned into Nishan's face, "Keep him warm, he'll be safe with you!"

The gunfire had amazingly died down. The only sounds were birds and swaying of trees in the warm wind. Walters cautiously marched forward into the forest. The natural sounds of the forest were now in the background. The lack of gunfire perturbed Walters. Walters wondered what had silenced the distant guns.

"You're a real bastard Walters, he'll die out there!" Watson angrily spoke. Walters remained silent. For the next ten minutes, Watson cursed at Walters. The anger in Watson's tongue violently cut through the peaceful forest. Walters mentally blocked out Watson's harsh words, he chose instead to concentrate on the mission in hand.

Walters abruptly stopped and raised his hand. Watson stopped and held his breath for a second. Anger filled Walters mind. He turned around and stood face to face with Watson. "Listen cowboy, if I call a medevac right now, it wouldn't make it within five miles of this place. It would be shot down in a heartbeat. We would have four more dead men!" Watson remained quiet. His anger slowly subsided, being replaced by the feeling of helplessness.

"JJ has a strong faith. Faith in God is much better in a situation like this than any sort of medical treatment. I know the strength of faith. Last year I broke my ribs in a mission. I spent 14 hours in the Siberian snow all by myself."

Watson curled his lips, "Broken ribs hardly compare to what JJ has right now."

"Hypothermia kills in minutes!" Walters snapped back.

Walters raised his head. The sound of a whimpering man echoed from some nearby brush. Walters marched forward with his rifle at eye level. A wounded Middle Eastern man lay beside his dead teammate. Blood seeped from leg onto the grass. "Is he dead?" Watson asked.

Walters pulled out his silenced Beretta 9mm pistol and fired several shots into the man's skull. "He's dead now," Walters coldly replied.

The two men traveled east to a large rock outcropping. In the distance, six buildings lay 6,000 yards from Walters' position. A large tank wandered the airfield at will. The two climbed down the steep cliff to a grass field below. They walked through the tall grass and jumped in a large ditch below. Mud and dirty water splashed the two men. Watson gave Walters a dirty look. Mud covered the faces of both men with mud.

A bullet cut through the air and crashed into the ground, mere inches from Walters. The two men headlong dived into the mud. Machine gun fire tore over their heads in the grass filed where they had been only minutes earlier. A mortar crashed into the ditch nearby, spraying the two men with dirty water and mud. More gunfire erupted over their heads. Watson screamed over the noise of gunfire, "So, what's our plan now?"

Walters aimlessly stared into the mud and silently spoke, "Checkmate!" Watson hung his head low in despair.

* * * * *

Alexandrovich watched the tank pummel Kotov's position with machine gun fire. Impulsively, he ran down from his safe position north, toward the edge of a deep ditch. The sound of nearby gunfire erupted all around him. Androvich instinctively dived to the bottom of the ditch. Strangely, no bullets fell nearby. The sound of gunfire continued to ring loudly around him.

Androvich looked up. A machine gun several thousand yards away fired into the west most portion of the ditch. The machine gunner remained unaware of Androvich's position so close to him. Androvich ran out of the ditch toward the building ahead with impunity.

Androvich walked between the buildings and made a left turn. He was now 300 yards from the machine gunner. Another soldier had joined him, attaching more belts to his ammo. Two more men walked over to a nearby mortar position. They carried an old green wooden crate.

Androvich lay down on the ground and set his sights on the men. He attached his last remaining belts of ammunition. Androvich fired a short burst at the men near the mortar position. The wooden box exploded into splinters. The two men fell to the ground grabbing their faces. Androvich fired several more short bursts into the twitching bodies.

Androvich poured automatic fire into the two machine gunners. The trigger man flinched and grabbed his leg. More bullets slammed into his position, knocking his assistant to the ground. The trigger man stood up and staggered, dazed by what just happened. Blood poured out of his leg at an ever increasing rate. The solder cried at the sight of injury. He pulled out a cigarette and lit it. Another bullet slammed into his heart severing his aorta. The man fell straight back onto his machine gun.

Androvich grabbed his gun and ran behind an old Jeep. An occasional bullet slammed into the ditch in the distance. Androvich looked up and saw a metal object twinkling in the west hill. Androvich rested the machine gun on the Jeep's hood and sprayed the hillside with his automatic gunfire. Androvich's machine gun fell silent after several hundred rounds. Piles of spent shells and links littered the nearby ground. Androvich scanned the hillside with his binoculars, the twinkling object was now gone. Androvich ran to the deserted machine gun position and madly grabbed as many ammunition belts he could carry.

Androvich ran to the ditch and looked down. Walters and Watson lay in a morass of ankle-deep mud and dirty water. The two men remained quiet, still shaking from the horrors they had just encountered.

Androvich immediately spoke, "Sergeant Walters, we must stop that tank. Sergeant Kotov is pinned down!" Walters shook out of his daze and jumped out of the ditch. Watson quickly followed behind.

Walters led the team between two buildings. The tank stood 2,000 yards away, still firing its machine gun. Several soldiers cowered behind the tank with their guns ready to fire. Walters huddled Alexandrovich and Watson. "The three of us need to rush that tank. Blast those guys with automatic fire. Give them everything you got. When we get near the tank, stay away from the turret. They can't touch you if you're near the same level of the tank treads. I'll throw a grenade into the hatch. That'll disable the tank in no time."

The team stormed out of the building. Androvich sprayed the men behind the tank with machine gunfire. The gun shook and rattled, Androvich pained to hold the gun still. Watson continually fired several single shots at the men ahead.

Rounds crashed into the tank with deafening sounds. The soldiers behind the tank turned around in shock. Disturbed by the metal clanging all around them, they sprayed automatic gunfire wildly into all directions.

Rattled by the rounds crashing into the steel hull, the tank crew immediately reversed direction. The massive tank crushed its own soldiers underneath its metal treads. The turret slowly swung around, spraying gunfire in all directions.

The team dove beside the tank and stayed underneath the turret's line of fire. The turret swept by, firing automatic fire above their heads. Androvich and Watson scampered around the tread, madly trying to avoid the rotating steel tracks. The tank turned right. The team dashed out of the way. The tank immediately reversed direction and turned to the left.

The team ran to the tank's rear. Gunfire poured out from one the buildings into the team's position. The turret rotated and fired more machine gun fire into the distance near the buildings.

The tank's driver opened the hatch and searched for his hidden foes. Walters sprayed the man with automatic gunfire. The driver fell back into the tank's open cavity. A blood trail covered the hull. Walters ran to the open hatch, he pulled a pin out and threw it into the open hatch. Men inside tank shouted several loud words in Arabic. The tank shook and rumbled with a loud boom, smoke poured out of the tank's openings. The engine fell silent for the very last time.

Walters ran to the tank's turret and sprayed a short burst of ammunition into a nearby building rooftop. A soldier fell out of the building to the ground with a loud thud.

Androvich ran to Kotov's position. Kotov lay bleeding and dazed. Androvich helped Kotov out of the ditch and laid him alongside the stricken tank. Kotov looked at Walters' dirt-covered face, "You fight hard Staff Sergeant Walters. You would do well in Spetsnaz."

Walters chuckled, "You and Androvich need to cover the airfield. I will root out Majeed from the buildings." Walters pulled out his flare gun and fire a colored flare in the darkening sky. The flare shot into the sky and exploded, hovering for a short time. Walters looked to Kotov again, "On of my men is badly injured. He is going to be transported here in a very short time." Walters handed Kotov his radio, "Call for a medevac!"

Unseen Warriors

Kotov grabbed the radio and madly called Spetsnaz headquarters.

Walters lead Watson to the northeast building. Walters kicked in the door and rushed in. The building had two floors. The bottom floor was littered with wooden crates. The top floor was only half the area of the first. Old rickety steps led the second floor behind a large steel box. The two men walked several feet into the room and scanned with their rifles. The room was dark. The only light penetrating was from the outside.

A large crate between the two men exploded into splinters. Walters was ejected forward and crashed into several large crates. Watson fell back and slammed his head into a steel box. The light came on, flooding the room with luminance. Dazed and confused, Watson and Walters shielded their eyes from the painful light. Footsteps thumped down the stairwell. The steel box blocking the steps' entrance immediately shifted aside.

The team's eyes grew huge at the sight. Babajhan stood with an angry look on his face. "Staff Sergeant Walters it is nice to meet you again," Babajhan said in a condescending tone.

Walters was now in shock. "You died in that cargo ship!" He quickly blurted out.

"No, I didn't. Allah had better plans for me." Babajhan cocked his MP-5. "Do you like my new toy? Your CIA agent brought it to on his last shipment to Pakistan." Walters remained silent, anger filled his mind.

"I'm glad you are here now, I can now go on to my next phase of my operation. You see this was all just a big ruse. I was using Mansoor and his stupid country to help me create the biggest terrorist attack since 9/11. Your forces will eventually defeat the Pakistanis and claim victory. After all Mansoor was the mastermind of all the attacks according to your President. I will leave this wretched country and set up shop somewhere else to do this all over again. That dictator will take the fall just like Mansoor, Saddam and Bin Laden did. Eventually America will become bankrupted by foreign wars."

"You are a butcher, murderer and liar," Walters shouted.

"Don't act so surprised. Did you really think that fool Saddam had connections to Bin Laden? Those two idiots can't even stand being in the same country together let alone the same room. Saddam didn't even have a program to manufacture fresh water. Do you really think he had a program to develop weapons of mass destruction after the first Gulf war? I planted all that information to the CIA so your President Bush would go to war. I am the one who planned out the 9/11 attacks and just like each case before, I walked away unscathed. After I finish you off I'm going to kill a few loose ends like General Majeed and Luck."

"Prepare to die!" Babajhan gave an evil laugh and pulled the trigger. The gun exploded, spraying him with hot brass and metal. Babajhan fell to the ground, his face bleeding. Watson watched with deep interest. Babajhan slowly died in front of his eyes.

Watson limped to Walters' side. Blood oozed out of Walters' arms and chest. Watson gave a confused look, "What caused that?"

Walters smiled, "Seems Collins finally got his revenge from the grave." Watson shrugged his shoulders. "Those rifles were all packed with cosmoline. Our buddy never cleaned out the barrel. I guess while he was planning on taking on the world, he forgot basic rifle care."

Watson laughed, "That Collins, even in death he came out on top." Walters nodded in agreement.

*****

Nishan crashed through the woods with JJ lying unconscious over his shoulder. JJ's weight bore down on Nishan's shoulders. Tears rolled down Nishan's cheeks. The horror of war had now taken a deeper, more personal toll than ever.

Unseen Warriors

Nishan trudged through the woods. He finally arrived to the forest's edge near the cliff. JJ's blood soaked his shirt and covered his face. Nishan put JJ down into the grass. Exhaustion filled his mind and body.

"I don't feel my arms anymore!" JJ cried.

"Don't worry JJ, the helicopter is coming! You're going to be okay," Nishan whispered.

"Nishan, will you be my friend if I get discharged?" JJ wondered.

Tears ran down JJ's cheek. Nishan wiped them with his hand and comforted him. "I'll always be your friend, no matter what happens."

"Just like I'm your friend," a voice boomed through the woods. Nishan turned his head and grabbed his rifle. A Pakistani general in camouflage fatigues stood nearby, an SVD Dragnov sniper rifle in hand. "We meet again Private Nishan!" The man said.

Nishan curled his lip with anger. "General Majeed, Mowia Mohammed or whatever you call yourself. You are a murder and liar!"

Majeed laughed, "How can call me that? You don't even know about your Mossad agents." Majeed gave an evil laugh and pointed his rifle Nishan. Nishan let his rifle fall to the ground. "Your stupid Jewish friends tried to steal the nuclear weapons shipment. Their plot was foiled and they died in the nuclear fireball in Multan. It was a pleasure to see my backpack nuclear project work so well. I have to say it was not as dramatic as the show in Seattle and Portland. My only regret is that I was not able to destroy your base the same way I destroyed your cities." Majeed pulled the charging handle on his rifle. "You Black Ops people have been a thorn in my side for long enough. Today you will die!"

Majeed reached for the trigger. A bullet slammed into Majeed's chest. Majeed fell backwards into the soil. Blood poured out of his chest and dripped into the ground.

Nishan quickly turned his face and looked at JJ. JJ's right hand shook, smoke gently rose out of his pistol. Blood had now completely soaked his shirt. Nishan grabbed JJ's head and cried, "JJ, are you alright?"

JJ shook his head and dropped the gun. Shaking violently, JJ reached out of his pocket and pulled out a black leather bound book. "Nishan please read out of this at Sarah's memorial." Nishan wiped the tears from his face looked down at the black leather bound Bible.

"No, JJ, you're going to be alright. You'll survive just like Sarah."

JJ shook his head. "No, Nishan, I see Sarah right now. She's holding out her hand, I'll be safe." JJ coughed up some blood and his eyes glazed over. Silently, his soul joined Sarah in heaven.

* * * * *

Androvich smoked a cigar. The taste and smell of fresh tobacco filled his lungs. The smoke helped calm his anxiety. He blew out a puff of smoke and looked down at Kotov quietly resting by the damaged tank's treads.

"I'm not sleeping!" Kotov replied with a booming voice. Androvich raised his eyebrows. "I wasn't saying anything."

"Yes, but I know what you're thinking!" Kotov angrily replied.

"How are you feeling?" Androvich meekly asked.

"I'm in a lot of pain, but I still can shoot my rifle."

Gunfire tore into the ground beside the stricken tank. Androvich fell to the ground beside Kotov. Slowly one by one, the two business jets exploded into huge balls of fire. A truck loaded with troops raced around the compound. The soldiers in the trucks box sprayed Androvich's position with wildly aimed gunfire.

Unseen Warriors

Androvich placed his machine gun on the tanks hull and sprayed the truck with machine gun fire. "Click," the machine gun was empty. Androvich madly searched the ground for additional ammunition. There was no more. Androvich fell behind the tank in sorrow.

The truck stopped several feet from the awaiting Mi-24. General Luck ran into the helicopter followed by several top Lieutenants. The helicopter's engines light off. The jet engine's harsh sounds cut through the air. Gunmen sprayed Kotov's position with more automatic gunfire. The helicopter's rotors turned at an ever-increasing speed. The gunmen ran into the open door seconds later. The helicopter shook and rattled, dust and dirt erupted into the air. The helicopter slowly rose into the sky and traveled forward.

Androvich immediately ran into the tank's turret and fired the machine gun at the helicopter. The helicopter banked hard, madly trying to avoid the incoming gunfire. Smoke and flames poured out of the open cabin door. Androvich led the machine gun and continued to fire. The helicopter's nose shook and vibrated. Smoke poured out of the cockpit and chin gunner's position.

The helicopter's nose rose high into the sky. Androvich poured the last remaining rounds into the stricken helicopter's fuselage. Bullets crashed into the fuselage and continued into the tail boom and rotor. The tail rotor exploded into a mass of high speed parts. The fuselage violently swung into the opposite direction of the rotor blades. The helicopter fell to the ground and exploded. Flames and burning aircraft parts ejected into the air. Black smoke poured out of the burning fuselage in the middle of the runway. The smell of burning flesh and jet fuel filled the air.

Watson emerged from the buildings with Walters over his shoulders. Androvich stood up and called to Watson. Watson smiled and waved back. Kotov struggled to stand up and peered into the distance.

After ten minutes Watson arrived and placed Walters beside the tank's treads. "Nice shooting," Watson joyously shouted.

Androvich smiled. "Thank you, Private Watson. Your men will no longer have to worry about their helicopters being shot down by the DMZ. General Luck is now dead."

Walters and Watson laughed out loudly. Androvich and Kotov looked on in confusion. Walters finally interrupted, "General Luck has been shooting down our helicopters from our side of the border for months now. This time we were one of the raiders. We shot down the general in his helicopter from his side of the border." The rest of the men broke out into laughter.

From the distance, Nishan walked forward carrying JJ's lifeless body. Nishan placed the body beside Walters and covered JJ's face with a cloth. The entire team became silent. Watson and Walters' faces sunk. Nishan sat beside Watson and cried into his arms. Kotov and Androvich quietly mourned JJ's death.

Walters came over to Nishan and comforted him. "JJ never died in vain. He died a hero like Private Matthews." Nishan gave a stern look to Walters. "Before we left, Griswalt told me Sarah's body washed up on the Azores last week."

Nishan fell to the ground full of sorrow. "I'm all alone!" Nishan whimpered.

Walters hugged Nishan, "No, you will never be alone."

Kotov walked over and hugged Nishan, "In the war on terror, you will never be alone." High in the sky, a Chinese turboprop approached the runway for landing.

Epilogue

Sioux city, Iowa
25-July-2010
1100 Hours Local Time

    The morning sun shone through the stained glass windows of the suburban Sioux City Church. On the front alter, an Army photograph of Sarah looked out into the sanctuary. An HK-rifle, barrel down, bore into her boots. Sarah's helmet topped the butt stock. The grand ceiling rose high in the air. Rows and rows of pews are brimming with men, women and somber children wearing their Sunday best church clothes.

    In the first row, Jonathan and Nancy Matthews sat. The weeks of mental anguish and lack of sleep had left them physically and emotionally exhausted. The news of Sarah's body washing up on shore became more of a relief than a disappointment. Life would finally be able to continue from the horrors of July 4th.

    Colonel Griswalt sat in a row across the aisle. He had been in many funerals in the last few weeks. For him, each one he went through was just as painful as the previous. A funeral for one of his fallen men would never become routine.

To Griswalt's right, Staff Sergeant Walters sat in his finest class a uniform. Medals bedecked his chest. His stomach and wrists were covered in bandages. Even though he had many physical injuries, His is spirit and faith remained stronger than ever.

Beside Walters, Corporal Carlson watched the comings and goings with rapt attention. On his collar, a brass cross gleamed in the light.

Behind Sarah's parents, Nishan sat holding his head, his eyes fixated at Sarah's photograph. Tears wet his eyes. JJ's bloodstained Bible was in tightly gripped his left hand.

Beside Nishan, Watson sat back with glazed eyes. JJ's death had changed his action movie life forever. The daily carnage of war had been nothing but a sideshow for Watson. Today, it shook him to the soul. The war now had a real personal face. Watson now confronted thoughts of his own mortality. The thoughts of death made him reflect on ways he lived his life. Watson knew that it was time for a change. It was time for him to live for the future.

Pastor Dave Steele walked up to the podium. The room immediately became hushed. Griswalt's team immediately sat to attention. Steele cleared his throat and adjusted his red stripped tie. The crowd's eyes immediately became transfixed on Steele's every action. Steele wiped his forehead and spoke to the crowd. "Ladies and gentlemen welcome to our memorial for Private Sarah Matthews. Today we gather not in a moment of sorrow; but in a moment in celebration. We celebrate the great life Sarah lived as a daughter, friend and fellow soldier.

"Sarah lived an exemplary life in which she always strived to do good for all. Doing such, she gave the final sacrifice that any one of us can – her life. But today we should not mourn or cry. Sarah spent her time here in a way we should strive for. Because of her willingness to dedicate her life to God, she will be rewarded with a life of eternity in heaven.

"I ask all of you to look at her life as a shining example of faith. Faith in God was the driving of her life." Steel put his microphone down for a second and stood still. The silence was deafening. Steele walked over to Jonathan Matthews and handed him the microphone.

Matthews stood up and faced the crowd, Steele stood by his side. Matthews wiped his face and spoke to the crowd, "I was twenty one when I came back from Vietnam. The horrors of war were still fresh in my mind. Stateside, I spent years fighting the demons that filled my mind afterwards."

Matthews rubbed his forehead, "In 1982, Nancy told me she was pregnant. I spent every night praying to God that my child would be a girl. I prayed that none of my children would ever see the horror that I saw in Vietnam." Matthews burst out crying; Steele hugged and comforted Matthews.

Steele helped Matthews down. Matthews continued to cry unable to control his despair. Nancy hugged Jonathan. Tears flowed down her cheek. Steele offered Nancy his microphone. She politely refused.

Watson stood up and begged Steel to allow him to speak. Steele offered the microphone to Watson, afraid to hear Watson's message. Watson stood up and faced the crowd. "Before this week, I lived a shallow life. A life in which all I wanted to do was indulge myself in an adrenaline high. For me combat was my drug and I needed a fix often. But no matter how often I got it, it never was enough.

"Next week I'm going to another memorial of one of my best friends. I began my Army career with three other friends. Unfortunately only one of them is left alive." Watson placed his hand on Nishan's shoulder. "I now realize the real meaning of life. I found the way that man is truly meant to live. Today, I decided to rededicate my life to God. Now I will live for his pleasure, not mine."

Steele hugged Watson. Watson sat down beside Nishan and whispered into his ear, "You won't have to bail me out of bar fights anymore." Nishan remained silent and stoic.

Walters stood up and spoke into the microphone. "I have been a professional soldier for almost 15 years. I have become numbed by the sights of blood, death and destruction. Nothing seemed to bother me anymore.

"That all changed after Sarah's death. Her death showed me that life is far too short to be wasted. My eldest daughter is now twelve. For most of her life, I've been far away fighting wars. No more, as of next week I will be leaving the Army. I need to spend more time with my wife and children before it is too late. This is the first step." Walters sat down and saluted Griswalt. Griswalt smiled and saluted back.

Corporal Carlson stood up. "Sarah and I shared a special relationship; she and I were first cousins. Sarah insisted that we kept that a secret. She never wanted to get special treatment for any reason.

"Sarah helped nurture my faith and allowed me to become the man I am. Tomorrow I enter Seminary school. I am going to be Pastor in the Army."

The Church erupted into applause. Smiles covered the members of the Parish. Steele walked up to the podium and spoke. "Let's return to the gymnasium for refreshments. May God bless you."

The crowd stood up and dispersed from the sanctuary. Jonathan Matthews stood up and whispered into Nancy's ear, "I'll join up with you in the gym. I need to take care of something first." Nancy nodded and walked out of the Sanctuary.

Matthews sat down beside Nishan. "How are you doing Mr. Nishan?" he asked.

Nishan answered in a quivering voice, "Not so good. You see Mr. Matthews, Sarah and I were more than just a couple of teammates."

"I know, you were a couple," Matthews answered back. Nishan's face turned white as a sheet. "I knew a long time ago. Sarah wrote a lot of letters home to me."

Nishan turned his face, "Would you have let us?"

Matthews smiled, "Let you? I would have made sure that you got married at this very church. I would have insisted Steele performed the ceremony." Nishan relaxed, confusion still covered his face. "Listen, as long as I'm head of the Matthews family. You'll always be a member, no less. This November, why don't you come down to my house for Thanksgiving. I know Nancy and Corporal Carlson would love to have you over."

Nishan smiled and hugged Matthews, "Thank you, Mr. Matthews."

Matthews sighed, "It's John and you're err…"

"Gian."

"Well, Gian, lets join Nancy for our luncheon." The two men walked out of the hallow Sanctuary. Sarah's photograph looked on.

Tacoma, Washington
28-July-2010
0200 Hours Local Time

Staff Sergeant Martin sat in his Tacoma Apartment. The TV played Jerry Springer. Martin poured scotch into the glass. He took a sip from the glass. The strong liquor did little to dull his pain.

The weeks after his release from Sadre had not been good to him. Martin had been plunged deep into a deep depression. Sights of the executions he witnessed haunted him day and night. Survivors' guilt continued to take its toll on his professional and personal life.

Martin had just started to recover when he found out both his children had been killed in the July 4th attack at the Portland Oregon airport. Now Martin was in the depths of a depression of unequaled proportions. Martin found no reason to live. Life was now just a boring trip to death.

Martin picked up his Ruger Sp101 Revolver. He placed on live round in the cylinder, the rest he filled with expended shells. Martin spun the cylinder and placed it into the gun's frame.

Martin pointed the gun to the TV and pulled the trigger. "Click." Nothing happened. Martin pulled back the hammer and aimed at his glass and pulled the trigger. "Click," nothing happened.

Martin pulled his bottle of Jack Daniels drank down the last ounce. He picked up the photograph of his children and kissed the photo. "I'll be there soon to join you," Martin whispered, tears rolling down his cheek. He pulled out the cylinder and spun it one more time. He carefully reinstalled cylinder back into the frame. Martin pulled the hammer back and pointed the gun to his temple and fired. A bullet shot out the barrel. The gun fell out of Martin's hand and fell to the floor. Blood covered the coffee table and sofa.

Two hours later a knock came at the door. "Hollywood, it's me Boxman. Open up." Boxman opened the unlocked door knob and flew the door open. Boxman rushed into the living room, horror filled his eyes. "Oh, my God," Boxman cried out. Boxman ran to Martin's side, "Hollywood, dude, why did you?"

Boxman checked Martin's pulse, tears rolled from his eyes. He shook his head and spoke to Martin's lifeless body, "Dude, you didn't have to do this. You had lots more to live for than this." Boxman wiped the tears his face, "Dude if you had waited, I could have showed you. It's all here." Boxman placed a Bible into Martin's lifeless body and prayed.

Arlington, Virginia
01-August-2010
0100 Hours Local Time

Lieutenant Townsend walked through the national cemetery. He slowly walked by rows and rows of crosses and headstones. After spending almost an hour searching, he came upon the headstone he was searching for. Townsend read out the inscription loudly, "Charles Skinner 1LT USMC 1983-2010"

Townsend placed a rose on the grave and Saluted. "You were a great officer. I wish I could have met you," Townsend spoke, tears wet his eyes.

The hair on Townsend's neck rose, a strange feeling came over him. Townsend flinched and looked back over his shoulder. Sergeant Gibson stood behind him, his face covered with an angry expression. "How dare you come here to Skinner's grave? If we it weren't for you, Skinner would still be alive. Because of you, my whole squad died. Some of the finest Marines that ever lived died to rescue you."

Townsend stayed calm and spoke to Gibson, "Can I say something in my defense?" Gibson angrily nodded. "My father sent you guys. The mission came directly from Chedwiggen and him. You have the right to be angry, but I'm not the man. Being locked up in that prison didn't allow me to dictate much of anything."

Gibson stayed quiet, anger still filled his eyes. Townsend sighed. "Listen, you can be bitter about the raid, you have full right to be. But bitterness does nothing but eat you up. Look at me, the bitterer I got about Iraq, the more I missed out on life. JJ died last month, a five-second apology for treating him badly were my last words to him. Do you really want to go through life like that?"

Gibson sunk his face for a second then saluted Townsend. Townsend returned the salute. "Now let's go into town and visit someone," Townsend calmly spoke. Gibson gave Townsend a confused look. "You have someone who needs to apologize to you."

"Who would that be?" Gibson meekly answered back.

Townsend smiled, "My father." The two men walked away side by side.

The Pentagon
Washington, D.C.
04-Aug-2010
0700 Hours Local Time

Griswalt pulled into the Pentagon parking lot with his black Volvo. The sights and smells of Washington, D.C. invigorated him. Griswalt continued on and wandered through the many corridors and passageways of the Pentagon. He watched hundreds of people shuffled by on their way for the start of their busy day.

Griswalt entered a plain office in an obscure corner of the building. An Army Colonel immediately greeted him and led him to a conference room. Griswalt entered, a smile covered his face when saw he Jonathan Matthews sitting at the head of the table. Griswalt sat down beside him and coddled his coffee.

Matthews was the first to speak, "So, General Griswalt, what does it feel like to have finally have become General of Black Ops. After all isn't this the Pentagon post you have always wanted."

Griswalt sighed, "I've got a lot of work ahead of me. Walters retired last week. I need to fill a corporal, two staff sergeants, a half a dozen privates and my position just at Camp Zulu alone." Matthews pulled out a Washington Post newspaper and placed it in front of Griswalt. Griswalt looked at the front cover and rubbed his graying hair. "I guess we both have lots of work to do Vice President Matthews." The two men raised their cups of coffee and drank.

The Washington Post newspaper fell to the ground reveling the day's headline. "Pakistani war death toll reaches 200. Major General Walter Douglas predicts the war will be won by spring."

Glossary

AAA - Anti aircraft artillery
AH-1 Cobra - heavily-armed helicopter, often referred to as a gunship.
Allah Akbar - Muslim saying for God is great
Aim-9 Sidewinder - Standard USAF and US Navy air to air heat-guided missile.
Aim-120 Amraam - Standard USAF and US Navy air to air guided missile. The launch aircraft designates the target with its radar. The missile launches from its aircraft and uses its onboard radar to room in on the target.
AKS-74U - Short barreled Russian assault rifle chambered for 5.45x39.5 mm. Often used as a replacement for a submachine gun in close quarter battles.
BRDM-2 - Russian, rubber wheeled armored personnel transport vehicle.
C-4 - Plastic explosive
Cluster bomb - Bomb which delivers thousands of baseball sized bomblets to cause damage to its target.
Condition lever - Lever in turboprop aircraft which sets maximum propeller speeds.
DMZ - Heavily defended border separating North and South Korea.
EICAS - Engine Indicating and Crew Alerting system – Modern warning system built into aircraft in conjunction with the FADEC. Warning lights are replaced by posted words on display screens color-coded to indicate their level of threat.
FADEC - Full authority Digital Engine Control – Electronic engine control system used on modern aircraft. No mechanical connections are used. Only electrical connections provide stimulus from throttles to the fuel control unit. Engine ECU will

provide various types of messages on display screens to indicate failure using FADEC Caution andWarnings

FLCS - Flight Control System-In modern jetfighters, there is no direct link from the pilot's control stick to the flight controls (Ailerons, elevators, rudder). Instead the stick transmits electronic inputs to a computer. The computer interprets the inputs to electronic signals which are sent to the hydraulic actuators. When any fault is found in the system, the FLCS message will appear.

Fox 3 - Call used by US pilots to inform wingman and element that pilot has fired an Aim 120 AMRAAM missile.

GBU-10A Paveway - 2000 pound laser guided bomb.

HK-21 - Belt fed 7.62x51mm version machine gun version of the famed HK-91 rifle.

HK-91 - 7.62X51mm battle rifle originally designed in Spain as the Cetme. Later Germany adopted a modified version called the G-3 which was manufactured by Heckler and Koch

HK-93 - Updated version of the HK-91 which is chambered in 5.45x45 mm. Most versions were only chambered for the lighter 55grain bullet.

HUD - Heads up display. Clear glass panel in front to pilots which displays critical navigation and attack information.

LZ - Landing zone

Medevac - Term used for medically evacuating personnel by means of helicopter or conventional fixed wing aircraft.

MIA - Short for missing in action

M-203 - 40mm grenade launcher that often mounted underneath the barrel of an assault rifle.

M-4 - Short barreled version of M-16 fitted with a14.5 inch barrel, extended chamber feed ramps and a collapsible multiple position buttstock

M-60 - Heavy 7.61x51mm machine gun that was used as a front line Infantry weapon as late as 1980's. It has since been replaced by lighter more versatile weapons such as the M-249 Squad automatic Machine gun. M-60s are still sparsely used in fixed machine gun nests on bases and some Blackhawk helicopters.

MK-19 - Automatic grenade launcher used to fire a projectile similar in size to the M-203

MP-5 - 9mm submachine gun based on a delayed blow back system similar to the HK-91

Nacelle - Structure mounted to wing which supports engine and subsystems for engine.

NCO - Non Commissioned officers – Senior Enlisted men such as Sergeants, Master Sergeants etc.

Power levers - Throttle levers in a turboprop aircraft. These levers control fuel to the engines which is directly controls the amount of torque. Torque is often referred to as power in turboprop aircraft and helicopters.

Punjabi - Language spoken by persons in Pakistan and Northwestern India.

PSG-1 - A Sniper version of the famed HK-91 assault rifle.

Raghead - Derogatory slang term used to describe person's of Arabic descent.

Red dot - Sight, usually non-magnifying, which uses an electronically generated dot by an LED.

Remington 700 - Bolt action rifle that is often used by snipers.

RPG - Rocket propelled grenade

SA-7 - Thermally guided surface to air missile used primarily by ground troops for protection from low flying helicopters and fixed wing aircraft.

SAM - Surface to air missile

SCUD - Russian medium range missile used to deliver various types of warheads.

Spetsnaz - The domestic Russian anti-terrorism agency

SPU - Standby Power Unit – Backup hydraulic pump, usually powered electrically with Alternating Current.

Submachine gun - Short barreled rifle, often automatic, which fires a pistol caliber cartridge. 9mm and .45ACP cartridges are the most popular.

T-55 - Russian tank from 1950's vintage. Completely obsolete compared to modern standards

TWI - Threat warning receiver – Display which is connected to dozens of antenna's on the outside of aircraft. The antennas receive radar signals which send information to the receiver ECU. The ECU then converts the signal in symbols on the display which the pilot uses to judge threat level.

UH-60 Blackhawk - Standard US Army transport helicopter.

Urdu - Written form of Punjabi used by Pakistanis.

UZI - A 9mm automatic submachine gun manufactured by IMI industries of Israel and used by various Police and Military forces around the world.

WIA - Short for wounded in action

Zil 135 - Standard Russian two axle truck used for transporting general cargo and troops.

ZSU-23-4 Shilka - Russian tracked vehicle loaded with multiple heavy antiaircraft cannons